The Legend of Robin Brodie

LISA SAMSON

HARVEST HOUSE PUBLISHERS
Eugene, Oregon 97402

THE LEGEND OF ROBIN BRODIE

Copyright © 1995 by Lisa Samson
Published by Harvest House Publishers
Eugene, Oregon 97402

Library of Congress Cataloging-in-Publication Data
        The legend of Robin Brodie / Lisa Samson.
            p. cm.
        ISBN 1-56507-306-1
            1. Man–woman relationships–Scotland–Highlands–History–18th century–Fiction.
        2. Young men–Scotland–Highlands–Fiction. 3. Highlands (Scotland)–Fiction. I. Title.
        PS3569.A46673L44 1995   95-11764
        813'.54–dc20   CIP

Printed in the United States of America.

95 96 97 98 99 00 01 02 – 10 9 8 7 6 5 4 3 2 1

To my mother,
Joy Ebauer,
for the foundation of
kisses upon which my dreams
were built.

About the Author

Lisa Samson has always had a keen interest in history. During a time of study at Oxford University, she fell in love with British history, and out of that love grew *The Highlander and His Lady*, her first novel. A graduate of Liberty University with a degree in telecommunications, Lisa lives in Virginia with her husband, Will, daughter, Tyler, and son, Jake.

Acknowledgments

First and foremost to my good friend Bill Jensen of Harvest House my gratitude must be expressed. Thanks for the many trips along *rabbit trails* of ideas ("bear with me, now") and showing me the importance of knowing the difference "between the lightning and the lightning bug."

James Byron Huggins, thanks again for your insight and valuable suggestions on crafting a book. Your love of the written word and your encouragement are priceless.

Lori Chesser, big sister, cherished friend, and queen of romance novels, your words of praise more than any others gave me hope that possibly I was on the right track.

Diane Raack, thank you for being the first person at Harvest House to read my writing. Thank you for liking it. Thank you for all the fun and encouragement along the way these past two years. It's my privilege to count you a friend.

To everyone else that gave me great encouragement, Joy Ebauer, Jennifer Hagerty, The Samson Bunch, The Danaher Clan, Evangeline Long, Joanne Sigmon, Greg Dowell, Anne Welborne, and Dawn Huth, thank you.

I would also like to thank Terry Miethe, Ph.D., for his influence, his dreams, and his example of hard work and study. Dr. Miethe, the Oxford study program which came about due to your inspiration and planning, made all the difference in my outlook on life, history, and God Himself, and that time will always be remembered as the greatest summer of my life.

A special word of appreciation goes to all the readers who bought *The Highlander and His Lady*. Thank you for the warm reception you gave my first book. I pray you will like this one just as much, if not more.

Appreciation also goes to my family. Will, thanks for being such a great husband—one who isn't afraid to let me do my thing. Tyler, you're a wonderful, loving child whose zest for life has kept me going many a weary afternoon. And to my baby son Jake, thanks for sleeping through the night, and smiling at me with eyes that put Paul Newman's to shame. I love you all.

And lastly to the Lord Jesus Christ. Another book upon the shelf and it is all due to You. Thank You. Thank You. Thank You.

A Word from the Author

Book 1 of this series, *The Highlander and His Lady*, was based on an actual historical event: the Jacobite Uprising of 1745. Some of the characters were real: the Duke of Perth, Lachlan Maclachlan, and the Duke of Argyll. Kyle and Jenny Maclachlan were characters completely from my imagination, although Lachlan Maclachlan's son Donald did get his lands back with the help of the Duke of Argyll.

As we venture back into the world of the Maclachlans and the Campbells, we witness the reconstruction of a war-torn land and meet Kyle and Jenny's daughter Alix.

You will notice poetry scattered throughout the pages of this book. The Scots have long been known for their lyrical natures—their love of song, story, and folklore. All of the poetry is Celtic, particularly Scottish, except for "In Shades of Forest Green," which is original to this book. All of the characters and events are completely fictitious, although actual clan names and their locations have been used.

Enjoy, my friends. I pray that this book will entertain you and provide a blessing to your soul as well.

Regards,

Lisa Samson
Virginia Beach, Virginia
January 1995

PART ONE

1746

After the Battle on Lena's Heath

Who can relate the deaths of the people?
Who the deeds of mighty heroes?
When Fingal, burning in his wrath,
Consumed the sons of Lochlin?
Groans swelled on groans from hill to hill,
Till night had covered all.

–James MacPherson
From "Fingal"

CHAPTER

1

The Scottish Highlands
April, 1746

Robin Brodie's fear was wordless. Snakelike, and wending its way through his tender mind like the fear of an opened wardrobe at midnight, it took on the form of misty moon devils, hags, and evil fairies. Unsought solitude, anger, and painful rage whispered voweled hauntings till his forehead felt it would implode upon its own frightened imaginings.

Darkness seeped into each pore of his face and neck, like water into black velvet, consuming him against his will. Nighttime flowered its slow, dark bloom as though the world had not changed, an entire nation had not been devastated.

The nightmare had only begun.

He was alone. Once he had a father—a man he had seen fight valiantly against the British on the field of Culloden three days before. But John Brodie slumbered eternally with Scotland's dead. An ill-fated warrior in a battle for freedom against the tyrannical English, leaving mouths to be fed and bodies to be sheltered and kept warm when winter came.

Robin was the oldest, the responsibility his. And that was more frightening than death to a lad who had seen but 11 new years. More terrifying than dodging Redcoats and foraging for food. Now all he wanted was to lay down his callow head, to let his black curls flatten between the hardened earth and his rounded cheek.

But it was not to be. The time had not yet come.

His eyes, deep pools of blackened brown, scanned the horizon to his left . . . in front of him . . . to his right. The tree line, black against the deepening blue of the new night sky, stood before him—unfamiliar, yet welcoming.

Sanctuary was near.

Please, please. Silent words were formed in desperation as the meadow before him seemed to lengthen under his leather-bound feet. *Please, please.* Over and over his mind intoned the silent, primal prayer.

At last he stood in the forest alone. Were Redcoats, England's vicious soldiers, waiting for him, a small Scottish lad? *Please, please,* he whispered now as a twig snapped under his foot. He jumped as though a musket had gone off beside him.

Steady, Robin . . . steady. His lips, cherublike and chapped from the long battle in hail and wind, mouthed the words silently as they pounded the command, forcing it through the channels of his brain. *Walk silently, tread silently.* His smallish hand, grimy and scraped, pushed a black curl, matted together with dust and sweat, behind his small ear.

He cocked his head to the left, jarring loose a bead of perspiration that had gathered on his right temple. It slid from its resting place, slanting down over his cheek to run beside his nostril and into the corner of his mouth.

He took a step.

Silence. Still all was bathed in silence.

Step by silent step, the leather-bound feet took him further into the forest, closer to home. Finally, in the hollow of an old, dead oak tree he curled into the tiniest ball he could make of himself.

Beside Robin his drum lay silent. A few days earlier the hide top had ceased its deadly reverberations. Along with the pipes, the instrument had called men to their deaths. A symbol of valor it was meant to be. Yet it had made this brave Scot boy who wielded the sticks a harbinger of doom. A siren singing an ancient song of death. Inside his brain, the drumbeats never stopped. And when he finally laid his smooth, unblemished cheek on soft green moss, mind full of misty nights, wild animals, isolation, and fear, Robin Brodie could only pray he would see the sunrise. . . .

• • •

The drumbeats never stopped. The battle raged and men died. Father swung valiantly. There was Father facedown, dead. The drumbeats never stopped. Bonnie Prince Charlie leading the troops. Bonnie Prince Charlie still alive. Mama cooking, making supper. Mama cooking, pounding meat. There was Father facedown, dead. The drumbeats never stopped. Deborah and Kathleen gathering flowers in the sunshine. Funeral flowers. There was Father facedown, dead. The drumbeats never stopped.

At last the sun arose and flickered in the cool April breeze across the laddie's face.

• • •

Into the meadow he trooped once again. *Home, I want my home.*

He fought back the tears remembering Mother, recalling the conversation that had taken place a week before he and his father had set off to meet with the forces that were gathering to rid Scotland once for all of England's iron bands.

There was Mother in the small, but extremely tidy Brodie kitchen. The jugs and platters had been stowed neatly behind the lower cupboard doors, and the plates and cups were stacked on top, ready for the next meal. A hewn table, strong and heavy, stood in the center of the clean-swept room. And a wide ribbon of sunlight spilled across most of the well-cared-for surface. A breeze, an August Highland breeze that blew in through the doorway, lifted the curls of the Brodie family as they sat together, their faces as serious as the discussion taking place.

Mavis Brodie looked at her husband, John, her soft brown eyes pleading. A work-worn hand, small but muscular, she placed on top of his large, knobby one. "Please, m'darlin', dinna take m'babe from me."

John's piercing blue eyes looked through his wife's, seeing her pain, her frustration. He reached his hand up to glide gently across the surface of her pulled-back, bright-red hair, seeking to apply a sympathetic salve to her aching heart.

They had married later in life. She had been a childless widow of 30, he a shy bachelor of 37, with prematurely gray hair that had once been as black as his son's, and eyes which told all and missed nothing. She was tall for a woman, and they stood eye to eye. She loved his arms, wood-carver's arms, muscular and defined. He loved her legs, straight and slim with graceful ankles and delicately arched feet. Every night he rubbed them, as much for his own pleasure as hers. And how they loved one another—two simple souls with beautiful, childlike faces and hearts with a deep capacity for love. And their children were just like them.

"But Mother," Robin laid his hand upon her arm, "Bonnie Prince Charlie has landed. An' we must fight. I want to go. Please."

John took his beloved wife into his arms and kissed her softly on the forehead. "He's not a bairn anymore, dearest," he whispered, caressing her rounded cheek with a calloused hand, warm and gentle. "If he wants to go, I think he should."

"But war and its horrors are na' for bairns. And he's still so young. Besides, the Brodie clan is stayin' out of it. No one else is goin' to fight."

"'Tis true, Mother," Robin's eyes were level, "but it's somethin' I have to do. I am half Maclachlan as well, Mother. True Jacobites, loyal to Scotland. 'Tis true I'm only 11 . . ."

"But he's a brave 11!" Kathleen, the youngest child and Robin's faithful admirer chimed in. "If anyone can take care o' himself, it'll be Robin!"

Mavis Brodie knew it was futile to argue anymore when Deborah, her eldest and usual ally settled her hands firmly on her brother's broadening shoulders. Robin would go to war and everyone in the family knew it.

"Well, then," she tried to be a bit cheerful, but her voice came out thick and husky, "come out into the woods with me, Robin Brodie, and help me fetch some berries an' roots. I'll need to make some dye if I'm to weave a new plaid for your sojourn." She shot her husband a look. "I suppose you'll be needin' one as well, Johnnie."

John laughed then and pulled his wife to her feet. "Thank ya', m'lovely bride." He kissed her soundly and quickly on the lips. "And I shall beg your leave an' go back into m'workshop. The chief wants those shelves carved an' up in his library by tomorrow."

His broad frame temporarily blocked the light in the doorway as he left.

Robin took her outstretched hand and grabbed a basket which sat beside the door. Mavis bit back tears, realizing that the most difficult part of parenting had begun so soon and without preparation.

She had to let him go.

They trudged into the woods. "Mind ya' keep warm while you're gone! Recall Scripture and pray every day. An' dinna' be gettin' involved with any of those ruffians that seem to be hangin' about army camps. An' if a strange lassie should come up to ya' . . ."

"Mother, please, I willna' do any o' those things. I promise ya'. As you've been remindin' us all this mornin', I'm but 11 years old!"

They came to a berry patch. As they gathered, their hands finding many berries, but feeling no thorns, Mavis continued to advise her son. If he indeed went to war, she wanted him to be fully equipped, not just with weapon and warm tartan, but with wisdom and the ability to see God each moment of the day.

Robin remembered the scene well and it sent an arrow of misery through him. He pushed it down and kept walking. *Home. Home.* It was all he wanted.

Finally, a familiar tree line appeared before his eyes as they blinked out the bright noontime sunshine. In four hours, he calculated, he would be in his mother's strong, wiry arms. In four hours he would share the news.

Father was dead.

He pictured his family even now. Deborah working her patch of garden, mother spinning or attending to other household duties, Kathleen learning to sew on her creepie stool by the hearth. He yearned to be there. But even as he had been a messenger of doom during the stormy battle, he had one more message to give.

Tears filled his eyes for the man who had loved him unconditionally, who had taught him what it was to be a man. He wept for his father as his journey turned from bitter to bittersweet.

Home.

It was so close now.

He entered the dense glade which surrounded the two-room cottage, walked by the stream, clear and catching the sun, where he caught his first trout. Father had scooped him up on his shoulders and carried him home. He could feel the string of fish hanging from his hand, biting into the middle bend of his fingers as it bumped against his father's arm below. The berry patch was visible up ahead. He had thought himself a man then as he had picked berries for the tartan dye. Now he knew what manhood was. Duty amid destruction. Responsibility amid pain.

The sights, the sounds, and especially the smells made him pick up his pace though his muscles, tired and worn, resisted.

The clearing was just a hundred yards up ahead. Voices filtered in his direction and he hastened even more, relief laying itself out across his forehead. The tones became stronger with each step as he hurried to let his family know he was home.

• • •

Weeping. Weeping. Open-handed slaps. And snarls. Cruel and angry taunts. There were four of them.

Redcoats.

The once-tranquil clearing became a terrifying riot of pain and lordship—cruel and vicious lordship. Robin blinked wildly as his feet became one with the forest floor. His mind protested, screaming behind his forehead. He knew not what to do as his vision blurred out the violent scene before him and his limbs quaked and his breathing became labored and gritty. He sought control but could not attain even the ability to blink out of his eyes the cold sweat that poured from his tightening scalp.

His mother and his oldest sister, Deborah, were being roughly forced by each man in turn. Little Kathleen, only eight. Her white, childish body was completely naked and shivering in the evening air as they led her around on the great stallion that had been Father's pride and joy. Her slim shoulders shook as she cried and tried to cover herself with frail hands. Leather thongs lashed at the horse, and the child clung with fear as the animal jumped. The tanned strap was aimed too high, biting into her innocent, alabaster skin as she passed in front of them.

"No!"

Robin screamed, running forward into the clearing. The sharp, metal rim of his drum pounded painfully against the small of his back and he threw himself at the horse, pulling Kathleen down and covering her with his plaid in one swift motion. The other soldiers pulled themselves off of Mavis and Deborah.

"Run!" he shouted, as he drew his dirk from his stocking and pushed her toward the forest. She wasted no time. Her smooth legs pumped hard below the slim, white buttocks. The strong muscles contracted visibly under the tender skin, ensuring retreat, guaranteeing relief, if just for a little while. Her long black curls swayed against the protruding bumps of her vertebrae. Robin watched her run as if in a dream. A cruel laugh turned his face toward a semicircle of debauchery and unfettered, condoned cruelty.

Their faces were weathered and pockmarked. One soldier was still young enough to sport a severe case of acne. Their hats were off. Their hair was caked with sweat and filth, having seen neither soap nor water in many weeks. They smiled the smiles of cruel children seeking a stray cat for sport. One grin was toothy, menacingly strong. One rotting and black. All emitted the fetid stench of stale alcohol and last night's meal. The odor struck Robin forcibly as the breeze ceased and the clearing became white-hot, even in April.

He was surrounded by them—an ever-constricting circle of blazing red. He crouched low, dagger forward, legs spread wide, eyes igniting rabidly with anger and fear. A boy against men.

"Run, Mother! Run, Deborah!" he shouted, and his voice sounded like it came from somewhere else.

His words were a sudden catalyst, setting each person into swift motion. Out of the corner of his eye, Deborah pulled together her torn clothes as she gathered her legs underneath her, scrambled to her feet, and made for the twilight dimness of the forest. A pain raced across Robin's back in a sweeping motion. Soon she was swallowed by the dense green, a bruised specter dissolving into a seeming oblivion. Mother stayed. And as she tried to pull the soldiers away from her boy, she was knocked unconscious by the butt of a musket.

He turned and shouted again as his back became inflamed, warm and sticky. "No!"

It didn't matter now what they did, he thought, as they descended mercilessly upon him. Father was dead and he had been too late.

• • •

Robin hit the ground hard, the impact sending jolts of pain up his spine as his body made contact with the earth.

"So, little Scottish boy," the leader drawled through his strong teeth, "I see you've lost your precious plaid."

They towered over him as he tried to scramble to his feet. A heavy boot made contact with his chest, sending him back down once again.

"Let's see what ye do once ye've lost yer kilt as well . . . laddie." The last word came out in a mocking brogue. "Strip 'im, Billy."

The youngest soldier laughed with a sloppy salute. "Aye, aye, captain."

"Niall, Harold, you help, too."

They pulled Robin roughly to his feet as Billy's strong hands yanked the homespun shirt over his head. The kilt came down next. He pulled up on the garment when it got to Robin's ankles. It sent him sprawling back down into the dirt once again.

Billy leaned forward, his face inches from Robin's. A cruel smile erupted amid the oozing face. It was soon ripped away as Robin, naked and defenseless, spit. It made its mark, right into the Redcoat's eye.

"Why you little piece of . . ." He raised his hand to strike.

"No, Billy," Henry interrupted. "I want this proud little man all to myself."

Robin lay wide-eyed, but garnered the courage to speak. "Man is right, ya' filthy piece of dirt. Ya' dinna' know what bein' a man really means. Any of ya'!" His eyes turned wild, his voice raised, the sharp, childish tones contrasting with the bravery of his words. "You're all nothin' but a bunch of stupid, ugly, foul-smellin' Englishmen!"

Henry's eyes narrowed, lit by smoking torches of danger. "Proud to the bitter end, are we? Ye lost, Scottish pig! *We* are your masters now."

A word was whispered.

"Never."

"Well then," Henry brandished a small knife, "let's see how a proud Scottishman behaves when British steel pierces his insolence. Hold him down, men."

With a man on each arm and one sitting down lower on his legs, the Redcoat's knife sliced into Robin's face. Blood spurted from his temple. Blinding pain exploded in his brain as the blade snaked down his cheek and neck, and onto his chest.

Screams filled his ears. His own screams. Sharpening his world into a pinpoint reality of pain. Agony in its basest of forms. Torture.

The knife stopped.

"What do ye say now, laddie? Still proud to be a Scot?

Say, lads," he looked up at the others, "it didn't take much to subdue this one, did it?"

Robin's eyes opened amid a scarlet haze of blood. "You'll never subdue me, Redcoat."

He laughed. Much too quietly. "No? We'll just see how much ye can stand. Turn 'im over men!" A cruel snicker issued from deep inside him as his eyes became happy. "You'll wear these marks forever, dog. And you'll never forget it was your pride which put 'em there."

The arm raised—a salute to sadism and everything man was never meant to be. Robin screamed as it slashed across his back. Again and again and again. The knife continued to wreak havoc on the tender flash, blood warmly spattering in countless crimson spots on the Redcoat's face, clothes, and hands.

The pain consumed him to the epicenter of all that he was, had been, or would ever be. And Robin Brodie fainted to the tune of a cold, soulless laugh, and the memory of eyes that were empty of anything but defilement and the love of someone else's agony.

"That'll teach the little scoundrel," one of them said, kicking Robin for good measure. "'e'll never rise against England again."

"Well, Henry, 'e'll never rise at all, thanks to ye! An' if he does, his back will always carry more lines than the plaid we stripped off of 'im."

"Let's go, men. We've done enough damage for one day." Someone laughed as they headed out of the clearing, wiping their brows and straightening their breeches. Another day's work done.

"They deserved it, the filthy Scots," the largest one with the rotted teeth spat back in the direction of the clearing. He looked with narrowed eyes at the mother and child lying in heaps and smiled a broad, spitty smile.

His booted feet turned in the dust.

• • •

Familiar arms carried the broken form into the hut and laid him on the kitchen table. Mavis's hands, gentle but shaking, cleaned the bayonet wounds and the snaking cut that disfigured the right half of the youthful face and continued down his neck to his chest.

A second pair of hands, younger, but equally as capable, fetched clean rags and kept refilling the basin with fresh water. Deborah's hands. Their own wounds would have to wait.

"Will he be all right, Mother?" the 14-year-old asked softly as she wrung out a fresh rag and placed it in the waiting palm. She pushed a strawberry-blonde curl back from her forehead with the back of her hand.

"He will live, child, if we can keep infection from settin' in." Mavis handed back the cloth.

Deborah stood ready with another cloth. "I canna' even see the mole on his cheek now. An I canna' help but wonder if when he heals and the scars are showin' if his cheek will still dimple when he smiles." Her voice revealed her pain, and fear of what the future would hold for Robin hung between them.

Tears flowed from Mavis's eyes. *If he ever smiles again*, she thought. But to Deborah she said. "Of course it'll dimple, m'love. Dimples are more than skin-deep. They're a reflection of the soul. Our Robin will recover."

Deborah nodded, but for the first time in her life she didn't believe her mother. No one was going to recover. Not really. The English had seen to that.

Kathleen, already bandaged and sleeping, cried out in her slumber. The panic in her voice shot through the two women's hearts. But they kept on at the task before them. It was all anyone could do now that the cause was lost.

Mavis finished his face and chest, and with Deborah's help she turned him over.

Stifling a gasp, her hand flew to her mouth at the pandemonium the knives had wreaked upon her son's once-smooth back. The maze of carvings stretched from the back of his neck to his buttocks. Deborah handed her more clean rags, and Mavis continued the process, cleaning, piecing the ribbons of flesh back together. Their slow tears mingled with the dirt and blood on Robin's tortured, shattered body. Finally they finished and ministered healing ointments to one another.

The sun set. The girls slept fitfully in between their anguished cries. And her mangled son still lay unconscious.

Mavis Brodie settled into the bed she and her husband had once shared.

John David was dead.

Robin's solitary appearance told the whole story.

Not bothering to pull down the covers, she lay on her stomach staring at the stitches on her bridal quilt, illumined by the moon.

But she was too tired. And too ashamed of the times her body had been forced to house the same men who had destroyed them all in the space of an hour. An hour in hell itself.

She didn't pray that night. She wanted to. But she couldn't. Instead she lay wide-eyed and aching in the darkness. And after several hours she slept a deep sleep—not of the dead, but of those who secretly wish they were.

• • •

"Mama! Mama!" The small boy with curly black hair pushed past his older sister through the door of the house. "I did it!"

Six-year-old Robin held up his first kill and set it on the table.

"A fine squirrel it is, my son," Mavis said, laughing as she patted his head. "You did well!"

"I saw him, Mother," Deborah's chest puffed out in pride for her little brother's accomplishment. "The arrow was straight an' true an' whistled through the air smoother than the wind. We waited quietly, almost afraid to even breathe," she continued. "Robin saw it first."

John stomped through the door after wiping his feet on the door-stone. Mavis hurried over to him and bestowed a kiss upon his cheek.

"It was a fine day for your son, Johnnie," she reported proudly and pointed to the table.

"Did ya' make that kill, Robin?" he asked, tugging on the lad's ponytail with three quick pulls.

The boy became serious, his shoulder stiffened martially, and he nodded. "Aye, Father."

"Well, then," John laughed, lifting his son into his arms, "I see we have two men in the family that will hunt for our supper."

"Aye, Father," he said, eyes glowing from paternal praise. The little boy's mind was made up, set to a new calling. By the time Robin was nine, John Brodie never had to hunt again.

Mavis jerked up out of her sleep, shivering. The dreams of their past happiness were so vivid, painfully poignant, and much needed if she was to make it on her own. Her eyes closed once more and she slept a sleep of blackness. No dreams. But no torment either. Just a simple, necessary oblivion.

The next day, Mavis Maclachlan Brodie gathered her girls to her to tell them of her decision. They had to leave. Their home was no longer safe. No longer home. The Red-coats could come back again and take the only thing left to them: their lives. The next time they wouldn't be so lucky. Especially Robin.

"I've made up my mind," she said focusing on Deborah, the child she had come to lean so heavily upon. "We can stay here in the woods as before, secluded from your father's people. Or we can go back to my home. Back to Strathlachlan."

"Will Grandfather take us in?" Deborah asked.

"Aye, Papa will take us in. An' if we're goin' to journey so far, we'll need to get started right away."

Wide-eyed and saddened, Deborah agreed and Kathleen stood mute, but nodded. They helped her pack their few belongings in silence.

• • •

The next day they began their long journey south. A crude cart held her kitchenware, sheets, clothing, and some meager provisions. The furniture stayed behind. All except the carven chest that John, a wood-carver, had lovingly made for her before their wedding. Father's furnishings would have to suffice. Robin lay in the back, sleeping on her quilt.

No soldier assaulted them. They saw practically no one. And Mavis remembered how to pray on those lonely days of travel. God protected them along the way.

CHAPTER

2

Strathlachlan, Scotland
April, 1746

The battle of Culloden was over. Their forces were destroyed. England was victorious.

Eight months previous the Maclachlans envisioned an outcome of glory and honor and victory. A spirit of excitement had rung through the clan when two clansmen, each wearing Maclachlan tartan, held aloft the fiery cross and summoned the men to battle. All through the region of Kilbride they had run in the time-honored tradition of the clans, covering the large barony which sat in the western Highlands with familiar quickness. And the Maclachlans responded by gathering in the great hall of Castle Lachlan to hear the chief's own bard give a rallying speech, encouraging them to brave deeds and recalling the valor of past times and past heroes when their clan had fought for the independence of Scotland time and time again. Kyle Maclachlan, the chief's own son and heir to the leadership of the clan, was the most inspiring, willing to leave his new wife for the cause he had come to love so deeply during his days at university in Edinburgh. The clansmen knew Kyle was solid and committed, willing to sacrifice all. And they responded in kind. Fergus, the clan piper, trained by the MacCrimmons themselves, played rallying tunes which resonated through the heart of each man present. Scotland called for their bravery, and the Maclachlans would answer.

And then the time of preparation had begun, each man setting his house in order, each woman spinning thread, weaving tartan, and gathering food from the household gardens for the journey to Glenfinnan, where Prince Charles Edward Stuart, "Bonnie Prince Charlie" himself, had raised the standard and declared his father, James III, king of Scotland and England. A title that was his by blood, his by birth.

On a misty summer morning they had ridden off with hope in their hearts and dreams of freedom and independence surging through their minds and bodies like a quickened pulse, heightened by passion and pride.

Bonnie Prince Charlie had sought to wrest back the throne of Britain from George II for his father, James Stuart. His movement failed. And his forces, "the Jacobites," had been devastated—were dead, scattered, or made prisoners by the English. King George's son William, the Duke of Cumberland, had done his job well. Culloden Moor, that final battlefield, had run red with the lifeblood of ancient Scotland. Men fighting for freedom. Men seeking to shed England's tyranny from their heavy shoulders once and for all. Now it was over. And they were fortunate to have made it home alive.

Scotland would never rule herself again.

But that was eight months and almost 2000 men ago. Now as Joshua Maclachlan and the new chief of the clan, Kyle Maclachlan, led their horses through the desecrated village of Strathlachlan, he wondered for a brief moment whether it had been worth the price.

He shook his head, clearing his strong mind of uncertainty, hopefully, but doubtfully, once and for all.

Kyle had seen his father, Lachlan Maclachlan, the chief, and his younger brother, Edward, shot down in their prime by British artillery. Joshua had no one to lose. But his heart wrenched when he looked over at the man whose "traitorous" activities stood to lose him the holdings his family had possessed here in the region of Kilbride for centuries. He would lose it all. A chief of nothing.

But Joshua knew something the British could not understand. The clans were not merely tribes of different people gathered together under one ruler. They were family. And the very blood that coursed through the veins of the chief flowed in the veins of the most humble clansmen. By this they were bound to each other and to the earth on which they toiled for their patriarch every day of their lives. Could the uprising have destroyed all of that? He doubted it. At least the Maclachlans would survive intact. And yet, what hope was there?

"It's almost better that Father didn't live to see this," Kyle spoke softly, looking at the half-destroyed village of Strathlachlan. Women wept and children cried from within the huts made wretched from the Redcoats' recent onslaught.

Joshua was silent. Before Culloden he had been merely a house servant. He glanced over at his new chief and his oldest friend. The auburn curls had grown well down Kyle's back. And as the wind blew them forward his large hand pushed the heavy hair back from the deep-set hazel eyes, so light in color they appeared golden. The long, straight nose sat in a regal manner above the wide mouth which was set in a grim line. In the past, Joshua had never known anyone as quick to smile as Kyle, but viewing his chief now, he wondered how much time would pass before his infectious humor would return to once again light up his ruddy countenance. They were both giant men, standing well over six feet in a time when the average Scot stood only four inches over five feet.

Joshua viewed the scene before him.

Against the lush, virescent springtime hills that provided a rolling background, the ruined village made him ache for his own past and everyone else's. How many had been killed during the pillaging of the English? Burial mounds told a grim story on the outskirts. The misery was great. They walked on.

"Master Kyle!"

Both men turned toward the voice. There stood a wizened old man, leaning heavily on a crutch, leg twisted and mangled from the Jacobite uprising 30 years previous. It had failed as well.

Kyle, gathering fortitude from the dregs of his nearly depleted reserves, stiffened his shoulders and walked over with a sad shake of his head. "It's not good, Thomas. The few survivors should be making their way home soon."

"Survivors?" Hope filtered through the sun-bleached blue of the man's irises. And his roughened fingers, white hair sprouting from beneath each knuckle, picked nervously at the homespun shirt he wore. "Jamie?"

Kyle nodded and tried to smile. "Aye, Jamie made it through."

Thomas smiled broadly, displaying a mouthful of crooked, but surprisingly strong teeth. "And Dougald?"

Laying a strong hand on Thomas's bony shoulder, Kyle could only say of the man's oldest son, "I'm sorry, Thomas. Dougald was killed."

Immediately his countenance fell, crushed amid the ultimate pain of parenthood. "I should be thankful that one will make it . . . home." The man's aged voice broke on the last word as he fought to control his emotions, fists curling into tight, arthritic balls. He didn't feel the pain.

Joshua found his voice for the first time. "Aye, sir. Most families here willna' be able to say the same. Your Dougald died valiantly. Rest assured, he fell in honor an' with the utmost bravery. Ya' would've been proud."

The old man leaned more heavily on his crutch and ran a shaky hand over his yellow-gray hair. " 'Tis a blessin' for m'Maggie that she didna' live to see this day. But it is as ya' say, Joshua," Thomas fought for something to tide him through the next minute, "he died for Scotland an' that canna' be seen as anythin' short of a privilege." Despite his brave words, Thomas turned away more stooped than before and with an iron will pushed down the aching sobs that yearned to come forth. "I'll go tell his wife."

"You do that, Thomas," said Kyle, his strength evident. Thomas didn't need to know yet that the chief and Edward were dead. He was glad when the old man turned to go.

They continued in silence, Kyle leading his horse. Joshua, more keen-sighted than most men, saw it first. Castle Lachlan, the ancient medieval fortress of the Maclachlans, stood before them.

Demolished.

Suddenly Kyle saw the destruction as well, his heart churning under the grindstone of merciless devastation. Without turning to Joshua, his tall form was running forward, his plaid flying behind him, parallel with his long hair. And he lifted up his voice in a grief so deep, so chilling, Joshua stopped in his tracks. But only for a moment.

He would not let Kyle mourn alone. Not now. Joshua knew too well what that was like. He picked up his pace and ran toward him. In silence his paces matched Kyle's step for step.

The gatehouse was a pile of rubble. The keep, that massive building which had housed the Maclachlan family for centuries, was gone, except for one corner of wall which rose in a sheer cliff almost four stories high. The stairs to the basements were still intact.

They stopped in what had once been the great hall.

"Kyle . . ." Joshua began, feeling at a loss for words, but wanting somehow to comfort his friend.

"I need to find Mother." The young chief's voice held a certainty his troubled heart did not reflect. His jaw muscles tightened visibly as he ground his teeth, fighting for control over the panic that broke out in a light, fear-filled sweat upon his brow.

"Perhaps she's in the basement," Joshua offered hopefully, yet his stomach sickened beneath the sour weight of doubt.

Without a word, the men descended into the darkened bowels of the ruined castle. They soon were in the kitchens. As Joshua expected, no one was there.

Joshua found a flint and with well-practiced fingers lit the torch that hung near the dry sink. His hand brushed the chain that looped from torch holder to wall, and it clinked softly, whispering against the stone. The gloom penetrated their senses fully, imparting the feeling that they were disturbing the very essence of the room locked in its own useless agony.

A whinny sounded from the corner as the smell of a living beast met their nostrils. Kyle reached for the torch as Joshua lit another.

The dim circle of light consumed the gloom slightly as it edged closer to the beast. And there she stood, white and beautiful. A reminder of all that was lost. Lachlan's horse.

"Father's mare." Kyle's voice was wistful and aching. "So she made it home all by herself." He couldn't bring himself to touch her, except to feel the warm breath—real, moist, and living—puffing faintly from her nostrils.

"She willna' leave th' basement. Has been here for three days."

They pivoted around to view the young man who had spoken. It was the gardener, Matthew Fraser. In happier times everyone had affectionately called him Mumbles behind his back, due to his habit of mumbling to himself as he worked.

Kyle grabbed the youth's thick forearms. "Matthew. Lady Alice. Where is she?"

"Your mother's stayin' at th' stone cottage down by th' loch." His clear blue eyes penetrated the shadows and a simple smile lit up his face, seeking to encourage. "She's well, sir. I've been makin' sure of it m'self." Evident was his childlike pride.

Saying nothing, Kyle ran up the stairs and into the sunshine once again. Thank God. She was still alive. He felt his boots pound deeply into the turf with each step as relief flowed down from head to heart.

"What happened, Matthew?" Joshua asked as they made their way outside as well. He hadn't realized how dank the castle had become until he breathed the keen air blowing off the loch. They stood in the courtyard. Matthew automatically bent down to pull a weed in one of the rose beds. He pointed across the water.

"A few days ago a British frigate sailed up the loch. The bombardment destroyed just about everythin', as ya' can see for yourself." The hand swept around in a semicircle.

Joshua sat down on a bench and stared vacantly at the greenery, trying to fight back an anger so strong it almost frightened him.

"Mary?" he asked Matthew of the housekeeper.

"She was killed in the blast, as were many others. I've been diggin' graves, buryin' folk for the past three days."

Across the courtyard and through the gatehouse, Joshua suddenly ran to escape the tidal wave of emotion surging strong and deep through his heart. He sought respite by the water—a lonely silhouette against the reddening sky. He stood in the breeze, looking out over Loch Fyne and Lachlan Bay. The red tartan of his kilt and plaid fluttered about him.

Twilight approached.

Joshua Maclachlan was a pensive man, though only 19 and raised in simplicity as a castle servant. He was as tall and nearly as broad as his chieftain. Promised to be even broader when he filled out to the powerful proportions of his father, the well-esteemed castle blacksmith, who died of a fever when Joshua was only nine. Sarah, his mother, died of the fever a week later. His arms were large and newly battle-scarred. His legs, long and thick, bore the same badges of honor and courage. He ran his hands over his forearms, relishing proudly in each snaking reminder of the past eight months of war. Scars. They were the only thing he could call his own.

Thick hair, so dark it was almost black, hung long and straight past his shoulders, and revealed the fact that the Maclachlans originated from Ireland. His skin was ruddy and glowed like the skin of his mother's family, the Stewarts of Appin. The two clans had fought side by side at Culloden.

Above the high cheekbones and beneath the fine brows, greenish eyes looked on the world forthright. And the strong set of his mouth and a jaw that was heavily bearded told of experiences far beyond his years. He had learned to lock away pain ten years ago when he was orphaned. And that skill was proving invaluable now that suffering was displayed so evidently everywhere his wearied eyes came to rest.

He turned to head back to the castle. To his pallet in a small room off the kitchen. Surprisingly, much of the basement was still as it was. Everything had fallen from its place from the force of the blast. But the great hewn table at which the servants had sat for generations still stood in the center of the kitchen. And there was wood by the massive fireplace. Mumbles had seen to that.

Hunger abruptly filled his belly with an ache.

He lit a fire and found some provisions in the large storeroom. Potatoes. Flour. Barley meal. And turnips. Swinging the great iron arm attached to the side of the fireplace, he hung a small caldron that Matthew had filled with water. Soon turnips were boiling, giving him time to meander again about the rubble-strewn courtyard, lost in the past.

It all came back so clearly. The hard life he had never minded. As a young servant, most of the unwanted jobs had been left to him. But fetching water and carrying firewood had strengthened him. Springtime blew around him and Joshua breathed in deeply, remembering his yearly ritual on the first morning of the year that the sun sweetened the air when he would linger at the loch much too long as he plunged his feet into the frigid waters. Mary, the house-keeper, always had something to say about his tardiness when he entered the castle whose walls stood golden in the morning rays of the sun. But the rare twinkle in her eye told him she understood. She had been young once, too.

They all had been young before Culloden. But now an ageless quality had stricken all of Kilbride's inhabitants.

A bit later Mumbles surfaced with two pewter plates of turnips, and they sat together in the hastily dimming twi-light. After a week of foraging for food, this simple fare was a meal fit for royalty.

"Is anyone else around the castle?" Joshua asked, his fork scraping, metal against metal, upon the plate's pewter sur-face.

"Nay," Mumbles answered between mouthfuls. "The rest have scattered or were killed by the blast, as I was sayin'."

"So you've been here by yourself?"

Mumbles nodded. "Perhaps the livin' will return to us someday."

"Perhaps. But as long as the castle isna' much more than a pile of rubble, the chances arena' good."

So they were the only servants left.

• • •

The next morning, the chief and his mother, Lady Alice, stood outside the castle, dressed in peasant rags. But even the tattered garments, the crude cart, and the old horses which were harnessed and waiting could not completely hide their nobility.

"Do ya' really think you'll make it to England without bein' caught?" Joshua asked. Doubt was splayed across his features and in his gestureless hands.

"I have to try. Jenny needs me, Joshua. She doesn't even know whether I'm dead or alive. Besides, Mother's in danger as long as the Redcoats are milling about. And I'm a wanted man."

"Will they be welcomin' ya' at her father's home?" Again Joshua doubted. Jenny's father was an English duke.

"Aye. That is the least of my worries. Getting there is not going to be easy. We've seen how Redcoats can materialize out of nowhere like the cursed wee vermin they are. But I believe we can make it." He turned to his mother. "Are you ready to start?"

She sighed heavily, looking about her ruined home through reddened eyes. "Aye, son. I'm ready to leave."

Joshua reached down into his stocking and pulled out his dirk. "Take it, m'lord. Ya' may need an extra one. Kill as many of them as ya' can along the way."

Kyle put his large hand upon Joshua's shoulder. "Nay, my friend. That time has passed."

Joshua nodded, but he didn't understand. Revenge now seemed the only reason for a Highlander to live.

"Besides," Kyle added, "you may need that dirk more than I." His eyes scanned the scene before him: the countryside, the castle, the village across the meadow in the distance. "Take care of things for me until I return."

They clasped forearms. A trust was made.

"Aye. I shall. You can count on me, m'lord."

Their eyes locked fast and hard.

"I know, Joshua. I've always been able to trust you to do what is right."

He turned and helped his mother up into the cart.

"Good-bye, Matthew." Mumbles stood mute at the chief's nod. "Good-bye, Joshua."

The air was solemn. Still.

"Good-bye, m'lord."

Kyle climbed up beside his mother and grabbed the reins. He didn't look back.

The chief was gone.

• • •

"All right then, Matthew," Joshua put his hand on the gardener's shoulder, "we've got our tasks set before us."

"What, sir?" The innocent blue eyes searched his master's.

"Let's walk a bit, over the countryside, into the village, and see what needs doin'. Ya' heard the chief, didna' ya'?"

"Aye."

"Well then, let's be about his business. Time is wastin' with each second we stand here jabberin'."

They began walking, over the meadow, to the village. Joshua brought the simple man into his confidence. He would need his help. And if Mumbles wasn't the brightest of men, he was certainly one of the most hardworking.

It was about half a mile to the village. Beyond Strathlachlan to the left a deep belt of woods shone green in the springtime sun. To the right the rolling hills began where a few sheep grazed and new lambs hopped about without a care.

" 'Tis a small village," Joshua said, now that he had seen the big cities of Britain during the war. "I wonder who will return?"

"Did Jacob make it through alive?" Mumbles asked about the blacksmith.

"Nay. But his son Edward did. We'll be relyin' heavily on him, to be sure."

Mumbles continued forward. "Mostly left are women an' children."

Down the main village street they strode, past the church, some huts, and Strathlachlan's only inn. Much was destroyed, too far gone for reconstruction. But some sounds of life could be heard. And where there was life, hope was planted.

"Do ya' really think the chief will return?" Mumbles asked.

"If he is not captured by the British. An' if he is, God help him. He'll probably end up rottin' in some disease-stricken London prison. The Crown surely willna' be kind to its enemies, Matthew."

"I suppose not." Mumbles sounded sad as they came to the end of the street.

"Let's go home," Joshua said, "and begin our duties. There's much to be done."

"Aye," Mumbles agreed. "Much to be done. An' the day is yet young."

They began by clearing the rubble and salvaging anything that looked worth saving into the vaults of the basement.

"...like buryin' old bones," Mumbles kept muttering over and over again until Joshua thought he would go mad.

But after two weeks the task was finished, and spring was waning into long, sunlit evenings. Winter preparations would need to begin, planting a garden for themselves and those in the clan whom death had left fatherless and husbandless.

The rebuilding must begin, thought Joshua. *And I am the man to do it.*

• • •

The sun set, its rays casting a golden glow over Joshua's face and neck. Joshua hated that daily event, lingering each evening in the safety of a grove of beech trees near Lachlan Bay, the body of water that Castle Lachlan sat beside in utter dejection. For as long as possible he would put off that solitary walk down the stone steps to his small room, insignificant within the phantom walls. The darkness depressed him, and wariness was still the order of life at all times of the day. Redcoats came occasionally. And at such times he would fade into the lightless passages he had loved as a child. Four thumps—two quick, two slow—from Mumbles against the storeroom cupboard in which the labyrinth began was the high sign. And he would emerge.

Joshua hated living like this. Fresh air and freedom were all he had ever asked in return for working hard on God's earth.

But nightfall was the most desolate time of day.

He rubbed the arch of his foot through the soft leather of his shoe. When the distractions of daylight faded, memories taunted him in the darkness.

And the fact that they were sweet memories, childish memories of careless afternoons and days when his biggest worry was angering Gertrude, the upstairs maid, made them agonizing in their innocence and naive optimism.

But he was a warrior now. Joshua knew that. He was a valiant, brave man. He had kept up with his chief measure for measure on the field of battle, tearing British soldiers to pieces with sword and ax. And if war seemed to somewhat haunt Kyle, it invigorated Joshua completely. He finally felt he belonged somewhere, was good for more than fetching wood and water.

And now he was home. And it was dark again.

• • •

They had been sitting at the kitchen table, a solitary candle aflame between them. Mumbles sorted through a sack of seeds, and Joshua whittled absentmindedly, not carving anything in particular, just working his hands. Neither wanted to retire to bed though midnight was fast approaching.

"What was it like?" Mumbles asked, hands moving automatically through the sack.

"Eh, Matthew?" Joshua glanced up, pulled from his introspections.

"The battle, Joshua. The final battle. Where was it? What happened?"

"It happened on the fifteenth of April, on Culloden Moor."

"Where's that?"

"About five miles west of Inverness. Way up north, Matthew." He didn't really want to talk about it and wouldn't have, but the look on Mumbles's face, so eager for the news, bade him go on. He cleared his throat.

"Culloden Moor is a wide, open field near Inverness. The skies were gray, promisin' a violent storm as we waited for the British regiments to march into view. The cavalry had naturally arrived first."

Mumbles pulled his bench closer, the slab-like legs scraping against the stone floor. The room faded from them as each word pulled their table from the quiet present to the thundering past.

"The entire night before we had marched. In two lines. We were to wage a surprise attack upon the enemy camp 12 miles away. Our stomachs had held but one biscuit the entire day. That was all they brought for provisions."

Mumbles's eyes were wide as Joshua continued, scraping the wood with his knife. "The Duke of Cumberland, Stinkin' Billy himself, was celebratin' his birthday. But the sky began to lighten an' we were still eight miles away. The surprise attack Bonnie Prince Charlie had planned was suddenly impossible, an' we turned back around. Back to Culloden Moor."

The candle on the table sputtered as Joshua recalled how the storm had broken during that final day of the rebellion. A hailstorm. His eyes blinked rapidly against the imaginary, well-remembered stones beating against his face.

"The battle had begun with the roar of artillery an' the spatterin' o' blood over m'face as the men in front an' beside me were shot down. And we fought as best we could havin' had no sleep the night before an' only one biscuit to go on. Lookin' back, Mumbles, I see that day as the travesty of war that it was. We were sheep led to slaughter."

"One biscuit?" he asked. Even slow-witted Matthew could see the futility of the endeavor. Charles Stuart's pride had been costly to his countrymen.

"One measly biscuit," he answered, pushing the knife away from him, down the block of wood with a violent thrust. He threw knife and wood on the table in disgust and sat back in his chair, sullen and brooding, angry at the world.

"What is it, sir?" Mumbles asked, eyes seeking to please.

"Oh, 'tis nothin', Matthew," Joshua answered. "Just wonderin'." He tried for a slight smile and succeeded for a brief moment.

"Wonderin' what?"

"Just wonderin' what it would have been like had we won."

Silence ensued as the kitchen became their reality once again.

Mumbles jumped up. "Just a minute, sir!" And he ran out of the room on his thin, bowed legs. He was back in a trice, arms stretched out.

The gardener handed him an old Bible he had found in the courtyard near what was once the stables.

"Here, sir. I forgot I found this!"

Joshua's fingers rubbed the stiff spine, the hard cover. They lightly traced the thick pages, uneven along the edge. The tanned leather felt warm to his touch. He loved God. And the feel of the sacred book beneath his fingertips brought back a flood of memories. Services in the small Presbyterian church in the village. Sermons which told him of God's love and forgiveness. Each Sunday he went, eager to hear the good news. And during the week he subsisted off the memories of the preacher's words and what Scripture his mother had taught him as a child. But there were no services now. The Reverend John Maclachlan, chaplain to the Jacobite forces, was rotting on a prison ship outside of London. Food for Joshua's soul was limited strictly to prayers said before bedtime, if exhaustion didn't overtake him first.

If only he could read.

He cleared his throat. "Thank ya', Matthew." Tears bit the corners of his eyes, and he quickly went to his room before Mumbles could see.

From that moment, the book sat on an upended wooden crate—the room's only furnishing besides his bed. And though the words inside were tightly locked away from his illiterate mind, he knew they were God's perfect gift to His created. A gift to him. Imperfect, wounded, aching, and alone.

Suddenly, the nights weren't so lonely. And placing his hands on the worn cover, Joshua learned anew what communion with his God could be.

After sunset he became a man of prayer. It was all he had. And strength for the tasks of a lonely life were found. Freedom and fresh air were given again without measure in the confines of the dank castle basement. He remembered the words John Maclachlan had spoken so often. He was free indeed.

• • •

Summer was in full swing as the cart creaked into the village.

"Oh, God," Mavis prayed, "let Father be alive."

He was.

Thomas Maclachlan folded his beloved daughter into his old, wiry arms and promised to take care of her and her children.

Jamie vowed to support his sister as well.

The news of her brother Dougald's death was just another tear in an already gaping hole inside her soul. She cried a little and ached to overflowing.

But for the first three days of her return to Strathlachlan, she was simply relieved just to be home.

• • •

A week later, having spoken not a word since he came to consciousness, Robin Brodie was gone.

CHAPTER

3

October, 1746

The summer passed more swiftly than the large brown hares which raced across the moor. Mumbles worked the garden each day, making sure they would have enough food for the winter. Joshua had been working since his return with the clansmen to assure some kind of harvest would be reaped. It would be meager. More and more were returning to Strathlachlan. And there were still some sheep left to graze upon the hills.

And now, autumn had rounded the corner, dressed in golden shades of serenity. He needed to start building shelter in the village for he and Mumbles.

Frequently he left the fields to hunt. Boar and deer were plentiful in the forest that lay behind the village. Already meat and fish from loch and stream were smoking in a makeshift smokehouse he and Mumbles had rigged from some of the rubble gathered in the courtyard.

The chief would not come home to complete desolation. Joshua would see to it. War had changed him, and he would never be content to be merely a servant again. The only place beside Kyle for Joshua was that of trusted friend and aide.

But this fall afternoon, procuring meat was the sole item on Joshua's agenda.

The forest swaddled him in golden-flecked green. On his back, a quiver of arrows bounced gently with each silent placing of his foot. No muskets were used now. No attention must be drawn to him or his clansmen. And who ever knew when Redcoats would appear, seemingly out of nowhere?

Arrow out and placed against the oaken bow, polished and tightly strung, he continued his search, watching, waiting, and listening. Always listening.

A muffled scream coming from over a small hill stopped Joshua. A woman's cry for help.

Arrow still in place he ran. The strong legs carried him swiftly and quietly. Again, the sound struck his eardrums. Faster he ran.

He saw red.

And he saw her on the ground, beating at the soldier atop her with ineffectual but well-aimed, fists. A basket of berries lay overturned beside her. He knew her. Joshua had seen her many times since she, her mother, brother, and sister had returned. The Redcoat, cruel and alone, raised a grimy hand to silence her. Her blue eyes were angry.

"Stand you up, Redcoat!" Joshua yelled. His voice echoed in deep strength under the treetops from his perch atop the hill. "I like to see a man's face before I send him to meet the One who gave him life."

The bow creaked softly as he pulled the arrow against the string.

Fear ignited the man's eyes, but just for a moment.

"You wouldn't kill an unarmed man, would you?" the soldier ventured, wiping smashed berries from the side of his face and sleeve. His accent proclaimed him from one of England's more wealthy houses. And his face, surrounded by dirty blond hair, was haughty with a small, beak-like nose and hooded eyes. His tongue licked the full lips as his mind clearly raced, seeking escape from the wild-eyed Scot who towered above him on the ridge.

"Ya' wouldna' rape an innocent girl, would ya'?" Joshua answered, his knees shaking with rage. "Ya' pig. Ya' filthy, rotten pig! You'll never take one of our women again, ya' know that, dinna' ya', man?"

"Let's talk about this, good man." The soldier, of medium height, stood up, took a step toward him. His black boots, highly polished, reflected the light coming through the trees. "Be reasonable. If my commander finds out about your actions, he will have this place surrounded in no time with troops."

Joshua smiled, arrow still readied. "Dinna' try an' play with me, son of the devil. You've deserted your regiment. We both know it."

"That could be," the Redcoat conceded slightly with a shrug. "But you cannot blame a man for relieving his frustrations now, can you?"

"Aye," Joshua's answer was soft and menacing. "I can blame ya', an' I will. She's only 14 years old, ya' stinkin' coward. Justice will be served here in these parts, Redcoat, an' your precious England willna' be doin' for us. So we've taken it upon ourselves."

Trying a new tactic, the Redcoat implored him, hands stretched forward, palms up. "Please, Mr. . . . ."

"No!" Joshua's anger deepened. Tears stung the backs of his eyes, daring not to come forward. "No! It's enough! We've had enough. Ya' knew better than to venture out alone. Ya' knew any Highlander worth the motto he bears would place sentence on ya' immediately. The savage behavior of you an' your fellow soldiers have assured nothin' less."

The bow string taughtened at Joshua's command as a soft breeze blew both men's hair.

"Say your prayers for soon you'll meet the demon that has spawned ya'."

In sudden desperation, the soldier ran toward Joshua, shouting curses.

Deborah Brodie stared in fascination, unflinching as the arrow made its mark.

...

The hunt was forgotten that day. Together they buried him. She wanted to help. To see the clods of dirt kicked in by her feet cover the face of her attacker. To bury all of them—the ones who killed her father, defiled her mother and Kathleen, and made Robin's life a living death.

She smiled the smile of one who has and always will survive. Forcefully their eyes locked across the shallow grave and strength flowed between them with a magnetic force, pulling them together and moving forward at the same time. *Aye*, he thought, *she's lovely, but there's more to that face than what I see.* He felt his stomach muscles tighten as the blue orbs looked steadily into his, and he took a step forward. Deborah would never need him, would never need anyone. But if she would ever come to want him as much as he wanted her in that instant, it would be enough, Joshua decided. And Joshua Maclachlan, still just 19, knew he would wait for her. In two years' time he would make her his. Deborah Brodie would be his wife.

"Thank ya' for comin' to m'rescue, Joshua." Her eyes were earnest, yet unapologetic.

"Ya' probably didna' really need me at all, Deborah Brodie. Knowin' you, that Redcoat's time was comin' to an end."

She smiled knowingly. They both knew what would have happened had he not found her, and in that moment she loved him. Her heart welled up and overflowed at the sight of him in front of her, standing so close now she could feel his warm breath upon her forehead.

Deborah held up the half-empty basket of berries with a grin. "Will ya' be comin' over tomorrow for some pie, Joshua Maclachlan?"

He bowed. "Aye, thank ya'."

She looked ruefully down into the basket. "If it hadna' been for that soldier, 'twould have been a much fuller pie."

"'Tis true, but if it hadna' been for the Redcoat, I wouldna' be comin' to enjoy it with ya' at all."

He took the basket from her hands and led her back to the village with his fingers twined mid hers. They stopped in front of her grandfather's house.

"They say, Joshua, that good sometimes can come from the bad."

"Always, Deborah. If we will it so."

• • •

"Aah," sighed Thomas as he hitched his old bones down onto the doorstone of the hut. "Daughter, ya' can fix a finer lamb stew than even your sainted mother could. An' after such a meal, I'll top it off with my last wee bit o' tobacco." He sighed, massaging the precious pouch. "Who knows when more will be comin' m'way?"

He lit his pipe as Mavis Brodie smiled from the doorway. "Thank ya', Father. 'Twas such a treat an' such a kindness on Joshua's part to bring us such a lovely bit o' meat." She leaned against the frame, wiping her hands. "Am I fancyin' things or . . ."

"Or has he taken on fancies of his own with our Deborah?" Thomas interrupted, puffing quickly to light the pipe, carved by John Brodie and given to him many years before.

"Aye, that is what I have been awonderin'."

"I dinna' think you're wrong on that account, daughter," Thomas agreed between puffs of smoke. "An' I think 'tis a good thing."

"But she's only 14, Father!"

"Well, your mother was the same age when she bore you, child."

"Father, that's different."

"And would ya' like to explain that, daughter?" His voice held the laughter of many years.

"There's really no good explanation, other than that she's m'daughter an' I dinna think I'll be able to let her go yet."

"Then dinna' let her go, Mavis. I dinna' think you'll have to for some time, anyhow."

"What mean ya', Father?"

"Joshua Maclachlan will take his time. He seems to be a strong, patient sort of man. He'll not want to scare her away."

"Aye, you're right. It's goin' to take a bit o' doin' to bring her round after what she's suffered under. She's a strong one, though."

"Aye. And then there's our Robin."

Mavis stood up suddenly, her lips tight with hurt, betraying a mother's heart. "Father, I'll not be hearin' anythin' said about m'Robin. The good Lord only knows what torment the lad is facin'."

She walked crisply into the house and finished cleaning the dishes. Robin had been gone for almost four months, and the only clue he had left was Mavis's mother's looking glass, broken upon the kitchen table. She bowed her head as she dried the plate with shaking hands.

Thomas came up from behind and put his large, arthritic hands upon his daughter's bony shoulders. "We'll see him again, daughter. With the first snow we'll see our Robin."

Deborah sat near the door embroidering an apron, pondering the conversation she had just overheard. And although Joshua had earned his place beside her, she had decided to wait. After all, he had killed the Redcoat. And she had kicked dirt down on the dead man's face.

But she buried her past that day with the devil who would have repeated her agony again and again. And she buried the four who had stolen her maidenhood as well. And Joshua Maclachlan had made the funeral, real and symbolic, possible. He of all men would understand the state in which she would enter their life together. She remembered the fire in his eyes as he called out from the knoll. And the moment she heard his voice she knew she was safe. There was no one to compare to Joshua. No one.

Deborah hummed softly to herself for a while until it was too dark to work. Then pulling her shawl around her shoulders and knotting the blue woolen under her newly budding breasts, she walked to the back of the hut. "At 16 we shall wed." It was decided.

Not 30 feet away in the darkness of the woods, Robin crouched with his kill. Waiting.

"Robin," she called into the darkness, startling him. "I know you're out there, Robin. Ya' canna' go on like this forever, brother. Ya' must be comin' home. Winter is 'round the bend."

Her voice sounded older, changed, he thought. His lungs stilled lest she hear his exhalations. And he bit back the tears as his legs ached to do her bidding. But forward he could not go.

"Ya' know, brother, I wasna' worried about ya' much before. Oh, 'tis true, I worry about your happiness, bu' I never worried much for your safety or bothered about whether or not ya' could take care o' yourself. After all, ya' must've learned somethin' about survival durin' the war, eh, Robin?"

He nodded mutely in the darkness.

"But," her voice lowered and she unwittingly took several careful steps in his direction, "Robin, things've changed. Be careful, brother."

Robin leaned forward on his haunches.

"A Redcoat chanced upon me in the forest two weeks ago, Robin. But for Joshua Maclachlan, we both know much too well what could've happened."

He already knew about it, had arrived on the scene as Joshua pulled his bowstring. Robin had shot as well, and he didn't know which arrow had done the job. Probably Joshua's.

"Ya' must be careful, brother. Ya' must be very careful."

Robin couldn't see her now, as she moved back into the dense shadow cast by the hut, but he knew she still stood in the dark. His muscles ached from their inactivity, yet he didn't want her to leave. Not yet. He sighed with relief as she spoke again.

"The chief returned today, Robin."

She paused for a moment to let that soak in.

"Aye, an' he brought Lady Jenny an' their wee bairn. Luckily, Joshua had the stone cottage down by the loch ready an' waitin' for their return for the past month. He caught word from one o' the clansmen southward that they were on their way home, so he ran over an' got a fire goin' in the place."

His eyes adjusted and he could see the lighter outline of her dress against the darkness of the house. She sat still, contemplating, then spoke again.

"I like Joshua, Robin. He's a wonderful man an' he's comin' over tomorrow for supper. We're havin' your favorite, Robin—beefsteak pie."

Deborah sighed with sadness, then brightened, humored by her own feeble attempt to rouse him. "I suppose it'll take more than pie to bring ya' round, eh, Robin? Dinna' worry, brother, I'll leave ya' a piece by the door." She drew her shawl more tightly about her.

"I'm goin' inside now. Good night, Robin." Her eyes searched the darkness, still seeing nothing. But she knew. Yes, she knew. "Dinna' forget about that pie now. I'll be talkin' to ya' tomorrow night."

A flutter of material in the breeze, she disappeared around the corner.

• • •

The squirrels he had killed and skinned were lying on Mavis's doorstep and he disappeared into the night, running with accustomed feet through the nocturnal forest and back to the empty seclusion of his cave. The wind was cold. Darkness had settled in thick completeness with no trace of a moon in sight. And Deborah was right. Winter was around the corner. Even so, Mother had left Robin another blanket and a goosefeather pillow. Slowly, Mavis was equipping her son for perennial survival. Previously she had supplied him with needles and thread, an iron tripod and hanging pot for cooking, a bucket, a small knife, and John David Brodie's exquisite bow with a staunch supply of arrows. He already had his dirk and his father's broadsword. And, of course, the drum was a constant reminder of his grief and deformity there in a dark cave called home.

He hastened, remembering an event earlier in the day. He had been walking near the stream when in his path lay a young pup—half wolf, half dog. Almost dead. She looked no more than three months old. Not knowing whether or not she was abandoned, he sat and waited for the mother to come and claim her. Three hours later, she had not. Robin made his move.

Gingerly, he picked up the unconscious beast, and immediately saw the musket wound in her side as he cradled her against him. Her breathing was faint and shallow. But warmth came from beneath the gray-brown fur. His hand rested on her back, and he could feel her. She was so real, so warm, with a beating heart. Holding her against him, his eyes closed involuntarily as his heart broke for the wee pup.

Once back at the cave, he washed her, applied a healing salve, and stitched her up. Then, after lighting a fire near the entrance and pouring water into his pot, he placed the dog on a blanket and sat down beside her as he cut up a potato and a partridge he had killed and cleaned earlier that day.

Aye, winter is just around the corner, he thought as he entered his cave. *But it might not be so lonely as I feared.* With the pup still unconscious by his side, Robin Brodie's hands whittled as his mind relived each trace of the Redcoat's knife upon his face, his back. Six months ago.

Soon he would take out his drum and remind himself of the battle and his father one more time. The sticks beat loudly against the skin top of the cylinder, as the 12-year-old played the wounded village to sleep.

• • •

The sun radiated without obstruction all over Scotland the next day. But not as blindingly as it shone over the region of Kilbride, particularly the village of Strathlachlan. The excitement broke out early in the morning when Deborah swept outside to gather eggs. Across the dirt street the blacksmith, Eddie, was stoking his fires.

"Good mornin' to ya', Deborah Brodie!" he called. "It's promisin' to be a fine day."

"Aye, Eddie. But not merely because the sun is shinin' are we to be most happy."

Setting down his tongs, Eddie, as broad as he was tall, and muscle through and through, came out into the morning light. He spread his arms wide. "What other reason could there be? The village has only half the people it once did, winter's comin' soon, and the harvest hasna' been as plentiful as it was before the blasted war."

Clearly Eddie had survived Culloden with a lion's share of disappointment. Though his smile had not faded, his eyes significantly clouded.

"The chief has returned."

The words issued softly from Deborah's lips.

"The chief has..." each massive hand encircled one of Deborah's shoulders as life, hope, and all the dreams of his youth sprang back into his large brown eyes with a blaze of all that was possible before Adam partook of the forbidden. "The chief has..." he repeated again, still unable to give voice to the complete thought which was ricocheting jubilantly about his mind. "When?"

"Yesterday afternoon. They're stayin' down at the stone cottage by the loch."

Eddie was galvanized. "We must tell the people! We must let them know!"

"Aye, Eddie. You tell the others. I'll run up to the castle to ask Joshua if he might convince the chief to come into the village today."

"Oh, he'll come. No doubt there. The chief will come to his people today or m'name isna' Edward Maclachlan." His smile was broad, stretched to its outer limits and framed by his warm brown beard and mustache. In seconds he was walking solidly up the street, hands cupped to the sides of his mouth.

"The chief has returned. The chief has returned."

The call sounded, echoing, throwing a much-needed lifeline to the Maclachlans.

And the village truly awakened for the first time in many months as Deborah lifted her skirts and ran toward the castle ruins.

• • •

The village huts shone white in the pale autumn sun, glimpses of some newly whitewashed walls flashed between tree trunks. Well over half were still nothing more than charred ruins. He ran as silently as he could over the curled up, fallen brown leaves, but faint crunches, puffs of sound, accompanied each step of his leather-bound feet. No matter. Robin Brodie simply needed to get to the edge of the wood, run across the clearing, and climb into the oak tree in the churchyard.

The chief had returned. He had heard the cry of the blacksmith earlier and, like a child called to a sweet treat, he had come. To see the man. To see for himself why hope had suddenly entered the land as tangibly as a royal messenger bearing good news.

A sigh of relief caught in his throat. He was clear now. And quicker than a cat, he climbed the tree, waiting for the clanspeople to gather.

Noise touched his ear. A noise he hadn't heard in months. Through the trees, a carriage was journeying upon the road. Not a cart. Not a horse. But a sound, beautiful carriage, shining and black, with polished brass hinges and red wheels. And such horses! Robin's eyes grew round. Bay horses. Brown coats and black manes were glistening and well-cared-for. This was wealth. And though Robin had never seen such luxury other than Bonnie Prince Charlie's finery, he knew it immediately.

The driver was a large man whose auburn hair, hanging almost between his shoulder blades, was caught at the nape of his neck with a dark-blue satin ribbon. He wore breeches, not a kilt. And his black cloak fluttered slightly around his top half. Dressed though he was, the fine clothing could not hide his ruggedness. Robin had witnessed the chief fighting valiantly during the uprising. Of course, then he had sported the blazing Maclachlan tartan. Why was he now wearing breeks? Come to think of it, Joshua Maclachlan, Uncle Jamie, and Grandfather had put aside their kilts as well. All of the men had.

Next to the chief sat his wife. So young, so fresh. Wispy waves of golden-brown hair escaped from the simple knot she wore at the back of her head. And her breeze-caressed skin glowed pink over her pretty features. Beneath her gray cloak, deep golden velvet peeped through. One hand sat possessively on her husband's thigh. The other cradled the third passenger of the vehicle.

In a daze, Robin continued to gaze at the vision before him. He couldn't take his eyes off the babe. Wrapped in pink wool, she was the most beautiful sight he had ever beheld. Sublime humanity in its most innocent form. Her darling face, framed with soft red curls, peeped out of her bunting as she sat alert on her mother's lap. Tiny hands, perfect in every way, pulled at her mother's cloak and batted at the protective arm in front of her.

And without warning, the village erupted with loud cries of "The chief! The chief is here!" The inhabitants thronged the streets, calling to others along the way, spreading the good news as the carriage stopped in the churchyard. Young boys bounded and cartwheeled their way over. Old men hobbled on their canes and rushed with bent backs and bony knees moving at impossible angles. The women laughed and called to one another as they balanced babies on their hips and corralled the rest of their broods toward the scene. They gathered together, every last inhabitant of Strathlachlan. And their eyes, how they sparkled! Their cheeks suddenly held the reddest of roses, and springtime was in every step of their worn, shodden feet.

Kyle stood in the carriage with a smile as wide as Loch Fyne upon his face. He held out his hands toward them, grabbing uplifted hands with his strength, and greeting them in turn. "Angus! Mary! Johnnie! Jamie! Eddie! Fergus! Martha!" He knew each one. "How are the children, Rachel? Where's your aged mother, George? Janie, are ya' still makin' the finest cheese in the village?"

"Who's the new little lady ya've got in your carriage, m'lord?" an ageless man asked through a face wrinkled by days and nights spent with his sheep in the brisk Scottish winds.

"This is my daughter, James. This is bonnie wee Alix."

Jenny held up the baby, and Kyle grasped the child around her middle and lifted her high above his head. The Maclachlans cheered and more than one woman wiped a tear from her eye.

"I see our prayers were answered!" Eddie called in a clear, booming voice.

"What mean you, Eddie?" Kyle asked, handing Alix back to Jenny.

"She looks like her mother after all!"

The crowd erupted in laughter, Kyle included. "We'll just see what manner of bairns you produce, Eddie. That is if you can find a woman who will have you!"

Joy was in evidence that morning. And hope previously sewn deep in the soil of misery and long forgotten sprang to life in Kilbride. All reaped of its benefits.

After the jesting was finished, the chief and his family alighted from the carriage to talk on a more serious note with the people. They brought forth their concerns.

"We need someone to run the mill."

"More shelter should be built before the snow falls."

"I'm afraid my garden didna' yield enough to feed us this winter."

And Kyle, with his hands on his people's shoulders, comforting, imparting strength, calmed their fears, and made plans to meet their needs. He called Joshua to him.

"This is Joshua Maclachlan," he said to the clansmen. "You may remember him from Castle Lachlan as one of the servant boys."

"He isna' a boy any longer!" someone yelled. "He's a giant, he is!"

"He's a giant and more. He saved my life at the battle of Falkirk-Muir. He is a just man, an honorable man, and I have made him my thane. Whatever comes from his lips is just as if it came from mine."

"Here, here!" Thomas yelled.

"Aye! Here's to Joshua Maclachlan!"

More cheers erupted as Joshua publicly took on great responsibility. Then and there he vowed to serve his clan with all the strength that waited inside of him. Deborah looked on in silent adoration.

The chief stayed for two more hours, listening to the wants and needs of his people. Yes, the rebuilding had begun. The chief had returned.

Up in the tree Robin sat in utter stillness, entranced by the scene before him. Entranced by the wee baby in soft pink wool. Then she laughed. The baby laughed despite all that had happened before, all that was necessary to take place to build up the clan once again. Clear, puerile tones echoed innocently across the destruction of the village, across the tattered garments of the clanspeople, across the aching plains of a country in subjection. For she knew not what Scotland had become, how much ardent toil lay ahead for her people. And for the first time in many months, Robin Brodie smiled.

• • •

August, 1748
Two Years Later

Joshua stood upon Mavis's doorstone with a bouquet of heather. Such a common, abundant flower. But it was his Deborah's favorite. Two years had passed since they had buried the Redcoat together. He remembered it well. They had turned away from the grave and smiled into each other's eyes. The smiles were ruthless, yet peaceful and without a trace of regret, and she had slipped her slender hand into his as he led her back to her home. She had been wearing blue then, and she was wearing blue now as the door opened.

Deborah Brodie, at 16, was completely a woman. Her hair, pulled up in the front, fell in bright, red-blonde curls down her back. She was quite tall and her figure was graced with the curves of womanhood—a body meant to bear and nurture children with its softness, to cradle a man at the end of a hard day. Joshua's eyes consumed her face, the eyes, bright blue, the peachy skin that seemed almost golden, the chin which jutted out defiantly when she was cross. Without realizing it, his hand reached out to caress the fine jawline which sported a spidery white scar along its edge. It intrigued him to know she had suffered; it thrilled him that she had survived. She didn't flinch as his gentle fingertips glided across the surface of her skin. The scar was as much a part of her, faded though it was, as anything she was born with. She liked it there. No one had to guess who she was.

A smile broke out on her face as she reached up to grab the large hand with a playful squeeze.

"Come in, Joshua Maclachlan." She eyed the flowers as she stepped away from the door with an inward sweep of her hand. "It's about time you started comin' around in such manner. I've been 16 for almost five months."

Joshua laughed. He had been visiting the Brodies' house for two years now, and everyone had acknowledged his place among them. Many evenings he had settled his tall frame on the doorstep to converse with Thomas, Mavis, or Deborah, or sat in warmth before a humble winter's fire. Even Kathleen had finally emerged from her speechless state and was always delighted when Joshua came to visit.

"I had much to prepare for," he said of the house he was building. Kyle had bestowed upon him, as his thane, 100 acres of land to do with as he pleased. Of course, upon Kyle's death it would be up to his son, Lachlan, only a baby now but future chief of the clan, whether or not he could remain there. But for now, he was considered a nobleman among the Maclachlans. Kyle had treated him well. And now sheep were grazing upon the land, and crops would be harvested soon. If all went well, a steady income was coming their way. "The house is almost finished. The crops are almost ready. And so the time has come, Deborah Jane."

Now it was Deborah's turn to laugh. She had no middle name, but Joshua insisted on calling her that. And it pleased her greatly, for it was his term of endearment.

She had been over to see the place built by his own hands. A fine house, built of stone and sturdy. Like her husband-to-be. And how she had grown to love him. His massive frame was comforting and made her, though large for a woman, feel childlike beside him. As strong as she was, he was stronger. And his gentleness toward her—the way his green eyes deepened with pleasure at the sight of her, or his fine dark brows arched in humor and surprise at her saucy ways—spoke to her mind and body in ways she didn't thoroughly understand. Yet she relished in the feeling. She already loved him with a lasting, steady love. And now the romance of man and woman would begin. Inside she felt shaky with anticipation. Soon she would feel his caresses, touch his hardened, weathered body, and feel him next to her every night. Her eyes could feast upon the beauty of him: the long, thick legs, the massive arms, the broad chest and muscled back, the straight, black hair, so thick and soft, meant for her hands alone. And it would all take place in the little house he had built for her, for their life together.

She would make their home an impregnable fortress in an everyday world torn by war of one sort or another. Would fasten his armor in the morning with loving affection, and tend his wounds and exhaustion at night with feverish passion.

"You're startin' out with a finer life than most women ever dare to dream of," Mavis had said one day when they walked out together to the property. "Dinna' take it for granted, Deborah. Use your blessin's properly an' give them back to the Lord."

And Deborah knew her mother was right. She looked at Joshua as he sat down at the kitchen table. He was a loving man, a giving man, a good man who loved the Savior. Their life would be filled with deeds pleasing to Him.

"Would ya' care to go for a stroll, Deborah Jane?"

"Aye, Joshua."

Suddenly she was nervous. Her future was beginning presently. What she had wanted for two years was finally happening. Could she measure up, or would she be found wanting? Joshua's hand was stretched across the surface of the table, and she placed hers in his. He squeezed it firmly, with a purpose. They were in this life together.

Looking into his green eyes, so tender and strong, she sighed in relief. Yes, they were in it together.

That night she told Robin all about it.

• • •

Late September, 1748

Cold mutton, partridges and duck, scones, oatcakes, and cheeses of many varieties were carefully arranged on the long, makeshift table in front of Joshua's new home. And now it was Deborah's as well. The well-wishers came with food in abundance, and the wedding festivities began.

The ceremony had been simple, held in the calm beauty of the forest. Deborah had been insistent, and only Joshua knew why. Villagers and clanspeople came to see their chief's most trusted man wed the fair Deborah Brodie. And so had Robin, tucked far above them in the top of a tree. But now the celebration, in the Highland style, was pushing on fervently. Spirits were high, and people enjoyed themselves more intently and loved more passionately. It was a wedding day.

After an hour of walking among the clanspeople, Joshua pulled Deborah inside the house and up the steps. The revelry filtered in with the midday sun through the closed window. He shut the simple muslin curtains with a swish and turned with a grin to his wife. It was lopsided and eager.

"Are you scared?" Deborah's brows were raised and her hands were clenched together under her breasts.

He had been. All night he lay in the bed and stared at the ceiling. Capable, respected Joshua Maclachlan, a leader in the clan, brave and responsible. He'd have been blind if he hadn't noticed other women's reaction to him when he went into Glasgow on business for Kyle. The propositions had been numerous for he was fair of form, of face, and of heart. But his heart belonged to Deborah. And it was easy to refuse them all. For her. And for himself. Now, as he looked at her, so lovely in the pale-green lawn dress she had made herself to wed him in, flowers and ribbon twined in her silky locks, the fear was gone. This was meant to be from before the world began. Just he and Deborah. Forever. And only unto each other.

He took a step forward and reached out his hand. "Nay, I am not afraid, Deborah Jane. For I love ya' so."

"And I you, Joshua. M'darlin', sweet Joshua." She reached forward and pulled the ribbon from his hair. "An' I wish for ya' to kiss me. Right now. For I dinna' know if I can last a moment longer."

"Are *you* frightened?" Joshua's hands ran from the sides of her face, down the length of her neck, and came to rest on her shoulders. He pushed her gown down over her arms. His question meant so much more than hers had to him.

"Nay, Joshua." Her gaze was level, deep and centered. "For I know ya' love me so."

"That I do, Deborah Jane," his lips touched hers. "An' I always shall."

She became a new creature in his arms, reborn underneath his expression of devoted love. Pure again and undefiled. He had accepted her, knowing it all, and it mattered not to him.

It was as if she had never known a man before.

And truly she hadn't. For those soldiers were not men. And Joshua, with strength and affection knit tightly within the very fibers of his soul, was more than just a man. He was her husband. And she was his wife. Would stand strong next to him, even as he had stood by her for the past two years.

The past was redeemed for Deborah Brodie Maclachlan.

• • •

A light tap sounded upon the bedroom door. It was Jenny, Kyle's wife.

"Deborah?" she called softly. "Are you all right?"

"Aye, m'lady."

"They're ready to start the dancing. And we need you and Joshua to open up the Wedding Reel. Do you know where he is?"

Deborah stifled a giggle as Joshua began to kiss her on the neck.

"Oh, I think I'll be able to find him. . . ."

Jenny knowingly smiled on the other side of the door. "Good. I'll tell them you're on your way." A few seconds passed. "See you there as well, Joshua."

Her footsteps thudded softly down the stairs, blending with the laughter of the newlyweds. They had been found out.

• • •

The following Sunday, the Reverend John Maclachlan announced the benediction and the race was on.

Two couples had been married in the same week. Joshua and Deborah, and the miller's daughter Anna and a crofter's son named Donald. Deborah had laughed when Joshua explained the custom earlier that day as they were getting ready for the Sunday service.

He handed her bonnet to her. "It works like this, Deborah Jane. If more than one couple gets married in a given week, the very next Sunday they must hurry home, for the first couple that enters their home is assured of a happy and prosperous life together."

"But we already know our life will be such, Joshua," she remarked with a laugh as he reached under her chin and straightened out the bow.

"Aye, but willna' it be amusin'?"

She caught the twinkle in his eyes. "Tha' it will. An' I say, let's win this race." Her competitive nature took over. "I'm sure we shall be able to do it."

"Aye, we shall for certain. Now this is what we'll do. . . ."

On the way to the church they planned their quick escape in hushed tones, though no one was around to hear them. And now they heard the same words uttered every Sunday, but never more anticipated before. "Let us go in peace, to love, honor, and serve the Lord, A. . . ," Joshua pulled Deborah to her feet, ". . . men."

Down the aisle they ran, even before the preacher had descended. The old ladies gasped and the children cried out in glee. But Anna and Donald were nowhere to be found, and suddenly everyone saw them thunder past in their cart.

The people thronged out of the church and began to cheer as Joshua and Deborah ran quickly to their buggy, her long legs easily keeping up with his.

"Take my horse, Joshua!" Kyle yelled as the couple started running for their carriage. "Let's make this a fair race."

Joshua helped Deborah up, then swung up behind her, wheeling Caleb, the chief's mighty war horse, around to face the right direction.

"Go, Caleb!" he whooped, as Kyle slapped the mount on his hindquarters, and they were off.

"Go, Joshua, go!" Mavis and Kathleen cried. The crowd yelled. And Deborah held on tight, exhilarated and ready for anything.

Ahead of them the trap bounced, Donald urging the horse to move faster. Anna held on to her hat, light-blonde curls bouncing in ringlets around her shoulders.

The cheaters, Deborah thought, the spirit of competition flaring up with a vengeance. *We'll just see who wins this race!*

Caleb's feet thundered down the road, through the village, amid the cheers of the clansmen, and out into the countryside. They were closing in quickly. Anna kept looking behind her and hitting Donald on the arm, yelling at him to hurry.

"Go, Caleb! Faster!" Deborah yelled. Anna and Donald's house was closer than their home. They would have to pass the other couple and then some. "Oh, Joshua, do hurry!"

Joshua laughed the laugh of a strong man as he pulled alongside of the cart.

"Good day, all!" he cried, overly cheerful, sickeningly indulgent. "Nothin' like a fair contest, is there?"

Donald looked ahead, smoothed his lank brown hair back, embarrassed. Anna hit him on the arm again. "We'll just see about that, Joshua Maclachlan!" she shouted, her voice vibrating with each bump in the road. "*You've* got farther to travel."

"Tha' means nothin', Mrs. Donald," he taunted and then lightly dug his heels into Caleb's flanks. "We'll be at home eatin' Sunday dinner by the time your poor old nag makes it to your door."

And they were off. Deborah whooped and hollered, swinging her bonnet over her head by its strings in great circles. Joshua's arms tightened about her as the stallion increased its speed, hooves thwacking the road. Suddenly he veered off the road—a shortcut only made possible by a single mount.

"You canna' do that!" Anna yelled in a shrill voice, clenching her fists and waving them into the air.

"A long an' happy life to ya'!" Joshua yelled behind him as Deborah laughed till she cried.

They were home in no time.

PART TWO

1762

The Cave

Written in the Highlands

Behold! it opens to my sight,
  Dark in the rock, beside the flood;
Dry fern around obstructs the light;
  The winds above it move the wood.

Reflected in the lake, I see
  The downward mountains and the skies,
The flying bird, the waving tree,
  The goats that on the hill arise.

The grey-cloaked herd drives on the cow;
  The slow-paced fowler walks the heath;
A speckled pointer scours the brow;
  A musing shepherd stands beneath.

But see the grey mist from the lake
  Ascends upon the shady hills;
Dark storms the murmuring forests shake,
  Rain beats around a hundred rills.

—James MacPherson

CHAPTER

4

May, 1762

"For your valor at Bannockburn, I, Robert the Bruce, King of the Scots, do proudly bestow upon thee the title of Earl of the Woods," 16-year-old Alix Maclachlan, the chief's daughter, chuckled, lightly dubbing her dog on top of his furry pate with her walking stick. She could have been 12. For underneath the voluminous, wine-colored skirt, the legs were still skinny with the knobby knees of childhood. Her arms were all elbows and wrists, jointy appendages that somehow moved with the grace of a willow tree. Yet her face contrasted with her body in the soft curve of her cheeks which always bloomed with the roses of health and the kisses of the Highland breezes which blew down from the hills.

Tail swinging unchecked, the wiry Russian sheepdog gazed at his waifish mistress with justified adoration. She hugged his neck ardently, her long, straight auburn hair flowing down her back.

Since he was given to her by her parents when she was six years old and he a bouncing, quivering pup, the loyal companion helped the quiet, curious child explore the fields and woods which surrounded the loch. They romped together everywhere.

The Maclachlan regions bordered upon Loch Fyne, a beautiful inlet that shimmered deep-blue and invited play. With a brother, two sisters, servants, and clansmen seeking out her father constantly, Alix often sought respite from the boisterous, noisy household in which she lived by walking alongside the peaceful, watery expanse. But today they were in the woods that lay a few hundred yards behind the village of Strathlachlan, where many of the clansmen made their homes and toiled their days away to happy tunes and crying, as well as laughing, children. Alix loved the woods as well. The moistened dimness. The secret places known only to her and Ivan. The silence.

In the woods she had never felt alone or vulnerable. Even as a child. It was a presence she could not explain. Just a feeling.

"Come on, then, Ivan," she said with a whistle, as she gathered her skirts with one hand and picked up the walking stick with another. The tyke stepped martially in line beside her, head in front, nosing out scents of danger. It was almost supper time, and Alix was eager to get home to the great manor house named Castle Lachlan, built to replace the family castle when she was a tot. The old fortress had already transformed itself into an enchanted, overgrown spot that the area children loved to explore after they had finished helping in the fields or around the house.

Alix continued on, ears tuned to the faint crunching of leaves and the soft pop of twigs on the forest floor. Leftovers from the fall. Spring was in full regalia, and the trees still wore cloaks of new green, brighter than the older green of midsummer. Evoking a fresh dose of optimism and hope in Alix's already bright outlook on life. Her step gained an extra measure of bounce. Alix relished the season, breathing in deeply on purpose, not wanting to miss a single particle of her favorite time of the year. Ivan, nose in the air, fur bristling, pushed against her leg, bidding her stop. But she didn't notice. And they continued on deeper into the forest until . . . a rustling sounded . . . and the dog stood motionless, growling deeply at the bushes to her left.

Fear sang in low decibels within Alix. Muffled snortings anchored her feet to the forest floor. Pacing from side to side, its base form flickered through the foliage.

A wild boar.

He was suddenly still. Ivan stood ready for the charge. Alix ceased to breathe.

But it happened so quickly.

In an instant, the hound was flying through the air with a yelp as Alix felt her legs move beneath her. The boar was running at her full force. Ivan, bleeding and wounded, struggled to get up as she ran in the direction of the village, but not before she had looked into its bright and beady eyes, mad with instinct. Its feral scream rang in her ears as she continued in flight, frail legs jarred with every step. Her large feet slammed painfully into the toes of her boots.

Get home! Get home! Terror urged her forward. She knew the clearing couldn't be far away. Her blood hammered forcefully through veins and arteries, resounding with each pounding foot as she sought escape.

Run, Alix, run! The devil's at your heels!

The trees caught at her long red hair. She didn't feel it. Didn't feel the briars and thorns tearing at her calves and arms. Didn't realize her skirt was ripping to shreds. The constriction of lungs and throat seemed to squeeze the life out of her brain. She became frantic. Eyes widened. Desperate with the will to survive.

Still, the boar advanced. Each stomping hoof brought him closer. In the throes of panic, all Alix could picture were those awful tusks and beady black eyes. A vision. A nightmare in front of the blurring foliage. Ivan was coming after it now, loping painfully in furious pursuit. His wounds, bleeding profusely, slowed him. Moving with an instinct as strong as the animal's that he chased, his barks echoed loudly, bounding off each tree, each leaf.

It leapt with a snarl.

The cloven hoofs made contact with her calves and, screaming at last, she fell from the force of the animal's dense weight. Darkness took over her mind as intense fear transformed itself into a benign anesthetic. A horrible, high-pitched scream pierced the forest as unconsciousness overtook her.

Fallen in a mossy bed of green, Alix lay in pallid oblivion. The roses were gone from her cheeks. Her tresses were wild and disheveled, arranged in confusion about the expressionless features. Vulnerable and childish she lay, eyelids thin and bluish, transparent skin showing the delicate blue veins of her throat. Her breathing was faint.

• • •

Beautiful.

Alix had been so to him since he first gazed upon her almost 16 years ago, merely an infant then, with smooth skin and happy, with wispy red curls. And over the years as she sojourned into his domain, her innocent laughter had played upon his heart. As vulnerable as he.

Tentatively, Alix's guardian of the forest reached out, wanting so badly to touch her cheek, her chin, the tip of her nose. The hand faltered, and yet he knew he might never have this chance again. Never before had he been this close to Alix Maclachlan. Years had passed since he had even spoken to, let alone touched another human being. Bear, the wolf-dog, now old and graying, around her face, sat breathing heavily, waiting patiently nearby.

His rough, weathered hand, young and strong, reached forward again. Beneath his roughened fingertips, her soft pink skin felt warm, and his eyes closed as they continued across her cheek to glide through the silky tresses which had long since lost their curl. The cool, moistened skin, the living human body he knelt over sent waves of warm pleasure through him. Basically human, instinctively needy. He had been watching over this maiden ever since she came back to Scotland with her parents almost 16 years before. Yet Alix had seen only glimpses of this youth of the woods, this local enigma. His face was somber, almost fearful of what this meeting could mean. The feel of her—real, alive, and breathing faintly—filled him with something he couldn't quite describe. Something his solitary existence defied him to understand.

Alix Maclachlan had always moved him, had drawn him to her. Touching her was like feeling a cool breeze after a summer storm.

She would awaken soon, he thought, with an unexplainable mixture of fear and elation. His emotions had been scourged by darkness, devoured by solitude. And every lonely year that he had excruciatingly lingered through pushed him down further into the darkened soil of despair. And yet Alix had always been there for him to guard, her blazing hair and warm ways bringing a light onto the horizon.

New emotions battered his heart, and he was powerless to resist their sweetness. Light dawned fully and warmly upon him as he stared at the vulnerable maiden and touched her lips with the tips of his fingers. When her small smile spread unconsciously beneath them, Robin Brodie knew that utter darkness had been banished forever.

He had saved her.

Alix Maclachlan lived and breathed because he had made her his responsibility. He knew these woods. He knew his weapon. She had never really been in danger, for Robin knew fully as he raced ahead of them, getting in position to fire his bow, that the boar would meet his doom. He had not been too late. And Alix was still unharmed because he, Robin Brodie, had made sure of it.

When her scream echoed off the treetops and over the embankment that separated them, he had raced through the trees, leather-bound feet familiar with the boulders and crevices, roots and gullies. At the same time he reached for an arrow and lined it up on his bow. Handmade and polished nightly to a high sheen, that was his weapon. His central means of pride, protection, and sustenance.

He had heard her running along a stretch near the small burn that crisscrossed the forest. Saw the wine color of her dress flickering through the leaves. Running to the small rise of ground that separated them, he pulled back on the arrow as the boar came in sight, feeling the tension strain from string, to wood, to fingers, to bicep. With an aim confident and practiced, he let go as the boar leapt. It hit right where he intended it should. And he ran forward as the pig squealed horrifically, the arrow entering its neck. Bear battered it broadside just as its front hooves reached Alix's calves.

Ivan now whined to him for help, eyes glazed, sides puffing with each breathless inhalation. Long ago the dog had become used to Robin's scent. As well as Bear's.

Robin laid down his bow, covered Alix with his plaid, and turned toward the faithful hound. "You're a brave one, boy," was all he said as he removed a clean cloth from his dependable knapsack, unfolded it, and wiped away the dirt. The profuse bleeding, now slowed, had done most of the cleansing. Next he brought out a flask. He poured Scotch whisky onto the wound. Ivan jerked as the fiery liquid burned a cleansing trail through the gore hole. Robin quickly bandaged the dog's chest with deft fingers, and turned back to Alix.

"M'lady!" he whispered, pushing his matted hair back from his eyes. "M'lady, wake up!" Knowing it had been fear and not the boar which rendered her unconscious, he realized she would awaken soon.

"Alix Maclachlan. Lassie. Wake up," he said again.

Tuned to the gentle force of his command, the blue eyes of his unknowing charge fluttered open. The woods were fuzzy and insubstantial to Alix as the world once again sharpened into focus. Silhouetted against a twilight sky that patched its way between the dancing leaves, she saw the form of a stranger kneeling over her. Then she remembered her fear as consciousness took complete hold of its rightful place.

She let out a cry. "No!" she screamed. He appeared to be half beast, half man, and for the second time that day her feet moved quickly beneath her, propelling her toward the edge of the trees to safety. But she stopped after gaining a safe distance and turned back around. Her companion had not followed.

"Ivan!" she shouted, beckoning the dog to come. "Ivan come here now!"

The scene before her caused her breath to stop as the man reached down and tenderly petted Ivan who tried to rise but couldn't. Her heart wrenched. He had fought so valiantly. Robin looked at her full face, standing up straight.

"Ivan!" she called again more softly, taken under the spell of the eyes which had locked into her gaze. Her fear dissipated under the weight of compassion, and she felt ashamed for running away like that. Ivan tried again to walk, but it was too much for him. He sat back down and looked up at Robin.

"He's in too much pain," the young man said with soft speech and kind eyes.

In one glance, it all became clear to Alix as the stranger stood mute and alone, save for the huge dog and his bow. Off to the side, the boar lay lifeless.

"It was you who killed the boar." The realization flooded Alix with relief as she walked back to her dog.

Robin simply nodded.

Her hands lightly fingered the bandages on Ivan's chest. "Did you do this as well?"

He nodded again.

"Thank you."

She now stood directly in front of him, and reaching down she picked up the plaid that had fallen to the ground and handed it to him. He looked down at the top of her head, at the burnished hair growing finely out of her white scalp, and he breathed in the scent of her, the clean sweat of the chase now drying on her forehead and under her clothes. Then she looked at him again, openly, curiously, benevolently. *He has the bearing of a Pictish king,* she thought. Middling of stature, lean yet strong, his limbs were filled with concentrated power. The purposeful scar was now white and faded from time's passage. Indeed, with his long black curls and unkempt beard, he looked wild and untamed, the last member of an angry race of fallen kings. But the dark eyes looked upon her with gentleness.

"You're Robin Brodie."

His kilt and plaid told the tale. Long ago Highland dress had been banned by the British to subjugate the Scots yet more. Only one person dared to wear Highland dress. He was the cause for local pride, and the villagers affectionately referred to him as the Last Highlander. They talked of his persistence, and wondered in what other ways he continued to rebel against the Crown. And now Alix, who had pondered the unknown ways of this mysterious, yet celebrated legend, found herself face-to-face with him.

He simply nodded, noting the gleam in her eyes as she continued. "I've seen only glimpses of you. I know your mother and your sisters. I used to fall asleep to your drums when I was a little child." Alix moved closer. "They comforted me for some reason, and yet they made me yearn. . . . I liked knowing you were out there. When they stopped some years ago, it saddened me. Hearing you made me feel safe."

Robin moved forward. Only slightly.

"Can you talk?" Alix asked, face open and nonthreatening.

Robin smiled. The brown eyes held a doe-like sheen. Unable to stop herself, Alix reached out to push away the black curls that fell into his eyes. He grabbed her hand with a hard squeeze, remembering only his scars, and pushed it away. "Aye, lassie," he said softly, finally answering her question in a low whisper, "but I dinna' do it much."

"I owe you my life," she said. "Thank you, Robin."

He bowed slightly, slowly. Each movement mesmerized her.

"Robin?"

"What, lass?"

"Would you meet me out here again tomorrow?" She could hardly believe she had dared to ask.

"I dinna' know if I can." His discomfort was evident, and he threw his plaid back over his shoulder.

"Why not?"

He shrugged, shifting from left foot to right.

"Please, Robin."

He still didn't answer.

"Well, will you walk me home then?"

"Aye, m'lady." He picked up Ivan. "Take my arm," he said to Alix.

His command was comforting, and her fingers curled onto the solid bicep. Years of survival, alone in the woods, had toughened him outside.

"Stay, Bear," he commanded the dog, lest there be more cause for fright upon whomever they should happen to meet.

Alix realized he had never said whether or not he would meet her again. But looking up at the fine features of Robin Brodie, the deep-set eyes, the small nose, the purposeful mouth, she thought he might.

Eventually.

Maybe not tomorrow.

But someday.

He walked firmly to the edge of the forest. And for the first time in 16 years he kept walking, not running, the light of the setting sun shining upon them. Each muscle tensed. He could feel it. Instinct. Honed to an animalistic point. His eyes darted warily. His heart beat as rapidly as that of a cornered fox, waiting for the hounds to lay siege. All around him was calm. A foreign world bathed in peace. Inside he raged with wary distrust of the world before him. But the feel of the small hand upon his arm kept him from bolting. He clung—her touch his anchor.

With Alix on his arm, Robin Brodie came to the chieftain of his mother's clan. Kyle was walking to the stables, getting ready to search for Alix. His face held no worry. It was something he had become accustomed to, having to search for his wandering daughter at least once a week since she was old enough to wander alone.

"John!" he called ahead of him to the stablehand, "Saddle Elijah. I must go searching for Alix again!" Near the door Mumbles puttered about the bulb beds, thrustful and jubilantly pointing their razored collection of leaves to the waning sun.

"Don't be too hard on her, Kyle," Jenny, Alix's mother, called laughingly from the doorway of the kitchens. The chief was nothing short of a pushover when it came to his girls, his wife included. Even his son, Lachlan, just a year younger than Alix, knew how to talk his father into almost anything.

"Papa!" Alix called. Kyle turned toward them, seeing his daughter on the arm of a stranger. Jenny stepped out into the yard.

"Alix!" he answered, instinctively laying his hand on his pistol, "are you all right?"

"Don't worry, Papa. I am all right. This is Robin Brodie."

"'Tis true?" he asked, his whole body registering his surprise. He looked wide-eyed at Jenny, whose reaction mirrored his own. Like everyone else he had been fascinated with the legend of this rebel Highlander. Robin Brodie's belligerence toward the Crown was an unending source of pride to the Scots who would forever consider themselves Jacobites.

By this time Jenny had reached Kyle, and the two walked toward them. "Alix, are you all right?"

"I'm fine," Alix said. "Robin saved my life!"

"Oh, Alix, what happened?" Jenny cried, as Alix ran into her arms. Alix's hair, in wild disarray, and her tattered skirt didn't give much of a clue other than a chase had ensued during whatever ordeal their daughter had survived. Jenny looked over her legs, scratched and sore, and hugged her daughter to her tightly.

"Look at poor old Ivan," Kyle said kindly as Robin laid the dog at his feet. Leaning down to pet him, he noticed the bandages on the dog's chest. "Did you bind him up then, Robin?"

Robin nodded.

"What happened?"

"A boar," was all Robin said. All he was capable of saying. His mind ached. This removal from the bowered harbor of his emotions was becoming too much to bear.

To the chief his family meant everything. He thrust out his hand. "Thank you, man. Thank you for saving her life."

Robin held his out and Kyle grabbed his forearm. Human contact. Man to man. Another barrier fell. Without another excruciating word, Robin Brodie, plaid flying behind him, ran back into his woods.

• • •

Eyes well accustomed to the darkness, he waited for the large brown hare that loped in graceful, yet erratic leaps across the moonlit moor. Bow poised, arrow in place, Robin released his fingers. His aim careful, the arrow struck true and the hare was down, tumbling over and over through the unblooming heather.

In no time it was skinned and ready to deliver to Mother. He bounded down the small hill at the edge of the woods and into the clearing. Bear stayed at the tree line. She knew the routine.

The tiny house looked warm and inviting as the golden, substantial light shone smooth and rich out of the windows. Quietly he looked in at his mother sewing by firelight. Grandfather Thomas had passed on last year, "traveled" as the Highland folk say, and she was alone.

A parcel waited for him, wrapped in a clean sack and bundled with twine. He picked it up, then placed the hare, cleaned and covered in cloth, on the doorstone. On top he arranged a small bundle of herbs and three flowers. Three quick raps on the window, and he was back at the edge of the woods where he sat and waited in the rustling of the night.

A warm light stabbed the darkness as the door opened. Mavis Maclachlan Brodie, hair now liberally laced with gray, reached down and picked up the bundle. Kissing the flowers, she looked toward the woods, eyes misting as usual. Her heart never stopped breaking for the tormented young man who was her son. The young man she didn't know anymore. Was he still out there? Watching? She didn't know. But she waved into the darkness anyway.

The door closed and Robin sat as one suspended in time, hand still raised in mute response to her gesture. When the light was extinguished two hours later and Mother was safe for the night, his muscles jerked back into motion. Slowly, under a lonely moon, he returned to his cave.

• • •

"Alix, I want you to be careful tomorrow," said Kyle after prayers as they walked up to their chambers. "The woods can be dangerous, as you've found out so painfully."

"Your papa's right. Besides, with these scrapes all over your legs," Jenny said as she lovingly stroked her daughter's hair, now clean and shining after a long, hot bath, "you'll probably not feel like walking much anyway."

"I think it would be best if you stayed in tomorrow," Kyle said with concern, his voice sterner than usual.

"But, Papa," Alix argued, "I doubt if another boar will . . ."

"Perhaps not," the chief interrupted his daughter, "but I'd still like you to stay here."

Alix bowed her head in submission. Staying in all day was a horrible fate. And what of Robin? She said she would meet him there tomorrow. But her father, although loving and sweet, had always made it clear he meant to be obeyed.

Her parents accompanied her into her room.

Alix sat on the edge of her bed, wincing as she bent her stiff legs underneath her. "Mama, do you think I'll ever see Robin Brodie again?"

"I don't know, love. That's the first time I've ever seen him up close." Jenny's clear, dark-blue eyes were thoughtful and deep.

"Aye," said Kyle. "It's all a very strange situation."

"Papa?" Alix asked.

"Yes, child?"

"For some reason, I feel like I've always known him. I mean, he's a frightful sight . . ."

"All that hair!" Jenny interrupted with a comment only a mother could make with such finesse.

"But his eyes," Alix continued, "they're like windows. Clear and smooth. He seems so gentle underneath that wild exterior."

The chief shook his head, still wary, and rightfully so. "That may be true, Alix. And then again, it may not. No one knows what he does in the woods. We only know he hunts game for his mother. He's chosen to be alone, and I think we should honor his choice. Don't force yourself on him, Alix. Robin is a scarred individual, and his wounds may run deeper than what you have seen on the surface."

"But, Papa, I asked him to . . ."

Kyle's eyes flashed and Alix knew she had argued one too many times. "I've spoken, child. You may not go near the woods tomorrow."

"Aye, Papa."

The chief reached out and put his arms around her. "I love you, Alix." He squeezed her shoulder. "And maybe one day when you have a child of your own, you shall understand."

Alix nodded mutely.

"You must be exhausted," Jenny said, tucking the covers up under her daughter's chin. "You sleep in tomorrow. Your lessons can be saved until the next day."

The bed felt so good as it cradled her exhausted body, and within seconds Alix's eyelids became heavy.

"What do you think of all this?" Kyle asked his wife as they shut the door behind them.

"I do not know quite what to think, truth be told. But I do feel utterly sorry for Robin, Kyle." The pretty face saddened.

"Aye, my love," he said, gathering her into his arms, "we cannot help but do that."

"Do you think maybe you're being a little too hard on Alix? She's wandered the woods for years, my love."

Kyle smiled down at his wife. "Maybe. But it will be better for her to start to heal up properly and to realize that although the woods may be Robin Brodie's home, peril can always lie in wait. She's too much like her mother when it comes to being outside."

"And like her father in every other way," Jenny laughed as they walked toward their own room, arm in arm. "We've been blessed, Kyle. Maybe we can share some of the love we've been given with that tortured young man."

"Robin Brodie may be beyond reach, my love."

For the first time in three years, the chief and his lady lay in each other's arms accompanied by the rhythms of a drummer boy. Alix heard them in her sleep and smiled.

• • •

With his plaid drawn over his body, the small cooking fire began to go red as Robin, still tingling from his brush with humanity, wafted off to sleep. The black eyelashes, long and curled, rested lightly on his cheeks, almost making the young man appear like the lad he was inside. The drum lay next to him.

Robin Brodie was, in fact, 27 that very day. He usually lost track of the exact date during the year. But he knew it was his birthday when the parcel waiting for him held a new kilt and plaid, as well as a snowy-white shirt. All sewn by Mother. He wasn't sure how she managed to weave the tartan without her loom, but he was grateful. He was a Scot, a true Highlander. And sometimes he felt as if he were the only one left. But as long as he wore the native dress of his people, he fought against them—the men, the country that killed his father, raped his mother, and disfigured him for the rest of his life. He would never wear breeches. And in his own private way, he continued fighting against the men that had haunted his dreams for years.

While Bear lightly slept in the bushes by Mavis Brodie's front door, her master—the ancient youth of the woodland, folk figure of Strathlachlan—slept in his cave. A nightmare raged through his slumber, but this night it was different. There followed a dream of hope, of spring freshets and laughing children. For he had touched Alix Maclachlan and his life would never again be what it once was. Robin Brodie had felt the touch of a gentle, strong, young woman.

Her eyes had sought his in friendship. And he knew that in some peculiar way, she needed him. And being needed made all the difference.

In their stone house a mile away, Deborah laid her head on Joshua's strong chest. And she prayed as she did each night that soon Robin would come back, that she would know her brother once again.

A tear escaped her eye and dropped onto her husband's warm skin. The great arm around her tightened gently. He had heard the drums as well.

"He'll come home one day, Deborah Jane. He'll come home."

CHAPTER

5

Alix sat straight up in bed with a cry, eyes opened wide. "Shhhhh!!" A finger was placed lightly over her lips.

It was her 15-year-old brother, Lachlan. His white-blond hair visible even in the darkness.

"What time is it?" Alix asked sleepily.

Lachlan stretched his long frame across the bed to push aside the curtain. He looked at the moon as its light spilled into the room.

"It isn't even two yet," he said in hushed, middle-of-the-night tones, then sat back up, cross-legged, in the center of the bed.

"It feels like I've been sleeping forever."

"You must have been tired after today." Lachlan punched her amiably on the arm. "I'm glad you're all right."

"What are you doing here?" Alix questioned. "I know you didn't come here just to tell me you're glad I'm all right."

Lachlan smiled sheepishly. "I came to find out about Robin Brodie."

"Ahhh," Alix sighed. "I fear I shall become famous in this region as being the only one to have come in close contact with the Last Highlander."

"What's he like?" Lachlan edged closer, eyes brimming with the love of intrigue. "They say animals aren't the only thing he hunts."

Alix sat up. "What?"

"Haven't you heard about that?"

"No. Never." A chill ran up her spine as she readjusted her pillow. "What are you talking about."

"They say he hunts Redcoats as well."

Alix shivered again. "Who told you that?"

Lachlan shrugged. "Some of the stablehands. They say he lives in a cave, and inside the walls are red with the blood of the men he has slain."

Alix laughed out loud, then stifled the noise with a quick hand and dart of her eyes. "I think you've been listening to too much gossip, Lachlan. Who has seen his cave? Who even knows where it is? And how do they know he even lives in a cave?"

"They say someone followed him once."

"Who?"

"How should I know, Alix?" Lachlan's voice held a slight tinge of irritation at his sister's persistence.

"Precisely."

"Oh, you think you're so logical, don't you?" His brotherly irritation became more pronounced.

"No, Lachlan," Alix sighed with a grin. "You simply have been prone to listen to such tales ever since I can remember. You believed in fairies until you were 13."

"That's nothing, Alix." Lachlan brightened instantly as he was wont to do. "Most Scots believe in them until the day they die!"

"There. You see? It's probably easier to believe in the fair folk than it is to believe Robin Brodie hunts down Redcoats in his spare time."

"Maybe." Lachlan still wasn't convinced.

"I'll tell you what, brother," Alix offered. "If I get the chance to see Robin Brodie again, I'll ask him to take me to his cave. Then we'll know if what you say is true."

"All right. But there isn't a chance that he will take you there."

"Who knows?"

"Well, we'll see, Alix." Lachlan's alabaster skin shone white in the moonlight. "Even if he doesn't hunt Redcoats, there has to be more to his story. We've all gotten glimpses of him. He looks wild, as untamed as the creature that runs with him."

"Bear?" Alix asked.

"Aye. Is that the wolf's name?" Clearly he liked getting the information—something he could share in the stables to-morrow.

"Aye. A gentle creature she is, too."

Lachlan leaned forward, his face inches from Alix's.

"Some of the men say that when they're alone in the woods they'll feel a presence behind them, can almost feel breath upon their neck. And when they turn around, they are as alone as they were before."

"I've heard it said his feet actually don't touch the forest floor when he walks," Alix said, feeding Lachlan's imagina-tion. "And that he runs faster than a deer."

Lachlan took her hand, getting excited. "He can make fire with his fingertips, and his wolf is actually a spirit."

This lost Alix immediately, and she began to laugh noise-lessly. "Oh, Lachlan, you really are pathetic!" She hit him over the head with a pillow. "Next thing you know you're going to tell me that he's really a ghost himself."

"Some people say that, too!"

"Go back to bed, my brother. Robin Brodie is flesh and blood, as are we all. You need a good sleep. It sounds as if your mind has become addled!"

Lachlan hit her back. "At least I'm not a literary snob like you are!"

"That's rich coming from a man whose only friends have four legs, manes, and a tail!"

"I'm going back to bed."

"I think you should."

Lachlan bounded off the bed in a huff and strode strongly to the door, pulling it open sharply. It had almost clicked shut when his blond head peered back inside the room.

"If you go scaring us like that again, Alix, make sure the beast that attacks you is something more comely than a pig!"

The door was firmly shut before Alix's pillow hit its paneled surface.

• • •

Alix awakened later than usual. The others were in the schoolroom, and the house was peacefully quiet.

With a sigh she dressed. And with another sigh she sat on her window seat, staring out at the woods. Never before had her room seemed so confining. Never before had the forest been so inviting. Alix smiled, thinking of Eve and feeling more akin to the mother of all men than she had ever felt before. And the more she sat looking out, the more tempted she became.

I could go for just an hour. Papa's probably out somewhere, and he'll never find out.

For half an hour Alix sat, her better half arguing with the other when a movement caught her eye. Running swiftly, Robin Brodie was entering his forest from the field. Where had he been? She had never seen him so clearly before in the light of day. A picture of a Redcoat formed before her eyes. Was it true?

Suddenly Alix was out of doors, all thoughts of Papa, right and wrong extinguished by overwhelming curiosity. Ivan stayed in the kitchen sensibly resting by the fire.

• • •

Finding a solemn, now-forbidden pleasure in the pathless woods, Alix made her way to a spot with more than its fair share of serenity. The weald took on a new role. What had been merely an area of nature's simplicity was now Robin Brodie's haven. In loneliness of heart and agony of mind, he moved along these shades. She had dreamed of him the night before. Of his kind brown eyes. And the melancholy lying therein.

Her soul tasted the sadness of him, and bitter it was. Happiness he well deserved. She wanted him to be rescued. And there was only one person who now could do it. Already she had conversed with him, looked into his eyes, and beheld what manner of man hid behind the roughened exterior. No one else could say that. She would sit in Robin's forest home, near the edge of the clearing, for an hour.

Hopefully he would come.

She sat in utter stillness, not quite so confident as when she entered the forest. *Would he show up? Why should he?* He owed her nothing. The precedent of mystery had been set for years. He didn't talk to anyone, not even his own mother. What would bring him down from his perch of isolation? Looking deep within, she could come up with nothing, only a feeling of pronounced inevitability.

And could Lachlan's legends about him be true? Alix pondered them. Yes. The more she thought about it, the more it made sense. They'd disappear with no one the wiser. In a breath of time, a man is gone. She shook herself, thinking, *Lachlan's ghost stories have affected me more than I thought was possible.*

But even as Robin had saved her, she knew she must do the same to him. Someone had to reach him. Had to find out what it was that caused him to shun humanity in the prime of his youth. He had been out in the woods for 16 long years. Why? Her heart constricted in pain at the thought of it. If only she could bring him out of exile. *Poor Robin,* she thought, *poor, poor Robin.*

She continued to muse as she sat crunching leaves with her booted feet. His scar hadn't been far from her mind since she saw him yesterday. She pondered how it came to be with the same fascination all humans have with scars and the watered-down mortality they represent. A scar like that didn't come from a skinned knee or some boyhood accident, she knew. And knowing history, she realized the snaking knife trail could have come only from a Redcoat, but how and why was still a mystery. It was all a mystery. Fascinating because of its obscurity, frightening in its severity.

She took out a cloth-covered book and began to read the handwritten pages. Her father's poems. Alix was like her father. Kyle saw things the way she did, through the eyes of the soul. He worked with her steadily, helping her learn to put those feelings into words. She would take her slate with her occasionally to write down what she felt. And like her father, she used the form of poetry, something that had burned within the Scots for centuries.

The wait continued as she read on through the collection Kyle had given her upon her fourteenth birthday. It was the story of his life told through rhyme and meter, masking nothing save his pride. There was still time for Robin to come.

• • •

He sat silently. Watching her. Not a leaf crackled, not a twig popped beneath his sensitive feet as he arose and walked closer.

She was waiting for him. Had been there a while. How long would she sit there?

He made a wide circle as she continued reading. Each muscle was tightened and strained, but still she did not know that her guardian was present. Soon he could see her face, bowed at the same angle of the book which she held. The long red hair hung in a braid down her back. *Hair that beautiful should be kept long and loose,* he thought, as his fingers ached to feel the glorious tresses once again. Her green dress blended in with her surroundings, making her hair flame even more brightly in contrast.

She had been there for so long. Would tomorrow find her waiting for him again? And was she there simply to read? How did he know whether she came expressly to see him? Doubts assailed him and he circled back once more and stood so closely behind her he could see the writing on the page. Inadequacy overtook him as he saw the words which meant nothing to him. She was educated. She was the chief's daughter.

He turned his back on her and started silently up the rise to keep quiet guard for one more day. With a sad shake of her head, Alix stood up from her spot of repose. She looked around her in a complete circle.

"Good-bye, Robin Brodie," she said just in case. "Thank you for saving my life. I trust we shall meet again someday." And with a weary sigh she walked out of the woods.

His heart leapt. *Please come back tomorrow,* he pleaded. When she was gone he called to his dog.

"Oh, Bear!" he said as the old beast fell in line beside her master as they walked quickly back to the cave, "how can a man like me hope to be befriended by a lady such as Alix Maclachlan?"

Bear looked at Robin with soft eyes and continued along beside him, her great flank pressing comfortingly against her master's thigh.

"Tomorrow," Robin spoke again, "I will go to her if she comes."

He promised himself it would be so. If she came.

•••

The kitchen was a warm, capable room, bustling with the usual supper-time preparations. Coming down after a long nap, Alix soon forgot her disappointment at not seeing Robin. Copper pots, reflecting the fire's glow, hung from the beamed ceiling. Huge cupboards lined one wall. Barrels filled with everyday staples such as flour, oatmeal, sugar, and salt pork stood in the corner. And the large, open hearth—the central focus of any proper Scottish kitchen—was hung round with cooking utensils: griddles, three-legged kale pots, tongs, and pokers. Nearby stood a wooden plunge churn and four three-legged creepie stools. After many an afternoon in the snow, Alix had crept up to the blazing fire to warm herself, perched on one of those stools.

A wooden door led down to the cellar where strings of sausages, hams, and onions hung in the cool dark. Smoked haddock, salt herring, and round kebbucks of cheese lay in wait as well. An ever-decreasing mound of potatoes stood in the middle of the floor, but summer would soon be providing them with vegetables fresh from their gardens: fresh kale, radishes, and other crisp offerings that they all dreamed about during the winter. Deeper into the cellars were the precious casks of claret and hogsheads of sherry imported from France.

Central to the kitchen was a mammoth hewn table with two long benches on either side, as well as two armchairs at either end. No one knew how old it was—it had been with the Maclachlans for ages, had been one of the few pieces that survived the frigate's bombardment. Therefore, it had become exceptionally special to them all. Most chiefs and their families rarely went into the kitchens of their houses. But that table, now a relic from another era, drew the inhabitants of the house around the polished surface marred with memories. It was a social place for the servants to commune with one another when their tasks were finished, and it provided a hub for the family as well—a center of warmth and belonging, the heartbeat of the happy home.

The family always gathered there for baby Mary Alice's dinner before going up to change for their own which was served in the dining room. Jenny was feeding Mary Alice. The chief's lady didn't take kindly to the idea that children should be raised solely by governesses and nurses, although the Maclachlans employed both. Her mustard-gold day dress reflected the firelight with a soft sheen. And her long hair fell well below the bench on which she sat.

"Here she is!" she said brightly, welcoming her oldest daughter into the room. "Are you feeling better after your rest?"

"Aye, Mama." Alix's cheeks were rosy from sleep and her eyes sparkled despite the disappointment the day held. "Hello, Mary Alice! Did you have a good afternoon?"

Mary Alice, dressed in pink, her short blonde hair curling around her face, smiled at her sister and batted the table with splayed, chubby fingers. Alix lovingly caressed the curls.

Without warning the delicious smells of dinner cooking sent signals to Alix's stomach. Roasting meat, potatoes, and pudding.

"I'm hungry. What's for supper tonight?"

"We got a surprise for supper tonight, lovie," said the cook. Martha was her name. She was still a relatively young woman, in her mid-thirties. Round and robust-looking, she had a pleasing face and shiny black-brown hair. Her voice was soft, gentle, and musical. She often sang as she worked, much to everyone's pleasure. Lachlan was always begging her to sing "Greensleeves" for him.

Inside the huge kitchen fireplace Alix saw what was turning on the spit at the hand of a plump servant boy. Its skin was brown and crispy. The juices popped and sizzled as they dripped into the fire.

"The boar!" she laughed, wondering how she had failed to notice right away, and suddenly knowing why she saw Robin running back into the woods. "I'll wager that pig wishes he had never laid eyes on me."

"I think you can safely say that!" Kyle, wearing tan breeches and a white shirt, black boots polished to a high sheen, strode into the room. He looked windswept and healthy as he always did when he returned from a day on the estates.

"And where did today find you, bonnie Alix? Didn't run into another boar, I trust?"

The chief looked meaningfully at his daughter. She was found out.

"No, Papa. Nor Robin Brodie either." She looked down, now ashamed of what she had done. "How did you know?"

"I was coming back from visiting Uncle John when I saw you emerge from the forest."

"I'm sorry Papa, it's just that . . ."

"I'm going to let you go back one more time, Alix. And if Robin doesn't show up, I want you to forget about this. If he chooses to live the way he does, it isn't up to us to force him to behave any differently, no matter how well-meaning our motives are. Is that understood?"

Alix smiled. "Aye, Papa."

"What prompted your change of heart?" Jenny asked Kyle, giving Mary Alice her last spoonful of pudding.

"I talked to Joshua about it and he told me how Deborah has been praying for years for her brother's return. Maybe this is a beginning. Maybe God will use Alix as His instrument." He turned back to Alix. "Instrument of God or not, Alix, I'm letting you off easy this time for your disobedience. But please be aware that next time I might not choose to show so much mercy."

"Thank you, Papa." Alix put her arms around his neck. "I'm so sorry."

"Did Robin bring the boar?" Jenny asked.

"It was on the back doorstep this morning," Kyle said, "all trussed and ready for roasting."

"Well, Father," Lachlan said later in the dining room as they were finishing up their meal, "maybe you should let Alix wander in the woods more often. We haven't had a boar like that on the table since Christmas a year ago!"

"Now, Lachlan, don't tease your sister," Jenny chided him.

"Who's teasing, Mother? Not only does it provide Alix an opportunity to meet Robin again, it puts meat on our table."

"What did you learn about Robin from Joshua?" Alix asked, shooting a sideways glance over to her brother.

"Nothing new, really. The Brodies have always been a very private family." The chief set down his fork. "There's more to Robin Brodie than meets the eye, lassie."

"What do you mean, Papa?"

Kyle looked at Jenny and wiped his mouth. She nodded.

"Shall we take a walk down by the loch, Alix? I'll try to explain what I can about Robin Brodie."

"Good," Lachlan said, "I'll go get my coat."

"No, son, trust me. I have nothing to add that the stable-hands have not already told you concerning the legend of Robin Brodie."

Alix put on a shawl and, holding hands, they walked in silence in the direction of forlorn old Castle Lachlan. She suddenly felt sad and held his hand a little tighter.

"What was it like to lose your home, Papa? It must have been terrible."

Kyle smiled sadly at his daughter as the old fortress stood before them. "It wasn't an easy cross to bear, Alix. But there are times in one's life that it becomes necessary to lean on others for support." The wind whispered in the small grove of ash trees through which they were passing.

"During that time the Savior became more real to me than ever before. And your mother was there also, Alix. She became my strength. My earthly pillar. I don't think I could have rebuilt the clan and come to peace regarding the horror of Culloden and its aftermath without her. The Scriptures tell us that in marriage two people become one flesh. During that time we became one mind, one spirit. Many men wouldn't care to admit that their wives are so important to them. But I am proud of it, Alix. I am what I am because she is so much a part of me."

"And it is the same with Mama," Alix said.

"How do you know that?" her father said in the darkness.

"It's evident in the way you look at one another. The way you speak paragraphs without uttering a word. I've seen you at social functions, and I've figured out there must be some code between you."

"What do you mean?"

"Well, 'This tea has a bit too much milk,' means 'I'm bored to death, meet me in the garden in five minutes.'"

Kyle laughed. "So we've been caught after all these years."

"And 'Did it suddenly get a little dark in here?' really means, 'Change the subject soon or I'll go mad!'"

"Any others?" the chief asked, smiling at how little there is that children miss.

"There are lots of them. Some I'm still not too sure of. But you repeat them too often for me not to realize there is something peculiar about them!"

They sat on the bank and looked out toward the island that sat in Lachlan Bay.

"Can you imagine what it would have been like after Culloden without Mama?" Alix asked. "God only knows what Robin has been going through, all alone for 16 years."

"Well, yesterday was the first time I've ever been face-to-face with him, the first time I've ever heard his voice. We don't know what has made him hide away in the forest. That's a mystery to all of us, lass. But we know it has something to do with the Redcoats and Culloden. That's all his mother will tell us. She doesn't want to discuss it further. And that's her privilege."

Alix picked at the grass.

"Papa? Why are the Redcoats still hated so after all these years?"

"Oh, Alix, if I could tell you what Scotland was like before the uprising. Each clan ruling its own. Freedom and independence of a nature we don't have now. . . ." His voice was wistful, filled with regrets.

"Weren't we still under the Crown then?"

"Aye, lassie, we were. But we had a voice in the government. Now, with the high taxes and tariffs we're forced to pay, the arbitrary laws placed on the books for our misery alone, it's all the people can do just to survive. The exodus has been quite extensive. Many who were not killed have left for the Colonies or Ireland, and I can't blame them. Some clan chiefs are not so benevolent either, I'm afraid. They've turned most of their tenants out and brought in sheep to graze."

"But you've done so well, Papa."

Kyle smiled. "We've been blessed, Alix. If it wasn't for your Grandfather Richard and the fact that my father planted many trees, we would have been hard-pressed to survive."

"God willed it, Papa."

"Aye, lass, that He did." Her devotion to the Lord, her simple faith, caused him to smile.

"But why does He make us prosper and leave others in torment?"

"You mean Robin?" he asked.

Alix nodded, moonlight illumining the concern written across her face.

"You've always been asking the difficult ones, Alix Matheson Maclachlan," he chided. "I'll do my best to answer it." He cleared his throat and began. "Some people refuse to be anywhere else, child. They don't know how. With Robin, he was just a boy, and I believe his mind never allowed him to get beyond whatever it was that happened, whatever it was that made him who he is. But you need to pray for Robin, lassie. He needs the Savior. Needs to know that he can overcome whatever it is that's been pulling him down for so long."

"It must've been horrible, Papa," Alix said, already empathizing with the Last Highlander.

"Aye, lass, it must've. I've known the horrors of war and how devastating they can be. When I lost a brother and a father within a 20-minute span, for a time I wished that I had died, too. But when my thoughts turned to you and to your mother, my will to live was renewed. Robin's father died during Culloden. He saw men fall dead next to him. Heard the thundering artillery and death cries from his compatriots. He was but a boy. Just 11."

"But there must be more to it, Papa," Alix theorized, "for him to stay away from his mother and sisters like that. Would battle produce a scar such as sits on the face of Robin Brodie?"

"No, lass. Who knows what his reasons are?" He placed a strong arm around his daughter's shoulders.

"Poor Robin. Poor, poor Robin," was all she could say as a tear streamed slowly down her face. Kyle, warmed by his daughter's tenderheartedness, pulled her close to him. Their thoughts, deep and plaguing, stole them from each other's company for a long while. Alix realized she might never know what happened to Robin Brodie. But she purposed in her heart to somehow bring him home again, to blot out his pain forever.

• • •

The loch in the moonlight. It was the only time he ventured down to the water's edge. The inky surface gleamed cold, like polished onyx. A jewel of nature in a Highland setting. How he loved the Highlands. He missed out on so much. Wouldn't it be nice to walk along here during daylight hours? To walk with her. Tomorrow. Tomorrow was the day. It had to be or he might never look upon her closely again.

They had been there earlier, sitting by the castle. Alix and the chief. He heard their voices murmuring as he waited silently in the shadow of the ruins. It was evident that they were close.

The moonlight glistened on his eyes as they narrowed against the gentle wind. How he hated the Redcoats! Life had been looted clean of all that he had held dear. And they were responsible. His fingers went to his face and he winced from the memory of it. Yes. He'd go to her tomorrow. He had to. For each day that he stayed away the Redcoats cut away more and more pieces from him. Soon there would be nothing left.

He raced for his home.

Once back in the cave he lit a fire and set out his new clothes for the following day. Slipping back to the loch, the moon now hidden by clouds, he bathed in the cold water for the first time in months. Pulling the leather thong from his hair, he washed the long curls with some lye soap made by his mother. He scrubbed his body free of dirt and perspiration, pinkening the smooth skin. For such a dark man, he had surprisingly little body hair, his chest smooth and hard. It was necessary preparation. He *would* see Alix. If he had to say it to himself a thousand times to make himself go, he would.

I'm 27-years-old, he thought as he toweled himself off with rough rubbings, *and it's time. Even if it's only Alix.*

Then he smiled, surprising himself. *I did save her life. If it wasn't for me, Alix Maclachlan might be no more.* The thought of his deed cheered him as he slowly made his way back to the forest. Lost in thought he passed by his mother's hut, candles still burning. He forgot to look in.

•••

In the village of Strathlachlan, Mavis Brodie said her prayers. Deborah and Kathleen had been by that day with their children. But how she longed for her son! He had looked like his father, John, when he was a lad. And from the fleeting glimpses she had gotten of him, he still did.

If only he would come. Was it in vain that she kept up with the parcels? Surely not! After all, he looked after her constantly. Game on the stoop each night. Fresh water from the well waiting each morning. And now there was finally hope, after 16 years. She could hardly breathe from her excitement when Deborah had rushed in with the news of Alix's rescue.

Mavis Maclachlan Brodie was a busy woman. She worked wherever she could. Laundering, cooking, sewing. But she was never too busy to pray. Looking in the direction of the forest as she picked up the pheasant that was waiting, she waved into the silent shadows as she always did. Breathing in deeply, she prayed to her Father in heaven with a simple, earthy faith. "Lord of lords, thank ya'. Thank ya' for sending someone to m'poor Robin. Please, God, bring him back to me. For I'm gettin' old an' tired, an' I dinna' know how much longer I can make it on m'own."

The door shut, the candles were extinguished, and Mavis Brodie, old for her years, cried herself to sleep. Work was harder than it used to be, and she didn't feel good anymore. She needed her son.

CHAPTER

6

Brooding and dark, the next day started dismally with rolling grumbles out of the western sky. It was difficult to concentrate on the lesson Miss Cawthorne, the governess, had given Alix. Her sister Violet loved her books. And practical Lachlan had faced up to the inevitable long ago. Alix usually enjoyed her studies. But today was different.

Kyle and Jenny were off visiting the Duke of Argyll, the nearby chief of the Campbells. She had left her children with their assignments, and with kisses and hugs they were off in the carriage. They wouldn't be back until after supper.

Outside the leaded glass-paned window, the sky still roiled over the landscape, churning up Alix's insides with each word that sped before her unseeing eyes. A storm had been promising its presence for the past hour and a half. Springtime in the Highlands sometimes brought on storms whose endings seemed doubtful after several days of rain. If she wanted to see Robin, she knew she must go immediately.

"I've got to get outside," Alix announced.

Violet looked up and looked back down at her history book. Lachlan kept writing.

"It's your brain," Violet, who looked exactly like her mother, mumbled, flipping the golden-brown braid over her shoulder.

"That's enough, Violet. As usual you are ever so tactful." Miss Cawthorne, tall, painfully thin, and quite nondescript, came back into the room. She had been down to the library. "I take it you wish to go outside, Alix?"

"Yes, ma'am."

"It's a good idea. We could all use a break." The young woman sighed and pulled a wayward piece of mousy brown hair back into her bun. "Besides, I haven't had a cup of tea yet." Miss Cawthorne usually stayed up too late reading and rarely made it to breakfast.

Lachlan stood up to his full height and stretched his arms with a loud groan. At 15, he was as tall as his father but thinner, long of limb and agile. His coloring and features were passed down from Jenny's great-grandmother, the daughter of a Danish princess. He had light-blue, almost transparent eyes and white-blond hair. He reminded Alix of what a Viking warrior must have looked like centuries ago when they raided the shores of the British Isles.

"Well, sister," he said, "if you're leaving this room, then so am I. Heidi is about to drop a colt anytime now. I should go to the stables before the storm breaks."

Lachlan's passion ran deep for the graceful beasts that made up the stable's expanding population. Already he was beginning to breed fine, hearty draft horses, Belgians, known for their stamina and immense proportions. Nevertheless, his love was for the horses that could run. Yet, knowing he would be chief someday, he diligently kept at the workhorses. They would be his family's means of sustenance.

Violet looked up longer this time, down her nose. As the self-proclaimed moralist of the family, her expression was one of mild disgust. "Well, go if you must. *I* shall stay here and continue with my reading."

Alix and Lachlan were used to their younger sister and, without acknowledging her remark, they sped from the room with a conspiratorial chuckle. They knew she'd be down by the loch within ten minutes playing with her dolls or sketching the countryside. But thoughts of her sister's future whereabouts were quickly stifled in Alix's haste. And she found her feet taking her quickly down the back staircase.

She stopped in the kitchen on her way out to let Martha know where she was going.

"Violet is upstairs in the schoolroom by herself. But I doubt if she will be there for long," Alix told the cook. "I'm going out now before it begins to rain."

"Then let me at least pack ye a lunch, Lady Alix," Martha said warmly, her big arms crossed over a bosom that must have always been large.

"Nay, Martha," she swung her cloak around her shoulders, "I need to be going right away."

"At least take some cheese and a piece of bread," Martha said, hastily cutting a chunk from the large kebbuck of cheddar that sat on the table.

An idea suddenly popped into Alix's mind. "Martha, I'll be right back," she said, hurrying out of the kitchen, up the big central staircase that started in the entrance hall, and into her bedroom on the second floor. The skies were getting darker, and in the distance she heard thunder. She went right to a small chest in her closet. Her grandfather, Richard, the Duke of Loxingham, had given it to her several years ago. How she loved Grandpapa! They wrote long, indulgent letters to one another with robust frequency. All her personal treasures were kept inside the intricately carved rosewood.

Opening up the carved lid that sported roses of a lacy, airy nature, she briefly fingered the blue velvet lining before reaching in to pick up her prize. She would give this to Robin, this doll. A Highlander in kilt and plaid. Her mother had played with the wee Scot when she was growing up in the tiny village of Bridgend near the city of Perth. Alix had loved him as a small child. He had been her favorite toy as she imagined him running through the woods or fighting Redcoats. But the tiny Highlander had been resting in this special box now for years. Robin had no use for him, but she wanted to take him something. *He saved my life after all.*

Back down to the kitchen she raced. Waiting on the table was a small sack of food Martha had prepared for her. The cellar door was open, so Alix called down.

"I'm going now, Martha!"

With that Alix opened the back door and flew out into the blustery day. It was cool but not cold, the air slightly humid. The brisk, April wind pulled at her cloak and sent her blue skirts milling about her legs. Walking into the breeze, she fingered through her long braid, loosening her hair, loving the feeling of the wind full on her face as it rushed through her waist-length tresses.

It appeared the storm would hold off for a while longer and she was glad. Maybe Robin would come. In response to her whistle, Ivan came slowly out from the stable, ready to start the trek. Tail wagging furiously, he waited until she had her satchel securely over her shoulder before going on ahead.

"Robin!" she called loudly as she entered the woods, the wind blowing her words back in her face. "Robin Brodie! Where are you? Don't make me pretend another boar is chasing me!" That morning while fidgeting at her studies, she had decided to take a bolder approach. She wouldn't leave it up to him. Maybe he couldn't just come up to her. Maybe he needed her to seek him out.

A rustling from behind caused her heart to jump.

Bear sauntered out of the brush.

"Bear!" Alix was delighted and put out her hand. The wolf-dog sniffed it and Alix stroked the massive gray head, realizing that Robin must be nearby. So far she had heard nothing. But that was no surprise. Suddenly Alix felt self-conscious. Focusing on the dogs, she didn't dare to look into the forest about her. She knew he was there, but did he view her as intruder or friend?

Robin watched as the dogs began to scamper together. Alix pulled out the tiny Highlander and began to study him as an older child studies a long-outgrown toy. A smile spread across her face at the memories his little face evoked. Robin breathed in deeply and purposefully popped a twig beneath his foot. It was now or never.

Alix quickly tucked the doll back into her pocket and turned around with hopeful eyes.

"Robin?" she said. To her delight he stood there. She hardly recognized him. The white shirt contrasted sharply with his tanned skin. Down his back his hair fell in soft curls, pulled back with the leather thong. Face now clean-shaven, kilt and plaid bright in the dreariness of the woods, he looked quite noble.

"You came!" Her joy was unmistakable.

"Aye." He came next to her, softly padding on his leather-bound feet. Inside he was shaking, trembling.

"I was hoping that when Bear bounded up you wouldn't be far behind. She's a beautiful dog." She studied him closely. "You look very nice today, Robin Brodie." Alix took in the new kilt in a glance. "That is a new kilt from the one you wore yesterday, isn't it? Your mother comes over to our kitchens every spring to use Mother's loom. And, of course, Mama is only too happy to let her, because everyone in the clan is quite proud of the fact that you refuse to wear anything but Highland dress. Why, Joshua told us how the first pair of breeches your mother left for you sat on the doorstone for two weeks before she got the idea!" Alix's nervousness propelled her speech forward, and Robin Brodie didn't mind at all. "Did you know that everyone calls you the Last Highlander? And you're known as far as Perth?"

Robin's eyes dropped in embarrassment. Deborah, during one of her night talks, had told him of his seeming fame, but it wasn't until now that he realized she had not been exaggerating for his benefit.

Alix looked up through the trees. The clouds were getting darker. "It looks as if we won't have much time. Could we walk a bit before I have to go back?"

"All right." His words were stiff.

He glanced down at her bag as he led her forward.

"Some lunch for us," she explained, noticing the direction of his gaze.

His eyebrows raised.

"Martha our cook sent it for me, but there's plenty here for two." She opened up the sack and peered inside, hoping there was more than bread and cheese. Martha delivered as Alix had hoped. "There are pork pies inside. Thanks to you!" she laughed.

Remembering his mother's meat pies, he reached out and took the knapsack, carrying it for her. Her small hand sought his bigger one. He turned his head away, his eyes closing briefly at the warm contact of her smooth palm against his.

And Alix began to talk again. Not so much out of nervousness anymore. "Bear is a wonderful dog. She has such long limbs. My brother Lachlan says she's a wolf! I told him she looked part wolf, part dog."

Robin nodded yes, that it was so.

"Good. I was right. I love it when Lachlan is wrong!"

Shades of he and Deborah as youngsters made him smile at her words as they made their way deeper and deeper into the forest. Alix felt adventure in the air. Suddenly she was on a new path, new ground being trodden under her booted feet. The forest seemed even more mysterious, softer, as the thunderheads continued to churn above the treetops.

Lightning forked above them, and the wind became driving and forceful. Robin held onto her hand tightly and quickened his pace. The young leaves rustled and all the animals and insects stilled at the nearness of the storm.

"Quickly, lass," he said, "let's hasten to shelter."

Before she knew it, they were by an ivy-covered, rocky hill. Robin pushed aside the concealing vines, and Alix realized they had come to the entryway of a cave. It was in a hillside overlooking a valley in which a small stream crisscrossed the woods. He had framed in the entryway and built a heavy wooden door, divided across the middle, to keep out the elements.

"Legend has it you live in a cave," Alix said with anticipation as she stepped inside. "I've never been in such a cave before!"

He shut the bottom half of the door as he came through, keeping the ivy back with the top half. Stepping into the dry cave, Alix looked around the small room. A pleasing symphony of aromas harmonized together in the little home. Fire and earth, herbs and straw, fresh clover and lye soap were mixed into a clean scent of natural beauty. Upon the dirt floor Robin had spread fresh straw and clover. The pallet on which he slept, nothing more than straw neatly arranged, was in the corner, a blanket and pillow resting on top. Against the far wall he had hewn out a fireplace and chimney. He lit several tallow candles and placed them on the mantel. Various woodworking tools hung on the wall. John David Brodie's tools. And a table and two chairs sat near the door.

"Where does the smoke go?" she asked, examining the fireplace curiously.

"There's a fissure above here tha' acts like a chimney." He bent down to add fresh logs to the smoldering coals. His tongue seemed to be loosening a bit.

Alix stood near the hearth. "Why, you can feel the air flowing!" she said in amazement.

Her eyes adjusted fully to the dim light and focused on the walls around her, stained red-brown. It was all she could do not to gasp.

Just then the sky opened up completely, cracking like an ancient cistern. The rain fell thunderously as she ran to the doorway and looked out, her mind now far from the talk of stablehands.

"It's a good thing we're in here!" Her eyes were shining. Alix loved a storm. Maybe too much. Robin's eyes echoed her pleasure. He thought his cave, overlooking the wooded valley where the burn traversed, was the perfect spot to be when the heavens opened to refresh the earth's bounties and the dry, parched soul of mankind.

Thunder he loved the most. The great, clanging blasts that resounded with firm reverberations across the hills. Nature at its noisiest, not content to exist quietly as usual. He always pictured thunderstorms as the wakings of a mystical behemoth stretching its muscles after a long sleep, fire flashing from its eyes. Then ... quickly spent, it sleeps again, leaving the rain to patter softly on its placid domain, to nourish and water the daisies and the heather. And when the sun finally deemed it safe again to peer through the clouds, the great being would smile widely with a closed, smug smile, in the mist of his deadened slumber.

Pointing to a beautifully carved chest standing against the wall of the cave she asked, "Did you make it?"

"Aye." Robin nodded, remembering. "When I was but a wee laddie, m'father would take me into his workshop on many a rainy afternoon. I still work with wood on most rainy days."

"Like today!" Alix was happy he was sharing part of himself with her.

"Aye, lass. Like today."

"So that was how you learned to make all of this furniture? From your father?"

"Aye. One by one, Mother left his tools out for me. Since then I've tried to make this cave a home."

"It's beautiful." Alix looked around her again. "It's true. This cave is like a little house. Do you enjoy your carpentry?"

"Aye, Lady Alix. But carpentry isna' my first love."

He got down on his haunches by the chest and carefully opened the lid. His hands sifted gently through the contents: extra shirts, clean rags, and a spare blanket, carefully folded and neatly arranged. Alix looked curiously over his shoulder. His hands quickly covered up a garment, bright red and folded tidily.

Once again, he found his tongue. "Do ya' want to see what I love doin' the most?" he asked, pulling out a parcel of soft material tied with leather strings.

"Robin, I would love to see anything you have made."

As he undid the bindings, the storm continued to roll in the background, and that safe feeling that Alix had always felt in the woods became strong as she stood so near him.

"Face the other way," he commanded. Alix complied, kneeling down, wondering what type of carvings would come from the mind of such a man. As he set up his artistry on the stone hearth where the two dogs were now sleeping, Alix suddenly felt awestruck. She was in the home of this legend. He was capable, talented, and giving. And he was opening himself up to her. Compassion for him filled her being, and yet she couldn't help but thrill to be near him. She was in the presence of the Last Highlander!

"All right, ya' can look now."

Alix turned around and time became suspended as she gazed upon Robin. The firelight illuminated with warmth the left side of his face and his handsomeness shouted forth from where he knelt. He was truly a man. Not the little boy she had always pictured when she thought of him or played with her doll. The scar that everyone talked about was now a thin white line that added yet another dimension of mysterious strength to his demeanor. He was a man, earthy, with feet that walked upon the ground, and well-formed hands that could aim an arrow, hew a fireplace out of rock, and carve wood as well. He was not a ghost, nor a woodland spirit that breathed in silence upon the necks of those that entered his domain. He was flesh and blood, so much more than any legend could ever speak of. Her hero worship of the Last Highlander came down to earth. He was man, and a man with whom she could trust herself without fear. Their gazes locked for what seemed an eternity as he studied her beauty as well. And when her eyes dropped under the directness of his gaze, the scene he had set up before her caused her to cry with delight, and she somehow had the feeling she was looking into the true nature of Robin Brodie's soul.

Before her eyes a perfect little whimsical woodland scene unfolded. Dryads, dwarfs, and centaurs. Fairy princes and princesses. Baby animals. Bunnies rolling with laughter. Squirrels hiding behind a tree with the face of an old man. Deer and fawns frolicking. Even tiny frogs with self-satisfied smiles upon their wide mouths looked ready to leap from their perch and onto Alix's lap.

She laughed and clapped her hands. "Oh, Robin! They're the most enchanting things I've ever seen!"

Robin scooped up a handful and thrust them forward with leftover boyish impulsiveness. "You may have them all, Alix," he said.

Laughing, she took only the rollicking rabbit. "I like him the best, Robin. May I just have *him*?"

"Dinna' ya' like them?" His brown eyes were transparent.

"Oh, Robin, of course I do! They are perfectly lovely!"

"Then why . . . ?"

"Because," she said gently, "they're yours. You must have spent a great deal of time on these. I couldn't take them all. Besides," she hesitated, and picked up a fairy princess, "I want them to look at if you invite me into your home again."

"Would ya' come again, Lady Alix?" he asked, eyes betraying his disbelief.

Her heart reached out to him. Alix put down the carvings. He was still kneeling as she leaned over and put her arms around his neck, hugging him tightly. They breathed in the clean smell of each other's hair, delighting in the scent, in the feel of each other's warmth.

Each felt reborn. And Robin relished in the closeness of her. Having her in his arms was so perfect. Unlike anything he had ever known. His hand shakily touched her hair. And suddenly frightened, he quickly pulled away.

Alix expected no less. And as the rain came down, the lunch of bannock bread, cheese, and cold pork pasties was eaten slowly, Robin savoring each bite, Alix relishing completely in his enjoyment. Friendship had smiled upon them. And as he walked her back home in the light drizzle, Robin Brodie emerged yet further from his twilight existence and remembered what happiness was like for the first time in years. All because of Alix, her warmth and her love.

"Will you come to the house?" Alix asked as they came to the clearing, the rain just stopping.

Robin nodded no.

"I understand" was all she said as she started out into the field. "I almost forgot!" She ran back to him. "Here!" She reached into her pocket, pulling out the doll. "I brought this for you. The people call you the Last Highlander, but from now on I shall always think of you as my Highlander." She looked down fondly at the wee figure before holding him out. "I played with him all the time when I was little, and I always pretended that he was you."

He took the doll and stared in amazement as Alix, followed by Ivan, ran toward Castle Lachlan. She had called him her Highlander. It pleased him much. All of those years he lived in solitude thinking she didn't even know he existed.

"To think I've been a part of her life for so long," he whispered to himself. The thought was hearty enough to live on for the rest of his life.

• • •

Back at the cave he changed into his usual kilt, whistled for Bear, and went on his hunt. Someday soon he would give the game to his mother personally. Indeed, life had changed. And all because of a lovely maid with flaming red hair and a heart with a wide capacity for love and acceptance.

That night as he looked in on his dear mother, he saw her anew. She looked aged, though only 57. Her loneliness, so evident in her rounded shoulders and saddened eyes, echoed his own. He didn't know how acute his loneliness really was until Alix came. And suddenly, life such as he was living became utterly unacceptable. Loneliness was painful, and he must attend to his mother someday soon. He must become her son again—her true son. The question was when.

• • •

Alix walked through the kitchens and headed straight for her room.

"Alix!" Lachlan called from behind her as she handed her coat to Gertrude, the housekeeper.

She placed one foot on the step. "What is it, brother?"

"Did you see any ghosts in the forest today?"

They began to walk up the steps together.

"Aye, Lachlan," Alix's eyes shone huge and blue, "I met Robin Brodie and he took me to his cave. And yes, the walls *are* red."

Lachlan studied his sister and opened the door to his room. "Oh sure, Alix," he said, "and King Arthur is coming back someday as well." With that he closed the door, leaving Alix alone in the corridor.

CHAPTER

7

In between the old and the young
Came a time for two who felt undone
To love in purity with friendship true.
A wild man and maiden fair who came
To a rescue in shades of forest green
Listening for a sign. Of what? Neither knew.

She had noticed the Duke of Argyll's grand carriage sitting near the stables when she went down to the kitchens after finishing up her studies. But before she went in to see the man she loved as a grandfather, she ran up to the schoolroom to write down the words. Her father had taught her to never "save it for later," but to write down immediately an idea or a poem that came to mind.

A poet's heart.

It's what she felt destined to have someday. To see people not as they are but as they should or could be. To love the unlovely because they are made in the image of God. The ability to see beauty not in the outward, but in the soul, and if not in the soul then through eyes of pity that God's light had not yet found that corner of darkness. She somehow knew the road would not be easy. Which reminded her. She must go to the orphanage tomorrow.

With the poem written securely down on parchment, Alix changed from her blue day dress into a yellow gown that she frequently wore for dinner. Of fine woven wool, the saffron material was soft and fell in loose folds almost to the ground. Sewn around the square neckline and cuffs was creamy lace. Vermilion bows at the corners of the neckline and the outside of the sleeves gave the dress a warm, rich aura. Its simplistic styling was perfect on Alix, whose straightforward nature needed little adorning. She went immediately down to the dining room where everyone was taking their seats.

"Uncle Archibald!" Alix cried, running across the room. The Duke of Argyll, the influential and very tall chief of Clan Campbell, twirled her around playfully, giving her a tight squeeze and a peck on the cheek.

"Alix," he said fondly with a voice like wine. "My favourite red-haired lassie in all of Scotland! How good it is to see you, sweet one!"

"Uncle," Alix was excited to see him, "indeed this is a wonderful surprise. I'm so glad you're staying for dinner."

Paneled and bedecked with intricately worked molding and wainscoting of polished maple, the dining room truly befitted Kyle's station as a chieftain. Jenny's stepmother, Lady Margaret, had seen to the decorating of the room. The Persian carpet, with its jeweled palette of red, green, and blue, had been a Christmas gift one year from the Duke and Duchess of Loxingham. At the large window hung draperies of rich green silk brocade. In chinoiserie bowls on the mantel and sideboard Jenny had placed large amounts of ivy. A polished brass chandelier hung from the ceiling, the two dozen tapers casting lights off the china and silver pieces arranged to perfection on the starched white linen tablecloth.

They all sat at one end of the long table. Kyle and Jenny sat across from one another, feet interlocked underneath the table. Lachlan and Violet faced each other, and Argyll was across from Alix, their eyes locked in mutual admiration. He was happy she would be coming into his household, he thought as he watched her. Waif-like and innocent now, he knew she would be as wonderful a woman as she had been a child. The Lord knew Inveraray Castle, the fortress he had built himself, needed some joy within its walls.

He enjoyed being here with the Maclachlans. He had lived a full life so far. But he was a hard man to those who crossed him unnecessarily. Had little time or patience with those who were unable to fend for themselves, whatever the cause. He expected unconditional obedience from his subordinates, gained utmost respect from his peers. Yes, the Campbell chief was an extremely powerful man. But he was getting old, his children were in London, and his wife was dead.

"I'm hungrier than I thought!" Lachlan eyed the food that was brought in.

The leek soup which began the meal was creamy and hot. The main course, ptarmigan in a creamy herb sauce, was prepared to perfection, succulent and juicy.

"Ah, Kyle," he said after tasting the delicious bird, "as loyal as I have always been to the Crown, I must say that as far as our cuisine is concerned, I'm glad Scotland was allied with France for so long!"

"Maybe that's what the uprising was really all about," Lachlan joked with the ease of the next generation. "We were afraid we'd have nothing to eat save pork pies and beefsteak with kidney."

Kyle quickly changed the subject to Lachlan's horses. He was a humorous man, but as long as he lived he would never be able to make light of the fact that he was once a Jacobite.

Dinner was soon finished and they retired to the drawing room. Just the duke, Alix, and her parents.

Kyle began. "Lassie, his grace has something he wishes to discuss with you."

"Indeed?" Alix sounded excited.

The duke smiled. What a striking man he was with his aqua-blue eyes and snow-white hair. The fact that he was an outdoorsman made these features stand out even more as his face was tanned year-round. Alix often wondered how old he really was. He had always been vibrantly ancient.

"It's about something that will take place in two years' time," he said, still smiling.

"It's about Duncan Campbell. Alix," Kyle said, taking a deep breath, "Alix, the time has come for your betrothal to become official."

"And here I thought you'd all forgotten about it," Alix said, masking her sudden uneasiness with a jest. For years she had known she was to be the bride of Duncan Campbell. But now it was taking shape, becoming real. Not some distant dream wrapped in a fog of vagary. What would the man be like that materialized from the mists?

"Oh no," Argyll said fondly. "I've been waiting for this day for many a year." The relationship between the two families was and always had been, extremely close.

Kyle and Jenny smiled down at one another, and Argyll's heart melted. His duchess had passed away years before. And now that he was "one of the ancients," as he heard a housemaid whisper last week, he knew he would never marry again. Marriage is for the young, he always said. He couldn't imagine, at his age, feeling infatuation, being in love again.

Kyle became serious as Argyll stood up to pour himself a glass of sherry. "Alix, you were promised to the Campbells when you were a wee bairn. You are young, and two years will pass before you will actually marry Duncan. But we are officially betrothing you now. You understand what this means, don't you?"

The mood shifted from merry to grave in a heartbeat.

"Aye." Alix nodded with the whispered word, eyes reflecting the seriousness of the conversation. "Of course I understand what this means."

"From this day on, you will promise yourself to no other, for now you are Duncan's."

As he spoke, her hand sought the recesses of her pocket and the treasure therein. She pulled out the little bunny, feeling the smooth wood in the palm of her hand, and taking comfort from Robin's creation. Papa waited for a response, but Alix could think of nothing to say.

The pause lengthened uncomfortably until Jenny, a proper hostess, intervened, conversing about the first thing she saw.

"What is that in your hand, Alix?" she asked. Alix uncurled her palm. "Why, it's lovely. So delicate. It looks so real, almost alive!"

"Robin Brodie gave it to me, Mama," Alix responded eagerly, smiling down at the little carving.

"You've seen Robin again?" Kyle asked leaning forward on the couch.

Argyll sat next to Alix. "Robin Brodie?" He looked at each occupant of the room in surprise. "You mean the Last Highlander?"

Alix nodded as their eyes locked with enthusiasm.

"Does he still wear kilt and plaid?" he asked eagerly.

"Aye, Uncle Archibald. He still wears the Brodie sett." She turned to her mother. "Oh, Mama, you should have seen him today. He wore a brand-new kilt and plaid, was well-groomed and clean-shaven. And he is one of the most handsome men I have ever seen!" The more she talked about her Highlander, the more animated she became. She was eager to answer all the questions that were being fired off about Robin.

"How old is he?" asked the duke.

"Twenty-seven."

"That's only two years older than Duncan," he replied. Then his eyebrows raised up even farther with the love of intrigue. "They say he lives in a cave whose walls are red with the blood of Englishmen!"

"I was there today!" She grabbed his hand. "And yes, the walls *are* red!"

"So the legend is true! How did you manage to see his cave?"

"He took me there for shelter from the storm. Has made it quite a lovely little home, actually. We were walking together in the woods. . . ."

"How did you come to know him in the first place, Alix? I've heard he hasn't spoken to a soul in over 16 years!"

"Robin saved my life, Uncle!"

"What?"

"Aye. 'Tis true. Robin Brodie killed the wild boar that chased me in the woods two days ago."

As she explained in excitement of the rescue, her face became filled with emotion for the Last Highlander. Argyll was engrossed in the tale, but Jenny sat back, watching her daughter's eyes. It was easy to see through those telltale mirrors into Alix's soul, to what lay in her heart.

"Well," said Argyll, "I'm glad Robin Brodie was there to protect you, Alix. Or my grandson would have been without a bride!"

"That's true," said Kyle, looking at his daughter. "We owe the Last Highlander much."

A stiff silence ensued. "Well, I guess that settles it," Argyll said quickly, glad the matter was settled once and for all. "Even though I don't understand your ways of wanting Alix to be educated before she marries, Duncan is just as glad to wait for marriage for a while. He's enjoying his stay at Cambridge. He's every inch a scholar."

Alix was leaving for England in August to be further educated at her grandfather's estate for two years.

"How old is Duncan now?" Jenny asked, glad they had made the decision for Alix not to be married until she was 18.

"He just turned 25 a few months ago."

"Well, I'm sure it will be a beautiful match," Jenny said optimistically. Her stomach felt a bit queasy when she thought about losing her firstborn, but a promise was a promise. And according to all she had heard about her daughter's groom-to-be, he would be kind to Alix.

"Before I go," he said to Alix as Beaton the butler, all five feet four of him, was summoned to bring his cloak, "I have a gift for you, Alix." He handed her a small, neat parcel.

Alix undid the paper. Her gift was a book, containing many old Scottish poems she had never read. She gasped, looking at her father.

"Papa!" She ran over to him. "Look!"

"These poems were translated from the original Gaelic by Duncan. It may not be as special as a gift from a legend, Alix, but know that it is given from the heart."

"Thank you, Uncle."

"And with that, I'll take my leave," Argyll said. Beaton helped him on with his cloak and opened the door.

"You'll be a much-welcomed addition to the family, Alix," he said to her as he placed a tender hand on her shoulder. Straightening up quickly, he gave them a brisk bow and a hearty, "Good night, all."

In the moonlight, the Maclachlans stood watching the man of power riding off in his carriage. The driver, a solitary silhouette against the night sky, typified Argyll's existence. Starlit and lonesome.

"Well, lass," Kyle said later that night as his wife lay in the comfort of his arms, "maybe our little Alix will give him some happiness when the time comes. Maybe she's being sent there more for his benefit than Duncan's. Argyll could certainly use a good dose of love and compassion."

• • •

Moonlight spilled onto her book as Alix sat on the window seat in her bedroom. She read with delight about the silver lady who illumined the pages before her. The words of James MacPherson. Her eyes became heavy as she continued to read. But a movement caught her attention. She looked out onto the clearing.

It was Robin Brodie, on his way to Loch Fyne. His hair was free and streaming wild. Like a deer he ran. Smoothly and quickly, with seemingly no effort, his muscled legs made each step look like joy unrestrained. She couldn't wait to see him tomorrow. To show him her poem. What would he think when he read it? For that matter, could he read at all?

Realizing sleep could be stayed no longer, Alix slid off the ledge and got into bed. Her last thoughts were not of Duncan Campbell, but of Robin Brodie with his long black hair and soft brown eyes.

CHAPTER

8

"Deborah!" Alix called through the morning air.

Deborah Brodie Maclachlan was rushing out of Mavis's front door, basket perched upon her forearm. Her head whipped around at the sound of her name. A smile erupted on her face.

"Lady Alix!" she called back, running toward her. "Joshua came back with the news the other day. Is it true? Robin saved your life?"

"Aye, 'tis true. Deborah, he met me in the woods yesterday, and we spent the late part of the morning together!"

"Miss Alix, I've been prayin' for him for years," she ushered her around to the backyard. "We all have. I talk to him almost every night into the darkness, an' sometimes I think he's listenin', other times I dinna' know if he's there at all. But I always hope he is." She put her hand on Alix's arm. "Joshua tells me to keep prayin' that God will intervene in some way. An' now my prayers are bein' answered. And the Lord is workin' through you, Alix!" She put a hand up to her mouth and squeezed her eyes shut to hold back the tears.

Alix rubbed Deborah's arm. "I don't understand it all myself Deborah. But I know that the Savior is using me in Robin's life. Already I see changes in him, and it is only the second time we have met!"

Deborah's eyes opened wide as the questions of many worry-filled years broke free.

"Tell me all about him, Miss Alix. What does he look like? How tall is he? Is he healthy? How are his teeth? Does he still have his dark curls?"

Alix was eager to answer. "His features are quite fair, and he's a handsome man. He's not extremely tall, but his form is well-muscled and lean. He looks very healthy. And his teeth are white and strong and yes, Deborah, he still has his dark curls. They hang down past the middle of his back and he ties them back with a leather strap."

"And what of his scars?" Her brows were furrowed. "How has his face healed? The last time I saw him . . ."

"The scar," Alix interrupted her, "has healed down to a thin white line that blends in with the natural curves of his face. For some reason, Deborah, it makes him even more attractive in my eyes, and it lends itself to his character."

Deborah sighed with relief. "Does he live in a cave?"

Alix nodded. "He took me to his cave yesterday. But you can hardly call it a cave. It was once a cave, but he has made it a home with a door, a fireplace, furniture. He has a table with two chairs, Deborah, as if he were waiting for someone to find him. It smells of fresh straw and clover. A sweeter place I have yet to see. Your father's tools hang on the wall, and look," she pulled the bunny out of her pocket, "he gave me this."

Alix handed Deborah the carving, done by her brother's own hand.

Deborah's fingers lovingly felt every crevice, each indentation left by Robin's knife, seeking to somehow feel the warmth of his hands as he worked, the critical scope of his eye as he examined what he had done. Then tears began to flow with a force that would have embarrassed her if they had been shed for anyone else but her brother. She cried as strong and deep as yesterday's storm, searching for healing, for a respite from the separation and its pain that had driven deep, clawing roots into her heart. Alix put her arms around her and sat her down on an overturned washtub.

She couldn't begin to understand. All she could do was lend support as Deborah continued to cry, turning the little carving over and over again in her hands. Finally the torrent waned.

"When will ya' be seein' him again, Miss Alix?" she asked with a sniff as she wiped her eyes with a white handkerchief.

"I don't know, but we've talked about seeing one another again. And I'm going to seek him out soon."

Deborah stood to her feet and gave Alix a hug. "Give him my love, Alix. Tell him we think of him constantly an' that we're still missin' him so."

"I will, Deborah. I promise you I will."

Alix could tell Deborah wanted to be alone and she began to go.

"Alix?" Deborah called to her.

Alix turned around. "Aye?"

"Thank ya', lass," Deborah's blue eyes shone clear. "Thank ya' for reachin' out to him."

"I owe him my life, Deborah!"

" 'Tis true. And he'll make it through now that you're here for him, Alix." Her eyes were beacons of hope.

"I believe he will. But we must continue to pray for Robin. Only the Savior can truly resurrect him from his lonesome existence."

"Always. Always we shall pray for m'brother." Deborah's firm commitment was evident. Thoughts of solitude were quickly replaced. "I must run an' tell Mother, Miss Alix. She's down cleanin' at the kirk. She'll want to know about all o' this."

"Here," she said, handing Alix the basket she had placed next to her, "take this to Miss Ferguson at the orphanage, if ya' please. Some fresh eggs from this mornin'."

Then she was gone.

In a few minutes Alix was knocking at the door to the small orphanage her mother had set up originally to house the children whose parents failed to survive the Jacobite rebellion.

A teenage girl with reddish-brown hair and dark, laughing eyes, two years younger than Alix, answered.

"Why, Lady Alix! Wha' a pleasant surprise!" she said as Alix handed her the basket.

"Hello, Rebecca. I just came to take some of the wee ones outside for some fresh air."

"Aye, miss. They're in the kitchen finishin' up their mornin' chores."

Alix walked across the small entry hall and into the kitchens where bread was baking for lunch. The luscious smell made her yearn to take a loaf to Robin. How long had it been since he had eaten hot bread? She vowed then to have Martha bake an extra loaf tomorrow. There were so many plans she had. Things she wanted to show him, words she wanted to say someday. Her mind had been racing all morning with the possibilities.

"Miss Alix! Miss Alix!" shrill, childish voices rang through the room, bringing a wide smile to her face. Presently there were ten children staying in the home. Two were doing dishes, two were drying. Three were sweeping. And three more were peeling vegetables for the noon meal.

"Hurry, children! It's a beautiful day and you should be enjoying the fresh air!"

"Where are we goin'?" Betsy, the eldest girl, raven-haired and about 12 years old, asked.

"I thought we should play along the loch today. Don't forget to bring some toys."

"May I bring a doll?" a shy voice asked above the carrots.

"Of course, Emily. It just wouldn't be the same without Louise along."

Soon they were enjoying the sunshine, running along the shore, and playing games that made their voices hoarse from laughter. She kept up with them measure for measure. Skipping rope and tag were played in separate groups. And

Alix's heart melted at the sight of the shining faces, scrubbed clean that morning, with their features spread in childish pleasure.

Hide-and-seek was next on their agenda, she was sure, and naturally she was always the first one to stand counting with her hands over her eyes. It was not easy to find ten mischievous children, and the game lasted until the bell rang for lunch. Alix shepherded her flock back to the house. After that would come lesson time for the children as well as Alix, and she needed to get back home.

"Will ya' be comin' again soon?" Ned asked as she turned to go. Freckled and carrot-haired, he was her favorite boy at the home. He had learned to read and write so quickly, the orphanage teacher was astounded. On rainy days, Alix and Ned would sometimes sit together and pore over poetry and volumes of great literature. Ned would someday make this orphanage proud. Alix just knew it. How that would be accomplished was another matter. Orphans, as a general rule, were not privy to higher education. These children were lucky they were merely learning to read.

"Aye, Ned. I just got a new volume of poems by Mac-Pherson."

"MacPherson!" his voice was awestruck. "Oh, Miss Alix, please bring it by for me. I so want to read it."

"I will. I'll bring it by tomorrow or the next day."

"Thank ya', Miss Alix. Thank ya'."

The bell was ringing and his heels thudded softly as he ran into the dining room. Alix smiled. She was going to miss them. England was less than three months away.

• • •

"You came back."

Alix wheeled around with a cry of delight. "Robin!"

After her meeting with Deborah, a week of rains had begun, and Miss Cawthorne had stepped up their schoolwork. It was the first time she had seen him in two weeks.

"I brought us some lunch," her voice said, its tone rising with each word.

"Pork pies?"

"Nay," she shook her head with a laugh, "just bread and cheese."

Robin closed his eyes at the thought. He hadn't tasted cheese since he left home. He took the bag from her. "Would ya' like to walk a bit? Or perhaps go somewhere to sit an' enjoy the sunshine?"

"Aye," she slipped her hand into his, just like before, "there's been precious little of it lately. Where are we going?"

"It's a surprise."

They walked in congenial silence through the forest, following the path of the burn. A small clearing opened up to a spot that Alix had never been. The stream fell over a succession of rocks making music for the birds that swooped overhead to sing with. And it collected in a shallow pool where fish darted to and fro, the late-morning sun catching on their silvery scales.

"I didn't know this place existed!" Alix cried, looking at the wildflowers which grew on the other side of the stream. Browsing bees added to the harmonic music of the clearing.

"Nay. Not many people do. I come here quite often, and am rarely disturbed."

Alix sat by the stream, taking off her boots and stockings. The water was cold, and she squealed as she plunged her feet into the water. Robin looked at her deeply . . . and smiled.

"Do you want to put your feet in, Robin?"

He laughed. "Thank ya' no, Lady Alix. It takes me too long to get my leggin's laced back up! But," he bent down, "I do believe I'll sit here alongside of ya'."

Between them he set down the knapsack. Alix grabbed it and undid the drawstring. "I have a surprise for you."

His eyebrows raised.

"It's a letter. From your sister Deborah."

He reached for the folded parchment. "When did she give it to ya'?"

"Just the other day."

His head dropped in sudden embarrassment. How could he ask her to read it for him? He felt her touch his arm softly and he looked up, eyes transparent. Alix's eyes met his, and she smiled a gentle smile.

"It's all right, Robin. I'll read it to you." She reached for the letter, but he held on tight.

"I've had no formal education, Lady Alix. I dinna' know what ya' must think of me." His words were barely audible.

"Oh, Robin!" Alix took her feet out of the stream and knelt close to him, putting one hand on his shoulder and the other on his forearm. "Just because you're not educated does not mean you've no intelligence. Education has nothing to do with the power that lies within your brain."

"I'm just a hunter, m'lady, and a wood-carver. There's nothing smart about that."

Alix laughed. "Really? Well, then let me ask you this, my Highlander: What is the one common factor between hunting and carving?"

Robin looked at her warily and shrugged his shoulders.

"Patience," she said simply. "That's all learning takes. The patience and willingness to listen and look."

"Ya' really do make it sound like huntin'."

"That's all it is, Robin. But instead of hunting animals, we hunt facts and answers."

"It canna' be so simple, Lady Alix." He clearly wasn't convinced.

"Oh, but it is," Alix became animated, knowing that she had a new, challenging task sitting before her. "As I said, all it takes is patience."

"When did Deborah learn to read and write?"

"My mother taught Joshua after Culloden, after he found a copy of the Scriptures in the castle ruins. He wanted to read the Word of God for himself, not just wait to hear it on Sundays. After Deborah married him, he taught her to read as well."

Robin looked thoughtfully at the small waterfall. If he could learn how to read, the evenings would not be so lonely.

"Robin?" Alix pulled him from his thoughts. "Would you like me to teach you?"

His eyes were earnest and filled with gratitude. "Aye, m'lady."

"Then we shall start right now." Excitement filled her voice. "Hand me Deborah's letter."

He did, the world unfolding before him as she opened the letter.

She pointed to a word. "This, Robin, is your name."

"Robin?"

"Aye . . . Robin."

• • •

Summer came, sweet summer, each leaf pregnant with the soft breath of the wind, each day filled with peaceful times spent together. Alix was right as far as Robin's intellect was concerned. He learned quickly and his patience at difficulties seemed to have no boundaries. Robin took her to many beautiful spots she had never seen, and ones she already knew and loved. Rainy afternoons were spent in the confines of the cave, but steadily he learned. And by July he had picked up all the fundamentals of reading and writing. Each night in his cave he would review the list of words he had learned so far, and practice his letters with the set of pens Alix had given to him.

Each time they met he brought something for her. Flowers. Berries. He had even made her an intricately carved set of combs. Picnics were a frequent setting for their learning sessions, and Alix delighted in bringing him delicious dainties from Martha's kitchen. Every day brought out a new dimension to Robin's personality; each moment in her presence warmed his very being. The awakening was almost complete.

* * *

August arrived with a heat most of the clansmen had never seen before. Alix sat in her room, stifled in the warm night air, trying to sleep but finding it not. The house was silent and all were slumbering.

Slipping a light wrapper on over her soft batiste nightgown, Alix padded silently down the steps and out into the sweltering night. The sky hung in a black dome above her head, and the tender moon left its magical trail across the inky surface of the loch. The lights in the blackness appeared as though a great lamp, white-hot and eternal, had been smashed across the vast expanse, broken in millions of pieces. Shattered light, scattered about in everlasting glory, each pinpoint of luminescence conveying the will of God. She walked along the water's edge, away from the direction of the castle as a faint breeze began to move the air around her.

And then she saw him.

Clad in his kilt, he faced the loch. His back glistened in the white moonlight, and Alix saw the deep scars with which time had been impotent, unable to soften the horror of what had been done so many years before. Pulling his shirt over his head, the coarse white material clung to the smooth hardness of his chest. His black curls, wet with the waters of the loch, glistened in the moonlight. He heard her approach.

"Lady Alix?" his eyes narrowed as he peered in the distance, knowing her immediately by the red of her hair.

"Robin." She walked quickly to him, her robe and nightgown fluttering gracefully around her. "I'm sorry. I didn't mean to disturb you. I couldn't sleep in this heat," she said shyly, looking upon his fair form.

He looked down onto her upturned face. "I was just finished." She looked so pretty in the moonlight. He had never seen her in the moonlight.

"You are so beautiful, Lady Alix." His voice was gruff, filled with the anguish of being so near, yet unable to tell her his feelings. The mood changed in an instant as his hand caressed her rounded cheek. The strange tune of gentle winds enveloped them in the cloak of Robin's emotions. Music, shared by the stunning silence of nocturnal repose, lilted between them, heart melting into heart, two different tunes becoming one symphony. Harmony. Duet.

Alix responded without thought, reaching forward to put her hand upon his chest, longing to feel the wet curls of his hair heavy in her hand. Her other hand complied with the wishes of her heart, as she thrust her fingers into the hair at the nape of his neck and sighed heavily.

The warmth of her breath upon his neck was more than Robin Brodie could bear, and forgetting all thoughts of station or caution, he bent his head in a movement so natural, so ordained, that Alix felt no fear, only a sense of need. His lips found hers without hesitation. They met his softly, and he felt their warmth as he pulled her closely to him and wrapped his arms about her tiny waist. She whimpered with pleasure as he kissed her mouth, her cheeks, and her eyes. Her hand traversed the corded muscles of his back, and she breathed in the clean scent of him. A newly created universe surrounded them, supernaturally fleeing the boundaries of time, place, and presupposition. A place where myth and reality clashed, then melded into one point of view.

The kiss was the first taste of passion she had ever known. But for Robin it was a feast that fed his very soul. And he gave his heart to her completely and forever.

They pulled apart, neither knowing quite what to do or say. Life had suddenly changed. Every part of their bodies was tingling, heightened by what both had just experienced for the first time.

"I'll walk ya' back home." He held out his hand. His heart soared higher and with more intensity than the moon overhead.

Alix put hers in his as he led the way. *How can I tell him I'm leaving in a week?* she thought, aching more for him than for herself.

• • •

All night she tossed and turned, searching for a way to tell him.

"I should never have kissed him," she admonished herself as she finally arose from her bed to sit at her window seat while the sun rose. "And yet . . ."

She couldn't help but thrill at the memory of it. And she had recalled it hundreds of times after she went back to her room. Her head had felt so light and her body was so aware. And Robin . . . she remembered his moonlit eyes, the longing in them as his head bent toward hers, the joy when they pulled apart.

It was no use. She had to tell him. And being forthright, she dressed and was on her way to the forest before the sun had cleared the horizon.

• • •

Sleep had evaded Robin as well.

All night he sat at his table, parchment stretched out before him. In childish letters he wrote her name again and again. His happiness kept him from sleeping, and he did not mind.

The cave door, open to the summer air, began to let in the morning light.

"Mother!" he said suddenly, realizing he hadn't yet drawn water for her. He had never missed a morning. *How can I go to the well and not be seen?*

"Perhaps there is yet time," he whispered to Bear.

Without further thought, Robin Brodie donned his leggings and bounded out of his cave. The morn was quiet yet, and the sun, though beginning to pinken the sky, had not yet come over the horizon. But it would soon.

Quickly he ran out of the woods and into the clearing. The village lay before him in silhouette, and no one seemed to be milling about the streets.

"Come on then, Bear," he said. "We'd best hurry."

His feet had never run faster. His arms had never pulled up the bucket in such haste. And he looked about him constantly, a sweat breaking out on his back and face. Still no one.

As quickly as possible without spilling the water, he walked the short distance to his mother's home, praying she had not yet awakened. Silently he set down the bucket, ran around to the back of the house and began the race across the meadow.

"Robin!"

He was in the middle of the clearing. But he stopped and turned around, watching Alix as she ran toward him, several books tucked under her arm.

"Lady Alix?" his eyes questioned her. "What are ya' doin' up an' about so early?"

His happiness exploded at the sight of her, and he forgot he was only several hundred yards from the village. But the somber expression upon her face brought him to his senses. He took the books from her hands.

"Robin, we must talk." She took his other hand. "Let's go into the forest where you will be more comfortable."

"What is it, Lady Alix?" he asked, afraid to find out the answer, but taking the lead in the discussion anyway.

"Robin," she sat down on a patch of moss and picked at a leaf, "there's something I have to tell you. That I should have told you about sooner, but just couldn't."

He looked at her, his brown eyes burning into Alix's soul. She could see the love there, and all the emotions that went with it. Pain. Confusion. Doubt.

"I'm leaving next week for London."

"How far away is London?"

"Much, much farther than Glasgow. It will take me many days to get there, Robin."

Robin brightened up. "That's all right, Lady Alix. I'm sure you'll be home soon. Ya' *will* be home soon . . . willna' ya'?" His instincts had taken over and he knew the answer.

"No, Robin," tears filled Alix's eyes. "I'm going away for two years."

* * *

Every day that next week Alix sought Robin out. In the forest. At the clearing. By the burn. At his cave. And nowhere was he to be found. She left some books for him, more ink, and more parchment. Each night she wept sorely.

"Alix," her mother came in her bedroom the night before she was to leave. Her trunks, packed and ready, were waiting by the door. Jenny put her arms around her daughter. "I know it's hard to leave, my love. But just think of the wonderful experiences you'll be having."

"Mama," Alix sobbed, taking some small comfort from her mother's caressing hand. "It isn't just that. I'm so disappointed. Robin has avoided me for a week. Ever since I told him I was leaving."

Jenny looked tenderly into her daughter's eyes, and she cupped her face in her small hands. "You cannot expect any less, love. You have become Robin's world. Try and imagine what he's expecting his life to be once you are gone."

Alix nodded. "Do you think he's angry with me, Mama?"

"Nay, daughter," Jenny's voice was warm. "He's just confused."

"Oh, Mama, who will bring him books, teach him to write? Was it all for nothing?"

"So it seems," Jenny replied. "But do not forget about the Savior, Alix. Who knows what manner of man our Lord has designed Robin to be?"

"You're right," she sighed. "Sometimes I feel as though Robin has depended only upon me," she confessed. "But he's a man. And a strong one at that."

Alix thought later just how much of a man Robin Brodie truly was, the remembrance of his kiss still heavy upon her lips.

• • •

I am leaving Scotland.

Alix wanted to cry. Her mother had never looked lovelier. Papa never stronger. Lachlan never more vital. Violet never more thoughtful. And Mary Alice had never looked more sweet. The pain of leaving heaved within her breast with each word said.

The coach pulled around, laden with her trunks, and much too soon, Beaton opened the door, his hair blowing forward in the breeze. He bent down to pick something up, then he handed it to Jenny.

"It's for Alix," she said, reading the name, then turning to give her the small parcel.

But before she could open it, her family was surrounding her and tearful good-byes were uttered.

"Oh, Papa, I'll miss you so."

The chief looked into his daughter's eyes. "My lovely Alix. Be careful. And know that we'll be waiting for you and thinking of you every minute of the day."

"I love you," she whispered, her face pressed against his coat.

"And I love you, lass."

Minutes later she was on her way to England. Past the village of Strathlachlan. Away from the loch. Past the forest. A patch of red caught her eye. And there, standing at the edge of the trees was the legend himself. She waved frantically out of the window, calling his name. He raised his hand, and stood unmoving until the carriage had passed over the hill and was out of sight. The picture was forever engraved upon Alix's mind of Robin with the wind in his hair, plaid blowing in the breeze. The Last Highlander had said goodbye.

With shaking fingers Alix opened the note attached to the parcel.

I will miss you.

The words were scrawled across the paper in childish figures. Inside the cloth a carving rested. A Highlander and a lady sitting side by side, a book resting between them. It was Robin's way of saying thank you, and Alix wept until the sun began its descent and the first inn sat outside her window.

• • •

25 December, 1762

The moon flew high and white behind the wispy clouds as the Christmas wind that enveloped him. Light snow, fine and delicate, landed on tartan. The well-oiled leather kept his feet dry as he trudged across the snow-covered clearing. In his newer kilt and plaid, white shirt, and a covering of warm fox skins, Robin Brodie slipped silently through the village of Strathlachlan. Hair tied back, and walking straight and proud, he looked forthrightly about him, glad the streets were deserted. Christmas night was not a time the village inhabitants milled about the streets. He had observed enough Christmas nights to know that. Most were enjoying the peaceful night and their full bellies. He had heard the bagpipes and drums, the singing and the laughter. Maybe next year he would join them.

Alix had made her feelings all too clear in regard to his hermit existence. But he knew that even she would never understand why he could not emerge from his twilight world. Yet tonight, this Christmas night, he had an urgent task set before him. Time was running out. Each month he noticed his mother was getting thinner and thinner.

The house was still lit. Inside Mavis sat in front of the fire. Knitting and humming softly, her face was pleasant and at peace. On the mantel were graceful carvings of the holy family fashioned by his father: watchful Joseph, gentle Mary cradling her beloved son.

For a moment longer he stood looking on, as he breathed in the last breath of his old life, knowing things would never be the same again. A silent good-bye was said to his youth forever when he walked to the door, raised his hand, and knocked.

He knew she must be wondering who it could be. Suddenly the door opened and she was there. So tiny and so much older than a woman her age should be. The inquisitive expression turned to one of tearful joy.

"Robin! Oh m'Robin!" Her hands went up to her mouth, her eyes were wide. She put her arms around him letting her tears flow, and hugged him with a strength that surprised even Robin. And finally, after 16 long years, Robin Brodie cried. In her arms he let go of the scars, the wounds, the death, and the shame. They crumpled to their knees there on the doorstone amid the Christmas snow.

"Oh m'boy, m'Robin," Mavis soothed as Robin sobbed with abandon in her arms. Time, so much time they had lost. Yet hope had come into the world that night. And what the terms of his coming would be, she knew not. But her arms were full of her child, as they had ached to be for the past 16 years of his cold seclusion.

PART THREE
1764

O'er the Moor Amang the Heather

Comin' through the craigs o'Kyle,
    Amang the bonnie bloomin' heather,
There I met a bonnie lassie,
    Keepin' a' her ewes thegither.
        O'er the moor amang the heather,
           O'er the moor amang the heather;
        There I met a bonnie lassie,
           Keepin' a' her ewes thegither.

Says I, my dear, where is thy hame—
    In moor or dale, pray tell me whether?
She says, I tend the fleecy flocks
    That feed amang the blooming heather.

We laid us down upon a bank,
    Sae warm and sunnie was the weather:
She left her flocks at large to rove
    Amang the bonnie blooming heather.

While thus we lay, she sang a sang,
    Till echo rang a mile and farther;
And aye the burden of the sang
    Was, O'er the moor amang the heather.

She charm'd my heart, and aye sinsyne
    I couldna' think on ony other—
By sea and sky, she shall be mine,
    The bonnie lass amang the heather!
        O'er the moor amang the heather,
           Down amang the blooming heather—
        By sea and sky, she shall be mine,
           The bonnie lass amang the heather!

—Jean Glover

CHAPTER

9

London
June, 1764

The open market was ablaze with many colors. Flower ladies walked about calling out their wares, large baskets filled with colorful blooms perched upon their arms. Produce was stacked about in wooden carts, hauled in from the country that very morning. Common people and servants of the gentry haggled for the best price, and two females walked among them all, dressed in old dresses and sporting extremely mussed-up hair.

"How did you talk me into this one?" Alix whispered to her best friend, and elbowed her sharply.

"Ouch!" Lady Philippa Lundly replied. "Stop that, Alix. No one held a knife to your throat." Her face took on a look of extreme distaste. "Besides, it was either sneak out this morning or go riding with Thomas Peterson."

"That's true enough. I get so tired of hearing about Thomas Peterson. 'Educated in France, worldly wise, the most sought-after young bachelor in England.' I wish all the girls would be quiet about that fop."

"Well, Alix," Philippa taunted, "how can he hope to compare with a dripping-wet Scotsman clad only in his kilt under a full moon?"

Alix laughed easily, yet her embarrassment surfaced. "Philippa, that was two years ago."

"Maybe. But the thought of it still sends shivers up my spine. I do not know how it fails to do the same to you." Her blue eyes were dreamy.

Alix looked over at her friend and felt a melancholy wash over her. Her years in London were coming to a close.

"I wish I didn't have to leave London yet."

"Is it true, Alix? Do you have to go back to Scotland so soon?" Her blue eyes testified to a sadness that was penetrating her heart more deeply with each passing day.

They sat down on the fifth step leading up to the opera house at Covent Garden.

"I'm afraid it's true," she responded sadly. "I cannot believe two years have gone by so quickly. I am going to miss you, Philippa."

Lady Philippa's mother, the Countess of Dorset, was a close friend of Alix's grandmother, Margaret. The two girls spent some of their time together up in the north of England, the location of her grandfather's duchy. But London was where the majority of their fun took place.

"What am I going to do with you gone?" Philippa asked. "Schooling is going to be such drudgery from now on. And who else could I talk so easily into trouble?"

Alix looked at her wryly, remembering all of their escapades.

"Oh, one never knows, Philippa. You might find someone even more gullible. After all, I did turn around on you at the last moment last year as we were boarding the ship setting off for France. Lucky for both of us we got home before the notes were found."

Philippa laughed. "Think of it, though, Alix. We would have been the toast of Paris!"

"Only because Grandpapa owns a house there. We would have been on the street otherwise, and who knows what would have happened?"

"Maybe." The blue eyes sparkled. Philippa would never concede defeat. "But it's not all my fault. Your temper has caused enough trouble on its own."

"I'm truly trying to get a hold on it, Philippa." Alix was a bit contrite. She had too many years of theological training to be proud of her easily aroused ire.

"I know, Alix, I know. But next time you feel like telling off the Earl of Braxton when he puts down his wife at a party, make sure I'm not around!"

"Don't worry. I had to stay indoors for a week because of it. Believe me, I learned my lesson."

Just then Big Ben tolled. Both girls gasped. Six o'clock!

"We'd better get back! You're going-away ball starts in three hours!"

Alix jumped to her feet and pulled Philippa up. "Oh no! I knew better than to let you talk me into . . ."

"Hurry, Alix!" Philippa had her by the hand, distracting her before she became angry. Alix always became angry when she thought she would be getting into trouble with her grandparents.

As they ran home, a storm erupted, soaking their clothes and hair.

The girls gasped afresh. "How are we ever going to get our hair dry in time?" Philippa wailed.

Alix should have gotten angry, but the sight of Philippa, so short and skinny, with her black curls plastered to her china skin, and the awful, dirty gray dress clinging to her 16-year-old frame was so comical, she could only laugh.

"You are a sight."

"Oh, yes? Well you don't look like Madame de Pompadour yourself, Alix Maclachlan."

They grabbed one another's hand and picked up their pace. Soon they were running up the steps to Grandpapa's townhouse in Hanover Square. They burst through the door, slid across the grand marble entrance hall, and ran up the steps.

Within minutes they were in dry shifts and sat in chairs near the fireplace.

"Let's hope it dries quickly," Alix said as she continually fluffed her fingers through her reddened tresses.

Philippa was much less optimistic. She stood up, bent over, and began shaking her head as quickly as she could.

"You're going to make yourself sick," Alix warned.

"I already am," Philippa said dryly. "I cannot fathom why we let time escape us like that!" They only had an hour and 15 minutes before the ball began.

Forty-five minutes later, Alix's maid entered the room and began to dress her hair.

"Your hair is getting more glorious every day." Philippa sat on the bed, already dressed for the evening's party. Twenty minutes earlier she had summoned her ladies' maid who had taken the damp curls and pulled them up in a simple chignon at the crown of her head. A few of the dark tendrils had escaped, and framed her adorable face. Philippa was a lovely girl. With green eyes that always sparkled with life and red, full lips, and a tip-tilted nose, she inveterately looked ready for anything or anybody.

Alix winced into the mirror as Clara pulled and teased, pinned and curled. "In Scotland a red-haired woman is considered unlucky. Besides, Philippa, your thick black curls with your fair skin are quite striking. And you're so petite. I only wish I had your figure."

"What figure! You are so statuesque I look like a child beside you." Philippa's tone was so droll Alix burst into laughter.

Philippa giggled. "I just hope old Duncan is taller than you are."

She still hadn't met her betrothed, Duncan Campbell, and much jesting was enjoyed by Philippa at the poor man's expense.

Alix gave her a smirk and changed the subject. "Your gown is lovely, Philippa."

"Yes, it is perfect for a girl my age, isn't it?" she said with disdain. "Mother picked it out, of course. One of these days, however, after you have gone and some fop has wagered high enough with Daddy for the honor of my hand, I'm going to pick out my own gowns. No more of these confectionery trifles. No more white. No more pink. No more mint greens and sky blues. I'm going to wear scarlet, and gold, and rich green, and royal purple! It stands to reason that if I must marry some revolting, effeminate dandy, he's going to have to pay the price!"

Laughing, Alix waved a hand at her, having heard it all many times before. "I'm sure you will not let him spend more on his wardrobe than you do on yours. Look in the dressing room. My trousseau was delivered this morning. It may give you ideas for your own wardrobe next year."

"Next decade, you mean to say." Philippa walked across the room. "I plan on holding out as long as possible," she said as she flung open the doors and let out a gasp. "Oh, Alix. You are simply horrible! Look at these gowns!" She fingered through the rich velvets and brocades. At least 30 dresses hung in splendor. The winter gowns were all the deep hues of which Philippa dreamed. And the summer gowns, though of lighter material, were still vibrant and carried over Alix's signature style of simple elegance. They befit her station as the future Duchess of Argyll.

Soon both young women were completely dressed and stood side by side, looking at themselves in the full-length mirror in the corner.

Philippa, in a white taffeta ball gown whose overskirt was pulled up with flowers and bows, was the essence of innocence. The neckline sported a lace edging, and the underskirt was covered in lace as well. Her eyes, however, sparkled unruly above the perfectly chaste attire. Alix had chosen an ivory gown of heavy silk. The scoop-necked bodice held no ornamentation, merely embroidery in gold thread and three small ivory rosettes that found their way down the front to her waist. The underskirt was embroidered much the same as the bodice.

Philippa's expression was sour. "I look like a cake."

Alix hugged her tightly. "You look adorable."

She pulled away, suddenly serious. "Philippa, I have been wanting to ask you this for quite a while, but it has never seemed the right time. Would you stand in attendance at my wedding?"

This time Philippa pulled Alix into a hug. "Of course, Alix. Of course. I'd be honored. That is..." her mouth curled in a smile, "...if old Duncan says its okay."

"Oh, you!" Alix chimed. "Poor old Duncan, he's not going to know what to think when he meets you, Philippa."

"I envy you, Alix," Philippa said later as they slowly descended the grand staircase of the Duke of Loxingham's townhouse. "You are finished with parties once this one is over. And I have a whole season to get through. Imagine it. Another summer of balls, fetes, dinner parties, and card games with the dowagers. I do not know if I shall be able to stand it."

"Dear Philippa. I hardly think I shall be through with parties. And besides, you are only 16."

"Almost 17. Next month I'll be 17," she was quick to point out, hating the fact that she was so young.

"Yes, you are right. Let us just hope that this season will yield a man who is worthy of you."

"I doubt there is one out there," Philippa said dryly.

"Then let's pray there is one that at least can tolerate you!" Deep inside Alix had to wonder whether or not there was a man alive who could handle being married to high-spirited yet antisocial Philippa Lundly.

They laughed together as their heeled slippers clicked across the marble flooring of the entry hall, and they made their way to the veranda out back to wait until the ball began.

Both drew in their breath at the sight before them. An array of shocking pinks and purples streaked across the sky, blending into a starry night. Silence enveloped them. There was no joking now as the beauty before their eyes invaded them, reaching down inside their souls to churn up all the human feelings of insignificance they had been taught to hold silent. Their hearts were painful even on so special a night when the majesty of the heavens glorified the One who created them. Alix held Philippa's hand and wondered just how dull life was going to be without her best friend to lead her astray.

• • •

Alix's grandfather, Richard, the Duke of Loxingham, looked wistfully out through the glass-paned doors that opened onto the back porch leading into the small but picturesque gardens. The townhouse was new. Margaret had hated the old one and, knowing how much she loved to decorate, he was happy to surprise his duchess with the house two years ago. Alix had been with them only a month when, after a mysterious carriage ride complete with draped windows, he handed Margaret the key and told her to open her eyes. And now that the house was fully decorated and had come into its own, his favorite granddaughter was leaving it behind.

In his mid-fifties, the duke cut a fine figure of a man. Of medium height, he was still in remarkable shape due to hours of riding each day. His blond hair, liberally scattered with gray, was pulled back into a simple queue and held with a gold ribbon that matched his coat. He was an intelligent man. A shrewd man. Had become quite powerful in the House of Lords. His life, his mistakes, and his victories as well had taught him where true strength lies.

Noiselessly he opened the door and stood behind the girls, as lost as they were in the heaven's twilight offerings. It was 8:30. The ball would soon begin.

"It's beautiful, isn't it?" he finally asked. Philippa and Alix responded with a start.

"Grandpapa!" Alix turned around. "I didn't hear you come out."

"Just admiring the view as you are," the duke smiled into his granddaughter's eyes, so like his own, so like Jenny's. Then he mischievously pulled on one of Philippa's ringlets. "The ball is almost ready to begin. And as the guest of honor, I suggest you make your way in before the others start to arrive. I am sure you will wish to greet everyone. Well . . ." he smiled sheepishly, knowing how overbearing some of the nobility could be, "almost everyone."

They walked up the grand staircase to the ballroom. Located on the second floor, its large balcony overlooked the park across the street. Inside, its black-and-white parquet flooring was waxed and polished till it shone, and three large chandeliers sparkled under their heavy load of slim, white tapers. Large mirrors in gilded frames stood sentinel at either end of the room reflecting the light of the chandeliers and sconces which lined the pale-yellow walls.

"I'll wait over there while you greet your guests, Alix, and do my best to blend in with the scenery," Philippa said, sauntering away to wait by the balcony. Lady Margaret, wearing a brocade gown of pale rose, was making her way up the steps.

"Well, Richard," she breathed out heavily, pushing a black curl back into place with a gloved hand, "all is ready. They should be arriving any minute."

Her husband kissed her on the cheek. "You look lovely, my dear," he whispered softly into her ear. "You always look lovely."

The startlingly light-blue eyes closed as the duchess turned away from the duke and Alix with a blush. An extremely capable woman, her husband was the only person in the world who had that effect on her.

Twilight had taken its final hold on the heavens, and the sky, gradated from a brilliant azure to a star-studded black, provided a breathtaking background for the carriages as they pulled up to the grand, marble-pillared entryway of the house. Laughter issued among the clopping of horses' hooves, and a springtime breeze freshened the foul air of London as lords and ladies in their finest jewels and silks made their way up the steps.

The duke, a magnificent host, stood between Alix and his wife, welcoming guests to the first party of the season. Young women came along with their parents, wearing their finest gowns and looking as pretty as they possibly could. Mothers pushed them toward the center of activity, encouraging them and hoping against hope their precious child would not be left seated against the wall all evening. Alix smiled and curtsied and had her gloved hand kissed numerous times.

The music began, and soon the floor became an undulating spectacle of beautiful shades of swirling silk brocades and taffetas. Diamonds, rubies, emeralds, pearls, and sapphires twinkled the spectrum in the bright candlelight. The men were as equally impressive as the ladies, clad in intricately embroidered coats and waistcoats of extraordinary hues. And once the final guest had arrived, Alix joined them on the floor with her grandfather.

What a striking pair they made. And more than one young man was sorry that this was Alix's going-away party. She never wanted for a dance partner. *My face shall crack from this smile*, she thought. But she was enjoying the attention nonetheless.

In and out, round and round, the minuets and reels bade them go. And more than once Alix caught the sarcastic glances of Philippa who hated to dance. She remembered asking her friend what it was she really wanted from life.

Philippa's simple answer of "peace" surprised Alix. And for a while Alix strove to share the love of the Savior with her in both word and deed. After reading Ecclesiastes upon Alix's urging, Philippa's favorite phrase had been "vanity, vanity, all is vanity." Alix also prayed that Philippa's future husband would be a valiant man of faith, and not the simpering fop Philippa feared she was doomed to spend the rest of her life with. Like Thomas Peterson.

Lady Margaret was chatting with a group of ladies. Grandfather was talking politics as usual. And Philippa was dancing with a particularly handsome gentleman in military uniform. Her stiff movements proclaimed every step a misery. It was a good time to slip away downstairs to the garden.

She breathed in. Good. No one had come down yet. The air cooled her overheated body and her breathing slowed to normal.

Looking down at her gown in the torchlight, at the tiny waist and full breasts, she shook her head in disbelief. So many changes. Life was different now. And she was as well. Gone was the wispy little Scottish girl, content to gambol about the countryside and the woods. She needed more. And yet . . . Scotland wasn't the edge of the world. The Campbells were a learned family, famous for their literary contributions. Surely she wouldn't stagnate. Surely her education would deepen. Being a duchess someday would give her ample cause to enjoy the conversation of many intelligent, well-read individuals.

Hopefully Duncan is as smart as everyone says he is, she thought ruefully.

Her mind filled with visions of heather and heath, the hills of Kilbride, the shimmering, moving waters of Loch Fyne. The woods. Robin.

A narrow stone pathway took her over a small Chinese bridge to a fish pond, complete with lily pads, frogs, and fish. Several lanterns hung from the trees, closing in the area unto itself. A city fairyland tucked amid London's bustle.

She sat on a wooden bench and removed her gloves. Lost in thought, memories of her childhood as well as her time in England mingled together in her mind. The future, though known, was still a mystery. That disturbed her. If Duncan had only come to call, her apprehension would not be so great.

A footstep behind her caused her to turn.

"Hello, Alix."

Immediately her face fell. So much for time alone.

"Good evening, Lord Peterson. I didn't realize you'd arrived already. Bad luck at cards?"

"No. Good luck. I thought I'd leave the club while things were still going my way. And please, Alix, I've asked you before, call me Thomas."

Fastidiously he arranged the frill at his neck. "May I sit down?"

Alix waved her hand over the seat next to her.

"I'm leaving London in a few days."

Thomas's expression became pained. Dramatically so. "And will you miss me?"

Alix laughed. "I have a whole new life ahead of me." She knew Thomas would think it hurt her too much to say yes.

"Back up to Scotland, eh?" his face registered his distaste at the thought. "Back to wild men in plaid and starving peasants. What a waste of such beauty."

It was the first time he had ever really complimented her. Alix looked at him sharply.

"Thomas," she questioned, "correct me if I'm wrong, but did you just say something flattering about someone other than yourself?"

"I'm a desperate man, Alix."

She looked at him sharply. His tone was different. And yet his eyes were not. Clearly he was up to something.

"And why is that?" With laughter in her voice, she tried to keep the conversation on a lighter tone.

"Because you are leaving me, and my feelings for you have yet to be satisfied."

"What feelings are those, Thomas?" Maybe she could get an admission of love from him. Philippa would just love that!

"Feelings for you, Alix." He turned in his seat and grabbed her by the upper arms. His breath was heavy with the smell of brandy. "You've evaded me for over a year now, despite my attempts at wooing. I'm not a man that likes to be put off forever."

"Oh, my poor Lord Peterson," Alix began to chide him good-naturedly, but his hands tightened. "You're hurting me!"

"It cannot be helped. You drive me into lunacy with your saucy comments and your laughs at my expense. I'm not a fool, Alix, although it may seem so to you. Most women want a man they can rely on to drink, gamble, and carouse, and leave them alone. I've seen it happen too many times. Why do you think there are so many dandies in society nowadays?"

Alix raised her brows in surprise. It was the first intelligent thing Thomas had ever said. "That may be, but . . ."

He squeezed even tighter and Alix resisted, trying to pull away. "I'm not a man to be put off, Alix. I will have you."

"No, Thomas. Stop it! Stop it right now."

Thomas Peterson dropped his head toward hers, but Alix twisted from side to side, trying to avoid his kiss. "Stop playing games, Alix," he laughed, his face touching hers, "you know you want this as much as I do."

"I do not. Please, Thomas, let go of me."

They struggled, now standing. Alix desperately tried to get away from him, but Thomas held on even more tightly, giving her arms a twist. She cried out in pain.

"I believe the lady said no."

They both wheeled around and Thomas Peterson immediately let go. Anger colored his face a deeper red. "And who are you to tell me what the lady wants?"

A man stepped into the circle of light. A tall man with sandy-blond curls and deep eyes. "I believe she said it herself."

Thomas stepped toward the stranger. "What women say they want and what they truly desire are usually two different matters."

"A typical response," the stranger said calmly. "I think you'd better get back to the ball now and leave the lady alone."

"Why you insolent..." Thomas's fist shot forward, but the stranger was quicker and, with a swift right to the jaw, Thomas was sprawled on the walkway. The stranger lifted him up by his coat collar and shoved him toward the house. "Get out of here. And if I were you, I'd be more careful next time I force myself upon a woman that the feelings are mutual."

With a dark glare and a soft, "You haven't heard the last from me," Thomas walked up the path, straightening his clothing.

"Thank you," Alix said calmly. Inside she was shaking.

"Don't mention it," the man smiled warmly, immediately taking her into his confidence. "It's fellows like him that give the rest of us rogues a bad name."

"Well, I'm glad you arrived," Alix admitted frankly with a sigh. "Thomas Peterson is usually quite harmless. Although his disobliging ways have become a matter of habit, I'm not sure what got into him tonight. Your timely arrival is greatly appreciated."

The man stepped closer to her. Now only several feet from her, he bowed. The lantern light reflected off his thick hair. "Thank you, my lady."

He stood straight again with a smile. A smile filled with confidence. She had met many men of his ilk since coming to London. Suave, self-assured, with perfect clothes and manners to match, incurably given to rove. Yet he didn't seem to take himself too seriously, or anyone else for that matter.

Alix proffered her hand. "I am afraid that we have not yet been introduced. I am Alix Maclachlan."

"Ah, the honored guest." He raised her hand to his lips. They felt soft, yet firm upon the back of her hand. Yes, he really was very confident. "Forgive me for arriving too late to make your acquaintance. I am Aaron Campbell."

His accent was as unmistakable as her own, although time had eroded its severity. Obviously he had been in England for quite some time. "You are from Scotland, are you not?"

The two Highlanders smiled into one another's eyes. "Aye. I didna' think tha' I'd be able t' hide it from ya'!" He spoke in a broad Scots accent which delighted her.

"Are you related to the Campbells of Argyll?"

Alix's voice caught on the last word. Just last year the old Duke of Argyll had passed away. It was the first loss Alix had ever experienced of someone she truly loved.

"They are relatives of mine. Yes."

"And what brings you here?"

"I came with a friend. I suppose he sought my company to rescue him from time to time from the clutches of the boring witticisms of the gentry."

"Then I'm glad you could come!" Alix laughed. "While you're at it, you could impart the same service to me as well." Just then she saw Grandfather come out onto the balcony, breathe in deeply, then reenter the ballroom. Obviously he felt the same as they did. "Perhaps I should be getting back inside. If anyone saw you come out after me, I'm afraid we should be the main topic of conversation for the next week and a half."

"Sad, isn't it," Aaron said with a wide smile, "when that's as good as the talking gets? Although I must say, it sure wins over the latest update on that horse toothed Lord Darlington's gout, or the Prince of Wales and his latest paramour."

"You like to give yourself a lot of credit, don't you, Mr. Campbell?" Alix's eyes sparkled.

"Yes, actually, I do. Because, unfortunately, no one else will jolly well do it for me!"

"A truer word was never spoken." Alix looked up at the ballroom. "Supper will be starting soon. I suppose we should go back in."

Even as the words were said, she felt disappointed. She didn't want to go back in. For some reason she wanted to stay anonymously tucked away here where the breeze played lightly across the nape of her neck and the sound of the fountain nearby rustled in aquatic softness.

Fighting off her natural wants, she turned to go, but was detained by a gentle hand on her arm. Alix looked down. It was a strong hand. Yet encased inside the golden flesh was a tender touch that squeezed her forearm lightly.

"May I dance with you, Lady Alix?" He was still smiling. And Alix took in his features at length. The long face with its straight nose and strong mouth, the clear-cut jawline and high forehead, were pleasing to the eye and so very masculine. Yet the curls which escaped his queue softened his overall appearance, making him approachable and friendly looking. But in a jaunty, swashbuckling sort of way.

"Certainly, Mr. Campbell. Would you care to walk me back up to the ballroom?"

"I meant here, and please call me Aaron."

Alix didn't understand. "What?"

He bowed. "Will you dance with me here. In the garden?"

Her eyebrows raised, and a smile burst upon her face at his request. So unusual. "Yes, Mr. Campbell, I will. No one has ever asked me to dance in a garden before."

"Now we shall really have people talking!" he laughed.

As they danced a minuet near the fountain, Alix saw that his eyes were brown and while they left her feeling exposed and incredibly naive, his smile thrilled her heart. In and out the dance bade them go. Circling, touching hands, touching shoulders. Warmth spread through her, radiating outward from each spot his hand had rested. Her face flushed, eyes sparkling, she became alive in his presence.

When the music stopped, Aaron Campbell reached forward to her ear, his fingers sliding down the lobe to play softly with the dangling pearl of her earring. His eyes were bright with feeling. "Thomas was right, Lady Alix. You are a beautiful woman."

Placing her hand upon the invisible trail of sensation left by his hand, Alix ran back into the ballroom.

• • •

The duke and duchess sat on a settee in the parlor, leaning back into the cushions. Exhaustion made its mark upon their middle-aged faces, but good humor still rambled about their eyes.

Alix collapsed in a chair.

"Well," the duke said with a weary smile, "was your going-away ball everything you hoped it would be?"

"Everything and more. Thank you Grandpapa, Grandmama."

"It was nice to see the Duke of Argyll again, wasn't it, Alix?" the duchess asked.

"Yes, that surely was a surprise. I didn't know he was coming."

"Oh, I sent him an invitation. He resides in London throughout most of the year, you know."

"Yes. I was rather hoping that Duncan would be with him." Alix's tired eyes fixated themselves glassily on the green walls.

"Well," said Grandpapa, "the duke tells me that since he's gone back to Scotland indefinitely for his research, London has probably seen the last of him, except for an occasional visit."

"I suppose I shall have to wait yet longer to meet my betrothed," Alix said with a sigh. "He certainly has kept himself a mystery."

The duke sat up suddenly. "Speaking of mysteries, a note came for you with your mother's last letter. I was instructed to give it to you tonight, at your going-away ball." He reached into his coat pocket and pulled out an envelope with her name written in beautiful script on the front.

Alix looked away from the wall with a start and reached forward, her expression curious. "Did Mama say who it was from? I do not recognize the handwriting."

"No. She didn't mention that. Well, Margaret dear," he stifled a yawn, "what do you say, shall we retire?"

"Yes, Richard," the Duchess said, "but do help me up. I'm entirely spent."

The duke arose and helped his wife to her feet. "Well then, Alix. We shall say our good nights." They kissed her on the cheek.

"Thank you again for the lovely party," Alix said as she hugged them. "I'm going to miss you both so greatly."

"And so shall we miss you, my love," he said tenderly.

"Yes, we shall," agreed the Duchess. "Good night, Alix."

The parlor was empty. Alix could hear the servants bustling softly upstairs as they cleared the mess from the ballroom, their soft chatter filtering through the air. Skirts swishing gently, she moved to a chair by a window that overlooked the street.

"It's all over," she said as she sat alone with the letter in her hand, thinking about London, the evening, and Aaron Campbell. She hadn't seen him again after their dance in the garden. *All the better I suppose*, she thought. Scotland was before her once again, and her youth would firmly be behind her once and for all. Marriage loomed ahead of her, and she didn't need Aaron Campbell to complicate matters further. She leaned her elbow on the arm of the green-and-ivory striped chair and cupped her chin with a sigh. She looked out over the scene before her. The crowded street had become an urban desert, debris swirling in an eerie dance with the wind. A lone soldier from a Highland regiment walked down the road. His plaid moved fluidly about in the wind, his head was held high, and his kilt swung gently as he sauntered home to his lodgings.

Without warning Alix felt a yearning so strong that dizziness filled her head and her heart became hot with homesickness.

"I am a Scot." She said the words aloud, and tears spilled from her eyes onto the letter in her hand.

Minutes later, Alix looked down and remembered she had yet to read the mysterious note. The name had smeared where her tears had landed, and she dried the beads of liquid with her hankie.

As she unfolded the parchment, a gasp emitted from between her lips as a world of fancy unfolded down the left side of the page. Drawn in black ink, fairies and elves and animals danced an artistic, sweeping reel intertwined with flowers and vines. The flowing composition was so detailed and fanciful Alix knew who it was from immediately.

But just as lovely as the drawings was the writing. Each capital letter a masterpiece, each lower case formed to perfection. Obviously, Robin Brodie had practiced many a lonely night on the fundamentals of what she had taught him, and before she read a word the Last Highlander had written, tears flowed again. Blinking them away quickly, she began to read the words of the only man that she had ever kissed.

Dear Lady Alix

It's been so long since I have seen your face or heard your voice. And shortly you will be coming home to Scotland, to Strathlachlan and all that you love. I am anticipating that with much joy, for my debt to you is great.

Over the past two years I have thought back many times to our moments together and to the day we first met. Many times you thanked me that summer for saving your life and, Lady Alix, it was my privilege to do so. You thought that it was I who saved your life, when, in fact, you saved mine. And for that I could never begin to repay the debt I owe.

What started that day has been continuing even as you have been in London. As you can see, I have completed learning to read and write, and learning brings me much joy and companionship, especially during the winter months. Joshua was good enough to ask the chief if I might borrow books from the castle library and he agreed. Every week he brings two books home when I come for supper on Wednesday evenings. Aye, I come out of the cave more often, but it is still home and I must admit I am more relaxed when I am sitting in front of my own hearth. Your mother picks out the books herself, and I am honored. She has a fancy for Shakespeare, does she not?

I cannot wait to show you all that I have learned. The puzzling part of learning to read and write is how differently one writes than one speaks. Upon reading this over, I sound almost educated!

Alix smiled and continued reading.

You will be back in Scotland soon, back from the land of England. I hope they treated you well, my lady. Maybe you are part English, but Scotland will forever flow through your veins.

I am eagerly awaiting your homecoming.

  Sincerely,

   Robin Brodie

CHAPTER

10

Castle Lachlan stood firmly against the starry night. Yellow light burned from the windows into the darkness, welcoming and warm. Excitement, anticipation, and the joy of coming home pierced Alix when the great front door opened to the sound of her carriage coming up the drive. *It seems as if these horses will never stop!* she thought. But they finally did, and four people came running down the steps. Their familiar silhouettes brought tears to her eyes.

As soon as the carriage came to a standstill, the door was pulled open.

"Papa!"

"Alix!"

They cried one another's name simultaneously, and he lifted her down and whirled her around as he always had. Her mother hurried over to her, jubilation etched with no mistake on her gentle features.

"Oh, my darling, you're finally home!" She hugged her daughter tightly and kissed her on both cheeks.

Joy spread contagiously as Lachlan, now filled out and even bigger than his father, hugged her so hard he lifted her off her feet.

"Look at her, Father!" he said proudly, standing back. "She went away as a waif . . . and has come home a woman."

"Aye, that she has, son."

"Violet!" Alix leaned over and embraced her sister. "You've grown so much!"

"Thank you," Violet said primly. "I am glad you are home, sister."

"And I am happy to see you also. Where is Mary Alice?"

"Here I am!" A tiny face peeped from behind Jenny's skirts. Alix suddenly realized how much life she had missed. Mary Alice was three years old—no longer the baby who had sucked on her two middle fingers as Alix rode away. Her eyes were a bluer blue, her hair a shinier gold, and she was dressed in an adorable little gown the color of a buttercup.

"What a big girl you are!" Alix gasped and knelt down to gather her littlest sibling into her arms.

"Alix. My big sister Alix," she chimed as she pointed into the entryway of the house.

Jenny chuckled, putting a hand on Violet's shoulder proudly. "Every day Violet brought her down and showed her your portrait. She didn't want her to forget you."

Violet's eyes dropped in embarrassment, though her family loyalty ran deep.

"Thank you, Violet," said Alix.

Still unable to express her joy fully like the rest of her family, Violet, now ten, simply put her hand in Alix's and led her to the entry hall where the staff filed in respectfully to welcome her home.

Soon after that they sat down in the dining room. Silver cutlery shimmered alongside the fine white Limoges china that Jenny had inherited from Mattie, the governess who had raised her. A linen cloth was spread over the beautiful table, and crystal goblets caught the light from the brass chandelier which hung over the table. It was still the same, just as Alix had remembered. Jenny had planned a party indeed. Just for the family. In honor of Alix's return.

"What's for supper?" Lachlan asked as he seated his mother.

The chief smiled. "It should bring back some memories for Alix!"

"What is it, Papa?" Alix asked as the door swung open and a servant she did not recognize came in with a large silver tray.

"Suckling pig!" Violet said loudly and quickly before anyone else could divulge the secret she had found so comical. Everyone looked at her in surprise.

"Aye," Kyle laughed, "it was the closest thing we could come to wild boar."

As they all laughed and began to eat, Alix realized how much she had missed this happy, boisterous family of hers. But the sight of the pig brought Robin Brodie to mind.

"Lachlan," she directed her question at her brother, remarking to herself how handsome he had become, "does anyone see anything of Robin Brodie nowadays?"

Lachlan having just stuffed his mouth with potato, smiled with his mouth closed and nodded. Taking a drink, he answered her question.

"I knew you would ask that question. He visits his family frequently and still hunts for them. Joshua takes books to him that Mama selects from the library."

"I know about that. He wrote me a letter."

"Oh good," Jenny said. "I'm glad Papa didn't forget to give it to you."

"That's nothing, Alix," Lachlan began, "I didn't tell you . . ."

Alix interrupted him, excited. "Did you see how beautifully my name was written, Mama?"

"Aye," she nodded with enthusiasm, her hands becoming expressive. "It is only fitting, Alix, that a man who can carve so exquisitely could also wield a pen so effectively."

"But Alix . . ." Lachlan started again.

"You should have seen the inside of it!" Alix continued, as Lachlan's eyes looked at the ceiling impatiently. "It was decorated with the most beautifully drawn creatures, and flowers and vines. I'll show it to you later."

"I cannot wait to see it. Another artist in Kilbride. Think of it!"

Lachlan was exasperated. "Are you both finished yet? I wasn't finished with my tale!"

Alix laughed, as did her mother. "Of course, darling," Jenny said. "You've been waiting for ages to tell Alix about this." She leaned over to her daughter and whispered, "It actually happened only two weeks ago."

"Go ahead, Lachlan. Tell me everything."

His blue eyes were bright with adventure. "Well, Alix, I was out hunting in the forest . . ."

"*You?* Sir Horseman?"

"Yes, *me,*" he said wryly. "A man cannot spend all his life in the stables, Alix. Anyway," he was not put off in the least, "I took the bow that Joshua made for me several years ago and headed for the forest to find a deer. Now comes the amusing part, I had been in the woods for about two hours when I spotted a young buck. I crouched silently, waiting . . . waiting. My arrow was lined up on my bow, and finally when the shot was clear, I pulled tight and let go!"

"What sort of sport did you have? Did you hit it?"

"Well," her father said wryly, "*he* shot perfectly, but God was very kind to the deer."

Lachlan laughed out loud. "Of course I didn't hit the deer. The arrow went so wide and high the buck didn't even *move!*"

"Oh no, Lachlan. That's not a good sign."

"It gets worse. I did the same thing two more times."

The chief laughed. "That's my son, for you, trying to tattoo the very sun with his arrows."

"I don't think your father would be so brash if we were talking about racing Lachlan's horse against his own!" Jenny said.

"*Anyway,*" Lachlan continued, "being the first one to admit the humor of the situation, I sat there chuckling as the deer ran away from me. Behind me I heard someone joining in my laughter. I turned around, and who should be standing there but Robin Brodie himself."

"Really?" Alix couldn't believe it.

"Aye, it was him all right, standing there as big as life in his kilt and plaid. He walked right up to me, Alix, took my bow, and began to give me pointers on aim and technique, which were quite helpful."

"But Lachlan will never be another Robin Brodie!" Violet piped in.

Lachlan ruffled her hair. "Thanks, Violet. There's no one like Robin. Even though he has come out of hiding to visit his family regularly, he still remains a legend."

"More so, probably," the chief joined in. "Before, everyone thought he was a wild, untamed boy, who was kin to the wolf he ran with. But now that he's a man with a house in a cave, a man who reads, writes, and carves toys for the village children, he's even more of a mystery. So close he is to each one of us, and yet he still seems worlds away."

"I wonder why he still hasn't taken that final step?" Alix asked, disappointed Robin's social tendencies hadn't ripened further.

"You know Robin, Alix," Lachlan replied. "He refuses to set aside the Brodie tartan."

"Aye," Kyle's voice was proud, "he's truly the Last Highlander."

"And I had the privilege of meeting him face-to-face," Lachlan beamed. "We made a deal out there, Alix. He will teach me how to hunt with bow and arrow if I bring him a horse every now and again and go riding with him. He says he hasn't ridden since they arrived in Kilbride, and he's been yearning to feel a horse beneath him for years. You should have seen his face when he recalled the days when he cared for his father's stallion. I could hardly believe it was Robin Brodie that was talking. He seemed so... so... human!"

"Aye," Alix said quietly, "is that so?"

Inside she was angry at Lachlan. She was the one who did kind things for Robin and he returned each kindness with a measure of his own. What business of Lachlan's was it, anyway? Her jealousy turned quickly to guilt, however. Robin was not hers. *I should be happy he had the fortitude to talk to the chieftain's own son and heir.* She couldn't blame her brother at all for his excitement.

Alix's mind flooded with regret. She hadn't thought much about Robin over the past year, only when she noticed the carving on her nightstand. She had stopped writing when the social whirl had swallowed her, and her studies engulfed her. And, of course, she felt guilty. But Scotland had been a long way off, and she had to make the most of her time in England, didn't she?

What was he doing right now?

I'll go see him tomorrow, she thought. Lachlan stood up.

"If I may be excused, I've got to get back to the stables," he announced, pushing a stray piece of straight blond hair over his ear with one hand and setting down his carefully folded napkin with the other.

"So soon, son?" the chief asked. "Alix has just gotten home."

"It cannot be helped, Father. I've got ten good draft horses I'm driving to Glasgow on Wednesday for sale. There is much left to do."

Alix studied her brother as he stood towering over her, looking even more like the proud Viking than ever, and she realized Lachlan, though only 17, had become a man. His voice now resonated with the full tones of manhood, and his movements were swift, smooth, and mature.

"Why don't you come out to the stables, Alix?" he invited. "You'd be surprised at the changes we've made since you've been gone."

"May I?" she asked her parents.

"Certainly, my love," Jenny answered, wiping her mouth delicately. "We'll have dessert in the parlor when you get back."

• • •

Alix sat on the bench with Lachlan as he polished his mother's saddle. His white hands were well-muscled and strong, automatically setting about the task he had done thousands of times before.

"You do this every night?" she asked, sitting on a stool.

He smiled. A great, wide grin that pulled taut the muscles of his jaw. "It's become a ritual. First Father's saddle, then Mama's, then mine. It helps to relieve my frustrations."

"Has Mama been riding again?"

Lachlan's face lit up. Putting aside the saddle, he guided her over to the new stalls, spacious and with clay floors spread liberally with fresh straw. "Aye, Alix. Father bought her a new horse just a month ago. She's beautiful. A white Andalusian."

They stood before the horse. "Mother always did like white horses. What is her name?"

"Flora MacDonald!"

Alix raised her hand to her mouth, stifling a laugh. "Leave it to Mama to name her horse after the woman who helped Bonnie Prince Charlie escape from Scotland."

Lachlan nodded and continued his tour. He had certainly done well as far as the Maclachlans' horseflesh was concerned. Two Cleveland Bay horses with their sturdy black legs were standing quietly. Their father's carriage horses. A few others stood patiently in their stalls, not as exceptional as the three Alix had been shown so far, but still beautiful and needed for Violet and others who came to visit their estates. Lachlan reached into his pocket and gave each of them a carrot. Elijah, the chief's black stallion, was looking almost yearningly out of the window near his stall. *That horse would run all day if he could,* Alix thought.

"This horse is my pride and joy!" Lachlan announced as they came to the largest stall. Even as all the horses recognized him, this one was no exception. Indeed, his eyes glowed at the sight of his master. "This is Storm."

Alix stood in awe. "Is he an Arabian, Lachlan?"

"Aye. Isn't he the most beautiful thing you have ever laid your eyes on?"

Reaching out her hand toward the great gray head, Alix ran it down the white stripe on Storm's nose. "He's lovely."

"He's a bit spirited still. But we prefer you that way, don't we, Storm?"

Storm whinnied and tossed his head back. Lachlan held a carrot up to the stallion's mouth and rubbed his face affectionately. His well-formed hands, though roughened, were tender as they caressed the great beast.

"Tomorrow I'll show you the draft horses."

"I'm eager to see them. I can hardly believe how you've grown up, Lachlan. These horses. Your studies. Why, you're already a man."

He sighed. "Let's go back to the tack room."

Alix could see that he was troubled.

"What is it, Lachlan? Your horses are thriving and becoming well-known for their quality, and the stables are filled with wonderful beasts. You seem to have everything you've always wanted."

"Seem to is right, Alix. My life is filled with dreaming but a little, and doing much. I feel more akin to these draft horses than any other beast that roams the hills of Kilbride. But there's so much more I want. Alix . . ." he began buffing the saddle to a high sheen, "do you know what it is like to love someone?"

The question took Alix by surprise. "Why, I've never really thought about it," she laughed self-consciously.

Lachlan looked up quickly. "Never?"

"Oh, Lachlan," she chided him, trying to hide her feelings, "of course not. I've been promised to Duncan Campbell officially for two years. Unofficially ever since I can remember. I have spent the last two years avidly avoiding love." She put her hand upon his strong forearm, thinking how glad she was that she had met Aaron toward the end of her stay in England. "Would you care to enlighten me on your plight?"

With a sigh he put down the cloth. Then standing up, he heaved the saddle and placed it back on its peg. "Let's go sit in Mother's new garden."

They walked slowly beneath the starlight, the scent of heather soaking into their clothes while the summer Highland breezes floated about them with fanciful meanderings. Lachlan led her to the back of the castle, down a brick path to a wooden bench sitting near a rose arbor. Working side by side with Mumbles, the chief's lady had been engaged in planning the formal gardens since the house was built. This rose garden was her newest addition.

Alix took both of his hands in hers. "Who is she, Lachlan?"

"Do you remember when you used to go to the orphanage?"

"Of course."

"Do you remember the older girl who used to help with the young children?"

"Rebecca?"

"Aye," his voice was filled with pained emotion, "Rebecca." Her name dripped off his tongue with all the passion his innocent heart could hold.

"But she's a lovely young woman!"

Even in the darkness Alix could see his eyes light up.

"She is. And she's even more lovely than when you left. Alix, if you could only see her. Her hair is as brown as chestnut, and thicker than a horse's tail. And she's strong and works hard. But it's the love she is capable of which draws me to her. She's like Mother. When she loves, it's whole-heartedly and forever, of that I am most positive."

Alix reached for his hand. "Does she know you feel this way about her?"

"I'm not sure. I find every excuse I can to go to the home, but it's always a pretense of some sort." He shook his head in self-disdain. "Last week I reduced myself to giving the children pony rides just to see her smile."

Alix's laugh rang through the garden. "Oh, Lachlan, you are having a terrible time of it, aren't you?"

Lachlan laughed at himself. "I told you it was bad."

"Have you talked to Mama and Papa about her?"

He shook his head from side to side.

"Why not?"

"They wouldn't understand."

He sounded like a 17-year-old again.

"They would, Lachlan."

"No, Alix. Rebecca is a commoner. And as much as I love our parents, I don't think they would understand a future chief marrying someone of low birth."

"Papa did," Alix said softly.

Lachlan's eyebrows raised. "Alix, Mama's father is the Duke of Loxingham. I'd hardly call her common."

"Who was her mother, Lachlan?"

He looked at her questioningly. "Well, I just assumed that her mother had been Grandfather's first wife."

"You need to talk to her. Her mother was a commoner, as common as your Rebecca, if not more so. Find out about her. And then judge whether or not to make yourself sick over your love for Rebecca Anderson. Trust me, Lachlan, you won't be disappointed."

"I'll go right now." Lachlan's voice held an excitement, and soon Alix was left alone in the new rose garden pondering the fact that maybe, just maybe, she wanted the chance to fall in love as well. Sometimes she hated being a

woman, having life mapped out for her. Lachlan didn't realize how blessed he was to be a man.

• • •

The smoke went whirling down the sky in an inky cloak
from the chimney of Castle Lachlan's kitchens as the dusk
settled over Loch Fyne. Sunk in silence, dark eyes alive with
yearning, Robin looked at the mansion which had grown so
over the past 17 years. It was well-lit and rightly so. Alix had
come home after two excruciating years. The day was almost done, night greeting light, transforming it from life to
unalterable memory.

What will she be like? he wondered as the darkness found
a dwelling place over the land. Upon her departure, she
uttered the words he had kept alive in his heart almost
every minute.

"I'll return to you, my Highlander," she called from the
carriage. But his heart had lurched within him. For he loved
her that day, though Alix had still thought of him as her
guardian, her beloved friend. And she was betrothed to
Duncan Campbell—a fact he had found out last year. Robin
Brodie had learned to love despair.

Though no communication had passed between them for
the past year, Alix was still his closest friend. For a time she
had written him faithfully. How he looked forward to those
letters that his mother would give him on the evenings he
ventured from his wooded shelter under the protection of
night. Indeed, it gave him even more reason to venture
forth.

Alix's handwriting was slanted and artistic, showing a
creativity that he himself possessed. And her letters were always filled with poems—her own as well as her favorites
from some of the great bards of the British Isles. One he had
even memorized. It was by William Dunbar.

Be merry, man! and take not far in mind
  The wavering of this wretched world of sorrow!
To God be humble, to thy friend be kind,
  And with thy neighbours gladly lend
    and borrow:
His chance to-night, it may be thine to-morrow.
  Be blithe in heart for any aventure;
For oft with wise men it has ben said aforrow
  Without gladness availes no treasure.

And indeed, as best he could, he tried to live with his neighbors in mind. Although he spent most of his days in the woods, he left his mark with the chief and the villagers. Many a night's hunt produced more game than was necessary, and many a time a Maclachlan table was graced with meat from Robin Brodie. It wasn't at all strange to see the children playing with the little wooden figures he created. Not so delicate, they, but perfect for a child's play. And yet, he still was as elusive with his clansmen as he was before. Still a mystery. Still a flash of tartan out of the corner of the eye.

The Last Highlander had left his mark upon the community, and now Alix was returning. He wasn't sure he was yet ready to make that final leap, coming out in daylight. Being a true member of the warm society which made up his mother's clan.

The wind blew slightly cool as he waited. He had watched with a wrenching heart as the shiny brougham with the Loxingham coat of arms proclaiming the identity of the occupant pulled up to the entryway.

She had grown. Was tall and lovely. And that hair! It was even more wonderful than he remembered. His thoughts were consumed with her as he waited until the last light of Castle Lachlan was extinguished.

• • •

Inveraray, Scotland
20 June, 1764

My Dear Johann,

Has it been a year since we last shared a cup together? Time is but a breath, truly. And soon I shall be making my way to that state of matrimony that some welcome with open arms, and others disdain while they cowardly march forward, thinking themselves sheep led to slaughter. As for myself, I am not eager nor apprehensive, but relieved that it has all been planned for me. Worrying about women is the last thing I desire upon my mind. Sometimes I wonder whether I should have gone into the priesthood. But since we are protestants, and have been so for ages, that was hardly an option. In any case, the wedding is in August, and your presence would be greatly appreciated.

Alix Maclachlan, I have heard, is a wonderful young woman, truly sweet, and most pure. I met her briefly when she was a child. My fortune is great that we were betrothed years ago. Being away in England at her grandfather's estates these past two years, she arrived home yesterday. Father and I are visiting Castle Lachlan this morning and so I must go. Already he is calling me. It will be most agreeable to see you in the autumn, perhaps to share in some wine and hearty conversation. Ever in my books, I still remain your compatriot in learning,

D. Campbell

After reading the letter over carefully, Duncan Campbell, future Duke of Argyll, sealed the parchment with nervous hands.

Curse it! he thought, spilling some of the hot wax on his fingers. He felt as nervous as a schoolboy. Brave words he had written concerning Alix Maclachlan, but he was nothing short of terrified.

He had always been uncomfortable around women, and soon he would be marrying one. His stomach lurched at the thought of being a husband. Yet he wouldn't have made a good priest, either. His knees were too bony, and he hated drafts. But a scholar. Oh yes, he loved knowledge. How he had thrived learning among the hallowed halls of Caius College at Cambridge. If only he had had the fortitude to say no to his father. *I want to teach!* his heart had cried out time and time again. But it was not to be.

Please God, he prayed silently, *please let me be able to speak to her.*

But in his heart, he had no faith in himself or in the God he served that the prayer would indeed be answered. And resigning himself to portraying a mute, nervous man before his betrothed, he put on his coat and descended to the castle courtyard.

•••

"Miss Alix! You've overslept!" Gertrude nudged Alix on the shoulder. It was a gray morning. A light rain that pattered on the glass panes had kept her sleeping well past her normal awakening time.

"What is it, Gertrude?" Alix asked the maid.

"You've got visitors. Your betrothed is comin' up the drive."

"What!" Alix's eyes rounded and she threw off the covers. "Oh no! Gertrude, pick out a dress. Any dress. Preferably one that is green. And my hair. It must be a sight!" This was not the way she expected to finally meet Duncan Campbell, even if her upcoming marriage wasn't much cause for celebration as far as she was concerned.

She ran over to the mirror, picked up a silver brush, and began to drag it violently through her long hair. Soon the wardrobe door stood open, and she deliberated while Gertrude retrieved her undergarments from her dresser.

In no time she had decided upon a silk day dress of emerald-green brocade. Cut simply, the scooped neckline was piped in dark blue, and the underskirt was striped in dark blue and green. A pair of green slippers completed the ensemble.

Next Gertrude pulled her hair in a simple bun, braided at the back of her head, and pinned on a small lace veil that covered the chignon. She was ready.

As ready as can be expected, she sighed as she trailed her hand lightly down the banister. What would he be like? Had Duncan inherited his grandfather's boisterous zest for life? Did he invade every room he entered with his remarkable presence like the old duke had? She knew she was being unfair to compare any man to Uncle Archibald. Yet the family had produced some remarkable scholars throughout the ages as well as political strongmen. Unfortunately, she hadn't known any of them except for Uncle Archibald. At the least, if he was so learned, he wouldn't object to her continuing in the study of poetry in which she had become deeply engaged since she left Scotland. Unless he was one of those men who felt women should sit all day embroidering in the garden. The sitting room stood before her. She shivered, breathed in deeply, then entered breezily.

Jenny sat serenely in her dark-blue silk day gown. Mary Alice was on her lap. The whole family was there except for Lachlan. Kyle immediately stood to his feet upon her entrance.

"Alix, you have visitors."

"So I see," she smiled pleasantly as she walked smoothly into the center of the room, remembering all that she had learned in London of decorum.

"The Duke of Argyll and his son Duncan are here."

"How do you do, your grace." Alix bobbed a curtsy.

" 'Tis a pleasure to see you again," the duke said pleasantly.

Alix turned to her betrothed.

Duncan, clad in black, looked at her shyly.

"It's a pleasure to finally meet you again after all these years, Alix," he said with all the nerve he could muster, as if he had practiced that simple line for hours. His accent was decidedly British, and with a shaky hand he raised hers to his lips.

He was nothing like she had pictured. It took all she had within to contain her composure at the sight of Duncan Campbell.

"Have we met before?" Alix asked, surprised.

"Just once," Kyle interrupted, much to Duncan's relief. "You were only five or six at the time."

Duncan Campbell, raised in London and educated at Cambridge, was hardly the stormy Scot she'd always imagined she would marry. He was tall and gangly, and his brown hair waved back from his forehead where it was caught in a black bow at the back of his neck. His skin was white and fragile-looking. His lips were spare and covered the slightly protruding eye teeth. And even though he wasn't at all handsome, Alix had to admire his eyes. Framed by long, black lashes, they were the same startling aqua shade his grandfather's had been. Even in his state of extreme discomfort, she could see the remarkable intelligence behind them.

They betrayed his shyness, and he dropped his gaze as soon as she looked into them.

"It's a pleasure to meet you, Duncan. Please sit down."

"Thank you." His voice was barely above a whisper.

Even as her heart went out to him in compassion for his discomfort, it sunk deeply into her abdomen. She hadn't come close to picturing him thus. She did her best to contain the deep sigh that sought to escape.

Kyle and Douglas Campbell began to converse. Jenny poured the tea. And as she distributed muffins and jam, Alix answered the duke's questions.

"Did you enjoy, London, Alix?"

"Yes, your grace, immensely."

"It's not Scotland though, is it, lass?" Kyle asked.

"Nothing is like Scotland, Papa."

In both hands, Duncan held his cup tightly by the saucer and stared at the brown liquid.

"Speaking of Scotland," Jenny said pleasantly, turning to Duncan, "your father has told us about your research of Scottish folklore up in the northern Highlands. It must have been fascinating."

"Yes, m'lady," Duncan's eyes lit up.

"I hope you shall someday share with us your findings."

"It would be a pleasure."

Male voices and the sounds of boots echoing on the parquet flooring of the entry hall brought Alix out of her daze. Both voices were recognizable. One startlingly so.

"Thank you for showing me the stables, Lachlan," Aaron Campbell said, thumping him on the back as they walked into the room. "You've done a remarkable job! Absolutely remarkable." For a brief span of time his eyes met Alix's as her heart stopped. His handsomeness rained upon her for a second time. But she quickly pushed those feelings aside. What was *he* doing here?

"This must be your sister." His smile was pure and joyful. "I'm afraid we have not yet been properly introduced."

Alix couldn't help but notice his slight emphasis on the word *properly*.

"Aaron, this is my sister, Alix Maclachlan. Alix, this is Aaron Campbell, the Duke of Argyll's nephew. Have you met before?"

"Aye," Alix nodded smoothly, as if nothing was amiss, "just the other day at my going-away ball. Although I didn't realize then that he was so closely related to the duke."

A poor relation! Indeed, it was true. She struggled to appear normal as he kissed her hand, bringing back the strong memory of the dance in her grandfather's garden. Aaron

Campbell! It all came to her, astounding in its clarity. How could she have forgotten the details?

Aaron Campbell. The grandson of the old duke whose parents had been killed at sea when he was only 11. Aaron Campbell. The bright hope and favored grandchild of his grandfather. Aaron Campbell. A runaway five years ago at the age of 18, leaving the old man brokenhearted and unwilling ever to speak of the lad again. He wasn't just a nephew of the duke, he had actually grown up within the walls of Inveraray Castle. He was a Campbell through and through.

"Won't you have some tea, *Mr.* Campbell?" she said, her face too red for her own liking. Alix felt a bit foolish. How could she have behaved so with her betrothed's cousin! She felt like a fool. And she hated feeling like a fool. But it was too late to go back.

"Thank you, Lady Alix. I should love a cup," Aaron answered her question, amused at the situation.

You have a lot of explaining to do, Alix thought dryly as she sat next to Duncan. After the necessary introductions, Aaron joined easily in the conversation at hand. Her disconcertment was becoming annoying, to say the least. When the conversation came to a lull and she could stand it no more, she turned to Duncan.

"Would you care to step into the gardens, Duncan?"

He was so startled, the now-empty cup went flying off his saucer. Aaron reached out a quick hand and caught it before it fell to the carpet. "Steady, old boy," he whispered to his cousin so no one else could hear, "it will be all right."

Duncan looked at him, eyes pleading for help anyone, much less Aaron, was powerless to give. He stood up, unfolding the length of his body, and soon he and Alix were out of the room and strolling through the gardens.

It began as a quiet stroll. Naturally. But Alix had learned much about the art of conversation in London. She wouldn't let Duncan off so easily.

Alix leaned forward to look at his face. "It must have been a wonderful experience to have traveled so extensively through the Highlands. I haven't been past Glasgow, which is most definitely Lowlander country!"

Duncan smiled, but could not return her gaze. "Yes, it is. I enjoy my research greatly, thank you."

"And your subject matter is so intriguing. Folklore! I think it's wonderful that you're recording it."

"Someone had to," he said. "The old ways are dying out."

"Aye. It seems you're right. Papa says Kilbride is nothing like it was before 1745."

His voice saddened a bit. "But you have a famous legend right here on these lands. A living legend . . . I would someday love to meet him!"

Alix's eyebrows raised. "Robin Brodie?"

"Yes, the Last Highlander. His fame has spread across Scotland. Many folk brought him up when I was asking them questions, and they asked where I was born."

"Were you born at Inveraray?"

"Yes. But my parents moved to London shortly afterward. But back to Robin Brodie," he sounded official, so serious, like he was researching. Alix stifled a laugh. *Oh well,* she thought, *at least he's communicating.* "Have you ever caught a glimpse of him?"

Alix laughed. "Caught a glimpse of him? Duncan, I know Robin Brodie!"

"You've met him?"

"Yes," she chuckled. "You *have* been up in the Highlands for the past two years, haven't you?"

His eager face had "please explain" written all over it.

"Four months before I went to England for my education, Robin Brodie saved my life!"

"What!" Duncan's face became intense.

"I was being chased in the forest by a wild boar, and Robin killed it just as it leapt to take me down."

"Did he use his bow and arrow?"

"Naturally."

"Oh my. I so wish I had pen and ink to write this down. Drat it all!" He was flustered.

"Duncan . . ."

"I always find myself ill-prepared at the most inopportune of times." He opened his coat to look inside the pocket.

"Duncan . . ."

"It happens time and time again. You'd think after all those years of university I'd be able to remember . . ."

"Duncan!" Alix grabbed his hand, "you'll have the rest of your life to get the story from me!"

Duncan froze and smiled shyly once again. "Yes, you are quite right."

Alix tried to draw him out again with other subjects, but all she could get were yes or no answers, or quick sentences. Still, she had seen a pleasant, though absentminded, side to him. It could have been worse.

Luckily, Lachlan came out announcing that luncheon was served. The Campbells left soon after.

With a hasty "Meet me at the castle ruins at 11 tonight" when no one else could hear, Aaron had mounted his horse and galloped quickly away before the Duke of Argyll or Duncan had stepped one foot in the carriage. Alix was puzzled at his request. But there was no doubt in her mind where she would be when the clock struck 11.

• • •

28 June, 1764

Delight my soul, O God, with the woman of Your choosing. Can it be true? How could I have known that You were preparing such a one for me? Many are the questions in my heart tonight, 'tis true. My heart constricts in radical joy. Who has felt this way before? Surely not anyone. For I am in love. Is it insanity? Have I finally driven myself over the edge by much learning and searching for truth? If so, welcome lunacy, if you bring with it this heady sensation of well-being and excitement. I want no other course than to be half-witted over my betrothed.

Duncan, a single-minded man, shut his journal, and closed his eyes. He didn't understand what was happening inside his heart. But he knew he would try and be the best husband he could be. Once they were married, it would be easier, he reassured himself. He would confide his feelings directly to her, and not to his journal as he had been doing ever since he was eight years old.

Someday, he thought, *I shall tell her face-to-face.* His own brave words surprised him.

• • •

Alix put her hand in his as they strolled along the hillside.

"Are you glad to be home, lassie?" Kyle asked.

"Yes, Papa. Although I did enjoy England immensely. The balls and the parties were so exciting! And the education I received was invaluable. I cannot wait to continue learning. I'm sure the Campbells have an extensive library!"

In her tone, her mannerisms, Kyle could see his daughter had changed.

"Your grandparents are wonderful people. I'm sure you learned much."

"Oh, yes! And the gowns that Grandmama bought me for my trousseau are simply wonderful."

Even as the words issued forth from her mouth, Alix knew her father's mind. And she didn't know what else to say that would not be hypocritical. Should she say she had grown closer to God? That the Bible had come to mean more to her than anything else due to her grandparents' godly example? That her prayer life had never been more sweet with the communion of the Holy Spirit? *No, I cannot.* In her heart she was frightened. Her whole life was set before her, and she had lost the joy of her salvation.

Where is the child that asked all the hard questions? the chief wondered as they continued along in silence, the sun making their hair glow like flame.

• • •

"You have a great deal of explaining to do, Aaron Campbell!" Alix's red-haired temper exhibited itself in full force as she stormily approached him in the castle ruins. Her embarrassment from earlier in the day had turned to anger.

"I can only imagine what you must think of me, Alix," his voice drawled from the darkened form his body made against the wall. He walked into the moonlight and her heart did a somersault as he spread his hands wide and bowed. "And I am truly sorry if I gave you any misconceptions."

Her eyes flashed and she felt her temper getting the better of her.

"You did. Oh, I realize I should have put two and two together. But when you came walking into Castle Lachlan this morning, I nearly lost any composure I had ever been blessed with! What were you doing at the party in London?"

He came closer to her and smoothly offered her his arm. "May we sit down by the bay? It looks as if that wall there could come crashing upon us any second."

Alix nodded and put her arm through his. She was still angry, but she might as well be a lady about it. A large rock that lay near the water was their destination. They sat upon its smooth, weather-worn surface.

Aaron breathed in deeply and stared at the glimmering surface of the bay. "It was really all quite innocent. Duncan, as you have seen, is painfully shy around women. He wrote asking me to go with his father to meet you. He wanted to know all about you before he had the pleasure of making your acquaintance."

"Why didn't he come himself?" Maybe Duncan had been away in Scotland. But that didn't mean he couldn't have come back.

"The meeting between you had been arranged with your parents. He didn't want to ruin that for them. And to be quite honest, Alix, social gatherings of that sort are not Duncan's cup of tea. He's a scholar. A student."

Alix could picture Duncan so vividly, and her ire began to wane at the thought of her shy fiancé. "He seems so reserved."

Aaron picked up on her change of heart. "Oh yes, but he's quite brilliant actually. Has always wanted to be a professor. But he wouldn't defy the wishes of his grandfather, the old duke."

No change of expression manifested itself when Aaron spoke of the old man. Alix realized what an actor he truly was. Or his estrangement from the man that had loved him so dearly really meant nothing. Either conclusion was somewhat disconcerting.

Aaron continued. "He's a man of honor and intelligence, Alix. Surely, you could do a lot worse. All the parties you frequented during your stay in London will tell you that much. Thomas Peterson was only one of many."

Alix wasn't quite ready to let him go that easily.

"That's probably true, Aaron. However, I feel quite the fool, having responded to you out in the garden so, only to find out you're Duncan's cousin!"

Aaron's eyebrows raised. "I need to mark this day on my calendar," he said suddenly.

"What do you mean?"

"You're the first candid woman I've ever met. Are you sure you were in London for two years? How could you have been and not have had the city rub off on you somehow? Truly I thought the only games women knew how to play were guessing games. Now you've come along and shown me there's hope yet for the female of our species, blast you."

Alix laughed. "I take it you enjoy your role as cynic of the female psyche?"

He spread his hands wide. "Enjoy it? I've made it an art form!"

"Well, I won't hold your secrecy about your identity against you then. After all, if you had told me who you really were, I may not have been myself. And then what would you have reported to Duncan?"

"Precisely."

"You didn't report everything to him, did you?" Alix asked, looking at him sideways.

"Aye. I certainly did." Aaron was smiling with a wide grin.

"You didn't!" Alix gasped.

"Yes. I told him you were warm, witty, intelligent, and beautiful. As I said, I told him everything."

Alix patted him lightly on the upper arm. "You are truly a cad, aren't you?"

"I try, Lady Alix. Lord knows, I try."

Without warning, Alix realized she had a friend in Aaron. And so did Duncan.

"You really love your cousin, don't you?"

Disposed just then to reveal his sentimental side, Aaron nodded and looked out over the bay. "Aye. There's an odd mixture of protectiveness and deep respect that I feel for him. I would do anything for him."

Alix leaned over and impulsively brushed Aaron's cheek with her lips. "Then I shall consider you an ally at Inveraray Castle."

Putting his arm around her shoulders, Aaron gave her a quick squeeze and let go to take her hand. "I hope you shall always view me as someone to count on. Although," he added jokingly, "I can be a bit foolhardy and impetuous."

"That's all right, Aaron. In this life one must take one's friends where they can be found. I've found it best not to be too choosy."

"I don't know whether to take that as a compliment or not!" he laughed.

"I wouldn't if I were you," Alix joked, "but know that I'm glad we met."

This time it was Aaron's turn to kiss Alix. His heart warmed toward her.

• • •

Inveraray Castle, Argyllshire

The clock ticked loudly on Aaron's dresser. Successive, hollow soundings bouncing off into emptiness. Another on the mantel echoed the first. Time. There was precious little of it these days. That bonnie little redhead of Kilbride started him thinking. Did life in London hold the same sparkle it did before? True, he had always disdained the crowd in which he rambled, but at least they were more amusing than being alone. Perhaps there was more.

Aaron drifted off into a deep sleep.

The door opened softly. And a woman stared longingly at him sleeping in the great bed.

Clementine Mackay, fair and gentle, loved Aaron. Had loved him ever since she could remember. But he was the duke's nephew and she, after all, was merely the housekeeper's daughter.

• • •

The Daughter of the Snow

The daughter of the snow overheard,
and left the hall of her secret sigh.

She came in all her beauty, like the moon
from the cloud of the east.

Loveliness was around her as light.
Her steps were like the music of songs.

She saw the youth and loved him.
He was the stolen sigh of her soul.

Her blue eyes rolled on him in secret;
and she blest the chief of Morven.

–James MacPherson
From "Fingal"

CHAPTER

11

Evening

The rayons of the sun we see
Diminish in their strength;
The shade of every tower and tree
Extended is in lenth.

Great is the calm, for every where
The wind is setting down;
The smoke ascends right up in the air
From every tower and town.

Thoughtfully, Alix turned the summer leaf over and over in her hand. The delicate network of veins flowing from the center stem that provided texture for her fingers to probe, provided depth to her thoughts as well, giving life to the cells of her mind which had been undernourished for two years. Far too long.

In the forest she was waiting for him now as the evening hours began their slow fade. The fallen log which had supported her so many times just two years ago, supported her now. It looked the same. Nothing about these woods seemed to have changed, except for Robin. And even he had become more akin to the forest than ever before. Strong. Independent. And growing. Always growing. Her thoughts stole back to the city which had claimed her the past two years.

London. She remembered visiting Westminster Abbey with Grandpapa for the first time. Walking among the graves of kings, queens, poets, scholars, and statesmen.

"It is as if all the history I have ever learned is raining down upon me in one great storm," she had turned to the duke, wide-eyed, breathless.

"I know," he had put his arm around her shoulders, "I still feel the same way. Even after all of these years."

The abbey had been silent then, their hushed whispers echoing almost irreverently in the building humbly begun almost a millennia before. And over those years it had grown in its size and in its intensity. But its intensity and homage was not paid to the God of the universe, but to His created ones. Each man and woman that lay in final repose. Each hand that had cut the stone or worked upon the great church in a time when such a project took decades to complete. And God had been forgotten. It was an edifice that now honored man and his human endeavor to please God with plannings of the mind, workings of the hands, and not the love of a heart broken and needing so desperately the salvation only He can give.

The sun continued to lengthen the shadows about Alix, and she sighed heavily as she looked up at the arched bows of the trees overhead. God's cathedral. Sprung forth from His very creation. Standing firm, yet flowing with the sap of which life is made, the substance given by God for survival and continued glorification to the Almighty. She was glad to be home.

Would Robin come?

She gazed longingly through the ever-darkening shadows and decided he must be far from where she sat. Perhaps his hunt had taken him in another direction. But twilight would soon come to its maturity and she needed to head for home.

Still, she thought, *I must find out more about Robin.*

Alix gathered up her skirts and walked into the clearing toward the home of Deborah and Joshua.

Again she couldn't help but compare London to her native land. So civilized it had been, the men wearing garments cut from as fine a cloth as the ladies' gowns. With their powdered hair, their shiny shoes, and their propensity to a regular pinch of snuff, they couldn't have been more of a contrast to Robin Brodie. How could she have forgotten the Last Highlander amid the false business and shallow bustle of England's most populous city? Even as the fops and dandies had become products of their society, she realized that Robin was the same. Quiet as the forest breeze. Strong, and seemingly hewn from the rock of which his home was made. He traversed about these shades in utter simplicity.

Rollicking laughter snatched her from her musings as she walked, and Deborah's house stood in sturdy fortitude against the orange sky. Never before had she heard such a laugh—free, bright, and loud in its full reverberations. It was infectious and answered by the older boy Robin had pinned, his nephew.

"That'll teach ya', Johnnie, to challenge someone twice your size to a wrestlin' match. Leave it to Uncle Robin to teach ya' what it means to be a man!" He laughed again.

Culloden was gone.

The smile was clear and filled with joy as he leapt to his feet. And Alix's hand went up to her mouth to stifle the laugh which sought to escape her lungs at the sight of him in his kilt, white shirt stained with grass, and hair worked loose and laden with stems and leaves. In becoming a man, he had retrieved his youth.

His skin glowed healthily from the slight exertion of the match, and he bowed in the direction of the small garden where Deborah, Kathleen, and most of their children sat applauding. "Here, here!" Kathleen, a miniature, female version of her brother, yelled. "Ya' better watch that one, Robin. He'll be bestin' ya' before ya' know it!"

Much to everyone's surprise, Johnnie, Kathleen's eldest, made a wild leap onto Robin's back. A primal cry sprang forth from the lad as Robin flipped him over his shoulder, grabbed him with a growl, and held him above his head.

"What was that ya' were sayin', Kathleen?" he called.

Alix walked into the circle of Robin's vision. The Last Highlander froze as the vision he had yearned to see each night stepped before his eyes.

She had come!

Joy flooded through him as Johnnie kicked and yelled to be put down. But Robin felt or heard nothing. She was lovelier than he had dared believe anyone could be. And how she had grown—a woman now, graceful, and sweetened by maturity.

"Lady Alix," he said softly.

She stepped toward him as his brown eyes bathed her with the deepest, purest waters of his soul.

"Put me down, Uncle Robin!" Johnnie's cries were becoming louder.

"Perhaps you had better free your captive, Robin Brodie."

Robin started, looked up at the boy, then smiled into her eyes. "Perhaps you are right, m'lady." He set down his nephew. "Luck was with ya' this night, laddie. Next time ya' willna' be gettin' off so easily! Run along to your mother, now."

"Shall we walk a bit?" Alix asked, waving hello to his sisters.

"Aye," he said, not waiting for her to slip her hand into his, but taking it gently and holding it.

Deborah and Kathleen watched as the pair walked away toward the loch. They both smiled, but inside they ached for they knew his heart.

"I didna' think you'd be comin' out so soon. I was sure your parents had many things planned," Robin began the conversation.

"They did. A horse buyer from Edinburgh came to call," Alix replied, "but after supper tonight, I begged to be excused. They understood."

"I'm glad ya' came, Lady Alix. I'm glad ya' came tonight." His eyes shone.

"Do you venture out much, Robin?"

"Nay. But once a week I come to Deborah's house for supper. I dinna' have to pass through the village to come here. And, of course, I visit Mother quite regularly after sundown."

"Is she well?"

Robin shook his head sadly. "She's beginnin' to fail. Ya' came into m'life at the right time, m'lady. Now I can do m'part in carin' for her as she gets older."

"But you still stay in the forest otherwise?"

Robin laughed at her tone. "Did ya' expect to come back an' find me mayor of Strathlachlan, Lady Alix?"

It was the first time she had ever heard him joke, and it suited him well.

She looked at him ruefully. "I suppose not."

"Someday, m'lady. But a man must live up to his legend. For now I am content to hunt, to carve, and to learn."

By this time they were sitting along the shoreline in a small copse of trees as the sun continued its downward climb. "An' when it comes down to it, Lady Alix, there is no reason good enough for me to exchange my kilt and plaid for English clothes."

"Will there ever be?"

"Nay. Perhaps not. Culloden, though it wounded me at first, has now defined who I am. I could never deny my heritage."

"But isn't simply going on enough? To continue life as before, showing the Crown that their laws and persecutions cannot touch our souls?"

"This plaid is my soul, m'lady. My childhood, my youth, and now my adulthood are intertwined with the black, red, and yellow of this tartan. It is who I am."

Alix nodded. "I cannot say that I understand completely, Robin. But I admire you for never giving up, for having the courage to keep from compromise. Perhaps one day the law will be changed."

"Perhaps," he said as he picked a piece of grass. "It can be the way of things. Laws have been changed before."

"Aye, Robin." The sky deepened and her heart did as well. "Thank you for your letter."

He looked shyly down. "I hope ya' didna' think it impertinent of me."

"Nay!" Alix grabbed his forearm. "It made me very happy. Your writing is beautiful, Robin Brodie. And your drawings were nothing short of wonderful!"

"Did ya' really think that, Lady Alix?"

"How could I not? You've practiced very hard, haven't you?"

"Aye. The nights dinna' seem nearly as long now that I have somethin' to work on other than my carvin's."

"You do wonderfully with pen and ink. Mama, quite an artist herself, was terribly impressed, Robin."

"Really?" his eyes lit up.

"Aye. You're truly gifted, my Highlander."

His eyes closed at her endearment.

"I read much about London while ya' were gone." His voice was gruff as he suppressed his emotions. "The Tower Bridge, Big Ben, the Houses of Parliament. It's all very fascinatin'."

"Well, Mama is thrilled that you are taking advantage of our library."

"And I am very grateful. Will ya' tell her for me?"

"Aye, Robin. I will."

Robin looked directly into her eyes. "I missed ya', Lady Alix. But ya' know that, dinna' ya'?"

Alix nodded. "I was afraid when I left that you would go back to what you were before we met."

"Nay," he shook his head. "As I've said many, many times, ya' saved m'life. There was no goin' back. Even after you were gone."

"I enjoyed London, you know."

"Did ya' now?"

"Yes. But now that I'm back, I realize how out of place I was there."

"We're all out of place in this world," he said earnestly.

Alix became puzzled. "What do you mean?"

"Joshua's been talkin' to me quite a bit this past year. About God. About the Savior. An' your mother gave me a copy of the Scriptures. Told Deborah to tell me I could have the book. The only book I own, Alix."

"But surely the most important for any man to own." He had called her by her first name. It pleased her greatly.

"Aye. It has made me a rich man. And it has also taught me how poor this world is compared to what is waitin' for us."

Alix's eyes moistened.

He went on. "Joshua answered any questions that I had as I was readin' through the Gospels. An' after I finished those precious books, I knew there could be no other course for me. I believed, Alix. And now I stand forgiven."

"Oh, Robin." Alix reached out her arms and pulled him to her. So much change. The ultimate transformation had taken place in the heart of Robin Brodie. God had answered her prayers by revealing Himself to the Last Highlander. And the legend embraced truth.

Even in her happiness, Alix felt rebuked. Robin was now a shining example of what it meant to love the Savior. And she was farther away from Him than she had ever been before. Still, as she pulled away to look fondly into the eyes of the man she owed so much, she couldn't help but thank the Creator for His mercy to one who needed it so desperately.

• • •

Duncan loved to walk in the mornings. By himself. Communing with his Lord.

Softly a tune issued from his mouth as the birds began singing, breaking the silence of predawn. Cutting through the darkness. And he knew that whatever God had planned for him, he would try his best to be worthy of the task. He praised his Savior for protecting him. From bitterness. From futile dreams of what he could have been, might have done to make a difference. It was all he ever wanted out of life.

Someday I shall be the Duke of Argyll, Duncan thought. And now that Alix Maclachlan was destined to be his duchess, the prospect was not nearly as unfulfilling.

• • •

It was supper-time at Inveraray Castle. Always a formal affair. Mrs. Mackay, the sweet-faced, dependable housekeeper, was a woman committed to detail. The meals were always delicious, colorful, and served at just the right temperature. Her knack with the flowers from the castle gardens made each room in the downstairs, and especially the dining room, a sight to behold.

The Duke of Argyll sat with Duncan and Aaron at the long mahogany table. Two servants waited on their every need as they conversed about the goings-on of the day.

Scotland was new for all of them. Or new again. Duncan had grown up, for the most part, in England. And the duke had only been back regularly since the death of his father. Aaron, of course, spent most of his time on the other side of Hadrian's wall himself.

Endemic to his personality, he led the conversation.

"Lachlan Maclachlan should be back in a few days from Glasgow."

"He's doing that well with his horses, eh?" asked the duke.

"Aye, Uncle. He's raising fine, strong draft horses now. He just drove several of them to Glasgow for sale."

"That's right," Duncan brought himself into the conversation, "he's building up quite a reputation for himself with the Belgians he started several years ago."

"Good for him, I say!" said the duke as the servants began to clear away the soup dishes. "The Maclachlans have always had my admiration. Belgians, eh? Leave it to that boy not to raise Clydesdales."

Duncan smiled, his tongue never tied around his family. He knew that his father loved him completely. And his mother's death only three years before had brought them even closer. "They certainly have my admiration as well. And it's a good thing he raises workhorses! Those thundering racehorses, well, they are simply disconcerting. How anyone can stand to go galloping around on one of them when a carriage does just the trick and is many times more comfortable, I simply do not know."

"Come now, Duncan," the duke said with a laugh, "you have hated riding horses ever since you took that nasty fall when you were eight years old."

"And rightly so!" Aaron defended his cousin. "We almost lost Duncan. I don't blame him an ounce for not getting up in the saddle again." He smiled at Duncan. "Although you may have to try it again, Cousin. Alix Maclachlan loves to ride. Or so I hear."

Later, after supper, Aaron and Duncan sat in the garden smoking their pipes. The scent of roses wafted around them, mingling with the darkness.

"Well, I suppose I should at least try to ride. There can be no harm in that." Duncan went a bit pale underneath his brave words as a puff of smoke wafted up into the night air.

He was glad it was dark. "And since I am going to visit her the day after tomorrow, I shall try and ride again then. If she asks, that is."

"Then let me come with you, Cousin. You may need my assistance." The thought of seeing Alix again wasn't a bad proposition at all. Besides, Inveraray Castle could be so dull. There wasn't a pretty face around except for the housekeeper's daughter. *What is her name?* Aaron thought. *Oh yes, Clementine Mackay.* She was much too shy. He liked women who could hold a conversation. Women like Alix Maclachlan.

"Thank you, Aaron. You are most kind. Blast my tied tongue. I can discourse with any don at Cambridge or Oxford, but up against Alix I become as silent as a tomb. It certainly would be a relief to have you there, not only to save me from a wild horse, but from my inability to communicate to the fair maiden."

They both settled back more firmly on the bench as the bushes rustled near them, presumably from the wind or a small animal.

"Aye," Aaron agreed. "She is that. Most fair, if you do not mind my saying so, Cousin. After all, she is your betrothed."

Duncan's smile stretched across his slightly protruding teeth, lighting up his eyes and making him seem almost handsome.

"Yes, she is, isn't she? She will make a most wonderful duchess."

The men settled down to enjoy the June breeze and the quiet evening.

• • •

Mrs. Mackay walked slowly back into the kitchens of the castle after her solitary saunter. She picked at the skin on her hands, chapped and sore from repeated washings throughout the day.

The small, bow-like mouth frowned as she pushed open the door. "A wonderful duchess, indeed!" she muttered under her breath.

• • •

26 June, 1764

Tomorrow I shall see my betrothed. I shall someday call her my wife, and this fact makes me happier than I ever dared to dream.

A teacher? Yes, I suppose I shall always yearn for that impossibility. But all is not hopeless, for I shall have Alix Maclachlan beside me.

Can she learn to love me? I do not know. Yet I vow to do all that is in my feeble power to make my happiness hers.

How faithful is our Lord God. How loving and how kind.

Duncan put his journal away and blew out the light.

CHAPTER
12

Sleep

Whilst the body is dwelling in the sleep,
The soul is soaring on the steeps of heaven:
Be the red-white Michael in charge of the soul,
Early and late, night and day
Early and late, night and day.

• • •

The green hills drifted by the carriage window as Duncan and Aaron made their way to Kilbride.

"I am relieved you are coming, Cousin," said Duncan as his head bobbed from the rhythm of the carriage. "Now there will be no difficult lulls in the conversation."

"Do not worry about that," Aaron assured him readily, straightening out the frilled cuff of his shirt. "You'll soon find plenty to talk about with Alix. She seemed extremely bright when I met her at the party. Once you start sharing experiences, there will be many topics of conversation."

"I hope so. I keep praying that marriage will make a difference in my behavior. I just do not know."

"Now, Cousin," Aaron looked at him disapprovingly, "who is it that is always giving me lectures about faith? You above all people must take comfort in that. Even though I don't believe as you do, I'll always encourage you to rest in your beliefs."

Duncan sighed. "You are right, of course. It is just that Alix is so fair and I am ... well, Aaron, my mirror does not come close to telling the same tale that yours does. I am sure she is disappointed that I am not a handsome, strapping man, such as you or her father and brother."

Aaron, although likable, was still a tad too conceited, and he inwardly agreed with his cousin. Still he sought to encourage him. "I believe you underestimate your betrothed, Duncan. She sees beyond the physical. And you must give yourself some credit. You must learn to talk to her! Show her what is inside your mind. Why, you know you can outthink practically anyone. She'll never find a smarter man so besotted with her. And believe me, I'm sure there were many besotted men left crying in their whisky."

Duncan shook his head from side to side. "Thanks, Cousin. I realize what you are trying to do, and I wish I could fall for it that easily. But we both know it usually is not what is inside a man's head that wins a lady's heart."

"I think you are wrong where Alix is concerned." Aaron tried yet more to comfort him. Perhaps he could encourage Duncan as far as Alix's character. "Just be Duncan, Cousin. Get her talking about the things you love. She's quite educated and, at any rate, will probably enjoy the discourse."

The future bridegroom simply nodded and went back to viewing the lush countryside. Aaron took his attention again after a while.

"I should be heading back to London soon."

Duncan's head whipped around to face him, panic shone in his eyes. "So quickly?"

"Aye. I must get back to the theater. Not all of us are heirs to dukedoms! I must earn my keep. But don't worry, Cousin. I shall be back at the end of August for your nuptials."

"If there are any ..." Duncan looked doubtful. "What shall I do without your help, Aaron?"

"I'm sure you'll do fine. Besides, it might be good for you to be on your own. And you have lots to plan. Have you thought about where you'll be taking Alix on your honeymoon?"

"Yes," Duncan's eyes glowed. "We shall start with Paris and wind our way down through Italy."

"Goodness!" The extravagance, so unusual for Duncan, surprised even Aaron. "How long do you expect to be gone?"

"Nine months to a year."

"Well, good for you, Cousin!" Aaron clapped him on the back. "Good for you! Wine and dine her among the wonders of the world, eh? Pure genius! And you said you couldn't win her with your mind!"

Duncan shook his head in mock derision and laughed quietly. "You really know how to say exactly what people want to hear, Aaron!"

"That's not what my circle of friends say. But maybe that's why we get along so well, Duncan. You are the only one who sees me as I am and still claims me!"

As the old Castle Lachlan came into view, they laughed together.

Duncan suddenly turned to Aaron. "Please say you will not leave until the wedding. It's only two months away. I need you to help me through the rough spots until then."

"Cousin . . . I don't know . . ." Aaron hesitated. "Sooner or later you'll have to . . ."

"Please," Duncan pleaded as the carriage drew them closer and closer to Alix, "just until the wedding."

Aaron's smile was a little too wide. "All right, Cousin. I shall stay. For your sake."

How shall I survive in this boring place until August?

• • •

Beaton opened the door with a start.

"M'lord, Mr. Campbell, do come in. I shall summon Lady Jenny."

Immediately it was apparent that something was wrong. The servants bustled to and fro with grim looks pasted on their weary faces. No family members could be found in the near vicinity.

They stood with hats in hand. Waiting. The minutes ticked by on the hall clock. Each beat suspended in isolation. Aaron stood mesmerized by the pendulum. Unease was clearly written in his stance. Duncan looked out the window at Loch Fyne, shifting from one foot to the other, then back again.

Finally after what seemed an interminable amount of time, Jenny appeared. She looked exhausted as she wiped her hands on a linen towel. Face pale and hair out of place, her light-blue silk dress was creased and forlorn.

"Oh, gentlemen! Forgive me for not sending word. Mary Alice has been taken ill and we've been up all night trying..."

"She's come down with a terrible fever." Alix walked into the room, pushing her hair back from her face. She was in much the same condition as her mother. "Dr. McCallister doesn't know what to do for her. The leeches don't seem to be working, and she doesn't respond to anyone or anything. Just writhed all night moaning."

She put her arm around her mother's shoulders. "You go get some rest, Mama. I'll take care of her for the next few hours." Jenny walked from the room, head and shoulders bowed in exhaustion.

Even in her weariness, her face glistening with perspiration, Duncan thought Alix was the loveliest creature he had ever seen. But his kind heart pushed those thoughts aside. "How is she now?" he asked, finding his tongue easily in adversity.

Aaron, now the one unable to speak, stood as though his shoes had been nailed to the floor.

Alix's eyes were dull and tired. "She's sleeping peacefully. Maybe a little too peacefully. It seems unearthly somehow, Duncan."

Heartbroken at the thought of the cherubic three-year-old so ill, he commanded Alix.

"Take me to her."

At his authoritative tone, her head jerked back to look into the aqua eyes filled with concern and charity. Aaron's did the same. Even still, he could not move. Death was sure to come to this household. He felt it. As surely as he knew it the night his parents died when they all sat at dinner in the captain's galley of the ship and the storm began to blow. And he had spent the rest of his life so far trying to forget.

Alix took Duncan up to the nursery as Aaron sought out the stables. A groom saddled up one of the extra horses and soon he was riding away at full speed back to Inveraray. Promises or no, he would head back to London tomorrow.

• • •

Her breathing was deathly faint. Almost ten hours had passed since Duncan arrived, and she had not yet awakened. The blonde curls were matted against her broad forehead, and the full cheeks, relics of her infancy, were deep red, her chin was rashed. Pure innocence. Complete vulnerability. Totally at the mercy of the Creator.

Daylight was waning.

The chief knelt by the bedside holding the tiny, chubby hand. He looked as vulnerable as his youngest child. Jenny quietly stood behind him. Hands upon his massive shoulders. Eyes closed.

Alix whispered as she gently massaged her mother's tightened shoulder muscles. "Go to bed, Mama. Papa. I shall stay the night here with Mary Alice."

Jenny started to sob. "Oh, Alix, I can't. What if she . . . ?" Her hands went up to her face as she wept.

Kyle stood up and took her into his arms. "Perhaps Alix is right, my love."

Jenny nodded from side to side. But Kyle picked her up and carried her weeping form downstairs to their room. Duncan sat in the corner, praying as he had been all day.

"Why don't you go get some rest as well, Duncan? There's no sense in both of us staying awake," Alix offered, even though his quiet, steady presence had been of such comfort to her since he had arrived.

"No, thank you, Alix. I shall stay by your side. I'll be right back."

He rose from his chair and left the room. But he was back in no time with a houseservant carrying a chaise between them.

"Put that next to the bed," he commanded.

"This is for you, Alix," he said, scooting a chair for himself next to the gold brocade-covered lounge. "You can get some rest and continue the vigil as well. I shall stay awake lest any changes occur."

Alix settled her form upon the chaise with a shaky sigh. "Thank you, Duncan. I'm so glad you came."

She sat up suddenly with the first semblance of a smile he had seen upon her face all day. She looked so tired. "I'm even more glad that you stayed. Thank you."

"Anything for you, Alix."

She sat back and closed her eyes. Her breathing became deep and steady. She sat up again, jerked out of her sleep.

"Are you still praying, Duncan?"

"Aye, my darling. I am still praying."

She went back to sleep for much longer and Duncan Campbell continued his vigil, replacing cool rags upon the burning forehead as strength continued to wane from the little body guarded by his beautiful eyes. Night dragged on, and when Alix awoke around 5 A.M. he was still petitioning the throne for Mary Alice's life.

• • •

"I'm leaving tomorrow," Aaron told Mrs. Mackay when he came in from his morning ride. She stood in the entryway with her daughter.

Her gray eyes smiled at Aaron, and she nodded. "As you wish, sir. I shall have m'Clementine fetch someone to pack up your things." She turned to her daughter, whose eyes were wide with pleasure at the prospect of being so near to him.

"Thank you, Clementine," Aaron said in his usual warm way.

"I'll go right away!" the dark-haired beauty said. And her wavy, warm-brown hair swished over her slim shoulders gracefully as she turned to fetch a footman.

Mrs. Mackay's eyes were benign as she took note of her daughter's reaction to the duke's nephew. Deep inside an evil seed of revenge fell on soil which had been fertilized for years by a pure and undiluted hatred.

Quickly looking up at Aaron, her words were kind. "Ya' be careful along the roads, sir. There's highwaymen about, so I hear. We wouldna' want anything happenin' to ya'!"

"Thank you for your concern, Mrs. Mackay." He gave a raffish bow and bounded up the steps to his room.

Clementine—graceful, lovely Clementine—fell asleep that night with a smile on her face.

• • •

Alix stared out the window as the sun rose. "It doesn't seem right that the day should dawn as usual," she said quietly. Duncan rose to stand by her side. His joints were stiff, and his back ached. His eyes were red and weary, but they held much tenderness.

She leaned her head back against his chest, and he thought he would die from the nearness of her. He hardly dared breathe lest he disturb this moment of closeness.

"The sun is red." Her words were simple.

On the sill of the window sat a tiny bird—a sign for centuries to the Maclachlan clan that death would surely visit. They both knew what the day held. He had known it during the night. Mary Alice would never rise up again.

• • •

A bit of sleep strengthened the chief's lady, and she came into the nursery looking a little better but still just as fear-stricken.

"Any changes over the night?"

"We would have summoned you, Mama," Alix said tenderly. "She hasn't woken yet."

"Duncan," Kyle came in, "have you been here all night?" He just nodded.

"Thank you." The chief put his hand upon his shoulder. "We'll take up the post now. Why don't you and Alix go get a little breakfast? I'm sure you could use it."

Alix put her arm in Duncan's and they walked slowly down to the kitchen, leaving Kyle and Jenny to be alone with their youngest child.

• • •

Alix heard footsteps descending into the entrance hall. She looked from where she sat in the dining room only to see Dr. McCallister make the last step. He was heading for the door.

"Dr. McCallister," she called as she rose from her seat. Duncan entered the hall with her, eyes as hopeful as his fiancée's.

The doctor shook his head sadly. "I'm sorry, miss. Truly sorry."

"There's nothing you can do?"

"I'm afraid not. She's getting weaker and weaker. I don't know how much longer she can last. It's useless to try blood-letting again. I'm so sorry."

He put his hat upon his head and the front door closed with a hollow click.

Alix turned toward Duncan, tears flowing freely. With his arms around her, Duncan led her to the parlor, where she sobbed in deep, groaning spasms.

• • •

Jenny's eyes brimmed with tears. "It's happening isn't it?"

Kyle put his arm around her shoulders and held her tightly to his side.

"Aye, love. It's happening. We must pray that she'll go peacefully."

They knelt by the side of the bed, hands intertwined, and poured out their prayers. What every parent dreads but refuses to discuss was happening to them. His hands squeezed his wife's more firmly. *Oh, God,* Kyle thought, *help me to be strong for her.* As their petitions and yearnings soared heavenward, Mary Alice's eyes opened, blue and strong.

They got up and lay next to her on the bed. Jenny cradled the small, weakened form. Kyle cradled his wife. "Three spoons restin' in a drawer," Jenny whispered into the blonde curls, remembering all the times this child had crawled into bed with them in the wee hours of the morning. Her tears caressed her little one's cheeks.

"When you see the Savior, Mary Alice," Kyle said as his eyes closed in grief, "don't be afraid. Go right to Him."

"Aye, Papa," her voice could barely be heard.

"We love you, wee Mary," Jenny cried harder.

"I love you," the small voice came back more strongly as she drifted off again.

They lay that way all morning as Mary Alice's breathing became fainter and fainter. The little forehead felt clammy and unreal against Jenny's ever-present hand. And the more she faded, the more focused Kyle and his wife became. Lest one precious second be lost to them. No time. There was just no time.

Violet, Lachlan, Alix, and Duncan prayed together in the next room.

By noontime, the tiny child had gone from them completely. And Kyle and Jenny sobbed together in their misery as they lay on the bed with what had once been their daughter.

• • •

The death ritual began.

In the drawing room they placed the body, stretched out on a wooden board and covered with a wrapper of coarse-woven, snow-white linen. Lachlan, Violet, and Alix set a wooden platter on the breast of their sister. On the platter they sprinkled a small quantity of earth and a small quantity of salt in separate piles. The earth symbolized the body, corruptible and born to someday rest below the ground. The salt symbolized the spirit, incorruptible, created for eternity.

The normal Highland custom of a "melancholy ball" which included dancing and merrymaking was not observed. For no one could rejoice that one so young was delivered from this life of misery.

Jenny allowed no one but herself to wash and prepare the body for burial. The next day little Mary Alice was laid to rest in the graveyard outside the village church next to Kyle's mother. Kyle's uncle, the Reverend John

Maclachlan, preached the simple eulogy as the black-draped group mourned together, each in their own way. Jenny cried openly. Tears streamed down Lachlan's ivory face. Violet and Kyle stood stoically, with eyes full of pain. The mourning women of the clan chanted the coronach, a lament eulogizing the little girl. Clan members from all around showered the day with their grief as well. One of their own had traveled from them.

Alix never let go of Duncan's hand. And he finally knew that strength was not found in brawn and stature, but in a loving heart full of faith, fortitude, and reliance upon God. In all actuality, her grief was not his. He could only be a means of devoted support. And he would not fail her.

Robin Brodie came. But no one noticed.

• • •

The next day Duncan led Alix by the hand into the gardens. The house was draped in silence. The chief and his wife had retired to their room. Lachlan was trying to forget out in the stables. And no one really knew what Violet was doing.

"I never would have guessed my homecoming would be met so soon by tragedy," Alix said, her head bowed. "I never really got to know her, you know."

She looked up.

"I was away in England for two of the three short years of her life. Suddenly all the balls and parties, plays, and operas seem quite worthless."

"You cannot blame yourself, Alix. You went away for an education."

"Aye, and I received one. But at what price?"

"No one could have known." He tried to comfort her.

"No. I suppose you are right. If we had known, we would have done things differently."

"Everyone comes to that conclusion many times during their lives."

"I haven't read the Scriptures for myself in over a year, Duncan. I don't even remember how to pray."

"That's why He's brought me into your life."

"You are such a strong Christian," she stated.

"That is what I strive to be, Alix. I came to know the Savior at Cambridge, and I love Him more than anything that this world can hold up before me. You must turn to Him now, during this time, Alix. As much as I am here to support you, I am but a man, insufficient, and not enough to see you through this tragedy."

His eyes were so earnest and Alix's heart softened. "I want to come back, Duncan. I just cannot do it on my own."

"I know, dear Alix. I know. I will do all I can to help you. The Savior is awaiting your return, my beloved."

He put his arms around her as tears of remorse, grief, and hope flowed from the depths of her harrowed soul. Lifting up his eyes to the heavens, Duncan thanked his Creator for using him and making him a fit vessel to do His will.

His prayers were answered as she cried. Words were free between them and, along with his arranged position in her life, a needy place in her heart was opened to him.

CHAPTER

13

Inveraray, Scotland
15 July, 1764

My Dear Aaron:

I write with the supposition that you have heard of the death of Mary Alice Maclachlan. If you have not, then you can now understand what heaviness has befallen the Maclachlans. Over the past two-and-a-half weeks the privilege has been granted me to be of guidance and comfort to the bereaved family, but especially to Alix. You were indeed correct, Cousin, when you said it would take a shared experience to bring us together. Unfortunately, it was a tragic one.

My reason for writing to you at this time is to make you aware of the fact that the wedding has been postponed until the spring. The reasons are obvious.

London seems awfully far from me now, yet I hope it is treating you kindly. I remain in all sincerity,

Your devoted cousin,
D. Campbell

• • •

The nursery was closed up for the summer. Violet was moved before her time to a bedroom on the second floor, and Lachlan wondered whether or not the doors to the room that held his childhood would ever be opened again.

In his work clothes, he stood before the closed door. With a deep breath he put his large hand upon the handle and turned.

The fireplace was dark where once a happy blaze had burned consistently. Dustcovers were thrown over the stuffed chairs that sat near the hearth. Books were put away neatly, curtains were drawn, and all the old toys were hidden away in the toy chests. No one was home.

"Oh, Drake," he sighed, sitting crosslegged on the floor next to his hobby horse, the only reminder of his childhood left in the room other than the small table and chairs in the darkened corner. "What will become of happiness for us all?"

Lachlan always loved children. The births of both his younger sisters he remembered vividly. The muffled cry coming through the closed door. The leap of his stomach at the sound. And then Father, opening the door, would say, "You have a sister." Then he would usher he and Alix into the bedroom.

Violet had been a quiet newborn, emitting soft cries and sucking on her hand as she was handed first to Alix then to Lachlan. Mary Alice had been another breed altogether, crying with a lusty squall until she was fed.

Her birth had been the most precious of all with the three older children staring in awe at the red, wrinkled miracle that let out such a hue and cry that the whole family burst into laughter, the sound of which filled the bedchamber.

And Mama. She always looked so weary, yet so happy. He could have stayed in the room all day, sitting beside her, propped up against the pillows. But Father would come along and shoo them off. "The baby needs to eat and your mother needs to sleep," he would say. Then he and Alix would go outside and talk of nothing else.

It was all over now.

Soon dust would settle. Cobwebs would gather in the corners. And he was powerless to stop the progression. But he would never forget.

"Someday your own children will bring this place to life again, my son."

He hadn't seen her in the room when he entered. But Jenny had been there, sitting in a straight-backed chair behind the door, rocking the empty cradle, hoping that Highland lore would prove true and a baby would soon occupy the little wooden bed. Lachlan turned and began to get up.

"No. Stay where you are, Lachlan."

The music was gone from her voice. Dressed in black, her face pale, her body weight had drastically reduced in the past two weeks. She walked slowly over and sat down next to him on the floor.

Lachlan put his arm around her and she rested her weary head against his shoulder, taking comfort in his presence.

"You feel like your father," her voice held a smile. "You don't look like him at all, Lachlan. But you feel like him."

"Mother," Lachlan's voice caught as he voiced yet again what he had said to her many times since the death of his sister. "I'm so sorry. I'm so deeply sorry."

He held her as she cried, and together they sat in the abandoned nursery as, behind the heavy drapery, the morning sun climbed higher into the azure sky.

"Mama?" a small voice behind them spoke. Violet was crying for the first time.

She ran over and sat on their laps as they folded their arms around her. In their misery they wept together. Their grief was shared and absolute, profound in its purity and release. A child had died, and though they would recover eventually, their eyes would never shine as brightly as they once did.

• • •

London
October, 1764

Why do I continue to do this?

Aaron sauntered leisurely toward Covent Garden, one of London's licensed theaters. He knew he was one of the fortunate ones, playing before a more "respectable" audience, not being doomed to the minor theaters such as Goodman's Fields or Sadler's Wells. God knew he had enough of them: waiting in the wings while two horses danced a minuet, a duck sang, or a man balanced on a wire, playing the trumpet, the violin, and the drum as he sat on a coach wheel.

Then, once he set his feet upon the stage, he was reduced to singing or pantomiming his part. Such was the life of an actor in the minor theaters. Heaven forbid they actually perform an honest play without licensure by the Crown! Aaron shook his head in disgust.

And though he could actually speak his lines nowadays, that still didn't suck the weariness from his bones. It was invigorating at first, but he soon realized the upper classes were just as boisterous as the lower ones. The uproar before each show could be unbearable. Orange peels, glasses of water, and other liquids were thrown down from the gallery into the pit and the boxes. Why people continued to buy tickets in those seats was a mystery to him. But that wasn't the worst of it.

Aaron entered the back of the theater.

"Afternoon, Mister Campbell," a stagehand said as he swept the hallway.

"Hello, Toby. Anyone here yet?"

"No, sir. Just yerself as usual, sir. Just yerself. An' old Gus there." He pointed to a mangy-looking cat.

"Come on, Asparagus," Aaron said to the cat with a click, using his full name. "I've got some milk for you." He turned back to Toby. "I need to gather my strength before curtain call."

Toby, a young man in his late teens, incredibly tiny with wiry arms, laughed the laugh of a giant. "Don't I know it, sir. Why do ye keep up with it? Why don't ye go on back to the cool greens of Scotland?"

Aaron chuckled realistically. "I've asked myself that question many, many times, Toby, and I do not know. I suppose there is something to the excitement of this life."

"Aye, sir. People keeps comin' back, that's for sure."

"Any notables showing up tonight?" He meant royalty.

"None that I know of. But still and all, I'm sure the seats'll be filled up nicely."

He thumped the lad on the back several times. "They always are, Toby."

Misery followed him with Gus as Aaron continued back to the large, communal dressing room where he readied his costume and proceeded to light his pipe. He thought of Mrs. Lyons-Parker. It had been a late night last night. Too bad the theater didn't pay more. He dozed off, and all too soon it was time to get ready for tonight's production of *Every Man in His Humor* by the great Ben Jonson.

Well, at least I get to play the part of "Well-bred," he thought as he shrugged into his costume, hoping there would be no riots tonight. He hated theater riots. Already the corridors backstage were crowded and noisy. *No wonder I've become so blasted cynical!*

"You'd better start for the stage, sir," Toby slipped his way into the room. "You're due to be on in five minutes."

This was the time of night that he questioned his calling the most. Opening the dressing room door, he began his nightly routine of push and shove, curse and shout. Backstage was crowded with so many people whose chief delight and major goal was to impede the actors' progress that by the time Aaron made it through the pits and boxes he had to bound quickly on the stage to deliver his line in a timely fashion. He was drenched with sweat as he began to speak.

"No Scots! No Scots!" the mob in the gallery suddenly began to yell, silencing him immediately.

Aaron wheeled about, eyes widened. Had he let his accent slip? He had always been so careful.

Apples were pelted heavily down from the gallery, but they were not aimed at him, he saw with relief. Two officers from a Highland regiment had come in late to the performance. Clad in kilt and plaid, they walked amid the shower with heads held high.

Without warning, a man jumped up from the benches, shaking his fist up at the gallery and roaring out in a broad Scottish brogue, "A curse upon ya', ya' rascals!"

Amid the bombarding vegetation, he made his way up close to the officers and brought them down to his bench. He seated them alongside himself while Aaron waited for the riot to begin. It never did. A sigh of relief escaped his painted lips and the play continued.

After the show Aaron found them talking by the doorway to the theater. Not bothering to hide his true speech patterns, he walked up to them.

"So sorry about those upstarts in there, gentlemen," Aaron bowed slightly. "If you've never been to London theater before, you certainly were baptized by fire. What regiment do you belong to?" He should have known by the tartan, but he had never been much interested in military affairs. Another difference between he and Grandfather.

The irate man, a man named Boswell, spoke for his guests. "They are from Lord John Murray's regiment and they have just come home from Havana."

"Aye, an' this is the thanks we get," one of the soldiers said scornfully, "to be hissed when we come home."

"Aye, James," agreed the other, "if we were French, what could they do worse? The rudeness of the English commoners is terrible. This indeed is the liberty they have—the liberty of bullying!"

"I couldn't agree with you more," Aaron put his hand upon the man's shoulder. "I surely do wonder why I keep up with the theater life." He sighed.

"Where were you sitting?" Boswell asked.

"I wasn't sitting anywhere. I was playing Well-bred up on stage and saw it all." He laughed for real. "When they started yelling 'No Scots! No Scots!' I thought I had let my accent slip and they were talking about me!"

The men laughed together heartily. An immediate bond was formed.

"Well, since we four Scots have found ourselves together and without a country on such a night as this," Boswell invited warmly, "let's go down to Mivert's and I'll host you a proper supper."

Thanking him, Aaron and the two soldiers agreed that it was a wonderful idea. Didn't they deserve it after all they had been through that evening?

The dining room was lit by many chandeliers and sconces. And beefsteak and kidneys had never tasted so good to him. Yet the company of these men gave him a yearning for his homeland such as he had not experienced since he moved away. It puzzled him, to say the least.

But there is no place for me there. He thought of Alix for the first time in a week. He was happy for his cousin . . . and yet. If only he were the one to be the duke, he could have had the fair Maclachlan girl for himself as part of the bargain.

Across the room he spotted her . . . Mrs. Lyons-Parker. How old was she really? Even in her widowhood, she certainly cut a charming figure. Small and dainty with a soft, high voice. He couldn't help but smile when he recalled their initial meeting. She had at least eight brooches pinned onto the bodice of her green indienne dress. When he asked her about them, she smiled and trilled a laugh in his direction.

"Why, my dear boy," she said, "if I do not have at least five brooches on, I feel positively naked."

Her eyes had said more. And they said so now as she spotted him sitting with his newfound compatriots.

I must earn my keep, his words to his cousin came back forcefully. Yes. This life was becoming tiresome, to say the least.

• • •

Inveraray, Scotland
2 October, 1764

How could it be that, even in grief, my darling Alix becomes more precious with each passing day? No, she may never love me in the same way that I shall always love her, overwhelmingly. Yet, she needs me. And I shall ever be waiting in the wings to aid her and comfort her no matter what trial befalls her.

She told me yesterday that she has never had a friend like me. Someone she can open her soul to, who knows her shortcomings, and not only loves her anyway but seeks to help her become stronger. It thrilled my heart to hear her words.

Black becomes her, setting her hair into an even more uproarious flame. And as I am usually clad in that color, we must look ghastly at times! God of heaven and earth, thank You for Your mercy upon me. What a wonderful life lies ahead of me. Keep me always faithful, ever true, and ceaselessly pure of heart.

• • •

It started in the late morning, a sunny sky and crisp coolness blowing off the loch in a tangy breeze. Before the wind picked up, and from where Alix sat upon her window seat, the beech and oak trees, the young saplings in Mother's gardens spewed their fall foliage toward the south at the whim of the strong gusts. It would have been Mary Alice's fourth birthday.

The sky darkened within a space of ten minutes and still Alix sat, mesmerized as always by the storm. She thought of her Lord as the first clap of thunder ricocheted across the landscape and lightning briskly snaked downward from heaven to earth.

She whispered the words of the disciples. "Lord, save us. We perish."

Almost four months had passed since Mary Alice had been taken away from them. The rain began. Would the suffering never end? Heavy droplets pelted against her windowpane. Almost horizontally they barraged the world around her. Was life meant to be lived hand in hand with the fear of death and pain?

"Why are ye fearful, O ye of little faith?" The words of the Savior resounded in her heart as the storm resounded over the hills. She could cry no more. No one cried anymore. It went deeper. She didn't move for many minutes as she watched the forked lightning and heard the thunderclaps. Her mind emptied and she swayed to the rhythms of the storm.

"Then he arose, and rebuked the winds and sea. . . ." The storm began to blow over and small patches of blue could be seen through the rain. After a while the sun awakened the storm-tossed countryside. Glittering drops on trees and grass caught its clear rays.

". . . and there was a great calm."

• • •

Duncan was waiting. And he could see something had changed within her as she made her way into the sitting room. Her face spoke of an inner radiance that contrasted sharply with her black gown.

"Did you arrive before the storm broke?" Alix asked him with concern.

"Yes. Just barely. I waited it out in the stables with Lachlan and his men."

"Could you do with a walk, Duncan?"

He smiled. "I'm always up for a walk, Alix."

"Of course." She had forgotten his daily habit of strolling the woods and hills around Inveraray and the shores of Loch Fyne.

Wrapped in their cloaks, they walked through the village, past the orphanage.

"There's someone I'd like you to meet," Alix announced, putting her hand in her fiancé's.

"And who is that?" Duncan asked, the sun glinting off his thick brown hair.

"Robin Brodie."

Naturally, he was intrigued.

"Don't expect him to say hardly a word," she warned him. "He has no trouble communicating to me, but I have no idea how he'll react to meeting someone new."

"I understand that completely," Duncan laughed, remembering what she had said at their first meeting.

"Yes, Duncan. I suppose you do!" Alix smiled wide. "Besides, he might not be around. He may be in his cave today. And I wouldn't think of barging in without warning. Hopefully he's out and about."

The smell of autumn was all around them, the smoke of chimneys mixed with decaying leaves and overturned earth.

"The air seems so different in the fall, alive somehow," she said to Duncan. "Robin showed me a beautiful clearing last spring. I'll take you there now. Perhaps he has gone there as well, to see the stream reflect the color of the leaves."

"You really are a romantic, aren't you?"

"Aye. As are you."

"Me? Why, I'm just a scholar. There is nothing romantic about that."

She raised her eyebrows. "Surely you are joking?"

"No."

Her laugh rang out as she tenderly laid a hand on his arm. "You are a man that loves literature, the beauty of poetry, and you have traveled the Highlands to record folklore. I would say that constitutes someone who is a romantic."

Duncan blushed slightly and cleared his throat. "Perhaps. I have always thought of those things as scholarly pursuits."

"Don't be embarrassed, Duncan. They are what you love. And it still makes you a romantic. Believe me, I know one when I see one."

"Oh you do, do you?"

"Aye. Papa is a romantic. And there's something about the way your eyes sparkle that reminds me of Papa."

"Well then," Duncan bent formally at the waist, "I shall bow to your expertise."

Alix laughed. They were at the clearing. And both drew in their breaths at the sight before them. The clear water ran joyfully over the rocks, yellow leaves floating along for the ride. The Michaelmas daisies shared their blue hue in the glory of the golden sun. And rustling in dry softness, the trees added their part to the visual and audible harmony the clearing was celebrating for, it seemed, their pleasure alone.

"Lady Alix!"

They turned to the sound of the voice.

"Robin!" She flew over to him. It had been so long since she had seen him.

"Robin Brodie?" Duncan was surprised. This clean-shaven man in a fresh shirt, clean kilt, with a plaid draped neatly over his shoulders for warmth, was not at all what he expected, what his research had bade him envision. That a book was clenched in his hand shattered the myth of local lore even more thoroughly.

Robin bowed. He knew this man was Alix's betrothed. "In the very flesh. And how is it that the future Duke of Argyll has heard of someone the likes of me?"

"Do you not know, man? The legend of the Last Highlander has spread far beyond the region of Kilbride!"

Robin laughed. "Surely the legend is an exaggeration, m'lord."

"Well," Duncan rubbed his chin thoughtfully as his brain recalled each piece of information it had garnered regarding Robin Brodie, "you could safely say that. I expected to see a man that was practically half animal. And here you are, groomed and holding a book!"

"Had ya' come upon me three years ago, m'lord, ya' would've found such a man. This lady ya' have the privilege to someday wed is actually responsible for ending the fanciful tales that have arisen over the years. Alix saved m'life, m'lord."

"Alix, what is Robin talking about?"

"Well, actually Robin saved my life over two years ago. A wild boar was chasing me and he killed it with his bow and arrow."

"So it is true, you use a bow?"

"Aye, m'lord."

Duncan began to laugh as he placed a hand to his forehead. "When my research led me to modern legends, I sought to find out information about the Last Highlander, and come to find out my betrothed is truly the expert."

"She knows me better than anyone, m'lord." He put his hand upon his chest. "She knows my heart."

"Would you grant me the privilege of someday seeing your cave, Robin?" Duncan asked, knowing what great value it would be to his work.

"I prefer to call it my home, m'lord. But yes, I'd be happy to." He turned to Alix. "I'm sorry about your sister, Alix. Unhappiness has clouded our region ever since her death. Perhaps the storm will break soon. I'll be prayin' it does."

"I believe it's starting to, Robin. Death is never easy."

A large hare bounded across the clearing, taking their attention. Robin bowed formally. "M'lord, it was a pleasure meetin' ya', but I must be goin'. Noontime is soon approachin' an' I must be gettin' about the hunt."

Duncan nodded. "It was a pleasure making your acquaintance as well."

"Alix," Robin turned to her, "feel free to bring his grace around to my home anytime." He turned back to Duncan. "The walls really *are* red."

And with those words and a deep chuckle, the Last Highlander slipped quickly and silently back into the woods.

Duncan looked shocked. "Is it true, Alix? Are the walls red?"

"Yes they are," her eyes sparkled mischievously.

"I'm afraid to ask."

"Iron," she said simply.

"Iron?"

"In the water, silly. He told me what it was before I left two years ago."

Duncan laughed louder than he had ever laughed before. In all his years of adulthood as respected scholar and future duke, he had never been called "silly."

"Only you, Alix," he shook his head.

"What?"

"Only you could call a man silly and make it the highest of compliments."

Hand in hand they walked back to Castle Lachlan. They blessed the hills of Kilbride with their friendly chatter, and all who passed them along the way smiled in answer to their cheerful countenances.

• • •

"All love is lost but upon God alone"–William Dunbar.

Robin read the words aloud, then set down the volume of poetry the chief's lady had sent for him that week. The burden of a lonely life weighed in heaviness upon him.

" 'Tis true," he sighed as he picked up the Bible he had been given over a year ago. He had already memorized many passages that he would recall as he hunted or roamed the woods. His fingers opened to one of his favorite verses, and his lips whispered the words quietly as comfort flo

oded his soul from the healing ministrations of the Great Physician.

"Come unto me, all ye that labour and are heavy laden, and I will give you rest. Take my yoke upon you, and learn of me; for I am meek and lowly in heart, and ye shall find rest unto your souls. For my yoke is easy, and my burden is light."

He realized he would not be alone. God was with him. And always would be.

CHAPTER

14

December, 1764

The sound of the carriage approaching Inveraray Castle was muffled by the storm. The small, capable hand of Mrs. Mackay held the delicate lace curtain of the entry-hall window aside. Her fading blonde hair, shot through with one streak of purest white above her ear, shook almost sadly even as a hardened, purposeful glint surfaced in the depthless gray eyes.

Speaking softly to herself she whispered, "No one said it was going to be easy. Well," the lace curtain fell back into place, "all one can do is try."

A smile appeared, although her eyes never changed.

She had stared into them in the mirror many, many times over the last 27 years. And only recently had she ceased being frightened by what she saw.

• • •

"Come in, come in!"

Mrs. Mackay welcomed the Maclachlans, all still clad in black, with much huffing and puffing into the warmth of Inveraray Castle. The entrance hall became a flurry of wraps and blankets as Billy and Charlie, two liveried footmen with powdered wigs, waited patiently to take them from the chilled family members.

"My, my! When we saw a storm was startin' I said to m'Clementine, 'We had best hope they make it soon, dear daughter, or they willna' make it at all!' "

"Thank you, Mrs. Mackay," Jenny said, relief in her voice as she straightened her hair with her fingers. "The wind and snow began about a mile and a half back. We're lucky to have been so close."

The housekeeper smiled at them all. "Go fetch his grace, Charlie," she ordered. "There isna' the slightest chance they heard ya' pull up. All anyone can hear is this wind!"

Alix's eyes lit up at the sight of Duncan as he hurried into the hall.

"Thank God, you all made it safely!" he said, grabbing both of Alix's hands. "I cannot tell you how worried we were. We were just sitting together in the drawing room wondering whether or not to send out a search party!"

Impulsively, he gave Alix a little hug.

Soon the Campbells surrounded the Maclachlan chieftain and his brood. Christmas cheer abounded in the grand entryway, and Kyle was glad Jenny accepted the duke's invitation to spend the holidays at Inveraray. Castle Lachlan was still a sad house. But now it was Christmastime and he would rejoice and honor the Savior's birth. They all would.

"Kyle!" The Duke of Argyll said as he welcomed them. "So glad you made it safely!"

They shook hands warmly.

"Come into the drawing room," Duncan invited.

"Yes, please do," echoed the duke. "The warmth there should permeate those bones! I imagine the carriage became quite cold toward the end of the journey."

"Actually," laughed Lachlan, "I think my feet are the only parts that suffered. We must be a family of talkers!"

"That we are, son!" Kyle clapped him on the back as they went into the blue drawing room. "You can't keep any of us silent for long. Except for Violet, of course."

The now-youngest member of the Maclachlans came shyly forward and gave a curtsy. "Thank you for having us for Christmas, your grace," she said politely.

Mrs. Mackay stepped in. "What a lovely child," she said, rubbing her hand over Violet's shining hair. "I shall take Miss Violet to the kitchen an' find her some special dainty. And I'm sure ya' could all do with a nice cup o' hot tea!"

"Yes. Bring some right away," the duke ordered brusquely.

"What a wonderful woman!" Jenny smiled at Mrs. Mackay's retreating figure. "You've found a gem there, Douglas!"

Soon they sat drinking the strong brew, forgetting all about the storm that was raging outside. Violet opted to stay in the kitchen with Mrs. Mackay and help make shortbread.

"Lachlan," the duke said after half an hour of general conversation, "would you like to see some new horses we've recently purchased?"

Lachlan's eyes lit up and he nodded exuberantly. "Aye, sir, that I would!"

"Come along, then. I'll take you myself! Kyle," he asked, "are you up for a walk to the stables?"

"Aye, Douglas. Although I can't say I love horses as much as Lachlan here, I still think they're the most beautiful creatures on earth." He looked over at his wife. "Except for you, Jenny, of course."

"Go on with you, you Maclachlan rogue, you! Such flattery will not fool me. I've lived with you for much too long!"

She turned back to her daughter. "These men and their horses!" she chuckled. "Alix, if you wouldn't mind, I think I shall rest in my room for a bit. Come fetch me before supper."

"All right, Mama," Alix agreed, kissing her cheek.

Suddenly Duncan and Alix found themselves alone. And Alix looked around the luxurious room done in shades of gold and blue.

"Why don't we sit before the fire?" he said, pulling two arm chairs in front of the roaring blaze.

"That would be lovely."

Alix gathered her black velvet skirts about her and tucked her feet up underneath her as the fire's glow rested on her and Duncan.

"Thank you for inviting us."

"Well, Father was the one who sent . . ."

"Come now, dearest Duncan. I jolly well know who put the idea into his head in the first place!"

In comfortableness she reached for his hand.

Around them they could hear the soft bustle of Christmas preparations going on in the castle Duncan's grandfather had built. Maidservants chattered softly as they polished the silver in the dining room. The cutlery clinked together musically. Smells more delightful than usual filtered from the kitchens. And around the warm community of the castle, the storm raged to most everyone's oblivion.

"Alix, I know it is only Christmas Eve. But I wonder if I might give you your Christmas present now?"

"Of course, Duncan. But why now?"

"I just cannot wait."

Alix smiled. Duncan had only recently begun to display an impulsiveness she found entirely endearing.

"All right. Do you wish to give it to me here?"

He nodded. "Close your eyes."

She did so, and heard him run to the door. He was back quickly.

Alix squealed with delight as a warm, alive, furry little body was placed on her lap. Her eyes opened immediately.

"Oh, Duncan. A puppy!"

Around the cocker spaniel's midsection her hands curled, and she lifted him up to rain kisses on the sides of his tiny nose. "How did you know I'd been longing for another dog?"

"Lachlan told me about old Ivan. This one is named Plutarch."

"Oh? A philosopher like yourself! The name is perfect."

"You are right. His siblings are Aristotle, Aristophanes, Plato, and Socrates."

Alix kissed the dog again and chuckled as she sat with him on the hearth rug. "I'd hate to hear what his parents were named." She cradled the puppy in her lap and stroked his soft fur.

Duncan joined them on the floor, making him look even more "all legs" than usual. "Their names were Buttercup and Swallow." His eyes were mischievous.

"No!"

"No. You are right." He smiled wryly and reached over to scratch Plutarch's head. "Their names were Portia and Falstaff."

"I love him. Thank you, Duncan." She held up the little mite to look into his half-closed, sleepy puppy eyes.

Duncan cleared his throat. "There is something else about him that is special. See his collar?" He was hoping she would notice it on her own.

"Why it's a lovely blue satin rib . . ."

Alix's hand flew to her mouth and she gasped as Duncan untied the bow. Along the ribbon he slid off a ring.

"Alix," he said gravely, praying that his tongue would not fail him now, "I know we have been promised to each other ever since we can remember. And I know that these past few months you have come to rely upon me as your friend."

"Yes, Duncan. I don't know how I could have made it without you there. You've been the most devoted friend I have ever known."

Taking a now sleeping Plutarch off her lap, Duncan set him on the hearth rug to doze near the fire's warmth.

"But there is so much more to me, Alix," he said earnestly, taking both of her hands in his. "Everyone has always told me how intelligent I am. I know that. It is something I have come to take for granted over the years. And because of that, I do know what manner of man I am perceived to be. Each morning when I comb my hair, it is evident that I am nothing in appearance like my cousin Aaron, or Lachlan."

Alix interrupted. "Duncan, don't be silly. You are . . ."

"Let me finish," he kindly interrupted her break-in. "You do not have to encourage me in this area, Alix. It is something I have accepted for years. What I am trying to tell you is that, while I have played the role of your friend, something deeper has happened in my heart as well."

The final admission sprang from his lips, echoing from a heart bursting with emotion. "I love you, Alix. I truly love you."

Alix opened her mouth to speak. She had known it for months. But Duncan continued. "Oh, I know what your feelings are for me. I know that you see me as your friend. And I am satisfied with that. I would never ask more of you. But I wanted you to know how I feel, dearest Alix. And I wanted to give you this."

Gently he slid one of the most beautiful rings Alix had ever seen onto her ring finger. Mounted simply in gold, the square emerald sparkled in the firelight. He raised her hand and kissed the finger on which it rested.

"Alix, I wanted you to know that had your father and my grandfather not arranged our marriage years ago, I would still have wanted you for my bride."

Tears moistened Alix's eyes as she held his hand tightly.

"Duncan, thank you. But what you don't know is that I don't ask for fairy-tale romance. I'm not looking for a knight of old. I want to live in peaceful harmony with my closest friend. I want to live safely here in Inveraray, with you."

She could hardly believe the words were coming from her mouth when she remembered how miserable she was at the thought of marriage just six months ago.

"Alix?" he looked into her eyes, knowing he'd be a fool to expect more from her just then. But he couldn't help hoping in the future her feelings for him would deepen. "Would you marry me?"

"Aye, Duncan. I will gladly marry you."

Tentatively he looked at her, and she put her hands upon his shoulders. Leaning forward, he touched her cheeks lightly with his fingers. He relished in the newness of love. She relished in the sweetness of friendship. Each knew that their life together would be well-spent.

After many moments had passed, Mrs. Mackay finally cleared her throat from the doorway, announcing in pleasant tones that dinner was served. Their happiness twisted within her darkened heart, and she realized she hadn't acted a moment too soon.

• • •

The inn was quiet. Everything was quiet. The storm had stopped around nine the night before. He didn't much care for the idea of working like this on Christmas morning.

His room was dark. It was well before dawn and he shivered into his breeks, a shirt, and a leather jerkin. This line of work just wasn't worth it. Cold mornings. Long waits. And for what? Gold?

No. It just didn't seem to be worth it at all. His food had stopped settling well on his stomach, and he noticed another patch of gray in the little hair he had left.

I'm getting old.

There was no one to fix him hot cereal or darn his socks. Maybe this job would be his last.

The stranger grabbed his musket and headed out to begin the dirty deed.

• • •

Putting on an old pair of boots, Duncan bundled up and ventured out of Inveraray Castle for his morning walk. The snow was almost knee-deep in places and the hills shone a frosty, glittering pink as the sun began to rise. It was still early. But he didn't want to miss a moment of Christmas Day with Alix, so he left for his walk sooner than usual.

The ringing tones of "The Holly and the Ivy," and "God Rest Ye Merry Gentlemen" resounded through his soul as the wind, whipping off Loch Fyne, refreshed his body. He was much stronger than he looked.

It was Christmas Day. And he was betrothed, truly, of his own volition, to his beloved. Alix wore his ring upon her finger. He had never loved his Lord more than he did just then. And he had never felt more unworthy of the blessings God had given him.

"Oh, heavenly Father," he whispered as each of his footsteps crunched through the icy surface, "thank You."

A shot rang out.

Pain ripped jaggedly through the back of his thigh. He turned as he went down. Into his vision fell a tall man holding a musket disappearing into the thick belt of fir trees that flanked the back of the castle.

His mind clouded under the pain of the musket ball and the weight of a thousand questions melting into one boiling state of confusion. Red appeared before his eyes. Duncan's face screwed up in initial agony as he grabbed his leg. The world seemed white and glaring as he tried to gather his senses about him.

I've got to get home.

The cold of the snow began slowly seeping through his clothing. But he needed to clear his head. The sun began to rise, just barely peeping over the horizon. He stayed in the snow for a while, gathering strength to rise. *Who would wish to do this to me?* It was more than puzzling. It was frighteningly disconcerting. *Thank God, the man was a terrible marksman.* Still, the pain was foremost in his mind.

Finally, leaning heavily on his walking stick, he made his way to a standing position. His leg had begun to bleed heavily.

Opening up his cloak, Duncan pulled the tail of his shirt out and ripped off a strip of the fine linen. Binding up the wound and feeling nauseous, he started off as his leg throbbed and began to go numb.

He retraced his steps as best he could, using the tracks he already made as he had ventured forth. The going was slow and labored. The snow was deep. He hadn't gone far.

He fell again and again into the deep snow. Such was the journey back.

Finally the door stood before him. The oaken surface had never felt more comforting to his fingertips as he pushed upon its surface, then fell into the entry hall. Much to his chagrin, he fainted.

• • •

"Alix!" Kyle stood over his daughter's bed. "Alix, wake up!"

Alix opened her eyes and smiled up at him. This was unusual, having her father awaken her. But, after all, it was Christmas, and anything could happen on Christmas.

"Merry Christmas, Papa."

Kyle didn't answer the greeting, but sat down next to her on the bed. He decided to be direct. "Alix, Duncan was shot this morning on his walk. It's not serious," he added quickly as she gasped and grabbed his hand. "He was shot in the leg."

Alix sat up. "What happened?"

"We're not sure. The duke said it was probably some poor peasant out trying to hunt up something for Christmas dinner for his family."

"Do they have any idea who it was?"

"No. But up you get now, lassie. He's being looked at by the surgeon who has already extracted the ball, and I know he'll want to see you when he comes back down."

Alix was still concerned. This wasn't the way she pictured Christmas Day starting. "Will he be all right?"

"The shot missed his bone and the main artery, so it looks like he'll be fine." The crow's-feet around his eyes crinkled deeply with his smile. "Get up then, and come downstairs. Breakfast is waiting in the dining room. And I'm sure Duncan can use all the encouragement he can get right now. As expected, he's lost quite a bit of blood."

He got up and walked toward the door as she threw off her covers. "All right, Papa. I'll be right there."

Kyle suddenly turned and answered her initial greeting. "Merry Christmas to you, too, Alix."

. . .

Well, the stranger thought, *so be it. I'm glad I missed.*

He trudged up the bank of the stream, leading his horse hurriedly. England called to him. He would go back home to Manchester. Put this dark side of life behind him forever. The woman who had hired him was disturbing, to say the least. Even if the rest of her seemed normal enough, he never wanted to look into her eyes again. Like looking into calmed death, it was. She'd seek him out to demand her money back.

It wasn't easy to forget her. When she had walked into the inn, the entire room became hushed. The innkeeper had pointed her in his direction. The Needful Crow was a pub sacred to the underworld. She had come to the safest place in all of Argyllshire to hire someone like him. No one would have seen anything.

"Jacko there will take care of ya', ma'am."

Her heels had clicked a crisp tattoo across the flooring, and she stated her need.

Jacko agreed and named his price.

Mrs. Mackay calculated quickly in her mind, counter-offered, and a price was set. She gave him the location and Duncan's description. Then she named the day.

He immediately argued. "Oh, ma'am, 'ave a 'eart! Not on Christmas Day!"

Her eyes flashed. "Just do as I say. Ruffians like you come cheaply! I'm payin' ya' well!"

Aye, he thought continuing up the bank, *she was disturbing.* He smiled a brown-toothed grin and said to his horse, "But she'll not be findin' us in the inn, will she now, Rosie?"

The mare neighed and tossed her head as he reached in his pocket to pull out a piece of carrot.

Aye, I've had all I can take of this life. Perhaps I'll find me a wife. Walk the straight and narrow. Aye, when she comes to find us, we'll be long gone.

• • •

Mrs. Mackay raised her hand in front of the paneled door and hesitated. The Maclachlans, or any other family of noble blood, had no idea what the duke could be like when it came to his servants. Charming to his peers, he was as equally harsh with his staff. He demanded obedience and distance. Each of them knew their place at Inveraray Castle.

Breathing in, she knocked upon the door of the duke's office.

"Come in!" he called.

With a quick turn of the knob, she entered the study with her head bowed. He was the only person she had ever cowered before.

"Oh," he looked disappointed, "Mrs. Mackay. What is it that you want?" The tones were crisp and cool.

"Your grace, I'm so sorry about what happened this mornin'," she said softly. "And to think that ya' could've lost your only son."

"My only child, you mean."

"Aye, your only son," she repeated as she turned around and left the room before he had dismissed her. Her heart beat wildly as the door clicked shut, leaving the Duke of Argyll with a puzzled expression upon his face.

• • •

Clad in a gown of black satin trimmed sparsely with lace, Alix ran across the drawing room to where Duncan reclined in a chair before the fire. His leg was propped up on several pillows on the footstool in front of him, and Plutarch slept in his lap.

"Duncan!" she cried as she took his hands in hers and knelt down in front of him. "I'm so glad you're all right!"

He looked pale but in good spirits. A grin lit up his face, and his wonderful eyes looked reassuringly into hers. "Yes, dearest Alix," his hands squeezed hers strongly, "the musket ball did not go in deep. It didn't hit any major arteries."

"That's what Papa said. Thank God."

"Yes, thank God is right, Alix."

She looked at him earnestly. "I'll take all my meals in here with you!"

"Thank you, Alix. I should like that."

A voice behind them spoke. "And I shall as well."

Aaron stood in the doorway.

"Oh yes, Alix. I forgot to tell you. Aaron arrived this morning, not quite an hour ago."

"Awfully early to be up and traveling about, isn't it, Aaron?" Alix asked.

He smiled easily. "I'm happy to see you as well, Alix."

"Forgive me," she said as she bowed her head slightly, playing the mannerly woman while she wanted to tell him what she thought of his cowardly flight the past summer. "I'm happy you made it here safely."

"I would have been here last night, but I was detained by the storm about five miles away."

Duncan smiled at them. "The three of us together for Christmas. It's wonderful, Alix, is it not?"

"Aye, Duncan. Simply wonderful." Disappointed at Aaron's sudden appearance, she felt Duncan's ring resting heavily on her finger, and for the first time she wanted his company all to herself. But she decided to make the best of it, and soon the three of them were laughing merrily at Aaron's witty tales of his life in London.

. . .

It was a Campbell family tradition to observe the Christmas feast at noon, the whole family having opted to eat with Duncan in the drawing room. His newfound affliction was cause to make the Maclachlans forget their own. And when Aaron sat down at the harpsichord and played carols, the mood was merry and festive.

"You should hear the two boys sing together," the duke said.

"Oh, Father, please," Duncan chided from his chair, "it's been years since Aaron and I have sung with one another."

"Nonsense. I'm sure you still sing wonderfully together!"

"Go ahead," Kyle prompted.

"Yes. Please sing for us!" Jenny sat forward on her chair.

Alix's eyes brightened. She was hopelessly tone-deaf and admired those with vocal talent. Aaron, of course, was used to singing and performing and was more than willing to give it a go.

"Come on, Cousin," Aaron turned around to face Duncan. "Why not? It is Christmas after all."

Alix pleaded with him gently. "Please, Duncan. I didn't know you could sing." The rest of the room echoed her sentiments.

"All right, Alix," Duncan finally gave in with a sigh. "But you choose the song."

When Aaron's baritone voice blended with Duncan's strong tenor in a soft rendition of "I Saw Three Ships," the whole family sat in silence. Alix was awestruck as the notes from her betrothed seeped into her heart.

Soon the duke's bass joined in to the tune of "The Holly She Bears a Berry." It was Violet's favorite carol. Without hesitation, she stood next to Aaron and in a clear soprano joined in the small choir.

Jenny and Kyle looked at each other with raised eyebrows.

After a bit, everyone became sleepy as the wonderful roasted goose and apples settled more firmly in their stomachs and the mince pie and other dainties filled them with cozy warmth.

• • •

Silence bathed the castle, except for in the kitchens. But the servants could not be heard on the top floor of the rounded turret that faced west. The round room was warm from the fire Aaron had started in the marble manteled fireplace.

It was a luxurious place. Rich carpets hid the stone floor, and tapestries hung over the plastered walls. His grandmother had furnished this room for herself when the castle had been built. Now only he ever stepped within its sanctuary. And Clementine, who made sure that it was always well-maintained.

Three o'clock chimed from the small clock on the bedside table.

The door opened and Clementine walked in carrying a tray.

"The mulled wine you requested, Mr. Campbell." Her voice was soft and musical. Her eyes danced in his presence.

Aaron really saw her for the first time as she stood there before him. She looked so lovely, so sweet with her fair skin, rosy cheeks, and wavy ebony hair, and she was so tiny. She had always seemed nothing more than a child to him. He had noticed her many times in a cursory way–the delicate bones, the deep, soulful greenish-blue eyes–but she seemed different standing so close. Clementine was truly a woman, fully ripened, and ready to love. He simply hadn't noticed that fact before.

"How old are you, Clementine?" he asked rather forwardly.

"Twenty-seven, sir."

"You look much younger."

She smiled the smile of woman hearing the ultimate compliment. "Thank you, sir." Her head suddenly bowed in shyness, and she held out the tray toward him. Aaron poured himself a cup and swallowed it quickly.

"Have you had your Christmas dinner yet, Clementine?"

"Not yet, sir."

She really is quite lovely. Innocent really. The room seemed a bit warm. *Not like most of the women in London. Certainly not like Mrs. Lyons-Parker.*

"Won't you join me for a cup of Christmas cheer?" he asked, surprising even himself.

"Why, Mr. Campbell," Clementine was taken aback, "'twould be unseemly for me to take a drink with ya'! I'm just a housemaid, after all."

"Please. I'm one of those old-fashioned people who hate to drink alone. And it's Christmas, after all."

Clementine hesitated, knuckles white as she clutched harder the handles of the tray. Her eyes darted round the room, looking for permission, disapproval, a sign, something, but all that could be found were she and Aaron. And for the first time in her life the decision was up to her.

"All right." She blessed him with the first wide smile he had ever seen upon her face. "I'll toast with ya', Mr. Campbell, and pray that no one else is the wiser!"

Aaron laughed and led her over to the bench which sat before the hearth. "That's the spirit, dear girl. We shall toast together." He refilled his glass and poured one for her. "To . . ."

He hesitated. "What shall we toast to?"

Clementine shrugged, her eyes filled with joy. "To a year of surprises!" she said.

"All right then," their cups clinked together, "to a year of surprises."

Clementine's eyes closed as the spirits wafted over her palate.

"Did you enjoy that?" Aaron asked.

"Aye." She was breathless.

Aaron poured more into each of their glasses. His hand closed over hers momentarily as he handed her the goblet, and he looked into her eyes.

"You are a beautiful woman, Clementine."

She dropped her eyes shyly, but did not stop him when he lifted his hand to push the stray curl from her temple. Self-consciously she lifted the goblet to her lips and drank a second cup. Aaron did the same.

"I need to be gettin' back downstairs, sir," she bobbed a curtsy, and toppled sideways a bit.

"No, Clementine." The hand on her arm was gentle, but firm and inviting. "One last toast, and then if you still wish to go you may do so."

The dark-haired beauty looked doubtful, but Aaron pulled her to him and kissed her gently but quickly on the lips. "For me?" he asked. "Please, Clementine. It's Christmas."

"All right, sir," she said softly. Her head was beginning to swim. In fact, Aaron felt a bit woozy as well.

Strange, he thought, *and after only two glasses.*

They toasted once more, the decanter now empty. Aaron helped Clementine down onto the hearth rug, and he joined her there seconds later. Again his lips found hers.

Within minutes the drugged wine had done its job, and Aaron and Clementine lay passed out upon the floor.

The curtains shifted as the silent intruder set to work.

• • •

Aaron sat up suddenly in the great bed, eyes wide, mind foggy. He looked about him as he rubbed his pain-filled head.

He was naked.

And alone.

And on the floor lay a telltale woolen stocking and nothing else. Clementine's stocking, no doubt.

As he raked his fingers through his disheveled hair, he stood up. "What have I done?"

"I think the answer to that is quite obvious, Mr. Campbell." A voice, calm and clinical, came from the straight chair in the far region of the room.

Aaron grabbed the spread from off the bed and held it around him.

Shock widened his eyes. "Mrs. Mackay. What are you doing here?"

"I came up to check on m'Clementine and what did I find but the scene ya' see before ya' plus another person. M'daughter. An' she was in the same state you are now, Mr. Campbell."

"I don't remember..." Actually, the last thing he remembered was kissing Clementine.

"Course ya' dinna'!" She arose from her seat and walked over to the tray Clementine had delivered and picked up the empty decanter. "Between the two of ya' it's a wonder ya' woke up so soon!"

"Where's Clementine?"

"Charlie an' Billy came an' carried her down to her room."

"Oh no . . ." Aaron rubbed his throbbing temples with his middle finger and thumb.

"Oh no is right, sir. And just how do ya' plan on makin' amends? She was pure before she stepped into this room to-day."

"Oh no . . ." Aaron sat down on the bed. This was turning into a nightmare. He looked up into the hardened eyes of the woman that now stood before him.

"How much?" he asked.

"How much?" she echoed harshly. "What price would ya' put on a virgin's purity, sir? I'm curious to find out."

"A hundred pounds. Five hundred?" *Where am I going to get that kind of money?* he thought.

"Five hundred? Surely ya' must be jokin', sir." Her humorless laugh squeezed his spinal column painfully.

"One thousand?" He swallowed hard as a sweat broke on his forehead and his back.

The laugh came again. "I canna' be bought, Mr. Campbell."

"What?" His neck hair bristled.

"Nothin' short o' marriage will suffice."

"You're jesting!" Now it was his turn to take control. She couldn't force him to marry Clementine.

"Nay, sir. I'm very serious."

"How will you make me carry it out?"

"I'll tell everyone the truth. That ya' seduced an innocent girl an' tried to buy her off afterwards."

"What if I say 'go ahead?' "

She shook her head and clicked her tongue. "Ya' know it would ruin ya', Mr. Campbell."

"But it would be your word against mine."

"My word. An' Charlie's an' Billy's."

Aaron shook his head from side to side wearily, feeling trapped. "All right. Let it be as you say. Hopefully Clementine does not remember what happened either. So all I ask

is that you let me court her in a normal fashion. And that what transpired between us will stay between us. I'd also like time to go back to London to get my affairs in order."
And I do mean "affairs," he thought wryly.

"As ya' wish, m'lord . . . I mean, Mr. Campbell."

Aaron looked at her sharply. "If that is all then, Mrs. Mackay, I should like to get dressed."

"Certainly," she rubbed the reddened hands together. "I shall leave ya' to your privacy."

She opened the door and looked back in his direction. "An' to think ya' behaved so on Christmas Day!"

The door closed softly behind her as she left.

Aaron ground his fist into his palm. In a matter of minutes his entire future had been decided. And all because he invited a housemaid to share a cup of wine.

•••

27 December, 1764

Deep foreboding accompanies me after the events of Christmas. I feel hunted and vulnerable. It was no mistake, that shot. There were no animals in the clearing. And if it was a mistake, the fragileness of existence—walking one minute in praise to God, floundering in bloodstained snow the next—is nothing if not mortally discomfitting.

Does God give His children premonitions? Vague feelings of the future that steal obscurely through heart and mind?

I do not know.

PART FOUR

1765

Morning

O perfite light! whilk I sched away
The darkness from the light,
And set a ruler owre the day,
Ane other owre the night.

Our hemisphere is polish't clean,
And lightening more and more,
Till everything be clearly seen
Whilk seemed dim before.

The golden globe incontinent,
Sets up his shining head,
And owre the earth and firmament
Displays his beams ahead.

—Alexander Hume

CHAPTER

15

May, 1765

The wind carried her hair in a glorious, heat-filled stream as she galloped across the hillside. Laughter, full and hearty, issued from her lips as she looked back at Duncan, a dot of black against the bright green of the spring landscape.

Alix commanded Flora to slow down to wait for him. Duncan began to slow up.

"No!" Alix cried, cupping one gloved hand beside her mouth. "Don't stop! I've finally gotten you on a horse, and we're going to keep going!"

"All right!" He kept old Delilah going, but they slowed up considerably as he pulled alongside her. His black lashes blinked over his aqua eyes as the sun shimmered off the loch. "I'm following your lead on this one, darling Alix. And I must say, I do not relish being at the complete mercy of you and this ancient beast underneath me. It's positively humiliating!"

They were trotting lightly, the horses' hooves thudding pleasingly against the turf. "You're doing wonderfully. Why, soon Lachlan will be letting you ride Storm."

"Thank you, no," he held up a hand, and quickly put it back on the reins. "I will not be getting on that Arabian anytime during this life."

They rode on, skirting the edge of the forest, enjoying the shade.

"Grandpapa and Grandmother should be arriving soon," Alix announced, excitement written in her posture.

His smile was warmhearted. "I know. It should be a wonderful way to celebrate your birthday."

"Mother's was just last week. She was complaining of feeling like a Roman ruin because she was turning 37. Papa just looked at her askance and asked her if she would like to trade places with him."

"How old is your father?"

"He just turned 41."

"Really?"

The pride was evident in her voice. "Aye. He's a vibrant man, isn't he?"

"Yes. A strong man, too. A man I respect considerably," he said as he brought the horse to a stop. "My grandfather loved him like a son, you know."

"I know. And Papa loved him in return like a father. Especially after Culloden."

Dismounting, he helped Alix down. They were at a rock formation not far from the village. Grass and shrubbery sprouted up between the boulders, and birds and insects hummed a spring etude of relief-filled buzzings and chirpings. The air smelled clean and sweet.

"It's hard to believe that we are here with each other because of that whole ordeal," she said, slipping her hand into his.

"What do you mean?"

They sat down near the formation. The grass was cool and lush and soft beneath her hands as she leaned back on them.

"On the very day your grandfather told Papa he could go back to Scotland, I was promised to the next Campbell heir. I was only a newborn."

The aqua eyes lit up in the May sunshine. "So you have been mine ever since I was ten years old?"

She squeezed his hand. "Aye, Duncan, that I have. Although I wish we could have known one another sooner."

Duncan nodded and took out his pipe. "I agree. I had not even a clue as to what you were like. That is why I had Aaron come meet you at your farewell party."

"He told me about that later on."

"Did he?" Duncan became slightly uncomfortable, and he leaned his head more closely to hers before he spoke. "Alix, I've never really been sure about him."

Alix's blue eyes narrowed. "What are you saying?"

"I've never voiced my reservations to anyone before, but Alix . . . I do not completely trust Aaron."

"Why?"

"When he left Inveraray six years ago for London, he hurt my grandfather terribly. It was like the old man, who loved him so dearly, who had raised him and cared for his every need, had never existed. It makes one question his loyalty." Out of his coat pocket he retrieved a tobacco pouch. "I've always felt like he looked at me with thoughts of envy. Like I possessed something he did not. Imagine that. Of course, I'm probably imagining *that* for I've no concrete reason to feel that way."

"It's probably just feelings of guilt on your part that you are the one who will be duke someday."

"You're probably right. After all, Aaron has always been more than kind."

"Aye," Alix nodded. "I think you are the one person he truly loves."

They sat for a while longer in the sunshine. The bleating of the lambs and the breeze's rustle of the new leaves behind them provided a peaceful orchestration as they sat, having to say nothing. Duncan puffed on his pipe and Alix mused about what life would be like. True companionship was theirs. They had never been so comfortable in their lives.

"Duncan?"

"Yes, darling Alix?" He turned to her, resting his pipe hand on his knee, and smiled.

"What would you do if you could do anything in the world?"

"Oh, that is easy to answer." He spread his hands wide. "I would teach."

"What would you teach?"

"Literature. Poetry."

"I thought so."

• • •

Lundly Park
April, 1765

My Dearest Alix,

London's been such a bore since you left. I haven't been able to get in trouble with anyone.

I realize that by the time you receive this you shall see me shortly. Your wedding is right around the corner and how excited you must be! But my own excitement cannot be constrained or contained, and so I must write and tell you everything.

I am engaged. And it is to a man of my own choosing. Last season, as you know, was a disaster. Mother and Father had reached a level of such distress over me that I wondered if the family would survive! I had offers for my hand, but I positively refused to marry any of them, no matter how rich or pretty they were. You would have been proud of me.

Your letters about Duncan's strength and kindness set me thinking about just what I wanted in a man. And what I wanted in a man did not coincide with who I was as a woman. So I retrieved the copy of the Bible you had given me two years ago. And that was when the excitement began.

I was reading the Scriptures in the park when a young man sat next to me. He asked if I understood what I was reading, and of course I said no because I did not. Well, things picked up quickly and soon he was coming to call on me each afternoon. Last week as Easter arrived, I contemplated the passion of Jesus. I couldn't help but be struck by the beauty of God's love to me through the death of His Son. And that He rose again made it all so miraculous I was drawn completely and utterly. I gave myself to the Savior. Oh, Alix, I finally found the peace for which I was looking. But our Lord had even more planned for me.

The young man's name is James Lewis, and he is wonderful. Tall, with wavy blond hair and blue eyes. He is the exact opposite of me! He is a quiet man, but when he gets engaged in conversation, his intelligence and graciousness come out completely. And I love him so.

We are to be married in September. James will be finished with his time in the Royal Navy by then. And after a brief honeymoon on the coast of France, we depart for the Colonies in the spring. James hopes to start a mission to the Indians someday! How wonderful is the Savior. Mother and Father aren't at all pleased, but they have accepted the inevitable. Of course, my prayers are that they, too, will come to believe on His name soon.

I cannot wait to see you, dear Alix, and thank you in person for the many prayers you offered up in my behalf. I still miss you terribly.

With all my love and affection,

Philippa

• • •

Castle Lachlan was settled for the night as the chief and his lady made their way to their bedroom. Kyle's arm was placed securely around Jenny's shoulders, and she leaned into his strength with her head on his chest. They walked slowly up the stairs, rhythmically and steadily from years of practice.

Jenny's other hand ran along the wall and over the door frame as they entered the room. Candles on the mantel and bedside table lamps were glowing warmly in the white room with blue trimmings. Kyle began to unbutton her gown.

"I've always wondered how you ladies can stand to dress the way you do," he laughed. "Layers and layers. Buttons. Hooks."

Jenny smiled gently. "Oh, we have our reasons, Kyle Maclachlan. As long as we're in our long dresses, it leaves the dirty work up to you men!"

Kyle laughed as Jenny reached around and pulled the bow out of his hair. The soft auburn curls spilled into her hand. "There's a little more gray in there, my darling," she whispered, looking up into his eyes. "We're growing old together, aren't we?"

"Aye, my love. That we are." He turned and finished undressing. Jenny did as well. She had forsaken the use of a ladies' maid in the evenings ever since their marriage. Kyle had always been there to do the job.

Once in their nightclothes, Kyle pulled back the sheets and they sat on the large bed as he brushed his wife's hair.

"Aaron's visit tonight was a surprise, eh, my love?" he said as the brush flowed over the brown tresses.

Jenny nodded. "Alix pulled me aside after dinner. He said he has forsaken the London theater and wants to come back to Scotland."

"To Inveraray?"

"I suppose. Alix didn't want to ask. She knows that Duncan will welcome his cousin at the castle for as long he wishes to stay."

"Duncan surely is a noble fellow."

"Aye," she agreed, her fingers rubbing back and forth over the coverlet. "Maybe a bit too noble for his own good."

He divided her hair into three sections and began to work it into a braid. "I like Aaron. He seems a congenial lad, but I'm thankful it's Duncan our Alix is marrying."

"I've grown fond of Duncan, Kyle. When his father came in with him last June, I wasn't so sure he'd be enough for Alix. I'm glad I was wrong."

Jenny handed him a ribbon to tie off her braid. When he finished the bow, she turned and stroked his cheek with her small hand.

"I love you, Jenny Maclachlan." He blew out his lamp.

"And I love you, Kyle." She blew out hers.

Sliding down amid the pillows and into the sheets, he took her into his arms.

"You're still uncommonly beautiful for a 37-year-old relic," he whispered.

A slap sounded in the darkness as she giggled. Kyle rubbed his backside with a chuckle.

• • •

"That was quite a revelation to spring on someone two days before his wedding," Duncan muttered to himself, looking out at the full moon that kept up with the carriage measure for measure. The countryside was lit up so, he swore he would have been able to read a book in its silver light. He was glad Aaron had chosen to ride ahead on horseback.

Aaron hadn't said he would be staying at Inveraray Castle. But Duncan knew he must extend an invitation. In any case, he'd be home soon, and a good night's sleep would do wonders in making the horizon with Aaron at Inveraray look somewhat brighter. It put a bit of a damper on what he had envisioned life there with Alix would be. But he wouldn't turn out his cousin. It wouldn't be right.

But even Aaron's appearance could not dull Duncan's joy. Alix loved him. His wildest dream was coming true, and soon she would be his. He looked up at the stars and whispered words of thanks to the One who created them.

"Thank You, Father God," his soul felt warm and weightless in his happiness. "Thank You for putting into the heart of fair Alix Maclachlan love for a homely scholar like myself." He could hardly believe it was happening.

A shout caught his attention as two large figures on horseback emerged from the woods to the left of the road and bounded over a stone wall.

"Halt, I say!" one of them yelled again.

Highwaymen.

Duncan sighed in wearied resignation. Usually they were quite harmless if the holdup was financially worth their while. "Stop the carriage, Kenneth," he ordered the driver. "Let's not try and be heroes. They just want money." He leaned forward and whispered into his ear, "Is your pistol loaded?" Kenneth nodded almost imperceptibly.

The carriage came to a standstill in front of the men. The road stretched before them, a ribbon of purple moonlight, and all was hushed. Duncan was dismayed when he saw the two ruffians before him. They were poorly dressed. Their skin was ruddy from a life of too much drink. Their hair fell in tangles from their caps, and their mounts were pathetically old. *Not your typical highwaymen*, he thought, feeling a bit disturbed. He had been held up once before, but not by men like these.

"First," said the tallest one, older with yellow-gray curls framing the angular, lined face, "we'll take yer money. Isn't that right, Bart?"

Duncan sought to find a region for the accent and decided he must be from along the border. He didn't resist. Money held no significance to him. Besides, he'd have the authorities after these men as soon as he returned to Inveraray. He handed over his purse to Bart, a fat man with stubby, greedy fingers who shoved mousy-brown curls out of his eyes with his other hand.

"Here ye go, Harry," he threw the purse to the old one. "And who would we be robbin' today, eh?" Bart opened the door and Kenneth went for the pistol, but Harry was surprisingly quick. In a flash the pistol was in his hand.

"Don't be tryin' any more o' *that!*" he laughed, and Duncan could smell the scotch on his breath. "Have ye got one o' these things?" he asked Ian, the footman still standing behind Duncan on the back of the carriage as he held up the pistol. The servant held up empty hands. He was unfortunately unarmed. But Harry took no chances and searched him thoroughly.

"Now," Bart said softly but unmenacingly, "it's time we took the second thing we came for." His hand curled around Duncan's forearm. Duncan pulled his arm away.

"Don't!" yelled Harry. "Not if ye want to come out o' this alive." He opened the wallet. "There's not much in here, m'lord. We'll just be takin' ye to a safe place until we get a little money from that duke father o' yours."

Duncan shook his head as Bart again grabbed his arm. "Ransom? You must be joking!" Their foolishness bespoke more than kidnapping. No one was that stupid. No one would ever get away with kidnapping the heir to the dukedom of Argyll, and even men such as they knew that.

"Nay, m'lord. Now don't do anything stupid, or old Kenny there will be wearin' a musket ball for a hat."

"Aye," Bart laughed a wheezy chuckle, "a permanent one."

He squeezed harder on Duncan's arm and shoved him out of the vehicle. Harry grabbed him and held the pistol to the base of his skull. "Come along, m'lord."

Out of the darkness an arrow whizzed by Harry's ear, barely missing. He looked up as a lone figure materialized eerily from the darkness of the trees. Another arrow was poised upon the polished bow. Ready to shoot, his biceps taut, his fingers frozen, the arrow aimed and ready to seek death, the Last Highlander hopped up onto the wall.

"If ya' value your life, you'll let him go," Robin Brodie said softy.

Duncan sighed in relief even as Harry pushed the pistol even harder against the back of his head. Fear mixed with the alcohol in the hoodlum's system to form a false bravery. "The Last Highlander, eh? An' what makes ye think your arrow will be faster than my bullet?"

"I am sober. And I am not owned by any man."

"Neither am I, Robin Brodie. An' I do what I please." Harry pulled Duncan's arm tightly behind his back. Duncan flinched as a scream filled his ears. Robin's arrow deeply embedded itself in Harry's shoulder, severing veins and nerves. The arm went loose. Duncan bounded free. And Harry fell writhing to the ground. Robin readied another arrow aiming directly at Bart's heart. He pleaded for his life amid his compatriot's screams. Ian grabbed a rope and, in no time, with Robin's help, the two thugs were bound tightly together. Duncan was shaken, but he hid it well.

"Kenneth, unhitch Lady and ride for Inveraray and get the authorities to come back for these two. Go at once."

"Aye, m'lord." He touched his forelock and set to work. The sound of the horse's hooves was soon disappearing in the distant night.

"Thank you, Robin. Thank God, you came along at the right time!"

Robin bowed. "It was nothin', m'lord. I saw their fire last night and came over to see who it was. Your grace, they werena' plannin' on just kidnappin' ya'. That was merely a ruse to get ya' out of the carriage. They were hired to kill ya'."

"Who . . . ?"

"I dinna' know who hired them, m'lord. I didna' even know who they were plannin' to abduct. They never mentioned any names. So I came back an' waited to see who it was they were lyin' in wait for."

"I cannot thank you enough."

"There's no need to m'lord. I was glad to do it. You're Alix's betrothed." The last statement told Duncan all. Robin had needed no other reason. Duncan led Robin out of earshot.

"Robin," he confided in the Last Highlander, "this is the second attempt on my life. The first happened at Christmas."

"Joshua told me about that, but everyone thought it was a peasant."

Duncan's mouth was grim. "It was no peasant, Robin."

Robin nodded. "What can I do to help?"

"Nothing right now. I'm going to try and find out who is doing this, but to be quite honest, I have not one clue where to start looking. I've made no enemies that I am aware of. What I need you to do is to keep silent about what happened tonight. Especially to Alix. She must not know. Not with the wedding so soon."

Robin nodded. "All right, m'lord. I shall keep your trust."

"Thank you," Duncan sighed. "And pray, Robin. Pray that I find who it is that seeks my life."

"Aye. That I shall do, m'lord. Do ya' think these two will talk?" he jerked a thumb in the direction of Bart and Harry.

"Perhaps. But my guess is that whoever actually hired them is not whom I am seeking. If I wanted someone dead, I certainly would not seek out a willing party in person."

"You're right, m'lord. And I shall do as ya' say. I shall keep the matter private. But please, m'lord," he laid a strong hand on Duncan's arm, "if ya' should ever need my help, I'll be waitin' to do whatever I can."

"Thank you, Robin."

"I'll be leavin' ya' now, your grace, just as soon as I retrieve my arrow."

Robin raced toward the carriage and Duncan heard a hellish scream.

In a flutter of plaid, Robin was gone.

Harry muttered in delirious pain from his wound as Bart cursed the day they, and everyone else he knew, were all born.

"Be quiet!" Duncan said harshly as he sat down on the grass. "Ian, fetch my pipe and pouch. I'm of a mind to smoke."

Ian complied and, as he handed Duncan the pipe and tobacco, Duncan handed him the pistol. "Keep it trained on them, Ian."

Suddenly Aaron came riding back, concern spread on his face as he viewed the confusing scene. "I stopped to wait for you, and when you didn't come I came back to look for you. What happened?"

By this time Duncan was puffing on his pipe.

He pointed with the smoking device. "See for yourself, Cousin."

Aaron looked around, his shocked expression turning to puzzlement. "What's going on, Duncan? Is everyone all right?"

"It is as you see. Kenneth has ridden back to Inveraray for help. Why don't you have a seat and join me? There is a pouch of tobacco in the carriage."

Soon two trails of smoke filtered up into the starlight as Duncan related the details, including Robin's information. The look on his cousin's face became more incredulous with each word. Aaron swore himself to secrecy as well. But finally after many questions and answers, Duncan became weary of talking about it and changed the subject.

"So you are finally tired of London life?"

"Oh, Cousin," Aaron sighed, looking up at the dome of the heavens. He was more than happy to talk about himself. "I couldn't begin to describe to you what life is like for me there. I sincerely do not know how some of the actors last as long as they do."

Duncan glanced over at him, his suspicions rising. "Is there something else which drives you back up north as well, Aaron?"

"Aye."

Duncan's eyebrows raised. He hadn't expected Aaron to admit as much.

"The theater doesn't pay much, Duncan, you know that."

He nodded as he drew in on his pipe.

Aaron fidgeted a bit, swallowed, and continued. "I'd been seeing a rich widow. She began to get a bit demanding, and when I tried to break things off, I suddenly found myself being stalked and threatened by a certain few ruffians."

Concern spread over Duncan's face. This wasn't quite what he expected Aaron to say. Actually, he wasn't sure what he expected Aaron to say.

"Are you certain this woman had sent them?"

"Yes," Aaron went on. "I may have my vices, but gambling is not among them. Mrs. Lyons-Parker is the only enemy I can think of!"

"Mrs. Lyons-Parker?" Duncan looked with surprise at his cousin and suddenly felt sorry for him. "Oh, Aaron, you should have written me if you needed finances. I would have gladly spared you any dealings with that viper."

Aaron's head whipped around and he stared hard at his cousin. "What do you mean? You've heard of her?"

"Aaron, the woman is nefarious. She comes off so sweetly, but do not cross her. And that doesn't just go for the young men whose company she seeks. She is like that with everyone."

Aaron was clearly embarrassed. "How do *you* know so much about her?"

"A friend of mine at Cambridge got in a bit of a tangle with her. Guess she caught him stealing one of her brooches!"

The cousins laughed together, but both felt uneasy.

"She was such a sweet thing, I could hardly believe she was capable of such actions." Aaron tried to explain himself.

"People are always capable of things we do not expect of them," Duncan whispered softly into the darkness.

Aaron looked at his cousin sharply. But Duncan puffed benignly on his pipe. *Did I imagine some kind of implication in his tone?* Aaron thought. *Did Mrs. Mackay tell him about Clementine?*

"What do you plan on doing?" Duncan asked.

"I thought I would start writing."

"Oh?" This was a pleasant surprise. "Plays, I assume?"

Aaron nodded affirmatively. "What else? Duncan . . ." he hesitated.

"Do not saying anything, Cousin," Duncan interrupted him graciously "You are welcome to stay with me at Inveraray Castle as long as you wish."

Aaron breathed a sigh of relief. "Thank you."

Duncan nodded, looking back up at the moon. He wondered just when it was that lunacy had taken over his mind.

• • •

16 May, 1765

It is late. The castle sleeps in darkened silence and I am yearning for Alix. Aaron is home and life here after the honeymoon will not be as I expected. Still, I look forward to life with her. She reminds me of an ancient poem—timeless, deep, and filled with a new, different beauty each time my eye rests again upon her loveliness, each time my heart fills anew with her sweetness, her goodness, her kindness.

Five more days and she shall be mine. I know that she loves me and will love me yet more. But she shall never love me as much as I love her.

Another attempt was made upon my life tonight. Thank God, Robin Brodie was there. At least now I know beyond all doubt that someone is seeking to take my life from me. I cannot afford to keep this a secret much longer or surely I am a dead man. And yet, the wedding is only days away. How can I destroy the happiness of my bride with the news of what has happened? No. I shall not do such. Alix must never know.

• • •

A letter, written in a bold hand, was held between Alix's fingers. She looked out on the setting sun. Her window seat cradled her softly as she reclined against the multitude of downy pillows. The sky faded gradually from gold to peach to pink to purple. Color infused into color underneath a canopy of deep, sparkling blue.

She loved his handwriting. So assured. So true to who he was inside.

And how he loves the Savior, she thought as she read Duncan's words of love to her.

On the eve of her wedding, Alix realized that she wanted to be his wife in every way imaginable.

I really do love him. And she threw her head back and laughed a laugh of pure happiness at the sudden, joyous revelation. She was completely restored to who she was meant to be; she was true to herself and to her Savior once again. All because of Duncan. In giving her back the real Alix Maclachlan, he had taken her for himself. All because of love.

• • •

They were the uttermost picture of serenity as they lazed on the bank of the loch. Duncan, in his normal somber colors, made a stark contrast to Alix's pale-yellow dress. A straw hat decorated with daisies and violets shielded her milky skin. Together they looked the image of a man and a woman at peace with each other and the world. A breeze blew mildly around them, cooling them with softly treading fingers.

Alix's fingers played gently with his clean brown hair as Duncan lay with his head in her lap. How could she have known the reserved, nervous young Campbell that visited her almost a year ago would become so fondly loving, so assured? As he continued reading, Alix smiled at his musical voice, the hushed, soft tones of the Gaelic verse vibrating gently in her inner ear. She leaned her head down closer, ear turned toward his mouth. Smiling at her close proximity to him, he read on, the words deliberately becoming softer and softer.

Without realizing it, Alix continued her descent to him as his tones waned to a mere breath. Duncan put down his book.

"That is a lovely ear I see before my eyes," he said almost inaudibly. Alix leaned down even more proximate, and Duncan brushed his lips ever so softly against her skin. At the unexpected touch, Alix jerked her head, a heavy cascade of hair falling upon Duncan's face. Scooping up handfuls of the silken mass, he relished in its fresh scent, its softness, as he brushed it against his cheek, eyes closed.

Alix spoke in her usual forward manner, her face inches from his. "Duncan Robert Campbell. I've been waiting for some time now, and I do not believe there could be a better time."

His eyes opened. "For what?" He was entranced by her tresses. Each little part of her intrigued him.

"For the meeting of our lips, as well as our hearts."

"Aye, Alix. You have had my heart since I saw you enter the drawing room that first time."

"And you've had mine ever since Mary Alice passed away," she said, pulling the heavy curls back over her shoulder. "I just didn't know it fully until yesterday, Duncan."

Slowly Duncan sat up, eyes never leaving hers. "Do you mean that, Alix?" His hand caressed her cheek. "Can that possibly be?"

She nodded and grabbed his hand, kissing its palm. Her eyes softened as she gazed into his.

"Alix," he said in simplicity, voice like wine, running smoothly and directly into her heart, "I love you."

"Then kiss me, Duncan." Her eyes danced with expectation.

"The kiss will have to wait," he said softly as his face came closer, lips almost touching as their breath intertwined, warming each other's faces. Alix pouted and pulled away.

"What mean you, Duncan Campbell? Why will it have to wait?"

Mischief sprang to the aqua eyes. "Because we have someplace else to go."

Alix's eyebrows raised. Duncan was becoming so surprising.

"We're going up to old Castle Lachlan," he said, taking her hand into his, their fingers laced intimately as they started walking along the shore of Loch Fyne toward Lachlan Bay where the old edifice belligerently stood on guard. Duncan stepped up the pace.

"I'm sure this all makes perfect sense to you, Mr. Campbell," she laughed, "so why don't you enlighten me as to why we're treading at top speed up to the old castle."

"Because I want to feel your lips on mine." Even though his voice was light, his eyes spoke of the future and all the joys anticipated by both of them. Alix shivered with physical expectation.

"But why the *castle*, silly? Honestly, I see I shall have to make my questions distinct and clear from now on. I'd hate to be misunderstood because of something I said."

"I'm going to enjoy being married to you, Alix. You think like a man." The light breeze blew his hair into his eyes.

Alix threw back her head and laughed. "You still haven't answered my question," she said, reaching up to push his hair back.

"The brounie."

"The brounie?" Alix questioned. "What does the brounie have to do with this kiss?"

They came up to the ruins and went into what had once been the great hall. The sun continued to shine upon them. Sitting down on the floor cross-legged, they faced each other, hands clasped together and resting on her knees.

"Don't you remember the story you told me last autumn?" Duncan began. "How the brounie of Castle Lachlan became furious when a Maclachlan first married a Campbell?"

"The way he made the wedding feast disappear?"

"Yes, exactly."

"Duncan Campbell," she scolded, "you brought me all the way up here to chaff that poor little brounie? Why, the poor dear doesn't even have a decent home anymore!"

"Aye, maybe he just should have kept quiet about it. He would not be eating his words as we speak."

Alix laughed, but the smile quickly faded and her eyes deepened as she looked at him. "What are you waiting for, Duncan?" her voice was thick.

"Oh, Alix," Duncan reached out his hand and caressed her hair.

When had he changed? When had he become capable of feeling an emotion so deep it felt as if his life had been looted clean of everything that had ever mattered before? And why did she come to love him so? He wasn't anything she ever imagined her husband would be. *Kiss her now*, a little voice inside him whispered, *before it all becomes nothing more than the shadow of a dream!*

His hand delicately tracked her cheek, fingertips moving featherlightly down her neck and over to rest on her shoulder. The other hand wound its way into the curls at the nape of her neck. The feel of a woman, the feel of *her*, was so new, but so natural. And his face moved ever closer to hers.

Joining in a pledge, their lips pressed gently together, and their hearts responded with a leap of faith. For there is no surety on this earth. But in that simple kiss, Duncan and Alix opened themselves completely to one another, no matter what the cost. Alix's soul was consumed with her bridegroom. She could never feel anything other than wholehearted toward this man. Duncan thought himself the most blessed man that ever kissed a woman.

"I love you. I never even knew feelings like this existed before I met you," he said earnestly, revealing the overflowings of an innocent heart.

"I love you, Duncan," she said simply. And they kissed yet again, happiness wrapping them up in a gentle hand as they ventured together on a tale of love.

Sitting on the floor of the old castle, they stayed in silence, gazing at one another. Enchanted by mind, body, and soul.

The descent of the sun was almost complete when they walked back to Alix's home. Hand in hand, the mellowed breeze cooled their brows lightly, and the loch echoed the brilliant colors of the sky. And when the loving couple sat down to dinner, Kyle and Jenny smiled happily. Their daughter would achieve a lifetime of love, and for that they were thankful.

"Of course," Kyle said later that night as he and his lady were getting into their bed, "did you think that our fair Alix would do any less?"

Jenny laughed as her chieftain pulled her into his strong arms. "Of course not, she's too much like her parents."

"Insatiable?"

"Aye, Kyle Maclachlan, insatiable." She thrust her fingers into his auburn curls, now laced with silver. Her actions echoed the hungerings of her heart, mind, and body. And they gave themselves to each other as they had countless times since their honeymoon night 19 years before. It had never changed. The love had never stopped, or even subsided a bit. And afterward, they prayed that their daughter would be as blessed.

CHAPTER
16

A wreath of springtime heather, twined with orange blossoms, encircled her head as she danced with her beloved. Highland reels and country dances. Bowing, curtsying, weaving in and out. Smiling amid the cloud of her veil to the happy pipes, the harp, and the drums. Inveraray Castle became a fairy-tale palace of enchantment for those that had gathered to celebrate the marriage of Alix and Duncan.

The village church had harbored their vows. Vows strong enough, clear enough, and meant so sincerely as to last more than one lifetime. *I, Duncan.* He had promised to care for her for life, to love her for all his days, to cherish her. *I, Alix.* The honor due him she would give. During sickness and adversity she would be by his side. She would love him beyond death.

The afternoon feasting was slowing for soon the games would begin. The duke's swiftest runners had covered the length and breadth of Maclachlan and Campbell land making known that a great wedding was taking place and that Highland games would be part of the festivities. The old bard of the Campbells was coming as well. When the fire in the great hall of Inveraray Castle began to glow and the children slept on benches in the corner, he would sing the ancient tales of bravery and fancy when the country was young and fought off the Viking hordes, or when Scotland's faithful rallied behind Robert the Bruce.

But for now the sun was out and burning brightly across

the meadow near the castle. Blankets were spread as clanspeople began settling down to watch the festivities. Their bellies were full. Their hearts were merry. And they wanted nothing more than to rest and enjoy the spectacle that would be shortly taking place before their eyes.

Oh, the banqueting tables had almost seemed to buckle under the weight of Scotland's bounty. Joints of beef from the small, black Highland cattle turned on spits accompanied by venison and boar. Grouse, ptarmigan, pheasant, and partridge were piled high on numerous wooden platters. And of course, succulent salmon, caught in the region's cool streams, melted in everyone's mouth and pleased their eyes with its pink flesh. There were also shameless spreads of sweets, much to every Scotsman's delight, all prepared in the French manner by Inveraray's baker.

Alix and Duncan hadn't eaten much. They were far too excited. She shielded her eyes against the glare of the sun as the perimeter of the field became more highly populated.

And now the piper was calling all the clansmen to assemble. The games had not been held for years by either the Campbells *or* the Maclachlans. For the chief purpose of Highland games was now obsolete. Scotland was under the heel of England, and there was no need to determine the swiftest runners, the strongest men, the bravest warriors. The level of excitement was high, however, as the people awaited the arrival of the contestants, clansmen hoping to prove themselves worthy not of the chief's war retinue, but of their sweetheart's favor.

Brightly colored pavilions, contrasting vividly against the green of the landscape, were set up for the gentlefolk, and Alix and Duncan sat in the seats of honor, accompanied by family members under a canopy of yellow and red stripes.

"When were the first games held?" she asked, leaning closer to him.

"There are conflicting opinions. One says the people of Ceres in Fife held games to celebrate their bowmen's safe return after their victory with Robert the Bruce at Bannock-burn."

"What is the other opinion?"

"Some say King Malcolm Canmore held the first games at Braemar to choose a new courier."

"Interesting." Alix settled back to wait.

The people were now settled, chatting together, causing a pleasant hum to meld softly with the breeze shifting off the blue waters of the loch. Smell of sun on grass perfumed the air, and clouds floated by regularly, checkering the meadow with sudden spots of shade.

From the direction of the castle the contestants filed out onto the playing field. The guests let up a cheer so loud, birds fluttered from the dense treetops behind them. In their shirtsleeves and wearing kilts, they walked proudly before the crowd. They walked with heads held high, proudly displaying the tartan they had been forced to set aside years before.

The older guests recalled the days when all men dressed in their native garb. The younger ones tasted the glory of their heritage in a manner they had never experienced. And those who had proudly worn their plaids in Scotland's last fight for independence shouted with lusty yells amid tears of remembrance. In that small corner of Argyllshire, the old Scotland was resurrected, if only for an afternoon.

Lachlan walked onto the field, blond hair loose and hanging to the middle of his back. His face was lightly tanned and already beaded with sweat. *What a beautiful creature,* Alix thought. A Norse god come to life. The muscles of his calves constricted in powerful definition with each step. His face creased with a large grin as he waved into the crowd. Rebecca's face shone from her seat among the commoners.

Duncan's father, the Duke of Argyll, stood up from his box.

"Members of clans Campbell and Maclachlan, esteemed guests, lords and ladies," he called in a loud, clear voice, "welcome to the games!"

Applause erupted from all those who had gathered for the festivities.

"We've come to honor the marriage of Alix Maclachlan to my son and heir, Duncan Campbell."

Again, everyone cheered as the duke bade Alix and Duncan stand.

"Alix," he said, "would you do the honors?"

"Aye, m'lord." And with her loudest voice Alix called, "Let the games begin!"

The events proceeded. Lifting the Clach Cuid Fir, the Manhood Stone, was the first event. This heavy stone had been kept in Inveraray's garden for several centuries. The next event was the Highland fling, or putting the shot. Called the Clach Neart, or Stone of Strength, it left many breathing heavily.

"How heavy are those stones?" Philippa asked. She had come from London as promised and was thrilled at the competition, having never seen anything like it.

Kyle answered. "Philippa, they weigh about 30 pounds."

"Goodness," Jenny said. "Why aren't you out there competing, my chief?" she whispered to Kyle.

"I wouldn't want to show up the youngsters. Besides, I get enough exercise carrying you to bed, fair maiden." His lips brushed her ear as he spoke in a whisper.

"What do you mean you get enough exercise? If we weren't here I'd give you a slap, Kyle Maclachlan."

The games continued as, much to the delight of the overheated contestants, an afternoon breeze began to blow down from the hills.

"Excuse me, Alix," Duncan said giving her hand a squeeze. "I'll be back shortly."

Alix's eyes glowed at the scene before her, so rich with tradition. She fingered the yellow silk taffeta of her wedding gown as she watched her brother who so far had been one of the top three men of each event.

The hammer throw was next, followed by the caber toss. Many wondered how anyone could balance the long, straight Scots pine trunk, let alone throw it to land accurately in the 12-o'clock position. Even Lachlan, still young compared to many of the contestants, had to laugh heartily at his own feeble attempt.

A tug-of-war between the Maclachlans and the Campbells was next followed by pole vaulting and finally, the footraces.

"Alix, look!" Philippa was tugging at her sleeve in excitement. "It is good old Duncan!"

Changed from his formal wedding clothes into the blue, green, and black tartan kilt of his family, Duncan, looking lean and tall next to the other contestants, lined up for the race.

Her bridegroom suddenly turned and walked over to her.

"What are you doing, Duncan?" Alix asked, taking the hand he offered to her.

"I may not be a true man of the games, but I am one who has always enjoyed a good footrace."

"With limbs that long, I'll bet you're fast, aren't you, Duncan?" Philippa asked enthusiastically.

Duncan smiled with a mischievous twinkle. "Let us just admit, fair ladies, that sometimes it is best to travel lightly!"

The route was called out as the runners lined up. "Around the perimeter of the field, down to the loch, circle around the castle and back."

At the shot of the pistol, the race began. The men started off swiftly as neither one nor the other broke free from the pack. Alix and Philippa were on their feet, trying to contain a ladylike composure, but cheering on Duncan with all their might as the group disappeared to make the run to the loch.

The crowd settled down a bit as they waited to see who would emerge first from behind the castle.

"Do you think he will win?" Philippa asked Alix excitedly.

"I don't know! This is such a surprise," Alix answered. "But I've never seen Duncan do anything he didn't excel in. Except ride. And he only did that because he loves me."

Philippa smiled. "And he does love you, Alix."

"I know. Isn't it wonderful?"

The crowd picked up again as a lone runner shot from behind the castle.

"Who is that?" everyone was asking, and when it became clear, the cheering erupted with such a force no one cared about circumspection any longer.

"Go, Duncan, go!" Alix yelled with all her might as Aaron, in second place, veered into sight.

Duncan Campbell, running the course with athletic grace and ease, destroyed the competition. Everyone under the pavilion, including both sets of parents, stood with their mouths open.

The Duke of Argyll turned to Kyle. "I didn't know he could do that!" He turned to Alix. "Did you know he could do that?"

"No, your grace."

Everyone else shook their heads from side to side. Duncan had surprised them all. He was walking toward them, breathing heavily, but thrilled with his victory.

Alix ran down to meet him on the field. "You were wonderful!" she cried as her feet hastened toward him.

They met halfway and he picked her up and whirled her around as he kissed her lips. Much to the delight of all who loved them.

• • •

Breathing heavily and sweating profusely, Aaron sauntered off the field toward a group of castle servants. Surprise registered on Clementine's face when he stopped in front of her.

"I shall fetch you some refreshment, sir," she said immediately, shyly dropping her eyes in his presence.

"Your hankie will do, Clementine," Aaron said.

With shaking fingers she reached into the pocket of her gown and drew it forth. Aaron bowed and held it up to wipe his forehead. Its scent was clean and smelled of honeysuckle. His eyes closed at the fragrance's innocent beauty. So unlike the heady perfumes of London.

He looked up into her eyes and bowed. "I shall accept this as a token of victory from a maiden fair. Even if I did only take second place."

Her eyes widened and her breathing stopped. With gentle fingers Aaron reached up and softly caressed her cheek.

"Sir?" she questioned his gesture.

"You really are a beautiful woman, Clementine."

Then he turned and walked toward the castle.

It had begun.

• • •

"Ya' love her, dinna' ya'?"

Forthright and to the point, Deborah Brodie Maclachlan inquired of her brother's melancholy behavior.

"Aye, that I do. But I never dared to even think that it would end up any other way than that which it has. And to be quite honest, when I found out it was Duncan they had been talkin' about kidnappin', I almost lowered my bow," he said with a twinkle in his eye.

Deborah laughed.

"Although I havena' seen much of the world, sister, I dinna' believe there is anyone more fair than Alix Maclachlan."

"Alix Campbell now, Robin."

"Aye. Alix Campbell."

"Well," she sighed, "there are other women in Kilbride."

He nodded, looking straight into her eyes, his own filled with the sweet, quiet ache of longing. "There can be no other woman for me."

Deborah stood over him and held down her hand. "Walk with me, Brother. I'm of a mind to take some fresh air."

"Ya might as well admit defeat and go," Joshua said dryly. "Ya' know how our Deborah Jane can be."

Robin complied, easily rising from his cross-legged position.

"I'm sorry, Robin," she said simply when they were a hundred or so yards away. "I canna' say I know what you're feelin' right now. I've loved my Joshua, it seems, ever since I can remember."

"You're one of the lucky ones then, Deborah."

"Perhaps there is something you could do to keep your mind off o' things." Deborah's voice was bright.

Robin turned to look at her.

"It's just a thought, really," she hesitated, thinking about it further as they walked along near the edge of the forest. "Sit down, Robin."

A soft patch of grass cradled them and she took his hand. "Open up your own shop!"

"What?"

"There's plenty of room behind Mother's house to build a shed. And ya' canna' help but admit that it would do ya' good to work with your hands more!"

Robin couldn't help but smile. They would never understand who he really was. But he wasn't going to argue with her. It wouldn't do any good anyway.

"I'll be thinkin' about it," he said, giving her hand a squeeze, then letting go. He had no intention of setting up his own shop. Not yet.

Deborah nodded absentmindedly, head full of plans. Lachlan would help, she was sure. And, of course, the chief.

It would be wonderful. Robin would have a place to call his own in the world.

He left for his cave a few minutes later.

• • •

The Trouble I Have Found

The trouble I have found
Is weighted with a stone.
For her who caused my grief
My wrathe and rage are great.
Her skin like froth of waves,
Ruddy and soft her hand,
Her lips like berries red,
My soul she gently seized.
Since I slept last night,
Sad indeed my state,
I thought she was beside me,
That I saw her smile.
She's not been since the day,
When began my grief.
She of curling locks,
And colour richly red;
Five jewels in a knot,
In the maiden's name.

—From "The Book of the
Dean of Lismore"
Translated by John M'Murrich

• • •

His eyes still startled her.

How could I have ever thought of him as average? Alix asked herself as she and Duncan looked out over the waters of the

Tiber. A transformation had occurred in her mate. The honeymoon had been doing wonders for him. No longer was his skin pale and sallow. And with the overabundance of fresh air, his appetite had picked up considerably. She remembered how wan and painfully thin he had been when they first met. Now, with blooming cheeks and ten pounds added, he was still lean, but was the picture of health. Already the day was warm, but their little villa let in plenty of air and the servants gave them as much privacy as they could wish for.

"You have the most beautiful eyes I have ever seen, Duncan."

He looked embarrassed and fumbled in his coat pocket for his pipe.

"No. I really do mean it. And I'm not the only one who thinks so."

"Oh?" His eyebrows raised in genuine surprise. "Who else thinks so—your mother?"

Alix laughed. "Philippa Lundly, it just so happens, agrees with me wholeheartedly."

"Ah, Philippa." He was puffing away. "She's a wonderful young lady. I'm sure you must miss her friendship, Alix."

"I do, but now that I have you I don't miss her nearly as badly."

It was Duncan's turn to laugh. "I love your honesty, my darling. You two must have made quite a pair. It's a shame she wears those ghastly dresses!"

Alix held her hand up to her mouth to stifle a chuckle as she stared at a barge trudging down the river. "She positively hates them! It's her mother who makes her wear them. And in any case, she won't have to be worrying soon about pleasing Lady Janet."

"That's so. When did you say her wedding was?"

"It's in October."

"Then we shall round out our honeymoon in London."

"Oh, may we, Duncan?" Alix was clearly delighted. "I didn't want to ask to shorten our trip."

"Of course, my darling. I'd do anything to see your eyes light up like that."

Alix leaned forward and kissed him soundly.

"Anything?" she asked him provocatively.

"Yes," he said as he lifted her into his arms. "Anything."

The sheer curtains fluttered into the room, borne on the summer breeze that cooled the bedroom as they shared their love in gentle tenderness.

• • •

July burned its way into Venice as Alix and Duncan traveled the wonders of Italy, their love blossoming with a fervor. An appreciation of each other's character and inner qualities ripened with sweetness. And their time was not only spent lazing in villas and inns but visiting the poorer sections of the cities and villages in which they stayed.

A dream was born late in September in Calais.

"We shall start a school," Duncan announced one afternoon as they walked down the street of a small village.

"What?"

"Father is due to be around for years. I have always wanted to teach. I simply cannot imagine rotting away at Inveraray until I inherit the title."

"What kind of school are you talking about?"

Duncan's voice held an excitement. "A school for unfortunate children. Orphans, children whose parents could never afford to give them an education and yet who show extreme promise."

"Children like Ned?" She had already told Duncan of the orphan boy's genius.

"Precisely."

"Where?"

"Around Inveraray, I suppose."

"Mama will be thrilled with the project," Alix said. "Oh, Duncan, it's something we can do together. For the Savior!"

Duncan's mind was already humming along, planning at a frantic pace.

Suddenly they missed the green hills of home even more.

"Would you like to get back to Scotland, my darling?" Duncan said.

Alix nodded. She had been feeling sick for several days now. She ran the back of her fingers down the side of his neck. "I should like that, my love."

"I shall find passage for us tomorrow."

She sighed with satisfaction. Life would be even better soon.

"A child is coming, Duncan," she whispered in his arms that night.

Duncan had never been happier. A new life, a fulfilling life was before them, and they would share it all with the visible evidence of their love. A child.

"How I do love you, Alix," he whispered in the darkness every so often as she slept soundly next to him. He couldn't sleep. And he didn't mind at all. There were many wonderful things to plan.

Yet a dry sense of foreboding permeated the fibers of his being, increasing each day that they drew closer to the woods and hills of Inveraray.

CHAPTER

17

Late October, 1765

"Look! It's snowing!" Alix pointed out the carriage window.

Inveraray was up ahead. Duncan's brain shivered even though he loved snow. What lay before them? Dread became increasingly real, incessantly strong with each revolution of the carriage's wheels.

He donned a smile and squeezed her hand as the hazy shades of winter embedded their papery shadows in the private recesses of his heart.

"It is beautiful isn't it, my darling?"

She turned quickly and kissed his cheek as they turned up the long drive to the castle. "We're home, Duncan."

"Yes, Alix."

In the dimness of the coach, lost in her joy, Alix failed to notice the pallor that had replaced her husband's healthy complexion, despite the smile in his voice. There was so much to lose now that he was no longer a bachelor.

Deep inside, the root of distrust that had begun growing years ago concerning Aaron flowered. The morning he had been shot, Aaron had conveniently rode up several hours later. The highwaymen? Aaron arrived from London that same day.

What a pleasant surprise, Aaron! Imagine you showing up at Castle Lachlan after all this time! Duncan smirked. He had always known Aaron wasn't exactly Cambridge material, but the timing of his attempts were nothing short of the plannings of an imbecile.

It was all too clear. Aaron was next in line to inherit the duchy. He had come from London, hired the assassins, and would be right there to take over Inveraray once Duncan's father died. Duncan's heart broke.

Doesn't he know I would gladly give him the dukedom if he would simply ask? he whispered in the recesses of his heart. "All I've ever wanted to do is teach."

"What did you say, Duncan?" Alix asked.

"Nothing, my love." He squeezed her hand. "Just thinking out loud. Look, there's Inveraray Castle now."

Alix looked excitedly out of the coach window.

Surely I've figured it out, he thought. *But I have to be absolutely certain. And catching Aaron could not prove to be difficult, could it? The trick will be keeping the whole thing from Alix. Yet in her present state of pregnancy, I have no other choice but to keep it a secret.*

• • •

"Here you are, m'lady. Where is his grace?"

Mrs. Mackay came in with a breakfast tray, setting it down with a clink. Alix looked at it hungrily as Plutarch jumped off the bed and ran down the hall. He had already been out with Duncan. The dog always accompanied him on his early-morning jaunts.

Mrs. Mackay eyed the young dog as he loped from the room.

"His grace is already in his study." Alix put her feet on the floor and grabbed her robe. They had been home for a month. "Do you know, Mrs. Mackay, that this is the first morning I have felt I could actually eat?"

The housekeeper smiled with her mouth. The warmth in her voice surprised even her. "I remember it well, m'self. It felt so wonderful just to feel normal."

"The thought of carrying a child is miraculous, isn't it?" Alix sat down at the table by her window and picked up a piece of toast.

"Aye," Mrs. Mackay sounded wistful, "it is. Bein' a mother has been the only real joy of m'life. I dinna' know what I would do without m'Clementine." She reached down and poured Alix's tea into a china cup. "The dear girl means everythin' to me. There's nothin' I wouldna' do to see her happy."

"I can see why. She's a lovely girl. Inside and out."

"There's no one who can hold a candle to her, m'lady, if ya' dinna' mind m'sayin' so."

"Not at all. You must be proud of her. What was her father like?"

"Ya' wouldna' believe me if I told ya', m'lady."

"And why is that, Mrs. Mackay?"

"Let us just say that she's closer to her father than you'd ever imagine."

· · ·

Alix couldn't have realized what life with Duncan would be like. Slow strolls in the afternoon. Quiet evenings in the library. Winter at Inveraray took on a fairylike quality in the beautiful castle which buffered the force of the Highland gales as the icicles added to their length. She felt safe. Just like at Kilbride. And because of him.

"Duncan?" she looked up from her book as the fire blazed before their propped-up feet. "When do you think we'll start the school?"

"When summer comes I'm arranging a trip for us to London. We should be able to do much of the planning from there and engage an architect as well."

"An architect?"

"Yes, Alix. I want to do this right. Two beautiful buildings to begin with, facing the loch. One for classrooms and the library. The other for dormitories."

Her excitement was growing. "I know the first person I want to be enrolled."

"Ned." Duncan guessed correctly.

"Aye, Ned." She reached out to stroke the back of his hand. "He's going to be thrilled. I can't wait to get started."

It was almost Christmas; spring seemed interminably future.

Duncan reached forward and placed a hand on her slightly protruding stomach. "After the birth, as soon as you feel capable, we'll go."

The babe would come in June, Alix knew. It would be a lovely month for travel with a wee one.

"Until then, there's much we can talk about," she said with enthusiasm. "Classes. Teachers. Endowment. There's so much to do!"

"Alix," Duncan's voice was tender, "I am a lucky man to be able to share my life with you."

"Nonsense!" Alix chided. "Luck had nothing to do with it. God called us to be together, my love. Make no mistake about it."

She leaned forward and kissed his cheek. "Duncan, I love you so."

"And I love you, Alix. I hate to admit it, but it certainly has been nice having Inveraray to ourselves with Father in London until January."

"Well . . . there is Aaron," Alix said with her mouth a bit twisted.

Duncan chuckled and put more wood on the fire.

"He certainly has kept to himself, though, hasn't he, Duncan?"

"Yes." Duncan said the word quietly.

"It makes me wonder what he's been up to." Alix voiced Duncan's feelings, but for different reasons. She had found out from Philippa about his reputation as a ladies' man. Still, she liked him, and made it a point to pray for him. There was something inherently longful about him.

"Oh, he sticks to a usual routine. Rides in the early morning. Before luncheon he stays in his room and writes. Then he wanders the countryside and the villages during the day looking, I suppose, for inspiration for his plays."

"Well, at least you don't have to worry about him," Alix said. "And to think I thought he would be intrusive on us!"

And so the months played on before them. Christmas came and went. Hogmanay as well. And Alix and Duncan had never known such happiness and contentment. Neither had Clementine Mackay.

• • •

28 February, 1765

The babe grows within my beloved Alix, and I am filled with much dread. So far Aaron has been behaving impeccably. If it is Aaron, perhaps he has changed his mind, for I have been home for four months now and there have been no more attempts. Obviously, God is watching over me.

My cousin surprised me tonight. I caught him kissing fair Clementine in the library.

• • •

Duncan set down his pen, blotted the paper, folded it crisply, and placed it in his journal. She said she loved his letters, especially finding them tucked away in unsuspected places.

Time to go to bed.

He blew the lamp out in his study. Alix said to wait until midnight, and the clock was just about to chime as he made his way up to her bedchamber. Soft light shone under the doorway and, pushing upon the door's surface, he entered the room, accompanied by the tinny tones of the burled mantel clock chiming in a new day.

The glorious smell of flowers wafted around him. But the sight before his eyes was yet more wonderful.

"Come to me, my husband."

She knelt in the middle of the bed. Candles were placed on every table or surface the room afforded. And all around her petals of flowers taken from the greenhouse were strewn. A wreath circled her hair, which flowed around her completely. Her belly, rounded and filled with his child, caught the dim candlelight upon its soft curve.

"Alix."

He could only say her name he was so overcome with love at the sight of her.

"Come to me, my husband," she repeated and he complied. Gently he knelt in front of her as tenderly they kissed. And for barely an instant, Duncan was sad for her.

"I loved you, Alix. Always remember that."

They looked at each other for a split second of confusion, and life became abruptly urgent as she pulled him tightly to her and kissed him with a passion she had never known.

She would always remember those words.

• • •

Our baby's cheek will not be any softer, Duncan thought as he leaned down and kissed her. Her breathing was soft and comforting to him, and he put the palm of his hand in front of her mouth to feel the evidence of life coming from her lungs. He thought of the conversation they had after they had finished loving each other, filled with all their hopes and dreams. Alix's face had shone with love as they talked about what to name the baby.

"How about Lachlan?" Alix asked, snuggling into the sheets and laying her head on Duncan's shoulder.

"I am not sure about that. What do you say we go against tradition and simply pick out a name we like?"

"Why not? There isn't a law against not naming your child after a relative."

"Precisely," he laughed. "Whom do you most admire?"

"That's easy. The apostle Peter. He's the most like me," Alix smiled. "How about you?"

"Well . . . since you have taken care of the Scriptural name, I shall think of something else." He hesitated, thinking. "I've always admired Alexander the Great."

"But that's a wonderful name. I love the name *Alexander*."

"Well, then," Duncan kissed her head, Alexander it is. Alexander Peter Campbell."

"That sounds nice, doesn't it?"

"Yes, my darling. And the matter was certainly settled quickly. I've heard some nightmares . . ."

"Me too, Duncan," Alix said. "I was hoping we wouldn't begin the age-old arguments of what to name the baby!" She kissed him soundly. "What are your plans for tomorrow?"

"I thought I should awaken, think about how much I love you. Go for a walk. Think about how beautiful I think you are. Eat breakfast. Think about how much I would like to be kissing you. Work on compiling my research. And think about how blessed I am to spend the rest of my life with you!"

Alix looked tenderly at this man she adored so. "You really are a busy man, and a romantic one, too. And this just proves it."

"I've been told that before."

He kissed her.

"Oh yes? And by whom?"

"Simply the most stunning, intelligent woman that has ever walked the hills of the British Isles." He kissed her again. Longer this time.

"She must be something. Should I be jealous?"

"Absolutely." And his lips found hers again, traveling down her throat to her shoulder.

"Duncan Campbell," Alix said. He looked up with smoky eyes. "Will you love me forever?"

"Alix Campbell, I'll love you beyond eternity."

. . .

The darkness of predawn covered him as Duncan set out on his morning stroll. Its ebony hue, shapeless yet charged with life, pulled him into its quiet world. It had been a mild winter. The snow was gone and the loch had thawed almost completely. He started off slowly, as he did every morning, praying as his day began.

The wind blew, softly dark, humid, and suddenly cold.

CHAPTER
18

The Nuns' Song of the
Shipwrecked Irish Queen

Smooth her hand, Fair her foot,
Graceful her form,
Winsome her voice,
Gentle her speech,
Stately her mien,
Warm the glance of her eye,
Mild the look on her face,
While her white breast heaves on her bosom
Like the black-headed seagull
> *on the gently heaving wave.*

Holy is the woman of the gold-mist hair,
With tender babe in the crook of her arm:
No food for either of them under the arch of the sky,
No shelter under the sun to shield them from the foe.

The shield of the Son of God covers her,
The breath of the Son of God guides her,
The word of the Son of God is food to her,
His star is a bright revealing light to her.

The darkness of night is to her as the brightness of day,
The day to her gaze is always a joy,
While the Mary of grace is everywhere
With the seven beatitudes compassing her,
> *The seven beatitudes compassing her.*

· · ·

A cry issued from her lips as the dream became vivid. Bright-blue vivid.

Alix awakened with a start, sitting straight up in bed. Anxiety shrouded her well-being, and even the feel of her rounding belly did nothing to comfort her. Reaching for the silken bell cord, she pulled tentatively, the feeling of the dream still surrounding her like the mists on the moors. The silence, thick and dense, challenged her peace of mind in loud hums within her ears. She pulled again on the scarlet cord.

Clementine came rushing in with a tray several minutes later. Her brows knit together in kind concern when Alix didn't speak.

"Is there anything amiss, m'lady?"

Alix nodded. "Do you ever dream, Clementine?"

"Nay. Not often. An' when I do I dinna' remember much. Bu' I do know that some people dream dreams as real as life. Sometimes even more real. Did ya' have an odd dream, m'lady?" She talked as she worked, spreading a napkin, setting out the cup and saucer on the side table, pouring the tea from the pot, through a silver strainer and into the bone china cup, adding one spoonful of sugar and just a dot of milk.

"Aye, I did," she said softly, watching Clementine's hands. "It was about Duncan. He was sitting in his study and the fire was getting low. His eyelids became heavy, and as he lay his head down, a draft of wind blew the papers, all of his poems, all of his plans for the school, everything he's ever done, into the fire. I yelled as the fire began to curl the edges and reached for the pitcher of water sitting on a table near the door. But when the water hit the pages, it dissolved the ink. All was lost. Desperately I tried to waken Duncan as the room took on the appearance of an inferno. But he would not stir. Then I awoke."

" 'Tis a strange one . . ." Clementine mused, rubbing her chin with her hand. "But it probably doesna' mean anythin', ma'am. Mother's always told me that when women are carryin' they are especially prone to queer dreams."

"I suppose you are right." Her sigh was wooden.

"Of course I am. How about getting dressed now? It will take your mind off of it."

"That's a good idea. I believe I shall take breakfast downstairs with my husband this morning."

"Of course, ma'am, 'tis a wonderful idea. Only he hasna' yet returned from his walk."

"I wonder where he is?"

"The sun hasna' yet come completely out o' hidin'. I'm sure tha' he'll be back presently. Now there, ma'am, let me help ya' on with your gown, an' I'll hand ya' your cup o' tea to sip on while I do your hair."

Once dressed in a plum velvet day dress, Alix sat down in front of the mirror at her dressing table.

"It really was a peculiar dream." Alix shivered slightly, even though the liquid of the tea steamed its way down to her stomach.

Clementine brushed gently, chattering softly. "Never ya' mind, ma'am. You'll be feelin' more like your old self when ya' go downstairs to the dinin' room an' see your husband sittin' there all refreshed an' hungry from his stroll."

"You're right, Clementine. Thank you."

Soon Clementine had pulled Alix's hair up in a braided bun. She ran down the main staircase and into the dining room. Aaron was sitting alone at the long table with a plate of eggs, bacon, kidneys, and toast. An English-style breakfast.

"Have some breakfast, Alix," he said with a tense kind of smile. Mrs. Mackay had come to him last night. She demanded he make a decisive move toward Clementine soon.

"Thank you."

Toast and jam were all she could imagine putting into her stomach at the moment, and soon she was sitting across from him, although she wished she had stayed in her room.

"Where's Duncan?" Aaron asked between bites.

"I suppose he hasn't returned from his walk yet," Alix replied. "Maybe he felt he needed a bit more exercise than usual today."

"Hmmm. I suppose he forgot our appointment."

Alix took a bit of toast. "Did you have plans to meet for breakfast?"

"Aye. He was going to go over the first draft of my play with me this morning. I don't think I could do this without him."

"He's brilliant," Alix said matter-of-factly.

"Yes. I believe I was the one who told you that first."

Alix smiled. Aaron seemed different somehow. Better. More settled. Perhaps the writing life agreed with him.

"So you did."

They smiled into each other's eyes. Both remembered the conversation at the castle ruins, and the friendship that had woven between them, especially since his return to Inveraray.

Just then Mrs. Mackay came in. She began to load up the tray with the food.

"Pardon me, Mrs. Mackay," Alix interrupted her task, "but my husband hasn't come back from his walk yet. I'm sure he'll be hungry."

She appeared startled, and quickly put the covered dishes back on the sideboard. "Not back yet? I wonder what is takin' him so long? He's usually been back at least half an hour by now. Do ya' suppose he's all right?"

"I'm sure he's fine."

"I'll just bring up some more hot tea then," the house-keeper said. "How are ya' feelin' this mornin', Lady Alix?"

Alix patted her stomach with a laugh. "As well as one can expect to in the mornings, Mrs. Mackay."

"Dinna' worry, m'lady, 'twill soon be passin'." She picked up the silver tea service and left the room as Alix settled back into her chair with a sigh.

"Alix," Aaron said, "do you want me to go look for him?"

"Perhaps in a bit. I doubt if there's anything to worry about. I'm going to try and write some letters."

"All right. I'm going riding later on this morning. Is there anything I can pick up for you in the village—some paper, a new quill?"

"No, thank you, Aaron. I have all that I need."

Breakfast was finished quickly, and soon Alix found herself at her desk catching up on correspondence. After several letters she looked at the clock. Noon. *I'll go down and see if Duncan is in his study.*

It was empty. And Duncan was nowhere to be found.

An hour later Aaron strode in, still windblown and dressed in his riding clothes. "He's not back yet, is he?"

By this time worry had creased Alix's brow, and she nodded from side to side.

"This isn't like him," Aaron began to pace on the carpet in front of Duncan's desk. "This isn't like him at all."

"Are you worried something has happened to him?"

"Aye. I rode all through the woods and by the loch. Through the fields as well. Been gone for three hours, Alix. Surely I would have seen him."

"But what could have happened? Why would he have just disappeared?"

Aaron sat down near the fire. "Have a seat, Alix. There's something I must tell you."

"What is it?" She gathered her skirts and sat on the edge of a chair.

"Duncan was hiding something from you. Something he didn't understand himself."

Her stomach felt weighted. "Tell me, Aaron."

"That shot in the clearing was no accident. And the last spring, on his way back home from Kilbride the evening I showed up from London, two highwaymen held him up in his carriage."

"What!"

"Yes. It's true. I came upon them myself. If it hadn't been for the Last Highlander who overheard the men in the forest, Duncan would be dead. They weren't highwaymen, but hired assassins."

"Didn't he notify the authorities?"

"No. He wanted to find out on his own. Only all the leads he turned up ended up being nothing. Whoever hired them covered his tracks well. Not to mention these people have a code of honor."

"So Robin saved him then? I wonder why he didn't tell me about it?"

"He promised Duncan he would not say a word."

Hope grew. "Well, if Robin saved him once, he can save him again." She was writing quickly on a piece of parchment. "Charlie!" she yelled to the footman in the entry hall who stood before her a moment later. "Have the stable's swiftest horse saddled and a messenger made ready immediately. I need to get a message to Kilbride with all possible haste! I'm sending for Robin Brodie."

Charlie bowed and headed to the stables. The smile didn't appear this time. The Last Highlander. Would he come when Lady Alix called? Fear wrapped itself possessively around his black heart.

Alix felt much better when she heard the messenger ride swiftly out of the courtyard. She knew Robin could track anything. And surely he would find her husband. Rescue him as he did before. Rescue him as he had rescued her.

The Duke of Argyll walked into the room. "Has anyone seen Duncan this morning? I need him to help me go over..."

"He has not returned from his walk, Uncle."

His concern was immediate. "It's not like him. Not like him at all."

"No, it is not," Aaron said in an agitated voice. "I've been all over the estate for the past three hours, and there isn't a trace. There's no explanation for it. Not with regard to Duncan."

"I'll send a search party. Right now."

"You will not have to," Alix said. "I just sent a messenger to Kilbride. Robin Brodie will be coming."

"The Last Highlander?" Douglas went white. "Do you think he'll come, even for you, Alix?"

"Aye, m'lord. He'll come. And he'll find your son."

Alix began praying as she never had before. Her hands shook, but she willed herself strong.

Two hours later Lachlan's prize horse, his fastest stallion, veered into the courtyard. Robin jumped off Storm as Alix opened the door, ran down the steps, and into the safety of his arms.

CHAPTER
19

Bonnie George Campbell

Hie upon Hielands, and laigh upon Tay
Bonnie George Campbell rade out on a day;
Saddled, and bridled, and gallant rade he;
Hame cam' his guid horse, but never cam' he.

Doun cam' his mither dear greetin' fu' sair;
And out ran his bonnie bride rivin' her hair;
"My meadow lies green, and my corn is unshorn,
My barn is too big, and my babe is unborn."

Saddled and bridled and booted rade he,
A plume in his helmet, a sword at his knee;
But toom cam' his saddle, all bluidy to see;
Hame cam' his guid horse, but never cam' he.

                     –Anonymous

• • •

The air was deathly still. Robin walked slowly.

It was easy to see that nothing had interrupted nature's cycle in the belt of trees across the clearing. Robin knew what the woods were, and what they were not. He could find nothing.

"Find him, Robin . . . please," Alix's eyes had pleaded with him earlier. Robin knew that Duncan's life was in danger.

The loch, with its shallow shoreline, stood before him, less than ten feet away. His heart ached for Alix, her words echoed silently in his mind as he walked along the shore, eyes sharpened, ears alert, body aware of each blade of grass, each stick, each stone.

Stones.

He knelt.

Into the hardened ground a stone was pressed, even with the level of the soil. Another was exactly the same an inch away. But there was no indentation. Something hard and flat, and of considerable weight had pushed the stone down. Not an animal, to be sure. A deer would have left a track. And a small animal's weight could not have done this. Suspicion brightened within him and he knew. Man had done this. A boot had made it such.

Slowly he walked to the water, looking down. Always looking down. Crouching down at the water's edge, Robin put his hand into the frigid waters. Careful not to touch the bottom, not to disturb the sediment, he swirled the water softly with one hand, feeling it flow against his closed fingers.

"Aye," he whispered to himself, " 'tis not natural at all."

Stones had been drug in one direction, deeper into the water. Animals never entered the water to drink. And animals never deviated from what came naturally. He stood to his full height and walked further out, oblivious to the chilly waters that saturated his leggings, then his kilt. The water deepened quickly and was waist-high after four or five steps. His mind rendered a possible scenario.

Down Robin looked into the water, searching. In the murky depths, a shadow. This was no stone or fallen log. Robin Brodie breathed in deeply and prayed as he submerged under the water.

• • •

"Duncan will live on . . ." the Duke of Argyll's voice sifted over the congregation gathered by the tomb. The mourning women cried louder. Alix stood as stone. Her Highlander stood beside her.

Douglas looked tenderly at his daughter-in-law. "You brought more happiness to his life than his studies ever did. You brought him true joy."

Tears filled her eyes. She squeezed Robin's hand, searching for strength, seeking to hold back the maelstrom of grief that had not ceased to beset her since the day before.

"Aye," the duke continued. "He did not leave us barren and lonely. For the Lady Alix will bring our Duncan back to us. In the form of his son. The future laird of Clan Campbell."

The servants had gathered for the funeral as well. From butler to serving boy. From housekeeper to scullery maid. Almost everyone stood with heads bowed, eyes glistening with unshed tears. Almost.

Mrs. Mackay took note of the duke's words. Her mouth formed a thin line. Her eyes froze. Her heart paused its rhythm momentarily, then speeded up. He was right. Alix's body held the next heir.

Her heart became a darker shade of black.

"Rest assured," Douglas's eyes blazed with unsatisfied, righteous anger, "the blood of my son *will* be avenged. We will bring the man to justice who has done this, I vow to each one of you. But the road ahead of us will not be an easy one. Duncan was a gentle man. A good, kind, giving man. Who would want to kill him? He was a simple scholar, a man who cherished the dreams and talents of the Scots, who preserved the workings of their hearts through his translations. A school he and Alix were planning to found. For orphans and children whose parents could not ever dare hope to have educated. And he did all these things knowing that someday he would take up where I left off. It would have been easy for him to have done nothing but wait until I died. But that was not Duncan. The title meant nothing to him if it was not a means whereby he could do some good, show some kindness. . . ." The duke took out a handkerchief and wiped his brow. He could not go on. The minister quickly intervened.

Prayers were said. And Duncan Campbell's body was laid in a box of cold marble bearing his name.

Finally, Alix cried. Clean and pure, her grief was absolute, blowing through her soul like a clear, heavy breeze. She ran quickly home to their room, buried herself between their sheets still carrying his scent, and wept until the next morning's light flickered outside her window.

The death knell tolled through the village as the funeral procession made its way back to Inveraray Castle. Hollow soundings proclaimed an unnatural death.

CHAPTER

20

The journal lay open before her. The tale was told in its entirety, of that she was sure. The book opened at the command of her thumbs as they dug into the contents. When she saw the familiar, strong, yet scrawly handwriting, she breathed a sigh of relief. She was doing the right thing.

Their initial meeting, the death of her sister, their engagement, the shooting in the clearing. The spring of bliss. The highwaymen, Robin's secret. Their wedding. The honeymoon and how fully her husband was in love with her. She read of it all. How could he have hidden it from her?

The entries raced before her eyes, taking her with them into Duncan's happiness and plunging her into his misgivings, his fear, his pain. Aaron.

Did he really suspect his cousin? Alix couldn't fathom it. Yes, the evidence seemed to point in Aaron's direction, but she knew Aaron better than that, didn't she?

• • •

Robin came back to Inveraray a month after the funeral.

"The fire is low," he said and crouched down to put on more wood in the drawing room fireplace.

"Yes."

"The babe still moves?" he asked.

"Aye. Fine and strong."

"Good."

"Robin, please sit down. I've been reading through Duncan's journal."

He sat on the footstool in front of her. How he still loved her. In her grief, with tear-stained cheeks and hollow eyes, he wanted nothing more than to take her into his arms, to shield her from the pain in her heart she felt each time the bairn kick in her belly. He could only be a support to her, and he would strive to keep her from going under here in the wintry confines of the castle.

Alix held Duncan's journal securely in her lap.

"What is that, Alix?"

"It is Duncan's journal. I've been reading it every day. Trying to learn something new. Trying to find a reason someone would wish to . . ." She handed the book to Robin with trembling hands. "Read for yourself. I cannot bear to say the words aloud."

Robin did as he was bid, a feeling of danger growing with each word.

"Two times . . ." he said softly.

"Aye, two times they tried, before. . . ."

"Perhaps I should have told you about the highwaymen."

"Nay, Robin. You gave your word to Duncan."

He read on through the autobiography of a man hunted, yet loved. The fear. The happiness. The heavy dread. The love of Alix. He looked up sharply.

"Do *you* think it was Aaron?"

"I don't know, Robin. It makes sense. He's the only person in the world who stood to gain from Duncan's death."

Robin nodded.

Resting her elbow on the armrest, Alix cupped her chin in her hand. The room was dark behind them, and she felt as if Robin was the only friend the world afforded.

"Alix," he touched her hand, "I'm takin' ya' back to Kilbride. I'm takin' ya' home."

He reached for her hand and looked with unaccustomed boldness into her eyes. "I know what's best for ya', m'lady."

As in the woods so many years ago, he became her protector once again. A shy knight. Valiant and devoted entirely. His love demanded it. His past required it.

He bowed his head, not knowing what else to say.

Looking down upon the black curls, she rested her hand gently on top of his head. "Take me home, my Highlander."

"Aye, I shall. It's where ya' belong."

Alix grabbed his hand tightly. A lifeline in a storm the likes of which she had never faced. "Thank you, Robin."

I love you, Alix, he wanted to say. But he merely nodded and held onto her hand until the fire burned low.

"It's time for bed, m'lady."

"Aye, Robin. It is that. But I do not wish to go up to that room."

They sat until the study was dark and cold.

"I saw Aaron and Clementine together." Alix finally spoke.

"Where?"

"Up in one of the turrets."

"Could ya' hear what they were sayin'?"

"Nay. I could only hear murmuring."

"Perhaps he just came upon her whilst she was cleanin' up there?"

"Robin, I peered around the corner when the conversation lulled, and they were kissing."

She shivered.

Robin was quiet as he wrapped his plaid around her. Taking his gaze away from her face, he looked trancelike into the now-cold fireplace. Alix's mind was engaged elsewhere as well.

"It probably doesn't matter anyway. Nothing matters." A sigh came from the innermost recesses of her heart. "There's nothing that we can do to bring him back."

"Nay, Alix," Robin said. "There isna' anything we can do. We just have to make sure ya' come through all of this."

Tears formed in her eyes. "Does it really matter anymore what happens to me?"

The feel of a warm body that was not her husband's, the sense of loss, the fear bore down upon her, and sobbing in her misery, she believed her statement without reserve. What did anything matter anymore? Innocence was gone. Hope was lost. And light was nothing more than an external means of seeing what was in front of one's feet.

Robin merely stroked her hair. He understood. More than she realized. And if his tale could help her . . . tell her he would.

"We could set ya' up in a nice cave somewhere, Alix," he said, a bit of a smile in his voice for the first time. Her eyes opened at this new tone.

"What?"

"Well, why deal with your problems like some normal lass? Go hide yourself away in a cave for 18 years an' try to forget."

Alix sat up. "Do not joke, Robin. It truly is how I feel."

"Aye, an' I understand what you're goin' through." He reached up, caressed a lock of hair. "But I also understand what it means to give up. I did, ya' know. For much, much too long. An' Alix, I hate to see the same thing happen to ya'. Believe me, I know how easy it would be to want to forget right now, for eternity."

Alix shook her head from side to side. "How could you, Robin? You were just a child."

The words were callous. And he knew it. He also realized she was incapable of tact and true concern in the midst of her own personal tragedy.

"I havena' spoken of it since the day it happened. But I will tell ya' now, dear Alix, so that ya' might know how I can understand what it means to lose someone that ya' love. And what it means for someone who holds up your world to be dealt with violently. Perhaps we'll be able to hold one another up durin' this lifetime, for surely this pain is a battle we'll have to face day by day for the rest of our lives."

"All right, Robin," she reached up and touched his scarred cheek. He made no move to stop her action. "Tell me."

The words came easily after so many years of internalization. And with each sentence, Alix's heart went out to Robin more and more deeply. She heard each detail. The battle of Culloden. His father's death. The journey back to his home. The torture of his mother, sisters, and himself and finally...

"An' then, after we made it back to Strathlachlan, I had hope for the first time," Robin wound up his tale. "Grandfather was a kind old man. Joshua Maclachlan was more than man enough to help me along the way. An' we had food to eat."

"What happened?" It was the first Alix had spoken.

"Grandfather came in one evenin' with a mirror that had been m'grandmother's. He proudly gave it to Mother. A cherished heirloom. She cried, of course, then set it on the mantel."

He became a little nervous, and began resting his scarred cheek in his hand. Alix removed his hand. "No, Robin. It is all right. I've seen your face many times."

"When I looked into the mirror, I realized what a monster they had made of me."

"Oh, Robin!" She reached forward to touch his face again.

"I smashed the mirror, and knowin' I would forever be a reminder of the Redcoats' cruelty, I panicked an' ran into the woods."

"But she would have never thought about it like that, Robin. She loved you and wanted you with her. Why didn't you come back home?"

"Once I got out there, I realized how comfortable it was. That I didna' need to worry about hurtin' others, or havin' them hurt for me. Deborah and Kathleen's scars could be covered up with their clothin', but mine would never cease to remind them of the horror they had been put through that awful day when I came home. My face would reveal without ceasin' that I had not been man enough to rescue them from those filthy Redcoats!"

"But no one expected you to!" Alix defended him. "You were only 11 years old!"

"It didna' matter to me then, Alix. I was doin' what I thought was the merciful thing for everyone concerned."

The point was driven home, and Alix nodded.

"You dinna' really wish to die, do ya', Alix?"

"No," she whispered.

"That's good, lass." He reached forward and held her tightly in his arms. "For I would not let ya'. I will always be here to protect ya'."

"What about Aaron?" Alix pulled back a bit.

"I'll watch out for him."

"Do you think I'm in danger by carrying Duncan's child?"

"Maybe. But if it is Clementine and Aaron, they'll probably wait first to see whether or not it is a girl. If it's the title he wants, Duncan had to be killed no matter what."

Alix leaned her head against his chest, feeling the soft wool of his tartan under her cheek. "Poor, poor Duncan."

"Aye, Alix," he soothed softly into her hair, "poor Duncan."

CHAPTER

21

Robin accompanied her to Kilbride. Her home. It had never looked so perfect before. Nothing unnatural ever happened here, it seemed. Just hills and trees and the loch with its blue deepness, cooling to the soul. Calming to the mind.

Alix couldn't help but feel a bit cheered when she thought about the tales of fancy and folklore Duncan had told her on their walks. The water beyond the carriage window made her remember the tale that had been his favorite during his research time in the northern Highlands. Her mind mused back to the afternoon he had kissed her for the first time. She could recall the musical voice drifting around her smoothly with its enchanted tale as they walked together. And her eyes became tender and peaceful as she thought about his eyes as they reflected off the water along which they strolled. She smiled.

"What made ya' smile, Alix?" Robin asked, taking her hand.

"I was thinking about a story my husband told me. A folktale, of course."

"I'm certain he had some fascinatin' tales to tell," Robin encouraged her, knowing fond remembrances were the healing oil to a wounded, lonely heart.

"Aye, but this one was extremely special."

"Do ya' feel like tellin' me?"

Alix looked at him, almost surprised at her own reaction. "Why, yes, Robin. Actually I do." She cleared her throat slightly and began. "A great many years ago ... Duncan always started his stories that way . . . in the western and northern waters of Scotland there swam happy, playful creatures. They were smooth, gray, and lovely in their carefree outlook on life. They were called the selkies."

"Seals, eh?" asked Robin.

"Aye. They may have appeared to be ordinary gray seals. But they were not. For some were half human and loved nothing more than to dance upon the seashore in their human form."

Alix's voice traveled far up to the wild north as she spoke, retreating more fully into her fanciful tale with each syllable uttered, her speech taking on words, phrases, and intonations used by Duncan. Robin could clearly imagine his voice.

"Once upon a time an especially beautiful selkie drifted up to the shore. She was smooth and sleek, and had the most lovely eyes in the region. They were brown and round and as deep as the waters in which she had grown. How much she loved to shed her skin upon the shore. And this she did whenever she could get the chance, for her mother made her work hard and do many chores on the small island where they lived with many other of their type. But even so, she was always glad to get back into the cool waters of the sea. Back to her home. For although much was expected of her, she was loved greatly as well. On this particular summer day she came near the shore. She looked to the north. She looked to the south. And no one could she see.

"With liquid, hoppy, sealish movements she left the water, and slowly, deliciously peeled back the furry, rubbery skin. It was wet and heavy. And underneath lay the softest skin a man had never yet caressed. A fully ripened peach had never blushed more beautifully. She pulled the living pelt back from her face to reveal a head of hair so glorious, so black, it appeared to shine with a blue light. Only upon closer examination could one see the individual glints of blue so bright they seemed to shine from their own source of energy. For surely she did not need even the sun to catch the glistening strands in order to reveal their glory.

"The selkie danced with the wind as nature sighed in pleasure at her graceful movements. The tiny feet left no marks so lightly she stepped, and her arms formed delicate circling arcs, more beautiful than any dancer could ever hope to execute. But someone else, besides the birds and deer, watched the selkie's magnificent performance. For sitting nearby was the son of the laird. Although he, too, was young, he fell in love as he looked upon the beauty of the selkie. 'If it brings misery upon me or no, I shall take the creature for my bride,' he said. For his mother had warned him as he grew up in their castle that to marry a selkie would bring happiness for a time, but misery would be sure to follow. He sat and pondered just how he would accomplish such a wondrous feat, when a young fawn wandered near the selkie. Entranced by the woodland babe's gentle, tender-eyed loveliness, the selkie followed him down the coastline a bit. Her dance was forgotten and so was her pelt.

"The laird's son wasted no time. For he was a crafty fellow, and he knew if he possessed her seal hide she would be in his power. He jumped up and ran toward the skin just as the selkie turned.

"Her hand flew to her lips as they mouthed the word, 'No!' For you see, her mother had warned her many times since her birth of the dangers of leaving her hide unattended. The selkie knew she was trapped. Suddenly she realized her nakedness and sought to cover herself with her hands. She had never felt so wretched in her life. Her freedom was gone.

"That day, he gave her his plaid and, holding her hand ever so gently, he took her home with him to his castle and made her his bride. He was a good man, and he treated her fairly and with much compassion. For ten years they were happy. She bore him healthy sons and daughters, and she never aged at all. Each night as he lay beside her he would marvel at his fortune in having the beautiful selkie as his bride. Ah, but his mother had been right. The happiness was not to last."

Robin frowned.

"One night, in the midst of summer, on a day that was warmer than usual, the selkie was combing her long hair. The children were asleep, and her husband, now the laird, had gone to council with the war leaders of his clan, and she was restless. Naturally, she went down to the shore and looked longingly over the cool waves as they splashed around her delicate feet. She had never felt so homesick in the ten years since she had been taken captive.

"She hung her head sadly as she went back to the castle. The next day she was cleaning out an old trunk her husband kept in their bedroom when her hand hit a hidden latch. The false bottom sprang up and underneath, looking more inviting and comfortable than anything she had ever seen in the past ten years, was her seal hide. 'Oh joy!' she cried, and danced that same willowy dance in the midst of their bedroom that she had danced upon the shore ten years before. Without a thought she ran to the shore, put on her pelt, and hopped as seals do back into the gray, familiar waters of the ocean. Her husband never saw her again. 'Tis a sad tale for he truly loved her. And true love should never be parted so quickly for it comes so rarely."

The recitation stopped, and Alix's eyes which had become glazed in the telling returned to normal. She looked longingly at Robin, but she could not cry.

"He shall live on, Alix," Robin sought to reassure her, "in his work, his tales, his translations."

She nodded. "Yes. I received request from the University of Edinburgh for the body of Duncan's work. The poems and papers are to be published and used for their literature studies. So, in a way, he ended up teaching. It is as you say—his memory will live on."

Robin didn't compare himself with Duncan. He never would again. He just thanked God that Alix had the privilege of being the wife of such a gentleman.

• • •

They passed by old Castle Lachlan. Even when violence took place, as it had so many years ago from the British frigate, Kilbride grew up to claim it back for her own. Ivy grew in abundance up the sides of the structure. Soft, green, frothy, and fluttering in the April zephyr that was gently airing out the last vestiges of winter.

Home. Mama and Papa. Gentle and witty. Strong and courageous. In love with each other. In love with their children. Alix could only pray she would love her own child as much.

I feel so helpless.

Castle Lachlan was in sight.

Helpless, to be sure. All she wanted was to rest in the comfort of the home her parents had made for her. To be free from all that haunted her. And free from the responsibility of being called "adult." She almost envied Violet. Stern, somber Violet. For truly the 11-year-old had not a care in the world that was not of her own imagining. How blessed to be a child.

She wanted to run in from a day in the woods to find a warm supper waiting. She wanted to wrestle with Lachlan. To stick her tongue out at Violet when no one was looking. Her feet ached to kick themselves up on the ottoman in the sitting room and read the entire evening without hauntings and fear and dreadful scenarios of death interrupting her.

"I'm being silly," she said softly.

"What, Alix?" Robin asked as he sat, still holding her hand.

"Nothing, dear Robin. I was simply wishing to be a child again."

He looked deeply in her eyes, understanding with a sympathy of those whose feet had trodden the long, dusty road of painful memories and undetermined fear. Without warning to even himself, he leaned forward and kissed her cheek softly. She did not move away or recoil, but held his hand more tightly as her desolation was punctuated by his innocent action.

"Someday, Alix, someday ya' shall know wha' it is like to emerge from the storm an' walk once again in the rays of the sun."

She smiled sadly and nodded from side to side at his poetic hope. "I wish I could believe you, my Highlander."

"Aye, m'lady. Someday ya' shall. I know it."

The drive lay before them, and soon she was enfolded in the arms of her parents as their tears relayed the deep emotion felt by them both.

But she was home where she could rest her head in peace. And wait.

• • •

Early May

"The babe should be comin' soon, aye?" Robin asked as they sat near the castle ruins.

"I still have a month and a half left. It seems like an eternity."

"Does the bairn move much?" he asked shyly, looking down at her stomach. In the past two weeks he had helped her up so many times, had been leaned on heavily physically and emotionally, so much so that a love for the unseen babe had grown within him. Already he was connected to the child by a commitment to care for its mother.

She grabbed his hand. "Would you like to feel the babe move, Robin?"

He quickly snatched it away, a shocked expression on his face. " 'Twould be unseemly, m'lady, for me to put m'hand upon your belly!"

Alix laughed out loud for the first time in months. "My dearest Robin, if you could only see the expression on your face!"

"Dinna' laugh at me, Alix," he smiled in spite of himself, "I'm just no' accustomed to goin' around puttin' my hand on women's bellies."

"The bairn is moving about right now."

He could see the black silk of her dress moving slightly with each movement of the child within.

"It could stop moving at any time. They're very contrary, these wee ones."

"Alix, are ya' sure?"

Alix nodded quickly, with eyes opened wide and a broad, close-lipped smile lighting up her face. She needed him to put his hand there. Wanted so badly for someone to share this with her.

"All right then."

Reaching forward his hand, he placed it gently on top of her stomach. And waited. Suddenly the babe kicked.

He quickly removed his hand with a small laugh filled with much wonder. "Was tha' a kick?"

"Aye."

"May I . . . ?"

"Of course you may put your hand back!"

He returned it to her belly, feeling the babe kick and move within her.

"Truly, 'tis a miracle. I've never felt anything like it in all m'life." He shook his head from side to side. "To think there's a livin' babe inside of ya'!"

"I know," Alix said wistfully, remembering Duncan. "It is a miracle."

Long after the baby stopped moving, Robin sat with his hand on Alix's stomach, hoping to feel more. They both lazed in a trance of comfortableness, each lost in their own thoughts.

"Ya' know, m'lady," Robin said after quite a while, "m'loyalty and protection will not end when the bairn is birthed. I swore to protect ya' long, long ago."

She turned and looked into his brown eyes. "It was you, wasn't it?"

"What do ya' mean?"

"In the woods. As a child." She put her hand under his and studied the tanned, weathered skin, the clean nails, the wrinkled knuckles, the light scattering of dark hair under them. Turning it over she studied the calloused pink skin of his palm. So work-weary, yet so gentle. The hands were like the man—a study in contrasts. "You used to watch over me, didn't you?"

"Aye. The woods are a dangerous place for a young lass, Alix. It was my duty. And carin' for ya' was the only reason I had for stayin' alive at that time, the only joy I knew."

She smiled into his eyes, his handsomeness raining upon her anew.

He turned his face away in embarrassment, then whispered, "There could be no other way for me, m'lady."

In that moment, Alix knew without a doubt that he had always loved her.

"Let's get goin'," he said gruffly. "Your parents will be worried if I dinna' bring ya' back in time for luncheon."

"Robin?" she asked as they walked up to the door of Castlelachlan. "Are you sure it won't all stop when the baby is born?"

In that moment, Robin knew that she needed him. It was enough.

"Nay. I shall always be there to protect ya'."

He left her in the care of her parents and went to eat with his own. Deborah and Joshua welcomed him gladly.

They sat down to a simple meal of oatcakes, jam, and tea. Deborah set the pot on the table.

"So, Robin, have ya' given any more thought to settin' up your own shop in the village?"

He nodded up and down, surprising everyone in the room.

"Truly, Robin?" Joshua looked at him earnestly. "You're considerin' it?"

"Aye. It's gone beyond consideration, Joshua. I've spoken to Mother about it. She doesna' mind at all me takin' up a little space in her yard."

"When will ya' be startin'?" Deborah smiled in satisfaction, her hands placed on her hips.

"Next week."

The thought didn't frighten him. He thought it would. But it made him feel strong, better able to someday care for . . . He mentally shook his head. Best not to hope just yet. He didn't want to be caught trying to catch shadows which were not there. Alix herself said he had enough patience for the entire clan. He would wait as long as it took.

CHAPTER

22

17 May, 1766

The jewel of death shines only in the dark. A black gem. Jet. Smoky. Enslaving to the very marrow. Misery's essence, hardened into loneliness, regrets, and never-agains. Three months. Almost three months had passed.

The face of Alix Campbell was not what it once was. She ate only for the child within. Her cheekbones were highlighted, bony slashes, the full mouth was stretched, the neck slimmed considerably, now long and swan-like. Childishness in both form and feature were gone. Perhaps they were suspended by grief. Perhaps they were gone forever. She didn't care, she thought, as she looked at her reflection in the mirror.

I don't want to go, a scowl spread across her face.

The invitation a week ago had surprised everyone at Castle Lachlan. Aaron Campbell was marrying Clementine Mackay. It was to be a small ceremony in the chapel at Inveraray Castle. Only immediate family was attending. In Aaron's case, the duke and Alix. And though every shaft of hair on her head stood stiff in its follicle at the thought of being in Inveraray Castle again, she knew she must venture back for the sake of her friend. He had been so faithful in his visits since she returned to Kilbride. She wondered how well-founded Duncan's doubt of his cousin had been.

Dressed in a black velvet gown, a black lace veil pinned over the bun at the back of her head, Alix sighed and looked out at the cool, overcast day. Flat gray. Gray-green. And brown.

"Hello, sister."

Alix wheeled around. "Violet! I didn't hear you come in."

"No," she shook her head and slid the thick brown braid over her shoulder, "most people don't. I just wanted you to know that I think it's nice to have you home." Her eyes scanned the floor at her feet. Hands were folded together in front.

"Thank you." Alix's eyes opened more fully, revealing her surprise at the rare apocalypse of Violet's heart.

"I also want you to know how sorry I am . . ." her feet shifted, "well . . . about . . . Duncan and . . . everything . . . and . . ." Her head stayed bowed and she reached forward her hand. "Well, I'm not the best at . . . saying what I'm feeling."

Alix walked over, took her sister's outstretched hand, and put her other arm around the slim shoulders. "It's all right, Violet."

"No . . ." she shook her head, "no it's not. I've been praying . . . yes . . . praying so much. But I still don't understand how God could let . . . Alix, why does it seem that death devours everything lovely?"

"Oh, Violet," Alix interrupted, hugging her more tightly, "I can understand how you would feel that way. But what happened to Duncan, to Mary Alice, is not God's fault. Why, think of all the *good* things He's done instead. Don't concentrate on the results of the sin which entered the world near the beginning. It only leads to frustration and disillusionment."

Violet nodded, but her eyes betrayed her doubts. Her salvation was going to be hard-won, Alix decided. And yet, God was merciful. In the end, after sin meted out its cruelty and humans were done shaking their fists at the heavens, God was always merciful.

"Just think about the baby coming," Alix squeezed her hand. "You're going to be an aunt. That's something very special. Have you thought about it at all?"

Violet's grin echoed a sudden lightening of heart, and she pulled away and sat on the bed. "Oh, yes, Alix. After you have her I'm going to run in, just like I did with Mary Alice. And I'm going to lift up her fragile little hands, feel the smooth, tiny fingers. And then, after you're rested and she's fed, I'm going to climb up on the bed and hold her in that pink blanket Mama's had around for ages."

"I see you *have* thought about it!"

"But that's not all. When she's old enough I'm going to take her down to the gardens, let her feel the sun on her toes, and smell Mama's roses. She's going to love her Aunt Violet the most."

Alix chuckled. "What if it's a boy?"

"A boy?" Violet's blue eyes look confused for a moment. "I've never considered that fact. Heaven forbid! I'd never be able to understand him. Boys are so . . . so . . . *peculiar!*"

"Aye, sister, they are a mystery."

"Why is that?"

"Oh, perhaps because they are so different."

Their mother sauntered in. "Who is different?"

"Boys . . . men . . ." Alix said with a womanly shrug.

"Ahhh . . ." she sat on the bed.

"Mama? Did Papa ever do anything you didn't understand?" Violet asked.

Jenny held a hand up to stifle a laugh. "If you were 20 and not 12, you wouldn't have to ask, dear daughter. Yes, many times. When he went off to fight the British during the uprising of '45, I could hardly understand how he was so easily willing to die for Scotland. But . . . off he went, and he returned to me. So, I suppose all ended as well as can be expected. If you had been alive when I was a girl . . . well . . . seeing all the Highlanders in their kilts and plaids. Now, that was masculine. And it made them even more mysterious, more heroic. Ahh...those were wonderful times."

"I wonder if Aaron will be wearing a kilt for his wedding?" Alix asked.

"I'm sure he won't look anything like the Last Highlander if he does," Violet piped up.

"No one looks like Robin Brodie, Violet," Alix said, matter-of-factly. "I don't know how I could have made it through the past three months without him."

"Speaking of peculiar," Violet kept the conversation alive, "doesn't this whole wedding seem a little strange? It's happened so quickly."

Alix agreed. "I think so. It's quite mysterious. I did catch the two of them kissing in one of the turrets a couple of months ago." She looked directly at her mother and patted the side of her belly out of Violet's view. "You don't think..."

"Oh, no!" Her mother rushed in to defend Clementine. "Why, she's a lovely girl, Alix. Just because she's a housemaid doesn't mean she has no scruples. No. No, I don't think that is it at all."

"Then what could it be?"

"It only takes one look at her to understand that, Alix. She's kind, gentle, loving, and if that weren't enough, she's beautiful, truly beautiful. Not one feature that's displeasing to the eye." The chief's lady spoke now as an artist.

Alix sighed. "I suppose you're right, Mama. Perhaps it's not so much *who* Aaron is marrying, but that he is marrying at all. He seems like the type who should never settle down."

"Now on that, Alix, I can't help but agree. What a rogue!"

A light knock signaled Gertrude's entrance into the room. "Excuse me, m'lady, but the carriage from Inveraray has just arrived to take ya' to the weddin'."

Alix's heart sank as she bit her bottom lip and took a deep breath. Her eyes met her mother's, saw the misgiving there, and sought to reassure. "It's all right, Mama, everything will be fine."

"Your father has gone to Glasgow. What if something happens, Alix? What if the bairn comes early?" Her hands twisted. "I'd still rather you'd not go."

"I know, Mama. I know. But I am a Campbell now, and I must attend."

• • •

Charlie held out his hand, his blond hair blew back from the low forehead, and he tried to smile convincingly at Alix as she came up to the door of the coach. "Good day, m'lady."

"Hello, Charlie. How is it that you're driving today?" Alix took his hand as he helped her into the coach.

"Several of the drivers came down with a light fever, m'lady, so his grace ordered me up onto the bench." He began to close the door.

"Why is there no footman?"

The door closed and Charlie, pretending not to hear, climbed up quickly, grabbed the reins, and gave them an exuberant snap. By sundown he would be a rich man.

• • •

Infinite riches enclosed in a small room. That was what Mrs. Mackay expected to find as she stepped into the outer confines of the duke's office. Mr. Stephenson's desk was vacant, the duke's personal secretary tending to a small disaster at the local mill.

She pushed on an intricately carved pocket door that led to the duke's office—a sumptuous room with cherry bookcases and a desk that once belonged to Mary Queen of Scots herself. On the paneled walls fine art was displayed: a Van Dyck, a Botticelli. But behind the room's single tapestry depicting Achan hiding the treasure while his family peacefully slept, lay a hidden room enclosed within the rounded turret. A heavy, rough-hewn wooden door, accommodating a massive iron lock, kept its treasures stowed safely away.

Into her pocket she reached for the key that would open up to her a new world. Unleash her once and for all. To finish her plan. To fulfill her destiny as well as Clementine's. It took quite a shove to open the door, but once inside, the gray light of the day illuminated the scene before her. Mrs. Mackay gasped. Coffers filled with gold and silver were piled on one side. Jewelry chests lay stacked upon several tables. Jewels fit only for duchesses and queens sat on their velvet-covered trays. Artwork: vases, paintings, sculptures, tapestries, ornamental swords were carefully stored away. The housekeeper quickly recovered from her initial thought.

"If God looks upon riches to be such a valuable thing," she whispered, looking around, "He wouldn't have bestowed them upon such a scoundrel."

She chuckled softly as her hands reached forward. Gold coins. They made their way into her cloth bag. *Not too much, Betsy,* she said to herself, *just enough to pay the boys well and keep you hidden for the next month or so.*

A dirk caught her eye. The hilt was made of gold, two snakes twisted. The bodies wrapped lovingly around each other. The heads met in a lethal kiss. The emerald eyes told of death unspeakable. She grasped it into her clutches and petted each precious snake with affection before slipping it into her bag. "And whoever knows what good use this might be put to?" she asked softly then turned on her heel. "An' now. I've a weddin' to attend."

• • •

The coach stopped and Charlie appeared at the window.

"M'lady," he said, "it looks as if the wheel is about to come off. I'm goin' to have to fix it before we can go further."

"Oh dear," Alix sat up straight, "I'm going to be late."

Charlie bowed. "Why don't ya' sit on that fallen trunk over there while I fix it?"

Alix alighted from the coach with his help.

"It's strange. I didn't feel anything amiss."

"Well, see for yourself, m'lady." His arm swept an invitation to the other side of the carriage.

"Nay," she shook her head with a heavy sigh and waved a hand as she lifted her skirts slightly and made for the tree. "I'm sure it is as you say."

Charlie disappeared behind the vehicle, and Alix looked up at the pewter sky, hoping the rain would hold off just a bit longer. Bangings were heard, and after several minutes Charlie resurfaced. "It looks like I'm goin' to have to go back to the castle. As fortune would have it, m'lady, it's only about a mile away."

"I know," Alix smiled. *I used to live here, remember?* she thought with irritation. "You'd best get going."

"All right, m'lady," he bowed. "Here's some water if ya' feel a thirst. I remember my mother in your condition...."

"Thank you, Charlie." She took the skin from him, irritation lacing her words. It was bad enough to be inconvenienced, but to be compared to someone's mother was more than she could bear. "Why don't you get going? The sooner you go, the sooner help will arrive."

"As you say, m'lady."

"Charlie," she suddenly felt guilty for being so impatient with the servant, "thank you for the water."

He nodded without smiling and was off.

It wasn't long before her thirst got the better of her. And as Alix pulled off the stopper, she blessed the day Charlie was born. She drank greedily. Quickly. Her abdomen felt so tight, and her back was aching on and off.

She reached a hand up to her brow, feeling sleepy.

Just for several minutes I shall rest, she decided, laying back in the grass. *Surely I have a little time to doze before Charlie returns.*

Charlie emerged from his hiding place in the forest several minutes later, having circled back around to wait for her to drink.

"Glad I didna' have to knock ya' over the head," he muttered as he pulled her into the trees. His fingers moved quickly as he bound her wrists together, as well as her ankles. He had to get her to the rendezvous point before she awoke.

• • •

Aaron gazed at his bride, dressed in buttery silk. It was one of many gowns delivered three days previous. Ribbons fell from the crown of her head and mingled with the mass of silken, black curls which flowed down to her waist. Shining softly pink, her face smiled at her bridegroom. Her aqua eyes shone with emotion.

Aaron looked magnificent in a perfectly cut navy-blue coat, cream breeches, and a gold waistcoat intricately embroidered with interwoven vines and grapes. His curly hair was pulled back and held in place with a navy ribbon.

How could she have possibly come from that woman? His gaze shifted to Mrs. Mackay, dressed in a cranberry-colored taffeta dress, without a trace of fashion to be found along its many seams. A black lace square covered her light hair, and her lips were pursed. Actually, the housekeeper looked quite nice. Aaron Campbell was beyond giving the woman anything but a less-than-objective opinion.

Aaron joined hands with his bride. The duke shuffled beside him from foot to foot, wanting only to get it over with. This wedding was something he simply didn't understand. Clementine was beautiful, yes, but she was not duchess material, even if she did have a regal quality about her that no housemaid he had ever known possessed. And that mother of hers! He shivered. *At least,* he thought, *she won't be the housekeeper anymore. Perhaps she would rather live somewhere else.*

He knew it was wishful thinking. *With my luck, I'll have to live in close quarters with the woman for the rest of my days.*

In a matter of minutes, Aaron and Clementine were man and wife.

"It was a lovely little ceremony," Mrs. Mackay beamed in satisfaction as she hugged her daughter. "You will make a wonderful duchess."

"Thank ya', Mother," Clementine whispered, her hands going up to her mouth to stifle her emotions. "I dinna think I've ever been happier."

Aaron looked over at his new wife. *True,* he thought, *I could have done much worse. Maybe one day I shall come to love her.* He looked at Mrs. Mackay, knowing only too well what was hidden underneath the facade of gracious dependability. *But in the mother-in-law category . . .* He shuddered and donned a stage smile as she came to embrace him.

"Mrs. Mackay."

She hugged him tightly and whispered softly into his ear. "You'll do right by her until ya' die, Aaron Campbell. You'll do right by her."

Just then Billy the footman ran into the room. Aaron quickly disengaged himself from her embrace.

" 'Scuse me, m'lord, but I've just received an urgent message for Mrs. Mackay."

The Duke's brows knit. "What is it?"

"Your mother is ill to the death, ma'am. Word has it she fell down a flight of stairs. You're to go to Wick at once."

Mrs. Mackay's hand flew to her mouth. "Oh, no!"

"Billy!" the duke barked, "have a carriage made ready immediately and take Mrs. Mackay to Glasgow to get the stage." He was relieved. Wick was two weeks' travel. Mrs.

Mackay would be gone for at least a month and a half, if not more.

"Clementine, I'm so sorry." Mrs. Mackay grabbed her daughter's hands, and gave her a privately glaring look even as she sweetly spoke. "But I shall have to miss the celebration dinner."

Clementine's eyes filled with tears of confusion. "That is all right, Mother. You go on. Ya' must. Tell Granny that I love her so."

"It's all right, darling." Aaron brushed his lips against her temple, mistaking the reason for her tears. "I'm sure your grandmother will be fine."

"I'll go pack some things for the trip. You get the carriage." She followed Billy out the door of the chapel and went up to her room. A bag was ready and waiting on her bed.

• • •

"Blast it, but you're a heavy wench!" Charlie hissed at Alix's unconscious form in his arms. They were halfway there, but he had to rest.

Setting her down, Charlie sat next to her and leaned his back against a tree as he huffed, fighting for breath. This had been the opportunity he had been waiting for all his life. He couldn't wait to get on that horse and go. He was heading to South Africa when all this was done. Diamonds. Easy money and wealth beyond anything he could imagine. It was all there waiting just for him.

Alix stirred with a moan.

"Blast!" he said, watching as she regained consciousness. He had thought surely Mrs. Mackay's herbs would have lasted longer than this. It was going to be a long haul to his destination now.

"What's going on? Oh, Charlie," she felt a bit relieved, "I don't know what happened."

She tried to sit up. Face first, she fell into the moss. Her belly hurt. Her back throbbed and, as in a dream when one's body will not respond to the will, her arms and legs would not move. Struggling now, she strained her arms and felt the leather straps bite into her flesh. Her brows knit in muddled confusion, but it slowly became clear—much too painfully clear. She was bound.

And now frightened.

"Charlie, why am I bound? Untie me this second! What are you doing?"

"It's not on my orders, m'lady."

"What do you mean? You take your orders from me. What's happening?"

"I believe what's happenin' is what some people call 'goin' home,' you're goin' home, Lady Alix, only with a little help."

Home? What did he mean, "going home?"

Realization. She gasped.

"What are you talking about? Who gave you these orders?" Her eyes flashed as basic instincts shot forth and filled her with angry strength.

"No, no, no. All in good time. I wouldna' want to be spoilin' the surprise, ya' see. Come on now, we'd best get goin'. There's still a quarter of a mile to go."

"Go where?"

"You'll see, m'lady," he said with a taunting smile.

"You surprise me, Charlie. I didn't think you were capable of such deviousness."

"Why?" he shot back, "because I'm a servant? Because I've spent my whole life polishin' shoes, sweepin' floors, and bowin' and scrapin' to keep from bein' reprimanded with the rod? An' sometimes ..." he gave a harsh laugh, "it didna' matter if I was belligerent or not. I was just present in the room, and it would warrant a good kick for a piece of imperfectly polished silver or an ill-hung drape. No, Lady Alix, I am capable. My brain works far better than anyone else's at Inveraray Castle. I vowed when I was ten that I would get away someday, but only with a little money behind me. I've been waitin' for this opportunity. And if killin' you is the only way to be m'own master, so be it. Nothin' is goin' to get in m'way."

Alix decided she would fight for all she was worth. Robin had been right; she didn't want to die. She wanted to live. To hold this babe in her arms someday.

"You're not even human."

He laughed again as he heaved her into his arms and she began to struggle, arching back in his arms, kicking her feet forward.

"If you dinna' settle down, m'lady, when we get there I could just show you how human I am."

Alix stopped her struggling. And Charlie smiled again. "There now, that's a good lass. It's a smart woman who knows who her master is."

Charlie cursed as Alix spat in his face. "Don't you ever speak to me like that, Charlie. You are vile. A pathetic creature. And you'll never be anything more."

"Blast you, woman!" he set her down, retrieved his handkerchief from his uniform, and proceeded to wipe his face. "You'll regret those words, mind you."

"Nay," Alix cried, "you'll be the one living with regrets, if you live at all after this. You're neck is going to be stretched so far, Charlie, they'll have to dig an overlong hole to throw your worthless body into."

"Shut you up. I'm not goin' to hear any more of this. Just think about it this way: Your final destination will reunite ya' with your husband. Just think—your little family, all together. Willna' it be just so sweet? He'll be proud o' ya'. You're puttin' up a struggle against me that he now wishes he had had the chance to."

She couldn't respond. Charlie had done the unspeakable.

He laughed at her silence. "You can talk bravely all ya' want, Lady Alix, but it willna' be me screamin' for mercy in the end."

"Oh, yes, you will, Charlie. You haven't heard the last of me. I'm going to watch you hang and be at your miserable, lonely funeral to throw in the first shovelful of dirt with my own hands."

Charlie grabbed a handful of her hair, worked his handkerchief around her head, and gagged her. "As I said before, I willna' hear any more o' this."

Alix didn't scream. But her eyes shone deep-blue and angry. Charlie knew she would be true to her word if given the chance. He would just make sure she didn't get it.

He sought to pick her up again, but her struggle was violent as she thrashed around on the ground. *If I'm going to be killed, I'm not going to make it easy on anyone!* she thought decisively.

"So be it!" Charlie yelled, his anger now boiling with white hot intensity. He grabbed her arms and began to pull her along the ground. Alix pulled against him the whole way, her silent struggle more profound than any loud curses or shouts of protest could ever be.

· · ·

The duke's knife scraped across the plate as he looked up at the bridal couple. Not until three weeks ago when Aaron had entered his office and told him of their plans did he get even an inkling of what was afoot. He had seen by the look in his nephew's eyes that it was inevitable. And he realized that he should have been looking for a wife for him long ago. But how could he have foreseen Duncan's . . .

The pain ripped through him afresh.

He cleared his throat gruffly. "I wonder what has delayed Alix?"

"Perhaps, m'lord, as she is carrying now, she felt unable to make the journey," Clementine offered softly, setting her fork down gently. "She's only a month or so from delivering."

"Hmm," the duke nodded. "I wonder if we should send someone over to Castle Lachlan? To find out if everything is all right."

"Why don't we wait a bit longer, uncle?" Aaron suggested. "If she isn't here by the time we finish supper and receiving the servants' well-wishes, we'll send someone. Perhaps, if indeed she has deemed herself unable to travel, we'll receive a message."

"Of course. You are right, Aaron." He picked up his glass of burgundy wine and drank deeply. His plate would not be getting any emptier, he decided, looking down at the remainder of the roasted lamb and potatoes. An appetite, once hearty and seemingly endless, had fled since Duncan's murder. "If she is not here in an hour, we'll send someone out. Hopefully, we'll hear word in a few weeks from your mother, Clementine, regarding your grandmother."

They all sighed collectively. For different reasons. Clementine thought her grandmother had died years ago.

$$\cdots$$

Billy touched the horses' backs with the whip. Inveraray Castle was soon behind them.

"I dinna' think anyone suspected anythin' amiss, ma'am." Billy looked on ahead with a face like stone. As soon as possible he was getting out of this.

"Good," she nodded, "good. We're almost there. Do ya' see the carriage?"

"Aye. There it is. Pulled over to the side." *Yes sir, as soon as possible, I'll be long gone.*

He pulled on the reins and the vehicle came to a stop. Billy backed the carriage into a hiding place behind five large fir trees. After he unhitched the horses, he arranged branches on the vehicle, making it impossible to see from the road.

"Grab that bag of clothin'," she commanded.

Deeper inside the forest, Charlie and Alix waited.

CHAPTER

23

In eerie decay the ancient edifice loomed tall and narrow before them. Mrs. Mackay grabbed a handful of skirt and picked up her pace as the forgotten keep of a forgotten castle rose sharply in the center of the dim woods.

"Whose castle is this?" Billy's eyes were wide, though this keep was small compared to Inveraray.

"It belonged to an ancestor of the duke's who lived four centuries ago. Built the keep here, but never constructed the curtain walls or any other buildin'. He never moved in an' was killed by a raidin' clan. No one has ever lived here."

The timeworn building looked forbidding and strangely hostile. Each stone, placed by human hands, seemed an entity unto itself, staying in its rightful place for its own good rather than some collective responsibility to the building as a whole. It rose in three stories, an arched doorway at the bottom. Its four corners were towered, although only one tower still retained its pointed top, jabbing belligerently, angrily through the treetops at the iron sky. The dark forest had taken it over centuries before, but the keep fought on to stay intact—a reminder of lost visions, untimely death.

One side was overgrown with vines, patches of it living, some of it dead. Insects buzzed in a droning roar all around them, and the smell of moist stone, dust, and ancient dreams gone awry attacked their noses as they walked under the arch and through the door. In the great hall, a hearth showed signs of decay, yet strangely was not blackened by the fires of the once-living. Sturdy beams crossed the room halfway up, shrouded by thick cobwebs. And high windows slit in crosses gloomily cast their holy patterns on the dusty floor.

Billy shuddered and pictured himself at that moment: a small, strong man keeping an appointment with death. His white-blond hair contrasted with the gloom around him. And he stood beside a woman he had always thought so kind, but now knew was evil. But the riches she had promised.... it was too tempting for him—a man who had grown up on a poor croft, had eaten practically nothing but potatoes his entire childhood. Who hadn't worn shoes until he was 17 and taken into the duke's employ. He would take the riches she offered and leave. Leave Inveraray. Leave Scotland. And then, Pennsylvania. To buy some land for his very own. Even so, the price for his freedom was much too high. He knew that. But it was too late to go back. He would hang with the others, though he never lifted a finger. The duke would feel pity for no one.

"Where is she?" Mrs. Mackay asked Charlie who was leaning against the mantel.

"In the scullery an' madder than a hornet. Drank the water. Made it easy on me at first, but them herbs didna' last long. It was like draggin' a banshee the whole way here."

"Well, at least ya' got her here. Besides, the herbs are meant to do more than just put her to sleep. It's time for ya' to head back to Inveraray Castle. Now, what are ya' to do once ya' get there?"

"Tell them Alix was taken away, abducted by highwaymen askin' for a ransom."

"What else?" she snapped.

"They will be gettin' in touch with the duke in two days. At which time a message will be given tellin' the time an' date of the rendezvous."

"All right. Now go! I want this matter settled once an' for all. Until it is finished, I'll not know a moment's peace."

"Did ya' remember to bring the changes of clothes?" Charlie's concern was justified. Once he left Glasgow, he'd never get anywhere in Campbell livery.

"Of course. Now go, an' hurry. If the timin' isna' right, we'll all be caught."

Back in the scullery, Alix, whose hands were now tied behind her back, struggled to free herself. As she dug her heels into the floor and pushed slowly across the floor, a sudden wash of moisture drenched her underskirts.

Oh, God, the anger was suddenly gone in that silent, two-word prayer. Minutes later a mild contraction followed.

• • •

"Good, you're back." Mrs. Mackay looked up at Charlie as he entered the great hall some time later. "Billy, come here," she commanded sharply, reaching for the precious bag of riches. "Here. Your payment."

An eager hand was reached forward. Into his palm she dropped the snake-hilted dirk and a small bag of gold coins. "Be gone now. Your work is done."

"But I thought I'd be goin' to Glasgow with ya', to catch a stage to London."

"No, you're leavin' now," she said coldly. "It's up to you to get there on your own."

Billy looked down at his booty. Misgivings previously pushed under surfaced as the gold glinted dully in the dim light. "Mrs. Mackay, are ya' sure ya' must kill . . ."

"Quiet! I dinna' want to hear this, Billy. Ya' sunk yourself into this up to your neck when Duncan was murdered! Be glad you're gettin' somethin' out o' this at all. It would be easy for someone to find out about your participation and, before ya' know it, you'd be hangin' by your neck as well! Now get out o'here before I change m'mind an' do away with ya' as well."

"Charlie hit him over the head, not me. All I did was keep guard. But the baby, wha' about . . ."

"Get out, Billy!" Her eyes flashed impatiently. "It's too late for second thoughts. And dinna' be thinkin' about sayin' a word to anyone. You'll be judged just as guilty. Now leave. I dinna want ya' around anymore."

"I'd get out of Argyllshire as fast as ya' can," Charlie drawled with a malicious smirk. "An' Mrs. Mackay is right—you'd best not be sayin' anythin' at all. Duncan Campbell isna' the only man restin' in peace on m'list. You'd be easy enough to get rid of as well. Now do as the woman says an' get out!"

Billy ran for the door, only too happy to leave by this time.

"Aye," she nodded. "We'll be long gone by nightfall. Long gone. Charlie, ya' go on out now an' keep watch. Just in case. I want to make sure things have progressed beyond any sort of turnaround before we get goin'."

"How long will it be?"

"I dinna' know." Mrs. Mackay looked down. "Keep watch, I tell ya'. We dinna' want to take any chances on her escapin'. Not that there's a good chance of it. I'd best go check on her and see if the pains have started."

Charlie did as he was bid.

• • •

Almost there.

Aaron pushed his white horse faster. Faster. The ride to Kilbride seemed to lengthen into days. He saw the ruined castle in the distance. Ten minutes. Ten minutes and he would be at Castle Lachlan.

• • •

Numbness veiled her world. And pain concentrically exploded in rings of scarlet behind her eyes. Alix tried to focus, but couldn't. The pains, though still seemingly far apart, seemed to tear her in two like a living piece of cloth.

She gagged against the handkerchief in her mouth as she sought to moisten her drying lips. Her eyes focused on the rough stones, the small slit window recessed deeply high up in the wall, the stone floor upon which she lay. The air was old. And the heavy wooden door vibrated as its bolt was drawn.

A shadow appeared in the doorway.

Mrs. Mackay quickly walked over to Alix and untied the gag.

"Mrs. Mackay?" Alix's mouth dropped open and she breathed a sigh of relief. "Thank God, you've found me."

"Aye, m'lady. I've found ya'. An' may God have mercy on your soul."

• • •

Joshua raced on his stallion toward the village, leading the Arabian Storm. The lean lines of Joshua's large frame were tensed and strung even more tightly than his jaw. Urgency pulsed in his temple, throbbing even as he ground his teeth together, making the muscles in his cheeks tighten visibly with each movement. The horses' hooves struck the turf with the force and speed of summer lightning. Horse and rider pushed forward over the expanse that stretched between Castle Lachlan and the village. It had always seemed such a short journey before. He had made it every day, several times a day, for the last 17 years. Aaron rode beside him, face flushed and urgent.

• • •

Robin's arm muscles tensed, then heaved the load of pine board he had hewn the day before. Built behind his mother's little cottage, his shop was nearing completion. He had done it. Entered the village in the light of noonday, took his place among them, and began to set up his business. He dropped the boards and set about making a door.

Ever so slightly vibrations shook the ground beneath his sensitive feet. Horses, several of them, were coming and coming quickly. Their speed was evident. But they were starting to slow. His scalp tightened. Something was wrong. Instinct declared it. Robin rushed around the cottage as the horses came to a straining halt.

Joshua dismounted, his black hair loose, the ribbon long gone. Eyes encumbered by distress, he looked heavily at his brother-in-law, gripping his arms tightly as he spoke. Aaron stayed put in his saddle, his foot kicking in its stirrup with agitation.

"Alix is gone, Robin." Joshua spoke quickly.

"What?"

"You know she was supposed to go to Inveraray Castle today for the weddin'?" Joshua asked.

"Aye, she wouldna' listen to any of us. Insisted on goin'."

Aaron broke in, his words tumbling quickly but clearly over one another. "Her coach driver, Charlie, came back to Inveraray about two hours ago. Said highwaymen kidnapped her and were holding her for ransom. I immediately became suspicious after what happened to Duncan."

"Where's Charlie now?" The look of the hunter ignited in Robin's eyes.

"As soon as he gave the message, acting quite distraught, mind you, my uncle told him to go down to the kitchens, eat something quickly, and get ready to join a search party. I told my uncle of my suspicions, but when he sent down for Charlie, he was already gone. We sent out a search party on the road toward Glasgow, just in case his story is true."

"Ya' dinna' really think they were highwaymen, do ya'?"

Aaron's face was grim. "Even highwaymen wouldn't abduct a woman carrying a child so heavily. And highwaymen aren't usually kidnappers. They just take the money and are off."

"So Charlie is part of it all," Joshua surmised.

"Aye. But I don't know who he's working with. If only I had been thinking more clearly, but with the wedding and . . ."

Robin reached up and placed a strong hand on his arm. "Ya' came now, and ya' came quickly. Ya' did the right thing, sir. I'll be right back. I must get my bow." He bounded around to the shed and in seconds was back and mounted on Storm.

They rode north, propelled by danger, expediency, and their own fear. Each man loved Alix in his own right, for different reasons. But Robin's love outshone them all. He would find her. If he used nothing but instinct, he would find the woman he loved. His throat tightened, though his outward appearance seemed as stoic as ever.

Finding Duncan. It was the only vision his mind could conjure. And all he could do as he raced along, cold sweat covering his back and running down his face, was remember the day he had pulled the body up from the frigid, murky waters of the loch. If the murderer succeeded in what was started that winter's day, more than one person would die before the sun set. Was Charlie's story of highwaymen really the case? His prayer was "let it be so." But his heart knew better.

Bolstering himself as Storm's hooves thundered underneath him, he was like a man pursuing his own demons. *I will find her,* he promised himself, and his Savior as well, *I* will *find her.* Peace miraculously settled on his shoulders, strengthening him as a sense of destiny, predetermined before his birth, came to light. For this he was born. To be here now. To save Alix.

But he couldn't do this alone.

The great beast moved swiftly along, and Robin lifted his heart heavenward with more strength, more conviction than if he had been prostrate and groveling in the dust across which he raced.

• • •

"Are ya' surprised?"

The confession was out, the words pulling Alix down into a quagmire of horror. Mrs. Mackay. Dear Mrs. Mackay.

"Did ya' think I was not capable of carryin' out such a simple plot?" The gray irises of Mrs. Mackay's eyes flared, gaping with the fires of hell itself.

"Why?" Alix wanted to keep her talking as long as possible. Hopefully help was on the way. But how? "What could Duncan, gentle Duncan, have possibly done to have made you want to kill him?"

"He was born."

"I don't understand."

The housekeeper laughed. "No. Ya' dinna'. Of course ya' dinna'. It was because he was the next in line to inherit the title."

"But what did that have to do with anything?"

If only I could think more clearly, Alix thought as another contraction stretched painfully.

"Aaron was my reason," she said simply. "Aaron and Clementine. Another one of my glorious plots. They are married now. I tricked him into it. It was a beautiful piece of work, if I do say so myself. And a brilliant plot. Absolutely brilliant. And now Clementine will be the next Duchess of Argyll." She looked back at a dead branch, black among the living leaves that danced in the breeze before the window. Alix shuddered at the dark pride of Mrs. Mackay's heart.

The sky grew even dimmer.

"It all became clear once she fell in love with Aaron," Mrs. Mackay went on, looking calmly out the window. "For years I didna' have a clue as to how I was goin' to manage gettin' her set up as the duchess. I just knew it was her destiny. Her right."

"But why *us?* Why the Campbells?"

Mrs. Mackay stepped away from the window, eyes now calm.

"Because she is a Campbell."

Alix looked at her in disbelief.

"The storm is goin' to break any minute." She sat down several feet from her captive.

Alix finally found her voice. "What do you mean Clementine is a Campbell?"

"Do ya' remember the day ya' asked me about her father?"

Alix nodded and recalled the answer: *She's closer to him than you'd imagine.* "The duke?"

"Aye. I was but a lass. And a handsome young man came visitin' the chief of the clan. I was just a servin' girl, but oh, I was so much more. So much more. The Mackay was m'father, ya' see. My mother worked in the kitchens. Fair she was. Looked just like Clementine, except for the eyes."

"They're just like the old duke's!" Alix gasped. "They're just like Duncan's."

"Aye, just like Duncan's. When Douglas sent for me that night, I didna' ask questions, just went to his chamber. Clementine is the result. An' I vowed on the day she was born, she wouldna' end up in a life of servitude such as I, the daughter of a chief, had to live."

"Does the duke know?"

"Does the duke *know?*" Mrs. Mackay laughed—a single, forceful exhalation. "He didna' even recognize me when I showed up at Inveraray Castle two years later lookin' for work. Stephenson hired me, and the first time I stood in Douglas's presence, his eyes just passed over me without a trace of recognition. That's how much it meant, Alix. That's all it ever means to men." She started to relax, her feelings, her pain anesthetizing her from the task at hand. "Ya' should know that."

"Duncan wasn't like that. My father isn't like that," Alix said softly.

Mrs. Mackay gave a grudging nod. "Duncan, well, he was different, I'll grant ya' that. How he came from Douglas I'll never know. I felt bad about havin' to take care o' him like that. But suffice it to say he didna' suffer, Alix. He never felt a thing."

Tears formed in Alix's eyes as she recalled her husband's body lying dead on the table. "How could you do such evil? He never was cruel to anyone. He was the most kind, gentle man that this earth had ever seen. And because someone was cruel to you and to your mother, you deemed it necessary to be cruel to someone else. And not just Duncan. You've made my life utterly desolate, Mrs. Mackay. You've given me a grief-stricken pregnancy. And a future of raising my child alone."

"Nay, lass, you're not thinkin' clearly. Today I'm savin' ya' from all o' that."

The horror of the woman struck Alix forcibly. "You really believe you're doing me a favor, don't you?"

"Aye. And we'll make sure along the way that no heir is taken back to Inveraray."

Alix began to panic. "But what if it's a girl?"

"It doesna' matter now. I'm leavin' ya' here to have your babe alone. And here you'll stay."

"Please," tears streamed down Alix's face, "kill me if you must, but keep the child alive."

"Now, Lady Alix, what good would that do me? It is the *child* that is in the way of fulfillin' Clementine's destiny, not you. The child must die. The child will die. As will you. No one will find ya' here."

Tears formed quickly in Alix's eyes, "Please..." she whispered, "please, do not do this...." Sobs wracked her body. "Please... give me the chance you had... the chance to be a mother."

Mrs. Mackay's breathing quickened, small tears filled the very corners of her eyes. "No!" she stood quickly to her feet. "No, Alix Campbell. I willna' let your tears or the sympathy I feel at your plight deter me. Do ya' hear me?"

She grabbed the satchel and marched up the small staircase to the door.

Walking through the portal, she shut the door slowly behind her. Dry wood scraped a lifeless tune against the stone floor.

CHAPTER
24

The bolt slid in place. Slowly grinding, snuffing out Alix's one last scream for mercy. Thunder clapped and the rain started falling. The pains of childbirth continued to increase.

Thirst assaulted Alix violently. Death stared at her from its hollow grave. She was alone. No voices came from outside. And still her hands were bound painfully behind her back. How would she care for the babe when it arrived?

Hopeless sobs wracked her as another contraction rent her body. The urge to push was getting too strong to resist. There had to be a way out.

If I can just free my hands! Alix thought as she began moving across the floor again over to the steps. She wondered how long it would take to cut through the leather straps. It didn't matter. Sitting there writhing in pain wasn't something she would allow.

As she worked her way into the right position, back toward the bottom step of the scullery, she found its edge and began to rub the leather strap.

Back and forth.

The methodical task was oddly soothing.

Back and forth.

• • •

"Blast it!" Aaron interjected, looking up at the rain, blinking as the dense, numerous drops assaulted his face. "Why now?" He turned to Robin "Will it affect your ability to track?"

"Maybe," Robin admitted, looking down in sharp attention at the road, "but I dinna' think so." He pulled Storm to a stop. Joshua and Aaron did the same.

"What is back in the woods here?" he asked, looking at the coach tracks going in numerous directions.

"An old keep. Unlived-in for centuries."

"Does anyone know about this place?"

"Yes," Aaron nodded. "Everyone in Inveraray. It's become a lovers' rendezvous over the years."

Robin looked sharply through the trees and shook his head from side to side. "Did Charlie say where the highwaymen came at them?"

"About a mile from the castle."

"And we are about a mile from Inveraray now, arena' we?"

"Yes."

Robin jumped off Storm. "I'm goin' in. Perhaps there is a clue as to where they've taken her. I dinna' like the feel of things here."

Joshua moved to get down, but Robin held up a hand. "Nay, Joshua. As much as I appreciate your help, I do better in the woods on my own. Besides, it may be nothin'."

"I understand."

"Why don't you and I head on to the castle," Aaron turned to Joshua, "and see if my uncle has received any news?"

"All right. Perhaps someone can be sent to Glasgow. The chief must be told. In fact, I'll go m'self."

"Good. We'll get you provisions for the journey."

The two men rode off quickly to Inveraray Castle. Robin led Storm just into the woods, walked directly behind the fir trees, and tied him to where the carriage had been. To the unpracticed, civilized eye of a normal man, nothing looked amiss. But to the animal eye of Robin Brodie, the mannish intrusion in the forest—broken boughs, flattened grass—was clearly visible.

Breathing in deeply, he found his suspicions confirmed. Her smell was in the air. As sure as he knew the place in which he walked, Alix had been here.

Robin drew his bow.

• • •

Sweat poured from her brow as she continued to fight back the urge to push. Alix arched her back, aching from birthing pains, from her bonds, from the utter despair which fogged her mind. It hurt too much even to pray. The leather seemed thicker than when she had begun. Her wrists were bloody and torn as she grunted in her urgency to be free.

The droplets of blood collected in a small, warm pool, as waves of pain washed over her continually.

The time had come. She knew it. And a contraction so strong built up inside that Alix screamed out.

• • •

The keep stood before him now.

A scream shot through the air around him.

Robin ran through the arched doorway, through the hall. Silence again. He turned his head from side to side, listening. Always listening.

Another scream.

Through the hall he made his way more swiftly than a fox.

And Alix screamed again as Robin Brodie shifted the bolt.

"Alix! I'm here!" he cried, seeing her at the bottom of the steps. He jumped down, reached for his dirk, and soon her wrists and ankles were free from the scarlet-stained straps.

"Robin?" Alix rasped through her pain. "You found me. I didn't think . . ."

"Of course I found ya', sweet Alix." He wiped the sweat from her forehead, and kissed her torn wrists as his tears mingled with her blood. "Of course I did."

She began to weep and Robin held her. "Shhhh, love," he whispered comfortingly, "everything is goin' to be all right."

Five minutes later, Alix entered the last stage of labor.

Robin laid his plaid underneath her, and upon the Brodie tartan, Christiana Maclachlan Campbell was born.

• • •

God with Me Lying Down

God with me lying down,
God with me rising up,
God with me in each ray of light,
Nor I a ray of joy without him,
     Not one ray without him.

Christ with me sleeping,
Christ with me waking,
Christ with me watching,
Every day and night.
     Each day and night.

God with me protecting,
The Lord with me directing,
The spirit with me strengthening,
For ever and for evermore,
     Ever and evermore
          Chief of chiefs, Amen.

• • •

August, 1766

The day after Charlie and Mrs. Mackay were hung in Inveraray, Alix and the chief walked the woods. Hand in hand, their feet led them deeper into the summer forest, darkened by the dense foliage, yet warmed by the bright sun which shone in splendor above the treetops. Soon the cave stood before them. They entered the open door.

All was bare.

Except the walls, which still were streaked the deep red she had remembered from four years previous.

"So this was Robin Brodie's cave, eh, Alix?"

"Aye," she sighed, "and 'twill always be, I suppose. I never thought he'd actually make it out, you know."

"You underestimate yourself, daughter."

She shook her head. "Nay. It was not me, Papa. It was the Savior."

The chief's eyes did a quick circumference of the barren interior. "I didn't realize the water here contained so much iron. Someone surely had an overactive imagination, didn't they?" her father asked. "Stained with the blood of Redcoats . . ." he mocked. "Leave it to Lachlan to believe it!"

Then silence took over as they continued to stare, lost in thought, lost in the events of the past.

"I must leave this place, Papa."

"All right, Alix. Let's get back then." He turned to go.

"No."

His feet stopped, and he turned to look at her with questioning eyes.

"No. I mean Kilbride. I mean Scotland."

For some reason, the chief understood, and he conveyed it with his soulful eyes as Alix tried to explain. "There are too many ghosts about now. Good ones and bad ones. Too many memories of fear. And too many memories of love and happiness with Duncan." Her voice lowered. "It wouldn't be fair, Papa. Not to me, little Christiana, or to Robin."

"Will you marry him then, Alix?"

"Aye. Someday. When I'm ready."

"And then you shall leave?"

"Yes, Papa. Then we shall leave together."

"Where will you go?"

Alix looked around one last time, and they walked toward the entrance. Once out, she shut the door forever. They started back in the direction of Castle Lachlan.

"To America, I suppose."

If Kyle was surprised by his daughter's desire, his eyes betrayed it not. "I understand. I felt the same way after Culloden."

"Sometimes I feel that it would be running away," she placed her hand in his. "But the truth is, Papa, these memories are not ones which can be worked through. They are ones which must simply be forgotten."

"Sometimes we forget because we must, not because we will." His eyes were kind, full of a deep, boundless love.

She knew he'd understand. "Besides," she continued, "there's nothing for me here anymore. Not really. Robin has opened up his wood-carving shop and will live in the village until we're ready to leave. He's expanded his shop so that he can live there as well."

"He knows then? That you have chosen to be with him someday?"

"Aye. And he will wait. His patience is boundless."

"That is true, child. That is true. When do you think you'll be ready?"

"I'm not sure. But when the time is right, I shall know it. Duncan has been dead but six months."

"He'd want you to be happy, Alix."

"Aye, Papa. He would. But I shall only be happy if I mourn him respectfully for a while, and give myself a little time to get over the nightmare. . . ."

The clearing came in sight.

"I'm sure you know what's best for you, Alix. Do you want me to tell your mother?"

"Nay," Alix shook her head, "it would be better if she found out gradually."

He nodded.

Alix stepped over the fallen log upon which she had sat in wait for Robin so many times, then out into the clearing. She looked at the position of the sun as it hung in the sky. "I should be getting back to baby Christiana."

"All right."

"You know, Papa, sometimes I feel she is all I have left."

Kyle stopped and looked into his daughter's eyes with a love so deep and unconditional she felt its warmth cover her like a velvet cloak.

"Right now you may feel that way, my love. But you are rich with the love of others. It just may take a while until you recognize that fact again."

Alix knew he was right. And father and daughter walked back home slowly, arm in arm, borne on generations of love and tenderness.

CHAPTER

25

June, 1768

"It's been a spring for weddings, hasn't it, Alix?"

Aaron Campbell sat down next to Alix as little Christiana, now two and clad in a white batiste dress with a wreath of yellow roses in her hair, bounded up onto her mother's lap. Alix nodded and smiled up into the face of her friend as he lit his pipe.

Her mother's rose garden was blooming in profusion, blessing them with its delightful spring perfume. Mumbles had done a beautiful job for the wedding.

"First my uncle and the young countess of Wyndham..."

"And now Lachlan and Rebecca," she finished. "They look ecstatic, do they not?"

"Aye," a blue trail circled up and disappeared as Aaron spoke, taking in her mature beauty. She was a wonderful mother and grew more lovely each day. "But what about you, Alix? It's been almost two-and-a-half years since Duncan died."

"Yes," she squeezed her daughter in a hug, "I suppose it's been long enough."

Their eyes went to the far end of the garden where guests had gathered in conversation. The Last Highlander stood among them, at ease and speaking freely with Joshua, Deborah, and the Duke of Argyll.

"Do you think he's ready, Aaron?"

At that moment, Robin looked up, his eyes locking onto her gaze. And a smile leapt across his lips. His smile was never far away, and he had learned to laugh again. Most heartily.

"The first time I heard him really laugh I nearly jumped ten feet!" she told Aaron with a chuckle. "His business is thriving, and he enjoys his work greatly. I'd hate to take him away from all of that."

"I know, Alix. But he'd give it up for you without having to think for even a moment. We both know that. Everyone knows that. You've given him time enough to become the man he was meant to be. He is ready. Has been for the past two years, truth be told. The question is, are you?"

Alix looked at him thoughtfully as Christiana hopped off her lap to run to her grandfather.

"Aye, Aaron, I believe I finally am."

"Tell him then."

"What?"

"Tell him, Alix. Go right now. Make this a happy day for everyone!"

She sat up straight, excitement flashing in her blue eyes. "Should I, Aaron? Should I really?"

"Aye, my friend," a hand squeezed her knee, "it's time."

Alix arose from the bench and didn't look back.

Aaron smiled, thinking, *This would make a wonderful play.*

• • •

Robin, clad as always in kilt and plaid, saw her walking toward him. Quickly he excused himself from his companions and met her halfway.

Grabbing both of his calloused hands in hers, she pulled him toward the garden gate. "Come, my Highlander," she said with a mischievous sparkle in her eyes, "let's walk a bit, shall we?"

"All right, Alix."

"Where shall we go?" she asked him.

"Anywhere but deep into the forest," he chuckled.

Her laugh twined with his, filtering off into the summer air, as they tread toward the loch.

"They look happy, don't they, sweet Alix?" Robin spoke of the bride and groom.

"Aye. That they do."

Robin put his arm comfortably across her shoulders. Alix had become used to his embraces. And for the last six months, his kisses as well. Sweet and passionate, they were a true picture of the man himself.

"Aaron told me yesterday that the new Duchess of Argyll is expecting already."

Robin's brow creased a bit. "And how does he feel about it? Chances are he'll not be the next duke."

"I think he's relieved. Clementine naturally wants nothing to do with being a duchess. His plays are the toast of London theater, and he's in love. What could a title possibly hold for him?"

The brown eyes caressed her. "A man in love needs nothin' more."

Alix stopped.

"Do you really mean that, Robin?"

"I should know, Alix. I've loved ya' for many years."

He was so strong. So masculine and so selfless. Alix put her arms around his narrow waist and laid her head upon his tartan-covered chest.

Tears filled her eyes as she looked up at him. "What would I ever do without you?"

"Alix, I love ya' so much more than a simple man like me could ever begin to express."

"I love you too, Robin Brodie."

They remained in peaceful proximity for several minutes, arms wrapped tightly around one another. Robin's hand moved with gentle caressings over her hair. She felt his lips on her temple next, felt their chests touch as he breathed in her scent and she breathed in his. He still had the smell of the outdoors upon him, but now it was mixed with fresh-sawn wood and contentment. The smells of sadness and shame were gone.

"Alix," his voice was strong and confident as a sweet summer breeze lifted his black curls and brushed them against the backs of her hands where they rested on his back. "I do believe the time has come."

"Aye, Robin. It has come."

Without hesitating, Robin Brodie dropped to one knee. He had been dreaming of this moment for what seemed a lifetime.

"Alix Campbell," his eyes, still mirrors of his soul, looked lovingly into hers, "will ya' marry this poor wood-carver?"

She looked down on his upturned face. At the tanned skin, the faded scar, the sensual mouth she loved to feel on hers. And an emotion so powerful, so deep, plunged into the inner confines of who she was always meant to be.

"Aye, Robin Brodie, my Highlander, marry you I shall."

She knelt down as well, twining her fingers into the thick black hair. And Robin pulled her against him, his lips finding hers without hesitation. Strong and loving, his kiss pulled her soul forward, to mesh with his.

He pulled back, brown eyes sparkling brightly. "I love it when ya' look like that, Alix."

"Like what, Robin?"

"All soft-mouthed and flushed. It's good to know my kisses do that for ya.'"

"Then kiss me again, Robin Brodie. For I didn't ask you to stop that last one now, did I?"

He complied. But pulled back again.

"Will ya' marry me, Alix?"

"Will I . . ." confusion erupted good-naturedly. "I just said yes, that I would gladly . . ."

"No. Now, Alix. Will ya' marry me right now?"

"Robin . . . I . . . well," she stammered.

"There's no better time, m'darlin' love. The minister is here, the people are gathered . . ." He pulled her to her feet.

Alix put her hand up to her mouth, catching his mischief and loving it. "I suppose there's no real good reason not to . . ."

His eyes became serious without warning as he tilted her chin up to look deeply into her soulful eyes. "And we have both been lonely for far too long, Alix."

"Aye," tears welled softly, "the nights have been cold . . ." she leaned forward and whispered into his ear, ". . . and my bed much too empty."

Leaning back, she looked into his eyes. Passion blazed in the brown depths, and he crushed her to him, kissing her deeply, hinting at times to come, at future joys only he could give her. No one had ever loved her more. No one had ever needed her as much.

"Come, my Highlander!" she grabbed his hand and started running back to the castle gardens. "Let us be married. And let it be now."

• • •

Alix had never known such passion. Robin took her to heights she didn't know existed. A fire burned in him, strong and true. He was a giving lover, tender at times, forceful at others. Always seeking to please her.

Robin had never known such contentment. Alix made him complete. With each loving caress from the soft, white hands of his wife, his memories of death and war faded farther and farther, mere whispers of thought in the most remote corners of his mind.

"I love ya, m'lady," he said softly in her ear the night of their wedding.

"You saved me yet again, Robin." She cried tears of joy, coming out of the blackness of her misery in his beautiful arms.

"Nay, Alix, you saved me."

She laughed softly at their ongoing argument, burying her face in his neck. "Then you need me as much as I need you, my Highlander?"

"I need ya' more."

"Nay, my love. You've been saving my life ever since I can remember. Promise me you'll always be there when I need to be rescued."

"Nay, Alix. I canna' promise ya' that."

"What?" Alix lifted her head up to look into his eyes.

"I can only promise to be there always, whether ya' need rescuin' or not."

Alix dropped her head and pressed her lips to his. Inside he prayed a prayer of thanks. Life had pierced them with many griefs, but the Savior healed, and healed in a loving way. Wild solitudes were now behind him. Through strife and hardships their slumbering souls awakened to love one another for life. In her eyes were breathless dawns, the scent and beauty of a rose, and sunsets shining their golden light to warm his heart until death closed his mortal eyes for eternity. The time for rescue was done; the time for loving had begun. And love they would. Wholeheartedly. Joyfully. Until the breath of life made its final journey from their lips.

"I still can hardly believe I'm the wife of a legend," Alix said dreamily as she drifted off to sleep in his arms.

"Nay, Alix Brodie," he whispered into the darkness, "you're merely the wife of a man."

EPILOGUE

Richmond, Virginia
23 July, 1776

"Christiana!" Alix cupped her hands to her mouth and called for her eldest daughter. "Have you seen your little brother?"

"Which one?" the child of ten looked up from the clothes-line. She pushed a deep-brown curl out of her aqua eyes, but the breeze blew it back again.

"Johnnie."

"Oh, he just ran into the woods a bit ago. He saw a squir-rel and off he went with that *blasted* quiver bouncing on his back."

"Christiana, don't use such language. It's unbecoming on a lady."

"But Papa . . ."

"Is a man. And much older than you."

"He'd think it was funny."

"Perhaps he would," Alix smiled, thinking how soft Robin was when it came to Christiana. "But your brothers aren't allowed to talk like that, and neither are you. By the way," she wiped her floury hands on her apron, "where's Kyle?"

"He took Richard down to the pond. Said he was going to teach him how to fish. He's certainly gotten a bit puffed up since he turned six."

"Hmm," Alix's brows creased, "I suppose he'll be able to take care of Richard. Christiana, the baby's in for his nap. Go get your brothers and I'll finish hanging out the clothes for you. Daddy will be home soon, and dinner will be ready in 30 minutes."

Alix lifted up one of Robin's shirts with a smile and took two wooden pins out of the basket. *This certainly isn't the life of a duchess,* she thought, *but it is wonderful all the same.*

Four more children they had besides Christiana. Four loud and affectionate sons. She thought of the baby sleeping peacefully in his cradle, only three months old. Robin had named him Duncan as soon as he slipped into the world. Alix had cried. Her husband became more precious with each year that passed. Life in the Colonies had been good to them. And now that they were at war with England . . .

She turned her head. The sound of horses' hooves and the rickety clack of Robin's wagon going at full speed brought her running around to the front of the frame house he had built for them on their arrival to Virginia.

"Robin!" she called, running up to him as he jumped down. "What's happened? Are you all right?"

Robin lifted her into his arms and whirled her around. "Alix. I've never been better. We just got word not an hour ago!"

"Word of what?"

Robin kissed her quick and hard. "We are free, m'darlin'. Oh, that's not sayin' there's not goin' to be trouble down the road, more fightin' to ensure what has happened. But . . ."

"Robin Brodie, what are you talking about?"

"The Continental Congress met in Philadelphia at the beginnin' of the month. We've declared our independence from England."

"Oh, Robin. Are you sure?" Alix's eyes were as wide as they could be.

"Aye. I was at the mill gettin' a load of wood when a messenger rode up."

"So the war will continue?"

Robin set her down. "Aye, it shall. An' I imagine old George the Third willna' be makin' things easy now that the declaration has been signed by all 13 colonies."

"But we shall win?"

"Yes, m'darlin', we shall win—of that I have no doubt."

"But how can you be so sure?"

"Because this rebellion has nothin' to do with kings, monarchies, and rights to a throne," his eyes shone. "It's men fightin' to be free. To rule themselves. When we fought at Culloden we fought, ultimately, for a man. Another ruler to govern us. This rebellion is different. We're fightin' to be free, Alix. Free! And that, truly, is somethin' worth fightin' for, worth dyin' for."

"Will you join the militia? Fight the Redcoats one last time?"

"Aye. That's what I'd like to do." His eyes searched hers.

Alix smiled broadly, knowing instinctively what he needed, and loving him all the more for it. "Then go, my Highlander. For I know you'll come back. There's nobody in the world who knows how to stay alive better than you."

"That's the truth, m'darlin', Alix. Ya' know me too well. Ya' always have."

So Robin Brodie went to war, fought valiantly, and came back home to his family. In 1783 at the Peace of Paris the independence of the Colonies was recognized. Robin lived as a free man, out from under British rule, until the day he died.